The Journey of Three Lifetimes

There has never been a book like *Imajica*. Transforming every expectation of fantasy fiction with its heady mingling of radical sexuality and spiritual anarchy, it has carried its millions of readers into regions of passion and philosophy that few books have even attempted to map. It's an epic in every way; vast in conception, obsessively detailed in execution, and apocalyptic in its resolution. A book of erotic mysteries and perverse violence. A book of ancient, mythological landscapes and even more ancient magic.

Most of all, it's a book of extraordinary characters. At its heart lies the great sensualist and master art forger, Gentle, whose life of excess comes unravelled when he encounters two other unforgettable individuals: Judith Odell, whose power to influence the destinies of the men besotted by her is vaster than she knows, and Pie'oh'pah, an alien assassin who comes from a dimension most of us don't even know exists.

That dimension—or Dominion, as it is known—is one of five in the great system called Imajica. They are worlds which are in many ways utterly unlike our own, but which are ruled, peopled, and haunted by species whose lives are intricately connected with us. As Gentle, Judith, and Pie'oh'pah travel the Imajica—from the darkness of its infernal regions into its visionary places—they uncover a trail of Dominion-spanning crimes and intimate betrayals that will lead them to a revelation so startling it will change the way you look at reality forever.

*Great Book

By Clive Barker

Sacrament
Everville
Imajica
The Great and Secret Show
The Hellbound Heart
The Books of Blood, Volumes I-III
In the Flesh
The Inhuman Condition
The Damnation Game
Weaveworld
Cabal
The Thief of Always
Incarnations
Forms of Heaven

Visit Clive Barker on the World Wide Web at
http://www.barkerverse.com

IMAJICA

CLIVE BARKER

HarperPrism
A Division of HarperCollinsPublishers

HarperPrism
A Division of HarperCollins*Publishers*
10 East 53rd Street, New York, N.Y. 10022-5299

This is a work of fiction. The characters, incidents, and dialogues are
products of the author's imagination and are not to be construed as
real. Any resemblance to actual events or persons, living or dead,
is entirely coincidental.

A hardcover edition of this book was published in 1991
by HarperCollins*Publishers*. A dual volume edition of *Imajica*
was published in 1992 by HarperPaperbacks.

HarperPrism books may be purchased for educational, business, or sales
promotional use. For information, please write:
Special Markets Department, HarperCollins*Publishers*,
10 East 53rd Street, New York, N.Y. 10022-5299

Printed in the United States of America

Cover illustration: Kirk Reinhert

ISBN: 0-06-105371-6

First HarperPrism trade paperback edition printing: August 1997

Visit HarperPrism on the World Wide Web at
http://www.harpercollins.com

00 RRD/CC 10 9 8 7 6 5 4

—BOOK I—
The Fifth Dominion

I

It was the pivotal teaching of Pluthero Quexos, the most celebrated dramatist of the Second Dominion, that in any fiction, no matter how ambitious its scope or profound its theme, there was only ever room for three players. Between warring kings, a peacemaker; between adoring spouses, a seducer or a child. Between twins, the spirit of the womb. Between lovers, Death. Greater numbers might drift through the drama, of course—thousands in fact—but they could only ever be phantoms, agents, or, on rare occasions, reflections of the three real and self-willed beings who stood at the center. And even this essential trio would not remain intact; or so he taught. It would steadily diminish as the story unfolded, three becoming two, two becoming one, until the stage was left deserted.

Needless to say, this dogma did not go unchallenged. The writers of fables and comedies were particularly vociferous in their scorn, reminding the worthy Quexos that they invariably ended their own tales with a marriage and a feast. He was unrepentant. He dubbed them cheats and told them they were swindling their audiences out of what he called the last great procession, when, after the wedding songs had been sung and the dances danced, the characters took their melancholy way off into darkness, following each other into oblivion.

It was a hard philosophy, but he claimed it was both immutable and universal, as true in the Fifth Dominion, called Earth, as it was in the Second.

And more significantly, as certain in life as it was in art.

Being a man of contained emotion, Charlie Estabrook had little patience with the theater. It was, in his bluntly stated opinion, a waste of breath: indulgence, flummery, lies. But had some student recited Quexos' First Law of Drama to him this cold November night he would have nodded grimly and said: All true, all true. It was his experience precisely. Just as Quexos' Law required, his story had begun with a trio: himself, John Furie Zacharias, and, between them, Judith. That arrangement hadn't lasted very long. Within a few weeks of setting eyes on Judith he had managed to supersede Zacharias in her affections, and the three had dwindled to a blissful two. He and Judith had married and lived happily for five years, until, for reasons he still didn't understand, their joy had foundered, and the two had become one.

He was that one, of course, and the night found him sitting in the back of a purring car being driven around the frosty streets of London in search of somebody to help him finish the story. Not, perhaps, in a fashion Quexos would have approved of—the stage would not be left entirely empty—but one which would salve Estabrook's hurt.

He wasn't alone in his search. He had the company of one half-trusted soul tonight: his driver, guide, and procurer, the ambiguous Mr. Chant. But despite Chant's shows of empathy, he was still just another servant, content to attend upon his master as long as he was promptly paid. He didn't understand the profundity of Estabrook's pain; he was too chilly, too remote. Nor, for all the length of his family history, could Estabrook turn to his lineage for comfort. Although he could trace his ancestors back to the reign of James the First, he had not been able to find a single man on that tree of immoralities—even to the bloodiest root—who had caused, either by his hand or hiring, what he, Estabrook, was out this midnight to contrive: the murder of his wife.

When he thought of her (when didn't he?) his mouth was dry and his palms were wet; he sighed; he shook. She was in his mind's eye now, like a fugitive from some more perfect place. Her skin was flawless and always cool, always pale; her body was long, like her hair, like her fingers, like her laughter; and her eyes, oh, her eyes, had every season of leaf in them: the twin greens of spring and high summer, the golds of autumn, and, in her rages, black midwinter rot.

He was, by contrast, a plain man: well scrubbed but plain. He'd made his fortune selling baths, bidets, and toilets, which lent him little by way of mystique. So, when he'd first laid eyes on Judith— she'd been sitting behind a desk at his accountant's office, her beauty all the more luminous for its drab setting—his first thought was: I want this woman; his second: She won't want me. There was, however, an instinct in him when it came to Judith that he'd never experienced with any other woman. Quite simply, he felt she *belonged* to him, and that if he turned his wit to it, he could win her.

His courtship had begun the day they'd met, with the first of many small tokens of affection delivered to her desk. But he sooned learned that such bribes and blandishments would not help his case. She politely thanked him but told him they weren't welcome. He dutifully ceased to send presents and, instead, began a systematic investigation of her circumstances. There was precious little to learn. She lived simply, her small circle vaguely bohemian. But among that circle he discovered a man whose claim upon her preceded his own, and to whom she was apparently devoted. That man was John Furie Zacharias, known universally as

Gentle, and he had a reputation as a lover that would have driven Estabrook from the field had that strange certainty not been upon him. He decided to be patient and await his moment. It would come.

Meanwhile he watched his beloved from afar, conspiring to encounter her accidentally now and again, and researching his antagonist's history. Again, there was little to learn. Zacharias was a minor painter, when he wasn't living off his mistresses, and reputedly a dissolute. Of this Estabrook had perfect proof when, by chance, he met the fellow. Gentle was as handsome as his legends suggested, but looked, Charlie thought, like a man just risen from a fever. There was something raw about him—his body sweated to its essence, his face betraying a hunger behind its symmetry—that lent him a bedeviled look.

Half a week after that encounter, Charlie had heard that his beloved had parted from the man with great grief and was in need of tender care. He'd been quick to supply it, and she'd come into the comfort of his devotion with an ease that suggested his dreams of possession had been well founded.

His memories of that triumph had, of course, been soured by her departure, and now it was he who wore the hungry, yearning look he'd first seen on Furie's face. It suited him less well than it had Zacharias. His was not a head made for haunting. At fifty-six, he looked sixty or more, his features as solid as Gentle's were spare, as pragmatic as Gentle's were rarefied. His only concession to vanity was the delicately curled mustache beneath his patrician nose, which concealed an upper lip he'd thought dubiously ripe in his youth, leaving the lower to jut in lieu of a chin.

Now, as he rode through the darkened streets, he caught sight of that face in the window and perused it ruefully. What a mockery he was! He blushed to think of how shamelessly he'd paraded himself when he'd had Judith on his arm; how he'd joked that she loved him for his cleanliness, and for his taste in bidets. The same people who'd listened to those jokes were laughing in earnest now, were calling him ridiculous. It was unbearable. The only way he knew to heal the pain of his humiliation was to punish her for the crime of leaving him.

He rubbed the heel of his hand against the window and peered out.

"Where are we?" he asked Chant.

"South of the river, sir."

"Yes, but where?"

"Streatham."

Though he'd driven through this area many times—he had a

warehouse in the neighborhood—he recognized none of it. The city had never looked more foreign or more unlovely.

"What sex is London, do you suppose?" he mused.

"I hadn't ever thought," Chant said.

"It was a woman once," Estabrook went on. "One calls a city *she,* yes? But it doesn't seem very feminine any more."

"She'll be a lady again in spring," Chant replied.

"I don't think a few crocuses in Hyde Park are going to make much difference," Estabrook said. "The charm's gone out of it." He sighed. "How far now?"

"Maybe another mile."

"Are you sure your man's going to be there?"

"Of course."

"You've done this a lot, have you? Been a go-between, I mean. What did you call it . . . a *facilitator?*"

"Oh, yes," Chant said. "It's in my blood." That blood was not entirely English. Chant's skin and syntax carried traces of the immigrant. But Estabrook had grown to trust him a little, even so.

"Aren't you curious about all of this?" he asked the man.

"It's not my business, sir. You're paying for the service, and I provide it. If you wanted to tell me your reasons—"

"As it happens, I don't."

"I understand. So it would be useless for me to be curious, yes?"

That was neat enough, Estabrook thought. Not to want what couldn't be had no doubt took the sting from things. He might need to learn the trick of that before he got too much older; before he wanted time he couldn't have. Not that he demanded much in the way of satisfactions. He'd not been sexually insistent with Judith, for instance. Indeed, he'd taken as much pleasure in the simple sight of her as he'd taken in the act of love. The sight of her had pierced him, making her the enterer, had she but known it, and him the entered. Perhaps she had known, on reflection. Perhaps she'd fled from his passivity, from his ease beneath the spike of her beauty. If so, he would undo her revulsion with tonight's business. Here, in the hiring of the assassin, he would prove himself. And, dying, she would realize her error. The thought pleased him. He allowed himself a little smile, which vanished from his face when he felt the car slowing and glimpsed, through the misted window, the place the facilitator had brought him to.

A wall of corrugated iron lay before them, its length daubed with graffiti. Beyond it, visible through gaps where the iron had been torn into ragged wings and beaten back, was a junkyard in which trailers were parked. This was apparently their destination.

"Are you out of your mind?" he said, leaning forward to take hold of Chant's shoulder. "We're not safe here."

"I promised you the best assassin in England, Mr. Estabrook, and he's here. Trust me, he's here."

Estabrook growled in fury and frustration. He'd expected a clandestine rendezvous—curtained windows, locked doors—not a gypsy encampment. This was altogether too public and too dangerous. Would it not be the perfect irony to be murdered in the middle of an assignation with an assassin?

He leaned back against the creaking leather of his seat and said, "You've let me down."

"I promise you this man is a most extraordinary individual," Chant said. "Nobody in Europe comes remotely close. I've worked with him before."

"Would you care to name the victims?"

Chant looked around at his employer and, in faintly admonishing tones, said, "I haven't presumed upon *your* privacy, Mr. Estabrook. Please don't presume upon mine."

Estabrook gave a chastened grunt.

"Would you prefer we go back to Chelsea?" Chant went on. "I can find somebody else for you. Not as good, perhaps, but in more congenial surroundings."

Chant's sarcasm wasn't lost on Estabrook, nor could he resist the recognition that this was not a game he should have entered if he'd hoped to stay lily-white. "No, no," he said "We're here, and I may as well see him. What's his name?"

"I only know him as Pie," Chant said.

"Pie? Pie what?"

"Just Pie."

Chant got out of the car and opened Estabrook's door. Icy air swirled in, bearing a few flakes of sleet. Winter was eager this year. Pulling his coat collar up around his nape and plunging his hands into the minty depths of his pockets, Estabrook followed his guide through the nearest gap in the corrugated wall. The wind carried the tang of burning timber from an almost spent bonfire set among the trailers: that, and the smell of rancid fat.

"Keep close," Chant advised, "walk briskly, and don't show too much interest. These are very private people."

"What's your man doing here?" Estabrook demanded to know. "Is he on the run?"

"You said you wanted somebody who couldn't be traced. 'Invisible' was the word you used. Pie's that man. He's on no files of any kind. Not the police, not the Social Security. He's not even registered as born."

"I find that unlikely."

"I specialize in the unlikely," Chant replied.

Until this exchange the violent turn in Chant's eye had never unsettled Estabrook, but it did now, preventing him as it did from meeting the other man's gaze directly. This tale he was telling was surely a lie. Who these days got to adulthood without appearing on a file somewhere? But the thought of meeting a man who even believed himself undocumented intrigued Estabrook. He nodded Chant on, and together they headed over the ill-lit and squalid ground.

There was debris dumped every side: the skeletal hulks of rusted vehicles; heaps of rotted household refuse, the stench of which the cold could not subdue; innumerable dead bonfires. The presence of trespassers had attracted some attention. A dog with more breeds in its blood than hairs on its back foamed and yapped at them from the limit of its rope; the curtains of several trailers were drawn back by shadowy witnesses; two girls in early adolescence, both with hair so long and blond they looked to have been baptized in gold (unlikely beauty, in such a place) rose from beside the fire, one running as if to alert guards, the other watching the newcomers with a smile somewhere between the seraphic and the cretinous.

"Don't stare," Chant reminded him as he hurried on, but Estabrook couldn't help himself.

An albino with white dreadlocks had appeared from one of the trailers with the blond girl in tow. Seeing the strangers he let out a shout and headed towards them.

Two more doors now opened, and others emerged from their trailers, but Estabrook had no chance to either see who they were or whether they were armed because Chant again said, "Just walk, don't look. We're heading for the caravan with the sun painted on it. See it?"

"I see it."

There were twenty yards still to cover. Dreadlocks was delivering a stream of orders now, most of them incoherent but surely intended to stop them in their tracks. Estabrook glanced across at Chant, who had his gaze fixed on their destination and his teeth clenched. The sound of footsteps grew louder behind them. A blow on the head or a knife in the ribs couldn't be far off.

"We're not going to make it," Estabrook said.

Within ten yards of the trailer—the albino at their shoulders—the door ahead opened, and a woman in a dressing gown, with a baby in her arms, peered out. She was small and looked so frail it was a wonder she could hold the child, who began bawling as soon as the cold found it. The ache of its complaint drove their pursuers to action. Dreadlocks took hold of Estabrook's shoulder and stopped him dead. Chant—wretched coward that he was—didn't slow his pace by a beat but strode on towards the trailer as

Estabrook was swung around to face the albino. This was his perfect nightmare, to be facing scabby, pockmarked men like these, who had nothing to lose if they gutted him on the spot. While Dreadlocks held him hard, another man—gold incisors glinting—stepped in and pulled open Estabrook's coat, then reached in to empty his pockets with the speed of an illusionist. This was not simply professionalism. They wanted their business done before they were stopped.

As the pickpocket's hand pulled out his victim's wallet, a voice came from the trailer behind Estabrook: "Let the Mister go. He's real."

Whatever the latter meant, the order was instantly obeyed, but by that time the thief had whipped Estabrook's wallet into his own pocket and had stepped back, hands raised to show them empty. Nor, despite the fact that the speaker—presumably Pie—was extending his protection to his guest, did it seem circumspect to try and reclaim the wallet. Estabrook retreated from the thieves, lighter in step and cash but glad to be doing so at all.

Turning, he saw Chant at the trailer door, which was open. The woman, the baby, and the speaker had already gone back inside.

"They didn't hurt you, did they?" Chant said.

Estabrook glanced back over his shoulder at the thugs, who had gone to the fire, presumably to divide the loot by its light "No," he said. "But you'd better go and check the car, or they'll have it stripped."

"First I'd like to introduce you—"

"Just check the car," Estabrook said, taking some satisfaction in the thought of sending Chant back across the no-man's-land between here and the perimeter. "I can introduce myself."

"As you like."

Chant went off, and Estabrook climbed the steps into the trailer. A scent and a sound met him, both sweet. Oranges had been peeled, and their dew was in the air. So was a lullaby, played on a guitar. The player, a black man, sat in the farthest corner, in a shadowy place beside a sleeping child. The babe lay to his other side, gurgling softly in a simple cot, its fat arms raised as if to pluck the music from the air with its tiny hands. The woman was at a table at the other end of the vehicle, tidying away the orange peel. The whole interior was marked by the same fastidiousness she was applying to this task, every surface neat and polished.

"You must be Pie," Estabrook said.

"Please close the door," the guitar player said. Estabrook did so. "And sit down. Theresa? Something for the gentleman. You must be cold."

The china cup of brandy set before him was like nectar. He

downed it in two throatfuls, and Theresa instantly replenished it. He drank again with the same speed, only to have his cup furnished with a further draft. By the time Pie had played both the children to sleep and rose to come and join his guest at the table, the liquor had brought a pleasant buzz to Estabrook's head.

In his life Estabrook had known only two other black men by name. One was the manager of a tiling manufacturer in Swindon, the other a colleague of his brother's: neither of them men he'd wished to know better. He was of an age and class that still swilled the dregs of colonialism at two in the morning, and the fact this man had black blood in him (and, he guessed, much else besides) counted as another mark against Chant's judgment. And yet— perhaps it was the brandy—he found the fellow opposite him intriguing. Pie didn't have the face of an assassin. It wasn't dispassionate, but distressingly vulnerable; even (though Estabrook would never have breathed this aloud) beautiful. Cheeks high, lips full, eyes heavily lidded. His hair, mingled black and blond, fell in Italianate profusion, knotted ringlets to his shoulders. He looked older than Estabrook would have expected, given the age of his children. Perhaps only thirty, but wearied by some excess or other, the burnished sepia of his skin barely concealing a sickly iridescence, as though there were a mercurial taint in his cells. It made him difficult to fix, especially for eyes awash with brandy, the merest motion of his head breaking subtle waves against his bones, their spume draining back into his skin trailing colors Estabrook had never seen in flesh before.

Theresa left them to their business and retired to sit beside the cot. In part out of deference to the sleepers and in part from his own unease at saying aloud what was on his mind, Estabrook spoke in whispers.

"Did Chant tell you why I'm here?"

"Of course," said Pie. "You want somebody murdered." He pulled a pack of cigarettes from the breast pocket of his denim shirt and offered one to Estabrook, who declined with a shake of his head. "That *is* why you're here, isn't it?"

"Yes," Estabrook replied. "Only—"

"You're looking at me and thinking I'm not the one to do it," Pie prompted. He put a cigarette to his lips. "Be honest."

"You're not exactly as I imagined," Estabrook replied.

"So, this is good," Pie said, applying a light to the cigarette. "If I had been what you'd imagined, I'd look like an assassin, and you'd say I was too obvious."

"Maybe."

"If you don't want to hire me, that's fine. I'm sure Chant can find

you somebody else. If you *do* want to hire me, then you'd better
tell me what you need."

Estabrook watched the smoke drift up over the assassin's gray
eyes, and before he could prevent himself he was telling his story,
the rules he'd drawn for this exchange forgotten. Instead of questioning the man closely, concealing his own biography so that the
other would have as little hold on him as possible, he spilled the
tragedy in every unflattering detail. Several times he almost
stopped himself, but it felt so good to be unburdened that he let
his tongue defy his better judgment. Not once did the other man
interrupt the litany, and it was only when a rapping on the door,
announcing Chant's return, interrupted the flow that Estabrook remembered there was anyone else alive in the world tonight besides
himself and his confessor. And by that time the tale was told.

Pie opened the door but didn't let Chant in. "We'll wander over
to the car when we've finished," he told the driver. "We won't be
long." Then he closed the door again and returned to the table.
"Something more to drink?" he asked.

Estabrook declined, but accepted a cigarette as they talked on,
Pie requesting details of Judith's whereabouts and movements,
Estabrook supplying the answers in a monotone. Finally, the issue
of payment. Ten thousand pounds, to be paid in two halves, the first
upon agreement of the contract, the second after its completion.

"Chant has the money," Estabrook said.

"Shall we walk, then?" Pie said.

Before they left the trailer, Estabrook looked into the cot. "You
have beautiful children," he said when they were out in the cold.

"They're not mine," Pie replied. "Their father died a year ago
this Christmas."

"Tragic," Estabrook said.

"It was quick," Pie said, glancing across at Estabrook and confirming in his glance the suspicion that he was the orphan maker.
"Are you quite certain you want this woman dead?" Pie said.
"Doubt's bad in a business like this. If there's any part of you that
hesitates—"

"There's none," Estabrook said. "I came here to find a man to
kill my wife. You're that man."

"You still love her, don't you?" Pie said, once they were out and
walking.

"Of course I love her," Estabrook said. "That's why I want her
dead."

"There's no Resurrection, Mr. Estabrook. Not for you, at least."

"It's not me who's dying," he said.

"I think it is," came the reply. They were at the fire, now

untended. "A man kills the thing he loves, and he must die a little himself. That's plain, yes?"

"If I die, I die," was Estabrook's response. "As long as she goes first. I'd like it done as quickly as possible."

"You said she's in New York. Do you want me to follow her there?"

"Are you familiar with the city?"

"Yes."

"Then do it there and do it soon. I'll have Chant supply extra funds to cover the flight. And that's that. We shan't see each other again."

Chant was waiting at the perimeter and fished the envelope containing the payment from his inside pocket. Pie accepted it without question or thanks, then shook Estabrook's hand and left the trespassers to return to the safety of their car. As he settled into the comfort of the leather seat, Estabrook realized the palm he'd pressed against Pie's was trembling. He knitted its fingers with those of his other hand, and there they remained, white-knuckled, for the length of the journey home.

2

DO THIS FOR THE WOMEN OF THE WORLD, read the note John Furie Zacharias held. *Slit your lying throat.*

Beside the note, lying on the bare boards, Vanessa and her cohorts (she had two brothers; it was probably they who'd come with her to empty the house) had left a neat pile of broken glass, in case he was sufficiently moved by her entreaty to end his life there and then. He stared at the note in something of a stupor, reading it over and over, looking—vainly, of course—for some small consolation in it. Beneath the tick and scrawl that made her name, the paper was lightly wrinkled. Had tears fallen there while she'd written her goodbye, he wondered? Small comfort if they had, and a smaller likelihood still. Vanessa was not one for crying. Nor could he imagine a woman with the least ambiguity of feeling so comprehensively stripping him of possessions. True, neither the mews house nor any stick of furniture in it had been his by law, but they had chosen many of the items together—she relying upon his artist's eye, he upon her money to purchase whatever his gaze admired. Now it was all gone, to the last Persian rug and Deco lamp. The home they'd made together, and enjoyed for a year and two months, was stripped bare. And so indeed was he: to the nerve, to the bone. He had nothing.

It wasn't calamitous. Vanessa hadn't been the first woman to indulge his taste in handmade shirts and silk waistcoats, nor would she be the last. But she was the first in recent memory—for Gentle the past had a way of evaporating after about ten years—who had conspired to remove everything from him in the space of half a day. His error was plain enough. He'd woken that morning, lying beside Vanessa with a hard-on she'd wanted him to pleasure her with, and had stupidly refused her, knowing he had a liaison with Martine that afternoon. How she'd discovered where he was unloading his balls was academic. She had, and that was that. He'd stepped out of the house at noon, believing the woman he'd left was devoted to him, and come home five hours later to find the house as it was now.

He could be sentimental at the strangest times. As now, for instance, wandering through the empty rooms, collecting up the belongings she had felt obliged to leave for him: his address book, the clothes he'd bought with his own money as opposed to hers, his spare spectacles, his cigarettes. He hadn't loved Vanessa, but he had enjoyed the fourteen months they'd spent together here. She'd left a few more pieces of trash on the dining room floor, reminders of that time: a cluster of keys they'd never found doors to fit, instruction documents for a blender he'd burned out making midnight margaritas, a plastic bottle of massage oil. All in all, a pitiful collection, but he wasn't so self-deceiving as to believe their relationship had been much more than a sum of those parts. The question was—now that it was over—where was he to go and what was he to do? Martine was a middle-aged married woman, her husband a banker who spent three days of every week in Luxembourg, leaving her time to philander. She professed love for Gentle at intervals, but not with sufficient consistency to make him think he could prize her from her husband, even if he wanted to, which he was by no means certain he did. He'd known her eight months—met her, in fact, at a dinner party hosted by Vanessa's elder brother, William—and they had only argued once, but it had been a telling exchange. She'd accused him of always looking at other women; looking, looking, as though for the next conquest. Perhaps because he didn't care for her too much, he'd replied honestly and told her she was right. He was stupid for her sex. Sickened in their absence, blissful in their company: love's fool. She'd replied that while his obsession might be healthier than her husband's—which was money and its manipulation—his behavior was still neurotic. Why this endless hunt? she'd asked him. He'd answered with some folderol about seeking the ideal woman, but he'd known the truth even as he was spinning her this tosh, and it was a bitter thing. Too bitter, in fact, to be put on his tongue. In essence, it came down to this: he felt meaningless, empty, almost invisible unless one or more of her sex were doting on him. Yes, he knew his face was finely made, his forehead broad, his gaze haunting, his lips sculpted so that even a sneer looked fetching on them, but he needed a living mirror to tell him so. More, he lived in hope that one such mirror would find something behind his looks only another pair of eyes could see: some undiscovered self that would free him from being Gentle.

As always when he felt deserted, he went to see Chester Klein, patron of the arts by diverse hands, a man who claimed to have been excised by fretful lawyers from more biographies than any other man since Byron. He lived in Notting Hill Gate, in a house he'd bought cheaply in the late fifties, which he now seldom left, touched as he was by agoraphobia or, as he preferred it, "a perfectly rational fear of anyone I can't blackmail."

From this small dukedom he managed to prosper, employed as he was in a business which required a few choice contacts, a nose for the changing taste of his market, and an ability to conceal his pleasure at his achievements. In short, he dealt in fakes, and it was this latter quality he was most deficient in. There were those among his small circle of intimates who said it would be his undoing, but they or their predecessors had been prophesying the same for three decades, and Klein had outprospered every one of them. The luminaries he'd entertained over the decades—the defecting dancers and minor spies, the addicted debutantes, the rock stars with messianic leanings, the bishops who made idols of barrow boys—they'd all had their moments of glory, then fallen. But Klein went on to tell the tale. And when, on occasion, his name did creep into a scandal sheet or a confessional biography, he was invariably painted as the patron saint of lost souls.

It wasn't only the knowledge that, being such a soul, Gentle would be welcomed at the Klein residence, that took him there. He'd never known a time when Klein didn't need money for some gambit or other, and that meant he needed painters. There was more than comfort to be found in the house at Ladbroke Grove; there was employment. It had been eleven months since he'd seen or spoken to Chester, but he was greeted as effusively as ever and ushered in.

"Quickly! Quickly!" Klein said. "Gloriana's in heat again!" He managed to slam the door before the obese Gloriana, one of his five cats, escaped in search of a mate. "Too slow, sweetie!" he told her. She yowled at him in complaint. "I keep her fat so she's slow," he said. "And I don't feel so piggy myself."

He patted a paunch that had swelled considerably since Gentle had last seen him and was testing the seams of his shirt, which, like him, was florid and had seen better years. He still wore his hair in a ponytail, complete with ribbon, and wore an ankh on a chain around his neck, but beneath the veneer of a harmless flower child gone to seed he was as acquisitive as a bowerbird. Even the vestibule in which they embraced was overflowing with collectibles: a wooden dog, plastic roses in psychedelic profusion, sugar skulls on plates.

"My God, you're cold," he said to Gentle. "And you look wretched. Who's been beating you about the head?"

"Nobody."

"You're bruised."

"I'm tired, that's all."

Gentle took off his heavy coat and laid it on the chair by the door, knowing when he returned it would be warm and covered with cat hairs. Klein was already in the living room, pouring wine. Always red.

"Don't mind the television," he said. "I never turn it off these days. The trick is not to turn up the sound. It's much more entertaining mute."

This was a new habit, and a distracting one. Gentle accepted the wine and sat down in the corner of the ill-sprung couch, where it was easiest to ignore the demands of the screen. Even there, he was tempted.

"So now, my Bastard Boy," Klein said, "to what disaster do I owe the honor?"

"It's not really a disaster. I've just had a bad time. I wanted some cheery company."

"Give them up, Gentle," Klein said.

"Give what up?"

"You know what. The fair sex. Give them up. I have. It's such a relief. All those desperate seductions. All that time wasted meditating on death to keep yourself from coming too soon. I tell you, it's like a burden gone from my shoulders."

"How old are you?"

"Age has got fuck-all to do with it. I gave up women because they were breaking my heart."

"What heart's that?"

"I might ask you the same thing. Yes, you whine and you wring your hands, but then you go back and make the same mistakes. It's tedious. *They're* tedious."

"So save me."

"Oh, now here it comes."

"I don't have any money."

"Neither do I."

"So we'll make some together. Then I won't have to be a kept man. I'm going back to live in the studio, Klein. I'll paint whatever you need."

"The Bastard Boy speaks."

"I wish you wouldn't call me that."

"It's what you are. You haven't changed in eight years. The world grows old, but the Bastard Boy keeps his perfection. Speaking of which—"

"Employ me."

"Don't interrupt me when I'm gossiping. Speaking of which, I saw Clem the Sunday before last. He asked after you. He's put on a lot of weight. And his love life's almost as disastrous as yours. Taylor's sick with the plague. I tell you, Gentle, celibacy's the thing."

"So employ me."

"It's not as easy as that. The market's soft at the moment. And, well, let me be brutal: I have a new *wunderkind.*" He got up. "Let me show you." He led Gentle through the house to the study. "The fellow's twenty-two, and I swear if he had an idea in his head he'd be a great painter. But he's like you; he's got the talent but nothing to say."

"Thanks," said Gentle sourly.

"You know it's true." Klein switched on the light. There were three canvases, all unframed, in the room. One, a nude woman after the style of Modigliani. Beside it, a small landscape after Corot. But the third, and largest of the three, was the *coup.* It was a pastoral scene, depicting classically garbed shepherds standing, in awe, before a tree in the trunk of which a human face was visible.

"Would you know it from a real Poussin?"

"Is it still wet?" Gentle asked.

"Such a wit."

Gentle went to give the painting a more intimate examination. This period was not one he was particularly expert in, but he knew enough to be impressed by the handiwork. The canvas was a close weave, the paint laid upon it in careful regular strokes, the tones built up, it seemed, in glazes.

"Meticulous, eh?" said Klein.

"To the point of being mechanical."

"Now, now, no sour grapes."

"I mean it. It's just too perfect for words. You put this in the market and the game's up. Now, the Modigliani's another matter—"

"That was a technical exercise," Klein said. "I can't sell that. The man only painted a dozen pictures. It's the Poussin I'm betting on."

"Don't. You'll get stung. Mind if I get another drink?"

Gentle headed back through the house to the lounge, Klein following, muttering to himself.

"You've got a good eye, Gentle," he said, "but you're unreliable. You'll find another woman and off you'll go."

"Not this time."

"And I wasn't kidding about the market. There's no room for bullshit."

"Did you ever have a problem with a piece I painted?"

Klein mused on this. "No," he admitted.

"I've got a Gauguin in New York. Those Fuseli sketches I did—"

"Berlin. Oh, yes, you've made your little mark."

"Nobody's ever going to know it, of course."

"They will. In a hundred years' time your Fuselis will look as old as they are, not as old as they should be. People will start to investigate, and you, my Bastard Boy, will be discovered. And so will Kenny Soames and Gideon: all my deceivers."

"And you'll be vilified for bribing us. Denying the twentieth century all that originality."

"Originality, shit. It's an overrated commodity, you know that. You can be a visionary painting Virgins."

"That's what I'll do, then. Virgins in any style. I'll be celibate, and I'll paint Madonnas all day. With child. Without child. Weeping. Blissful. I'll work my balls off, Kleiny, which'll be fine because I won't need them."

"Forget the Virgins. They're out of fashion."

"They're forgotten."

"Decadence is your strongest suit."

"Whatever you want. Say the word."

"But don't fuck with me. If I find a client and promise something to him, it's up to you to produce it."

"I'm going back to the studio tonight. I'm starting over. Just do one thing for me?"

"What's that?"

"Burn the Poussin."

He had visited the studio on and off through his time with Vanessa—he'd even met Martine there on two occasions when her husband had canceled a Luxembourg trip and she'd been too heated to miss a liaison—but it was charmless and cheerless, and he'd returned happily to the house in Wimpole Mews. Now, however, he welcomed the studio's austerity. He turned on the little electric fire, made himself a cup of fake coffee with fake milk, and, under its influence, thought about deception.

The last six years of his life—since Judith, in fact—had been a series of duplicities. This was not of itself disastrous—after tonight it would once more be his profession—but whereas painting had a tangible end result (two, if he included the recompense), pursuit and seduction always left him naked and empty-handed. An end to that, tonight. He made a vow, toasted in bad coffee, to the God of Forgers, whoever he was, to become great. If duplicity was his genius, why waste it on deceiving husbands and mistresses? He should turn it to a profounder end, producing masterpieces in another man's name. Time would validate him, the way Klein had said it would: uncover his many works and show him, at last, as the visionary he was about to become. And if it didn't—if Klein was wrong and his handiwork remained undiscovered forever—then that was the truest vision of all. Invisible, he would be seen; unknown, he'd be influential. It was enough to make him forget women entirely. At least for tonight.

3

AT DUSK THE CLOUDS OVER MANHATTAN, which had threatened snow all day, cleared and revealed a pristine sky, its color so ambiguous it might have fueled a philosophical debate as to the nature of blue. Laden as she was with her day's purchases, Jude chose to walk back to Marlin's apartment at Park Avenue and 80th. Her arms ached, but it gave her time to turn over in her head the encounter which had marked the day and decide whether she wanted to share it with Marlin or not. Unfortunately, he had a lawyer's mind: at best, cool and analytical; at worst, reductionist. She knew herself well enough to know that if he challenged her account in the latter mode she'd almost certainly lose her temper with him, and then the atmosphere between them, which had been (with the exception of his overtures) so easy and undemanding, would be spoiled. It was better to work out what she believed about the events of the previous two hours before she shared it with Marlin. Then he could dissect it at will.

Already, after going over the encounter a few times, it was becoming, like the blue overhead, ambiguous. But she held on hard to the facts of the matter. She'd been in the menswear department of Bloomingdale's, looking for a sweater for Marlin. It was crowded, and there was nothing on display that she thought appropriate. She'd started to pick up the purchases at her feet when she'd caught sight of a face she knew, looking straight at her through the moving mesh of people. How long had she seen the face for? A second, two at most? Long enough for her heart to jump and her face to flush; long enough for her mouth to open and shape the word *Gentle*. Then the traffic between them had thickened, and he'd disappeared. She'd fixed the place where he'd been, stooped to pick up her baggage, and gone after him, not doubting that it was he.

The crowd slowed her progress, but she soon caught sight of him again, heading towards the door. This time she yelled his name, not giving a damn if she looked a fool, and dove after him. She was impressive in full flight, and the crowd yielded, so that by the time she reached the door he was only yards away. Third Avenue was as thronged as the store, but there he was, heading across the street. The lights changed as she got to the curb. She went after him anyway, daring the traffic. As she yelled again he was buffeted by a shopper, on some business as urgent as hers, and he turned as he was struck, giving her a second glimpse of him. She might have laughed out loud at the absurdity of her error had it not disturbed her so. Either she was losing her mind, or she'd followed the wrong man. Either way, this black man, his ringleted hair gleaming on his shoulders, was not Gentle. Momentarily undecided as to whether to go on looking or to give up the chase there and then, her eyes lingered on the stranger's face, and for a heartbeat or less his features blurred and in their flux, caught as if by the sun off a wing in the stratosphere, she saw Gentle, his hair swept back from his high forehead, his gray eyes all yearning, his mouth, which she'd not known she missed till now, ready to break into a smile. It never came. The wing dipped; the stranger turned; Gentle was gone. She stood in the throng for several seconds while he disappeared downtown. Then, gathering herself together, she turned her back on the mystery and started home.

It didn't leave her thoughts, of course. She was a woman who trusted her senses, and to discover them so deceptive distressed her. But more vexing still was why it should be that particular face, of all those in her memory's catalogue, she'd chosen to configure from that of a perfect stranger. Klein's Bastard Boy was out of her life, and she out of his. It was six years since she'd crossed the bridge from where they'd stood together, and the river that flowed between was a torrent. Her marriage to Estabrook had come and gone along that river, and a good deal of pain with it. Gentle was still on the other shore, part of her history: irretrievable. So why had she conjured him now?

As she came within a block of Marlin's building she remembered something she'd utterly put out of her head for that six-year span. It had been a glimpse of Gentle, not so unlike the one she'd just had, that had propelled her into her near-suicidal affair with him. She'd met him at one of Klein's parties—a casual encounter—and had given him very little conscious thought subsequently. Then, three nights later, she'd been visited by an erotic dream that regularly haunted her. The scenario was always the same. She was lying naked on bare boards in an empty room, not bound but somehow bounded, and a man whose face she could never see, his mouth so sweet it was like eating candy to kiss him, made violent love to her. Only this time the fire that burned in the grate close by showed her the face of her dream lover, and it had been Gentle's face. The shock, after so many years of never knowing who the man was, woke her, but with such a sense of loss at this interrupted coitus she couldn't sleep again for mourning it. The next day she'd discovered his whereabouts from Klein, who'd warned her in no uncertain manner that John Zacharias was bad news for tender hearts. She'd ignored the warning and gone to see him that very afternoon, in the studio off the Edgware Road. They scarcely left it for the next two weeks, their passion putting her dreams to shame.

Only later, when she was in love with him and it was too late for common sense to qualify her feelings, did she learn more about him. He trailed a reputation for womanizing that, even if it was ninety percent invention, as she assumed, was still prodigious. If she mentioned his name in any circle, however jaded it was by gossip, there was always somebody who had some tidbit about him. He even went by a variety of names. Some referred to him as the Furie; some as Zach or Zacho, or Mr. Zee; others called him Gentle, which was the name she knew him by, of course; still others, John the Divine. Enough names for half a dozen lifetimes. She wasn't so blindly devoted to him that she didn't accept there was truth in these rumors. Nor did he do much to temper them. He liked the air of legend that hung about his head. He claimed, for instance, not to know how old he was. Like herself, he had a very slippery grasp on the past. And he frankly admitted to being obsessed with her sex. Some of the talk she'd heard was of cradle-snatching; some of deathbed fucks: he played no favorites.

So, here was her Gentle: a man known to the doormen of every exclusive club and hotel in the city; who, after ten years of high living had survived the ravages of every excess; who was still lucid, still handsome, still alive. And this same man, this Gentle, told her he was in love with her and put the words together so perfectly she disregarded all she'd heard but those he spoke.

She might have gone on listening forever but for her rage, which was the legend *she* trailed. A volatile thing, apt to ferment in her without her even being aware of it. That had been the case with Gentle. After half a year of their affair, she'd begun to wonder, wallowing in his affection, how a man whose history had been one infidelity after another had mended his ways; which thought led to the possibility that perhaps he hadn't. In fact she had no reason to suspect him. His devotion bordered on the obsessive in some moods, as though he saw in her a woman she didn't even know herself, an ancient soul mate. She was, she began to think, unlike any other woman he'd ever met, the love that had changed his life. When they were so intimately joined, how would she not know if he was cheating on her? She'd have surely sensed the other woman. Tasted her on his tongue, or smelled her on his skin. And if not there, then in the subtleties of their exchanges. But she'd underestimated him. When, by the sheerest fluke, she'd discovered he had not one other woman on the side but two, it drove her to near insanity. She began by destroying the contents of the studio, slashing all his canvases, painted or not, then tracking the felon himself and mounting an assault that literally brought him to his knees, in fear for his balls.

The rage burned a week, after which she fell totally silent for three days: a silence broken by a grief like nothing she'd ever experienced before. Had it not been for her chance meeting with Estabrook—who saw through her tumbling, distracted manner to the woman she was—she might well have taken her own life.

Thus the tale of Judith and Gentle: one death short of tragedy, and a marriage short of farce.

She found Marlin already home, uncharacteristically agitated.

"Where have you been?" he wanted to know. "It's six thirty nine."

She instantly knew this was no time to be telling him what her trip to Bloomingdale's had cost her in peace of mind. Instead she lied. "I couldn't get a cab. I had to walk."

"If that happens again, just call me. I'll have you picked up by one of our limos. I don't want you wandering the streets. It's not safe. Anyhow, we're late. We'll have to eat after the performance."

"What performance?"

"The show in the Village that Troy was yabbering about last night, remember? The Neo-Nativity? He said it was the best thing since Bethlehem."

"It's sold out."

"I have my connections." He gleamed.

"We're going tonight?"

"Not if you don't move your ass."

"Marlin, sometimes you're sublime," she said, dumping her purchases and racing to change.

"What about the rest of the time?" he hollered after her. "Sexy? Irresistible? Beddable?"

If indeed he'd secured the tickets as a way of bribing her between the sheets, he suffered for his lust. He concealed his boredom through the first act, but by intermission he was itching to be away to claim his prize.

"Do we really need to stay for the rest?" he asked her as they sipped coffee in the tiny foyer. "I mean, it's not like there's any mystery about it. The kid gets born, the kid grows up, the kid gets crucified."

"I'm enjoying it."

"But it doesn't make any sense," he complained, in deadly earnest. The show's eclecticism offended his rationalism deeply. "Why were the angels playing jazz?"

"Who knows what angels do?"

He shook his head. "I don't know whether it's a comedy or a satire or what the hell it is," he said. "Do you know what it is?"

"I think it's very funny."

"So you'd like to stay?"

"I'd like to stay."

The second half was even more of a grab bag than the first, the suspicion growing in Jude as she watched that the parody and pastiche was a smokescreen put up to cover the creators' embarrassment at their own sincerity. In the end, with Charlie Parker angels wailing on the stable roof and Santa crooning at the manger, the piece collapsed into high camp. But even that was oddly moving. The child was born. Light had come into the world again, even if it was to the accompaniment of tap-dancing elves.

When they exited, there was sleet in the wind.

"Cold, cold, cold," Marlin said. "I'd better take a leak."

He went back inside to join the line for the toilets, leaving Jude at the door, watching the blobs of wet snow pass through the lamplight. The theater was not large, and the bulk of the audience was out in a couple of minutes, umbrellas raised, heads dropped, darting off into the Village to look for their cars, or a place where they could put some drink in their systems and play critic. The light above the front door was switched off, and a cleaner emerged from the theater with a black plastic bag of rubbish and a broom and began to brush the foyer, ignoring Jude—who was the last visible occupant—until he reached her, when he gave her a glance of such venom she decided to put up her umbrella and stand on the darkened step. Marlin was taking his time emptying his bladder. She only hoped he wasn't titivating himself, slicking his hair and freshening his breath in the hope of talking her into bed.

The first she knew of the assault was a motion glimpsed from the corner of her eye: a blurred form approaching her at speed through the thickening sleet. Alarmed, she turned towards her attacker. She had time to recognize the face on Third Avenue; then the man was upon her.

She opened her mouth to yell, turning to retreat into the theater as she did so. The cleaner had gone. So had her shout, caught in her throat by the stranger's hands. They were expert. They hurt brutally, stopping every breath from being drawn. She panicked; flailed; toppled. He took her weight, controlling her motion. In desperation she threw the umbrella into the foyer, hoping there was somebody out of sight in the box office who'd be alerted to her jeopardy. Then she was wrenched out of shadow into heavier shadow still and realized it was almost too late already. She was becoming light-headed, her leaden limbs no longer hers. In the murk her assassin's face was once more a blur, with two dark holes bored in it. She fell towards them, wishing she had the energy to turn her gaze away from this blankness, but as he moved closer to her a little light caught his cheek and she saw, or thought she saw, tears there, spilling from those dark eyes. Then the light went, not just from his cheek but from the whole world. And as everything slipped away, she could only hold on to the thought that somehow her murderer knew who she was. . . .

"*Judith?*"

Somebody was holding her. Somebody was shouting to her. Not the assassin but Marlin. She sagged in his arms, catching dizzied sight of the assailant running across the pavement, with another man in pursuit. Her eyes swung back to Marlin, who was asking her if she was all right, then back to the street as brakes shrieked and the failed assassin was struck squarely by a speeding car, which reeled around, wheels locked and sliding over the sleet-greased street, throwing the man's body off the hood and over a parked car. The pursuer threw himself aside as the vehicle mounted the pavement, slamming into a lamppost.

Jude put her arm out for some support other than Marlin, her fingers finding the wall. Ignoring his advice that she stay still, she started to stumble towards the place where her assassin had fallen. The driver was being helped from his smashed vehicle, unleashing a stream of obscenities as he emerged. Others were appearing on the scene to lend help in forming a crowd, but Jude ignored their stares and headed across the street, Marlin at her side. She was determined to reach the body before anybody else. She wanted to see it before it was touched; wanted to meet its open eyes and fix its dead expression; know it, for memory's sake.

She found his blood first, spattered in the gray slush underfoot, and then, a little way beyond, the assassin himself, reduced to a lumpen form in the gutter. As she came within a few yards of it, however, a shudder passed down its spine and it rolled over, showing its face to the sleet. Then, impossible though this seemed, given the blow it had been struck, the form started to haul itself to its feet. She saw how bloodied it was, but she saw also that it was still essentially whole. It's not human, she thought, as it stood upright; whatever it is, it's not human. Marlin groaned with revulsion behind her, and a woman on the pavement screamed. The man's gaze went to the screamer, wavered, then returned to Jude.

It wasn't an assassin any longer. Nor was it Gentle. If it had a self, perhaps this was its face: split by wounds and doubt; pitiful; lost. She saw its mouth open and close as if it was attempting to address her. Then Marlin made a move to pursue it, and it ran. How, after such an accident, its limbs managed any speed at all was a miracle, but it was off at a pace that Marlin couldn't hope to match. He made a show of pursuit but gave up at the first intersection, returning to Jude breathless.

"Drugs," he said, clearly angered to have missed his chance at heroism. "Fucker's on drugs. He's not feeling any pain. Wait till he comes down, he'll drop dead. Fucker! How did he know you?"

"Did he?" she said, her whole body trembling now, as relief at her escape and terror at how close she'd come to losing her life both stung tears from her.

"He called you Judith," Marlin said.

In her mind's eye she saw the assassin's mouth open and close and on them read the syllables of her name.

"Drugs," Marlin was saying again, and she didn't waste words arguing, though she was certain he was wrong. The only drug in the assassin's system had been purpose, and that would not lay him low, tonight or any other.

4

I

Eleven days after he had taken Estabrook to the encampment in Streatham, Chant realized he would soon be having a visitor. He lived alone, and anonymously, in a one-room flat on a soon-to-be-condemned estate close to the Elephant and Castle, an address he had given to nobody, not even his employer. Not that his pursuers would be distracted from finding him by such petty secrecy. Unlike *Homo sapiens*, the species his long-dead master Sartori had been wont to call *the blossom on the simian tree*, Chant's kind could not hide themselves from oblivion's agents by closing a door and drawing the blinds. They were like beacons to those that preyed on them.

Men had it so much easier. The creatures that had made meat

of them in earlier ages were zoo specimens now, brooding behind
bars for the entertainment of the victorious ape. They had no grasp,
those apes, of how close they lay to a state where the devouring
beasts of Earth's infancy would be little more than fleas. That state
was called the In Ovo, and on the other side of it lay four worlds,
the so-called Reconciled Dominions. They teemed with wonders:
individuals blessed with attributes that would have made them, in
this, the Fifth Dominion, fit for sainthood or burning, or both; cults
possessed of secrets that would overturn in a moment the dogmas
of faith and physics alike; beauty that might blind the sun or set
the moon dreaming of fertility. All this, separated from Earth—
the unreconciled Fifth—by the abyss of the In Ovo.

It was not, of course, an impossible journey to make. But the
power to do so, which was usually—and contemptuously—referred
to as magic, had been waning in the Fifth since Chant had first arrived. He'd seen the walls of reason built against it, brick by brick.
He'd seen its practitioners hounded and mocked; seen its theories
decay into decadence and parody; seen its purpose steadily forgotten. The Fifth was choking in its own certainties, and though he
took no pleasure in the thought of losing his life, he would not
mourn his removal from this hard and unpoetic Dominion.

He went to his window and looked down the five stories into
the courtyard. It was empty. He had a few minutes yet, to compose
his missive to Estabrook. Returning to his table, he began it again,
for the ninth or tenth time. There was so much he wanted to communicate, but he knew that Estabrook was utterly ignorant of the
involvement of his family, whose name he'd abandoned, with the
fate of the Dominions. It was too late now to educate him. A warning would have to suffice. But how to word it so it didn't sound like
the rambling of a wild man? He set to again, putting the facts as
plainly as he could, though doubting that these words would save
Estabrook's life. If the powers that prowled this world tonight
wanted him dispatched, nothing short of intervention from the
Unbeheld Himself, Hapexamendios, the all-powerful occupant of
the First Dominion, would save him.

With the note finished, Chant pocketed it and headed out into
the darkness. Not a moment too soon. In the frosty quiet he heard
the sound of an engine too suave to belong to a resident and
peered over the parapet to see the men getting out of the car
below. He didn't doubt that these were his visitors. The only vehicles he'd seen here so polished were hearses. He cursed himself.
Fatigue had made him slothful, and now he'd let his enemies get
dangerously close. He ducked down the back stairs—glad, for once,
that there were so few lights working along the landings—as his
visitors strode towards the front. From the flats he passed, the

sound of lives: Christmas pops on the radio, argument, a baby
laughing, which became tears, as though it sensed there was danger near. Chant knew none of his neighbors, except as furtive faces
glimpsed at windows, and now—though it was too late to change
that—he regretted it.

He reached ground level unharmed, and discounting the
thought of trying to retrieve his car from the courtyard he headed
off towards the street most heavily trafficked at this time of night,
which was Kennington Park Road. If he was lucky he'd find a cab
there, though at this time of night they weren't frequent. Fares were
harder to pick up in this area than in Covent Garden or Oxford
Street, and more likely to prove unruly. He allowed himself one
backward glance, then turned his heels to the task of flight.

2

Though classically it was the light of day which showed a painter
the deepest flaws in his handiwork, Gentle worked best at night: the
instincts of a lover brought to a simpler art. In the week or so since
he'd returned to his studio it had once again become a place of work:
the air pungent with the smell of paint and turpentine, the burned-
down butts of cigarettes left on every available shelf and plate.
Though he'd spoken with Klein daily there was no sign of a commission yet, so he had spent the time reeducating himself. As Klein
had so cruelly observed, he was a technician without a vision, and
that made these days of meandering difficult. Until he had a style
to forge, he felt listless, like some latter day Adam, born with the
power to impersonate but bereft of subjects. So he set himself an
exercise. He would paint a canvas in four radically different styles:
a cubist North, an impressionist South, an East after Van Gogh, a
West after Dali. As his subject he took Caravaggio's *Supper at Emmaus*. The challenge drove him to a healthy distraction, and he was
still occupied with it at three-thirty in the morning, when the telephone rang. The line was watery, and the voice at the other end
pained and raw, but it was unmistakably Judith.

"Is that you, Gentle?"

"It's me." He was glad the line was so bad. The sound of her
voice had shaken him, and he didn't want her to know. "Where are
you calling from?"

"New York. I'm just visiting for a few days."

"It's good to hear from you."

"I'm not sure why I'm calling. It's just that today's been strange
and I thought maybe, oh—" She stopped. Laughed at herself, perhaps a little drunkenly. "I don't know what I thought," she went
on. "It's stupid. I'm sorry."

"When are you coming back?"

"I don't know that either."

"Maybe we could get together?"

"I don't think so, Gentle."

"Just to talk."

"This line's getting worse. I'm sorry I woke you."

"You didn't—"

"Keep warm, huh?"

"Judith—"

"Sorry, Gentle."

The line went dead. But the water she'd spoken through gurgled on, like the noise in a seashell. Not the ocean at all, of course; just illusion. He put the receiver down and—knowing he'd never sleep now—squeezed out some fresh bright worms of paint to work with, and set to.

3

It was the whistle from the gloom behind him that alerted Chant to the fact that his escape had not gone unnoticed. It was not a whistle that could have come from human lips, but a chilling scalpel shriek he had heard only once before in the Fifth Dominion, when, some two hundred years past, his then possessor, the Maestro Sartori, had conjured from the In Ovo a familiar which had made such a whistle. It had brought bloody tears to its summoner's eyes, obliging Sartori to relinquish it posthaste. Later Chant and the Maestro had spoken of the event, and Chant had identified the creature. It was known in the Reconciled Dominions as a voider, one of a brutal species that haunted the wastes north of the Lenten Way. Voiders came in many shapes, being made, some said, from collective desire, which fact seemed to move Sartori profoundly.

"I must summon one again," he'd said, "and speak with it," to which Chant had replied that if they were to attempt such a summoning they had to be ready next time, for voiders were lethal and could not be tamed except by Maestros of inordinate power.

The proposed conjuring had never taken place. Sartori had disappeared a short time later. In all the intervening years Chant had wondered if he had attempted a second summoning alone and been the voiders' victim. Perhaps the creature now coming after Chant had been responsible. Though Sartori had disappeared two hundred years ago, the lives of voiders, like those of so many species from the other Dominions, were longer than the longest human span.

Chant glanced over his shoulder. The whistler was in sight. It looked perfectly human, dressed in a gray, well-cut suit and black tie, its collar turned up against the cold, its hands thrust into its pockets. It didn't run but almost idled as it came, the whistle confounding Chant's thoughts and making him stumble. As he turned away the second of his pursuers appeared on the pavement in front of him, drawing a hand from its pocket. A gun? No. A knife? No. Something tiny crawled in the voider's palm, like a flea. Chant had no sooner focused upon it than it leapt towards his face. Repulsed, he raised his arm to keep it from his eyes or mouth, and the flea landed upon his hand. He slapped at it with his other hand, but it was beneath his thumbnail before he could get to it. He raised his arm to see its motion in the flesh of his thumb and clamped his other hand around the base of the digit, in the hope of stopping its further advance, gasping as though doused with icewater. The pain was out of all proportion to the mite's size, but he held both thumb and sobs hard, determined not to lose all dignity in front of his executioners. Then he staggered off the pavement into the street, throwing a glance down towards the brighter lights at the junction. What safety they offered was debatable, but if worst came to worst he would throw himself beneath a car and deny the voiders the entertainment of his slow demise. He began to run again, still clutching his hand. This time he didn't glance back. He didn't need to. The sound of the whistling faded, and the purr of the car replaced it. He threw every ounce of his energy into the run, reaching the bright street to find it deserted by traffic. He turned north, racing past the underground station towards the Elephant and Castle. Now he did glance behind, to see the car following steadily. It had three occupants: the voiders and another, sitting in the back seat. Sobbing with breathlessness he ran on, and—Lord love it!—a taxi appeared around the next corner, its yellow light announcing its availability. Concealing his pain as best he could, knowing the driver might pass on by if he thought the hailer was wounded, he stepped out into the street and raised his hand to wave the driver down. This meant unclasping one hand from the other, and the mite took instant advantage, working its way up into his wrist. But the vehicle slowed.

"Where to, mate?"

He astonished himself with the reply, giving not Estabrook's address but that of another place entirely.

"Clerkenwell," he said. "Gamut Street."

"Don't know it," the cabbie replied, and for one heart-stopping moment Chant thought he was going to drive on.

"I'll direct you," he said.

"Get in, then."

Chant did so, slamming the cab door with no little satisfaction and barely managing to reach the seat before the cab picked up speed.

Why had he named Gamut Street? There was nothing there that would heal him. Nothing could. The flea—or whatever variation in that species it was that crawled in him—had reached his elbow, and his arm below that pain was now completely numb, the skin of his hand wrinkled and flaky. But the house in Gamut Street had been a place of miracles once. Men and women of great authority had walked in it and perhaps left some ghost of themselves to calm him in extremis. No creature, Sartori had taught, passed through this Dominion unrecorded, even to the least—to the child that perished a heartbeat after it opened its eyes, the child that died in the womb, drowned in its mother's waters—even that unnamed thing had its record and its consequence. So how much more might the once-powerful of Gamut Street have left, by way of echoes?

His heart was palpitating, and his body full of jitters. Fearing he'd soon lose control of his functions, he pulled the letter to Estabrook from his pocket and leaned forward to slide the half window between himself and the driver aside.

"When you've dropped me in Clerkenwell I'd like you to deliver a letter for me. Would you be so kind?"

"Sorry, matc," the driver said. "I'm going home after this. I've a wife waiting for me."

Chant dug in his inside pocket and pulled out his wallet, then passed it through the window, letting it drop on the seat beside the driver.

"What's this?"

"All the money I've got. This letter has to be delivered."

"All the money you've got, eh?"

The driver picked up the wallet and flicked it open, his gaze going between its contents and the road.

"There's a lot of dosh in here."

"Have it. It's no good to me."

"Are you sick?"

"And tired," Chant said. "Take it, why don't you? Enjoy it."

"There's a Daimler been following us. Somebody you know?"

There was no purpose served by lying to the man. "Yes," Chant said. "I don't suppose you could put some distance between them and us?"

The man pocketed the wallet and jabbed his foot down on the accelerator. The cab leapt forward like a racehorse from the gate, its jockey's laugh rising above the guttural din of the engine. Whether it was the cash he was now heavy with or the challenge of outrunning a Daimler that motivated him, he put his cab through its paces, proving it more mobile than its bulk would have suggested. In under a minute they'd made two sharp lefts and a squealing right and were roaring down a back street so narrow the least miscalculation would have taken off handles, hubs, and mirrors. The mazing didn't stop there. They made another turn, and another, bringing them in a short time to Southwark Bridge. Somewhere along the way, they'd lost the Daimler. Chant might have applauded had he possessed two workable hands, but the flea's message of corruption was spreading with agonizing speed. While he still had five fingers under his command he went back to the window and dropped Estabrook's letter through, murmuring the address with a tongue that felt disfigured in his mouth.

"What's wrong with you?" the cabbie said. "It's not fucking contagious, is it, 'cause if it is—"

"... not ..." Chant said.

"You look fucking awful," the cabbie said, glancing in the mirror. "Sure you don't want a hospital?"

"No. Gamut Street. I want Gamut Street."

"You'll have to direct me from here."

The streets had all changed. Trees gone; rows demolished; austerity in place of elegance, function in place of beauty; the new for old, however poor the exchange rate. It was a decade and more since he'd come here last. Had Gamut Street fallen and a steel phallus risen in its place?

"Where are we?" he asked the driver.

"Clerkenwell. That's where you wanted, isn't it?"

"I mean the precise place."

The driver looked for a sign. "Flaxen Street. Does it ring a bell?"

Chant peered out of the window. "Yes! Yes! Go down to the end and turn right."

"Used to live around here, did you?"

"A long time ago."

"It's seen better days." He turned right. "Now where?"

"First on the left."

"Here it is," the man said. "Gamut Street. What number was it?"

"Twenty-eight."

The cab drew up at the curb. Chant fumbled for the handle, opened the door, and all but fell out onto the pavement. Staggering, he put his weight against the door to close it, and for the first time he and the driver came face to face. Whatever the flea was doing to his system, it must have been horribly apparent, to judge by the look of repugnance on the man's face.

"You *will* deliver the letter?" Chant said.

"You can trust me, mate."

"When you've done it, you should go home," Chant said. "Tell your wife you love her. Give a prayer of thanks."

"What for?"

"That you're human," Chant said.

The cabbie didn't question this little lunacy. "Whatever you say, mate," he replied. "I'll give the missus one and give thanks at the same time, how's that? Now don't do anything I wouldn't do, eh?"

This advice given, he drove off, leaving his passenger to the silence of the street.

With failing eyes, Chant scanned the gloom. The houses, built in the middle of Sartori's century, looked to be mostly deserted; primed for demolition, perhaps. But then Chant knew that sacred places—and Gamut Street was sacred in its way—survived on occasion because they went unseen, even in plain sight. Burnished by magic, they deflected the threatening eye and found unwitting allies in men and women who, all unknowing, knew holiness; became sanctuaries for a secret few.

He climbed the three steps to the door and pushed at it, but it was securely locked, so he went to the nearest window. There was a filthy shroud of cobweb across it but no curtain beyond. He pressed his face to the glass. Though his eyes were weakening by the moment, his gaze was still more acute than that of the blossoming ape. The room he looked into was stripped of all furniture and decoration; if anybody had occupied this house since Sartori's time—and it surely hadn't stood empty for two hundred years— they had gone, taking every trace of their presence. He raised his good arm and struck the glass with his elbow, a single jab which shattered the window. Then, careless of the damage he did himself, he hoisted his bulk onto the sill, beat out the rest of the pieces of glass with his hand, and dropped down into the room on the other side.

The layout of the house was still clear in his mind. In dreams he'd drifted through these rooms and heard the Maestro's voice summoning him up the stairs—up! up!—to the room at the top where Sartori had worked his work. It was there Chant wanted to go now, but there were new signs of atrophy in his body with every heartbeat. The hand first invaded by the flea was withered, its nails dropped from their place, its bone showing at the knuckles and wrist. Beneath his jacket he knew his torso to the hip was similarly unmade; he felt pieces of his flesh falling inside his shirt as he moved. He would not be moving for much longer. His legs were increasingly unwilling to bear him up, and his senses were close to flickering out. Like a man whose children were leaving him, he begged as he climbed the stairs.

"Stay with me. Just a little longer. *Please....*"

His cajoling got him as far as the first landing, but then his legs all but gave out, and thereafter he had to climb using his one good arm to haul him onward.

He was halfway up the final flight when he heard the voiders' whistle in the street outside, its piercing din unmistakable. They had found him quicker than he'd anticipated, sniffing him out through the darkened streets. The fear that he'd be denied sight of the sanctum at the top of the stairs spurred him on, his body doing its ragged best to accommodate his ambition.

From below, he heard the door being forced open. Then the whistle again, harder than before, as his pursuers stepped into the house. He began to berate his limbs, his tongue barely able to shape the words.

"Don't let me down! Work, will you? *Work!*"

And they obliged. He scaled the last few stairs in a spastic fashion, but reached the top flight as he heard the voiders' soles at the bottom. It was dark up here, though how much of that was blindness and how much night he didn't know. It scarcely mattered. The route to the door of the sanctum was as familiar to him as the limbs he'd lost. He crawled on hands and knees across the landing, the ancient boards creaking beneath him. A sudden fear seized him: that the door would be locked, and he'd beat his weakness against it and fail to gain access. He reached up for the handle, grasped it, tried to turn it once, failed, tried again, and this time dropped face down over the threshold as the door swung open.

There was food for his enfeebled eyes. Shafts of moonlight spilled from the windows in the roof. Though he'd dimly thought it was sentiment that had driven him back here, he saw now it was not. In returning here he came full circle, back to the room which had been his first glimpse of the Fifth Dominion. This was his cradle and his tutoring room. Here he'd smelled the air of England for the first time, the crisp October air; here he'd fed first, drunk first; first had cause for laughter and, later, for tears. Unlike the lower rooms, whose emptiness was a sign of desertion, this space had always been sparely furnished, and sometimes completely empty. He'd danced here on the same legs that now lay dead beneath him, while Sartori had told him how he planned to take this wretched Dominion and build in its midst a city that would shame Babylon; danced for sheer exuberance, knowing his Maestro was a great man and had it in his power to change the world.

Lost ambition; all lost. Before that October had become November Sartori had gone, flitted in the night or murdered by his enemies. Gone, and left his servant stranded in a city he barely knew. How Chant had longed then to return to the ether from where he'd been summoned, to shrug off the body which Sartori had congealed around him and be gone out of this Dominion. But the only voice capable of ordering such a release was that which had conjured him, and with Sartori gone he was exiled on earth forever. He hadn't hated his summoner for that. Sartori had been indulgent for the weeks they'd been together. Were he to appear now, in the moonlit room, Chant would not have accused him of negligence but made proper obeisances and been glad that his inspiration had returned.

"Maestro . . ." he murmured, face to the musty boards.

"Not here," came a voice from behind him. It was not, he knew, one of the voiders. They could whistle but not speak. "You were Sartori's creature, were you? I don't remember that."

The speaker was precise, cautious and smug. Unable to turn, Chant had to wait until the man walked past his supine body to get a sight of him. He knew better than to judge by appearances: he, whose flesh was not his own but of the Maestro's sculpting. Though the man in front of him looked human enough, he had the voiders in tow and spoke with knowledge of things few humans had access to. His face was an overripe cheese, drooping with jowls and weary folds around the eyes, his expression that of a funereal comic. The smugness in his voice was here too, in the studied way he licked upper and lower lips with his tongue before he spoke, and tapped the fingertips of each hand together as he judged the broken man at his feet. He wore an immaculately tailored three-piece suit, cut from a cloth of apricot cream. Chant would have given a good deal to break the bastard's nose so he bled on it.

"I never did meet Sartori," he said. "Whatever happened to him?"

The man went down on his haunches in front of Chant and suddenly snatched hold of a handful of his hair.

"I asked you what happened to your Maestro," he said. "I'm Dowd, by the way. You never knew *my* master, the Lord Godolphin, and I never knew yours. But they're gone, and you're scrabbling around for work. Well, you won't have to do it any longer, if you take my meaning."

"Did you . . . did you send him to me?"

"It would help my comprehension if you could be more specific."

"Estabrook."

"Oh, yes. Him."

"You did. Why?"

"Wheels within wheels, my dove," Dowd said. "I'd tell you the whole bitter story, but you don't have the time to listen and I don't have the patience to explain. I knew of a man who needed an assassin. I knew of another man who dealt in them. Let's leave it at that."

"But how did you know about me?"

"You're not discreet," Dowd replied. "You get drunk on the Queen's birthday, and you gab like an Irishman at a wake. Lovey, it draws attention sooner or later."

"Once in a while—"

"I know, you get melancholy. We all do, lovey, we all do. But some of us do our weeping in private, and some of us"—he let Chant's head drop—"make fucking public spectacles of ourselves. There are *consequences,* lovey, didn't Sartori tell you that? There are always *consequences.* You've begun something with this Estabrook business, for instance, and I'll need to watch it closely, or before we know it there'll be ripples spreading through the Imajica."

"The Imajica . . ."

"That's right. From here to the margin of the First Dominion. To the region of the Unbeheld Himself."

Chant began to gasp, and Dowd—realizing he'd hit a nerve—leaned towards his victim.

"Do I detect a little anxiety?" he said. "Are you afraid of going into the glory of our Lord Hapexamendios?"

Chant's voice was frail now. "Yes . . ." he murmured.

"Why?" Dowd wanted to know. "Because of your crimes?"

"Yes."

"What *are* your crimes? Do tell me. We needn't bother with the little things. Just the really shameful stuff'll do."

"I've had dealings with a Eurhetemec."

"Have you indeed?" Dowd said. "However did you get back to Yzordderrex to do that?"

"I didn't," Chant replied. "My dealings . . . were here, in the Fifth."

"Really," said Dowd softly. "I didn't know there were Eurhete-mecs here. You learn something new every day. But, lovey, that's no great crime. The Unbeheld's going to forgive a poxy little tres-pass like that. Unless . . ." He stopped for a moment, turning over a new possibility. "Unless, the Eurhetemec was a mystif. . . ." He trailed the thought, but Chant remained silent. "Oh, my dove," Dowd said. "It *wasn't,* was it?" Another pause. "Oh, it *was.* It *was.*" He sounded almost enchanted. "There's a mystif in the Fifth and—what? You're in love with it? You'd better tell me before you run out of breath, lovey. In a few minutes your eternal soul will be wait-ing at Hapexamendios' door."

Chant shuddered. "The assassin . . ." he said.

"What *about* the assassin?" came the reply. Then, realizing what he'd just heard, Dowd drew a long, slow breath. "The *assassin* is a mystif?" he said.

"Yes."

"Oh, my sweet Hyo!" he exclaimed. "A mystif!" The enchantment had vanished from his voice now. He was hard and dry. "Do you know what they can do? The deceits they've got at their disposal? This was supposed to be an anonymous piece of shit-stirring, and look what you've done!" His voice softened again. "Was it beautiful?" he asked. "No, no. Don't tell me. Let me have the surprise, when I see it face to face." He turned to the voiders. "Pick the fucker up," he said.

They stepped forward and raised Chant by his broken arms. There was no strength left in his neck, and his head lolled forward, a solid stream of bilious fluid running from his mouth and nostrils. "How often does the Eurhetemec tribe produce a mystif?" Dowd mused, half to himself. "Every ten years? Every fifty? They're certainly rare. And there you are, blithely hiring one of these little divinities as an assassin. Imagine! How pitiful, that it had fallen so low. I must ask it how that came about." He stepped towards Chant, and at Dowd's order one of the voiders raised Chant's head by the hair. "I need the mystif's whereabouts," Dowd said. "And its name."

Chant sobbed through his bile. "Please," he said. "I meant . . . I . . . meant—"

"Yes, yes. No harm. You were just doing your duty. The Unbeheld will forgive you, I guarantee it. But the *mystif,* lovey, I need you to tell me about the mystif. Where can I find it? Just speak the words, and you won't ever have to think about it again. You'll go into the presence of the Unbeheld like a babe."

"I will?"

"You will. Trust me. Just give me its name and tell me the place where I can find it."

"Name . . . and . . . place."

"That's right. But get to it, lovey, before it's too late!"

Chant took as deep a breath as his collapsing lungs allowed. "It's called Pie 'oh' pah," he said.

Dowd stepped back from the dying man as if slapped. "Pie 'oh' pah? Are you sure?"

"I'm sure. . . ."

"Pie 'oh' pah is alive? And Estabrook hired it?"

"Yes."

Dowd threw off his imitation of a Father Confessor and murmured a fretful question of himself. "What does this mean?" he said.

Chant made a pained little moan, his system racked by further waves of dissolution. Realizing that time was now very short, Dowd pressed the man afresh.

"Where *is* this mystif? Quickly, now! *Quickly!*"

Chant's face was decaying, cobs of withered flesh sliding off the slickened bone. When he answered, it was with half a mouth. But answer he did, to be unburdened.

"I thank you," Dowd said to him, when all the information had been supplied. "I thank you." Then, to the voiders, "Let him go."

They dropped Chant without ceremony. When he hit the floor his face broke, pieces spattering Dowd's shoe. He viewed the mess with disgust.

"Clean it off," he said.

The voiders were at his feet in moments, dutifully removing the scraps of matter from Dowd's handmade shoes.

"What does this mean?" Dowd murmured again. There was surely synchronicity in this turn of events. In a little over half a year's time the anniversary of the Reconciliation would be upon the Imajica. Two hundred years would have passed since the Maestro Sartori had attempted, and failed, to perform the greatest act of magic known to this or any other Dominion. The plans for that ceremony had been laid here, at number 28 Gamut Street, and the mystif, among others, had been there to witness the preparations.

The ambition of those heady days had ended in tragedy, of course. Rites intended to heal the rift in the Imajica, and reconcile the Fifth Dominion with the other four, had gone disastrously awry. Many great theurgists, shamans, and theologians had been killed. Determined that such a calamity never be repeated, several of the survivors had banded together in order to cleanse the Fifth of all magical knowledge. But however much they scrubbed to erase the past, the slate could never be entirely cleansed. Traces of what had been dreamed and hoped for remained; fragments of poems to Union, written by men whose names had been systematically removed from all record. And as long as such scraps remained, the spirit of the Reconciliation would survive.

But spirit was not enough. A Maestro was needed, a magician arrogant enough to believe that he could succeed where Christos and innumerable other sorcerers, most lost to history, had failed. Though these were blissless times, Dowd didn't discount the possibility of such a soul appearing. He still encountered in his daily life a few who looked past the empty gaud that distracted lesser minds and longed for a revelation that would burn the tinsel away, an Apocalypse that would show the Fifth the glories it yearned for in its sleep.

If a Maestro was going to appear, however, he would need to be swift. Another attempt at Reconciliation couldn't be planned overnight, and if the next midsummer went unused, the Imajica would pass another two centuries divided: time enough for the

Fifth Dominion to destroy itself out of boredom or frustration and prevent the Reconciliation from ever taking place.

Dowd perused his newly polished shoes. "Perfect," he said. "Which is more than I can say for the rest of this wretched world."

He crossed to the door. The voiders lingered by the body, however, bright enough to know they still had some duty to perform with it. But Dowd called them away.

"We'll leave it here," he said. "Who knows? It may stir a few ghosts."

5

I

Two days after the predawn call from Judith—days in which the water heater in the studio had failed, leaving Gentle the option of bathing in polar waters or not at all (he chose the latter)—Klein summoned him to the house. He had good news. He'd heard of a buyer with a hunger that was not being satisfied through conventional markets, and Klein had allowed it to be known that he might be able to lay his hands on something attractive. Gentle had successfully re-created one Gauguin previously, a small picture which had gone onto the open market and been consumed without any questions being asked. Could he do it again? Gentle replied that he would make a Gauguin so fine the artist himself would have wept to see it. Klein advanced Gentle five hundred pounds to pay the rent on the studio and left him to it, remarking only that Gentle was looking a good deal better than he'd looked previously, though he smelled a good deal worse.

Gentle didn't much care. Not bathing for two days was no great inconvenience when he only had himself for company; not shaving suited him fine when there was no woman to complain of beard burns. And he'd rediscovered the old private erotics: spit, palm, and fantasy. It sufficed. A man might get used to living this way; might get to like his gut a little ample, his armpits sweaty, his balls the same. It wasn't until the weekend that he started to pine for some entertainment other than the sight of himself in the bathroom mirror. There hadn't been a Friday or Saturday in the last year which hadn't been occupied by some social gathering, where he'd mingled with Vanessa's friends. Their numbers were still listed in his address book, just a phone call away, but he felt squeamish about making contact. However much he may have charmed them, they were her friends, not his, and they'd have inevitably sided with her in this fiasco.

As for his own peers—the friends he'd had before Vanessa— most had faded. They were a part of his past and, like so many other memories, slippery. While people like Klein recalled events thirty years old in crystalline detail, Gentle had difficulty remembering where he was and with whom even ten years before. Earlier than that still, and his memory banks were empty. It was as though his mind was disposed only to preserve enough details of his history to make the present plausible. The rest it disregarded. He kept this strange fallibility from almost everybody he knew, concocting details if pressed hard. It didn't much bother him. Not knowing what it meant to have a past, he didn't miss it. And he construed from exchanges with others that though they might talk confidentially about their childhood and adolescence, much of it was rumor and conjecture, some of it pure fabrication.

Nor was he alone in his ignorance. Judith had once confided that she too had an uncertain grasp of the past, though she'd been drunk at the time and had denied it vehemently when he'd raised the subject again. So, between friends lost and friends forgotten, he was very much alone this Saturday night, and he picked up the phone when it rang with some gratitude.

"Furie here," he said. He felt like a Furie tonight. The line was live, but there was no answer. "Who's there?" he said. Still, silence. Irritated, he put down the receiver. Seconds later, the phone rang again. "Who the hell *is* this?" he demanded, and this time an impeccably spoken man replied, albeit with another question.

"Am I speaking to John Zacharias?"

Gentle didn't hear himself called that too often. "Who is this?" he said again.

"We've only met once. You probably don't remember me. Charles Estabrook?"

Some people lingered longer in the memory than others. Estabrook was one. The man who'd caught Jude when she'd dropped from the high wire. A classic inbred Englishman, member of the minor aristocracy, pompous, condescending and—

"I'd like very much to meet with you, if that's possible."

"I don't think we've got anything to say to each other."

"It's about Judith, Mr. Zacharias. A matter I'm obliged to keep in the strictest confidence but is, I cannot stress too strongly, of the profoundest importance."

The tortured syntax made Gentle blunt. "Spit it out, then," he said.

"Not on the telephone. I realize this request comes without warning, but I beg you to consider it."

"I have. And no. I'm not interested in meeting you."

"Even to gloat?"

"Over what?"

"Over the fact that I've lost her," Estabrook said. "She left me, Mr. Zacharias, just as she left you. Thirty-three days ago." The precision of that spoke volumes. Was he counting the hours as well as the days? Perhaps the minutes too? "You needn't come to the house if you don't wish to. In fact, to be honest, I'd be happier if you didn't."

He was speaking as if Gentle would agree to the rendezvous, which, though he hadn't said so yet, he would.

2

It was cruel, of course, to bring someone of Estabrook's age out on a cold day and make him climb a hill, but Gentle knew from experience you took whatever satisfactions you could along the way. And Parliament Hill had a fine view of London, even on a day of lowering cloud. The wind was brisk, and as usual on a Sunday the hill had a host of kite flyers on its back, their toys like multicolored candies suspended in the wintry sky. The hike made Estabrook breathless, but he seemed glad that Gentle had picked the spot.

"I haven't been up here in years. My first wife used to like coming here to see the kites."

He brought a brandy flask from his pocket, proffering it first to Gentle. Gentle declined.

"The cold never leaves one's marrow these days. One of the penalties of age. I've yet to discover the advantages. How old are you?"

Rather than confess to not knowing, Gentle said, "Almost forty."

"You look younger. In fact, you've scarcely changed since we first met. Do you remember? At the auction? You were with her. I wasn't. That was the world of difference between us. With; without. I envied you that day the way I'd never envied any other man, just for having her beside you. Later, of course, I saw the same look on other men's faces—"

"I didn't come here to hear this," Gentle said.

"No, I realize that. It's just necessary for me to express how very precious she was to me. I count the years I had with her as the best of my life. But of course the best can't go on forever, can they, or how are they the best?" He drank again. "You know, she *never* talked about you," he said. "I tried to provoke her into doing so, but she said she'd put you out of her mind completely—she'd forgotten you, she said—which is nonsense, of course."

"I believe it."

"Don't," Estabrook said quickly. "You were her guilty secret."

"Why are you trying to flatter me?"

"It's the truth. She still loved you, all through the time she was with me. That's why we're talking now. Because I know it, and I think you do too."

Not once so far had they mentioned her by name, almost as though from some superstition. She was *she,* her, the woman: an absolute and invisible power. Her men seemed to have their feet on solid ground, but in truth they drifted like the kites, tethered to reality only by the memory of her.

"I've done a terrible thing, John," Estabrook said. The flask was at his lips again. He took several gulps before sealing it and pocketing it. "And I regret it bitterly."

"What?"

"May we walk a little way?" Estabrook said, glancing towards the kite flyers, who were both too distant and too involved in their sport to be eavesdropping. But he was not comfortable with sharing his secret until he'd put twice the distance between his confession and their ears. When he had, he made it simply and plainly. "I don't know what kind of madness overtook me," he said, "but a little while ago I made a contract with somebody to have her killed."

"You did *what?*"

"Does it appall you?"

"What do you think? Of course it appalls me."

"It's the highest form of devotion, you know, to want to end somebody's existence rather than let them live on without you. It's love of the highest order."

"It's a fucking obscenity."

"Oh, yes, it's that too. But I couldn't bear . . . just couldn't *bear* . . . the idea of her being alive and me not being with her. . . ." His delivery was now deteriorating, the words becoming tears. "She was so dear to me. . . ."

Gentle's thoughts were of his last exchange with Judith: the half-drowned telephone call from New York, which had ended with nothing said. Had she known then that her life was in jeopardy? If not, did she now? My God, was she even alive? He took hold of Estabrook's lapel with the same force that the fear took hold of him.

"You haven't brought me here to tell me she's dead."

"No. *No,*" he protested, making no attempt to disengage Gentle's hold. "I hired this man, and I want to call him off."

"So do it," Gentle said, letting the coat go.

"I can't."

Estabrook reached into his pocket and pulled out a sheet of paper. To judge by its crumpled state it had been thrown away, then reclaimed.

"This came from the man who found me the assassin," he went on. "It was delivered to my home two nights ago. He was obviously drunk or drugged when he wrote it, but it indicates that he expects to be dead by the time I read it. I'm assuming he's correct. He hasn't made contact. He was my only route to the assassin."

"Where did you meet this man?"

"He found me."

"And the assassin?"

"I met him somewhere south of the river, I don't know where. It was dark. I was lost. Besides, he won't be there. He's gone after her."

"So warn her."

"I've tried. She won't accept my calls. She's got another lover now. He's being covetous the way I was. My letters, my telegrams, they're all sent back unopened. But he won't be able to save her. This man I hired, his name's Pie—"

"What's that, some kind of code?"

"I don't know," Estabrook said. "I don't know anything except I've done something unforgivable and you have to help me undo it. *You have to*. This man Pie is lethal."

"What makes you think she'll see me when she won't see you?"

"There's no guarantee. But you're a younger, fitter man, and you've had some ... experience of the criminal mind. You've a better chance of coming between her and Pie than I have. I'll give you money for the assassin. You can pay him off. And I'll pay whatever you ask. I'm rich. Just warn her, Zacharias, and get her to come home. I can't have her death on my conscience."

"It's a little late to think about that."

"I'm making what amends I can. Do we have a deal?" He took off his leather glove in preparation for shaking Gentle's hand.

"I'd like the letter from your contact," Gentle said.

"It barely makes any sense," Estabrook said.

"If he *is* dead, and she dies too, that letter's evidence whether it makes sense or not. Hand it over, or no deal."

Estabrook reached into his inside pocket, as if to pull out the letter, but with his fingers upon it he hesitated. Despite all his talk about having a clear conscience, about Gentle being the man to save her, he was deeply reluctant to part with the letter.

"I thought so," Gentle said. "You want to make sure I look like the guilty party if anything goes wrong. Well, go fuck yourself."

He turned from Estabrook and started down the hill. Estabrook

came after him, calling his name, but Gentle didn't slow his pace.
He let the man run.

"All right!" he heard behind him. "All right, have it! Have it!"

Gentle slowed but didn't stop. Gray with exertion, Estabrook
caught up with him.

"The letter's yours," he said.

Gentle took it, pocketing it without unfolding it. There'd be
plenty of time to study it on the flight.

6

I

Chant's body was discovered the following day by ninety-three-
year-old Albert Burke, who found it while looking for his errant
mongrel, Kipper. The animal had sniffed from the street what its
owner only began to nose as he climbed the stairs, whistling for
his hound between curses: the rotting tissue at the top. In the autumn of 1916, Albert had fought for his country at the Somme,
sharing trenches with dead companions for days at a time. The
sights and smells of death didn't much distress him. Indeed, his
sanguine response to his discovery lent color to the story, when it
reached the evening news, and assured it of greater coverage than
it might otherwise have merited, that focus in turn bringing a penetrating eye to bear on the identity of the dead man. Within a day
a portrait of the deceased as he might have looked in life had been
produced, and by Wednesday a woman living on a council estate
south of the river had identified him as her next-door neighbor,
Mr. Chant.

An examination of his flat turned up a second picture, not of
Chant's flesh, this time, but of his life. It was the conclusion of the
police that the dead man was a practitioner of some obscure reli-
gion. It was reported that a small altar dominated his room, decorated with the withered heads of animals that forensics could not
identify, its centerpiece an idol of so explicitly sexual a nature no
newspaper dared publish a sketch of it, let alone a photograph. The
gutter press particularly enjoyed the story, especially as the artifacts
had belonged to a man now thought to have been murdered. They
editorialized with barely concealed racism on the influx of per-
verted foreign religions. Between this and stories on Burke of the
Somme, Chant's death attracted a lot of column inches. That fact
had several consequences. It brought a rash of right-wing attacks

on mosques in greater London, it brought a call for the demolition of the estate where Chant had lived, and it brought Dowd up to a certain tower in Highgate, where he was summoned in lieu of his absentee master, Estabrook's brother, Oscar Godolphin.

2

In the 1780s, when Highgate Hill was so steep and deeply rutted that carriages regularly failed to make the grade and the drive to town was sufficiently dangerous that a wise man went with pistols, a merchant called Thomas Roxborough had constructed a handsome house on Hornsey Lane, designed for him by one Henry Holland. At that time it had commanded fine views: south all the way to the river; north and west over the lush pastures of the region towards the tiny village of Hampstead. The former view was still available to the tourist, from the bridge that spanned the Archway Road, but Roxborough's fine house had gone, replaced in the late thirties with an anonymous ten-story tower, set back from the street. There was a screen of well-tended trees between tower and road, not sufficiently thick to conceal the building entirely, but enough to render what was already an undistinguished building virtually invisible. The only mail that was delivered there was circulars and official paperwork of one kind or another. There were no tenants, either individuals or businesses. Yet Roxborough Tower was kept well by its owners, who once every month or so gathered in the single room which occupied the top floor of the building, in the name of the man who had owned this plot of land two hundred years before and who had left it to the society he founded. The men and women (eleven in all) who met here and talked for a few hours and went their unremarkable ways were the descendants of the impassioned few Roxborough had gathered around him in the dark days following the failure of the Reconciliation. There was no passion among them now, nor more than a vague comprehension of Roxborough's purpose in forming what he'd called the Society of the Tabula Rasa, or the Clean Slate. But they met anyway, in part because in their early childhood one or other of their parents, usually but not always the father, had taken them aside and told them a great responsibility would fall to them—the carrying forward of a hermetically protected family secret—and in part because the Society looked after its own. Roxborough had been a man of wealth and insight. He'd purchased considerable tracts of land during his lifetime, and the profits that accrued from that investment had ballooned as London grew. The sole recipient of those monies was the Society, though the funds were so ingeniously routed, through companies and agents who were unaware of their place in the system, that nobody who serviced the Society in any capacity whatsoever knew of its existence.

Thus the Tabula Rasa flourished in its peculiar, purposeless way, gathering to talk about the secrets it kept, as Roxborough had decreed, and enjoying the sight of the city from its place on Highgate Hill.

Kuttner Dowd had been here several times, though never when the Society was assembled, as it was tonight. His employer, Oscar Godolphin, was one of the eleven to whom the flame of Roxborough's intent had been passed, though of all of them surely none was so perfect a hypocrite as Godolphin, who was both a member of a Society committed to the repression of all magical activity, and the employer (Godolphin would have said *owner*) of a creature summoned by magic in the very year of the tragedy that had brought the Society into being.

That creature was of course Dowd, whose existence was known to the Society's members but whose origins were not. If it had been, they would never have summoned him here and allowed him access to the hallowed tower. Rather, they would have been bound by Roxborough's edict to destroy him at whatever cost to their bodies, souls, or sanity that might entail. Certainly they had the expertise, or at least the means to gain it. The tower reputedly housed a library of treatises, grimoires, cyclopedias, and symposia second to none, collected by Roxborough and the group of Fifth Dominion magi who'd first supported the attempt at the Reconciliation. One of those men had been Joshua Godolphin, Earl of Bellingham. He and Roxborough had survived the calamitous events of that midsummer almost two hundred years ago, but most of their dearest friends had not. The story went that after the tragedy Godolphin had retired to his country estate and never again ventured beyond its perimeters. Roxborough, on the other hand, ever the most pragmatic of the group, had within days of the cataclysm secured the occult libraries of his dead colleagues, hiding the thousands of volumes in the cellar of his house where they could, in the words of a letter to the Earl, *no longer taint with un-Christian ambition the minds of good men like our dear friends. We must hereafter keep the doing of this damnable magic from our shores.* That he had not destroyed the books, but merely locked them away, was testament to some ambiguity in him, however. Despite the horrors he'd seen, and the fierceness of his revulsion, some small part of him retained the fascination that had drawn him, Godolphin, and their fellow experimenters together in the first place.

Dowd shivered with unease as he stood in the plain hallway of the tower, knowing that somewhere nearby was the largest

collection of magical writings gathered in one place outside the
Vatican, and that among them would be many rituals for the raising and dispatching of creatures like himself. He was not the conventional stuff of which familiars were made, of course. Most were
simpering, mindless functionaries, plucked by their summoners
from the In Ovo—the space between the Fifth and the Reconciled
Dominions—like lobsters from a restaurant tank. He, on the other
hand, had been a professional actor in his time, and fêted for it. It
wasn't congenital stupidity that had made him susceptible to
human jurisdiction, it was anguish. He'd seen the face of Hapexamendios Himself and, half-crazed by the sight, had been unable to
resist the summons, and the binding, when it came. His invoker had
of course been Joshua Godolphin, and he'd commanded Dowd to
serve his line until the end of time. In fact, Joshua's retirement to
the safety of his estate had freed Dowd to wander until the old
man's demise, when he was drawn back to offer his services to
Joshua's son Nathaniel, only revealing his true nature once he'd
made himself indispensable, for fear he was trapped between his
bounden duty and the zeal of a Christian.

In fact, Nathaniel had grown into a dissolute of considerable
proportions by the time Dowd entered his employ, and could not
have cared less what kind of creature Dowd was as long as he pro-
cured the right kind of company. And so it had gone on, generation after generation, Dowd changing his face on occasion
(a simple trick, or feit) so as to conceal his longevity from the withering human world. But the possibility that one day his double-
dealing would be discovered by the Tabula Rasa, and they would
search through their library and find some vicious sway to destroy
him, never entirely left his calculations: especially now, waiting for
the call into their presence.

That call was an hour and a half in coming, during which time
he distracted himself thinking about the shows that were opening
in the coming week. Theater remained his great love, and there was
scarcely a production of any significance he failed to see. On the
following Tuesday he had tickets for the much-acclaimed *Lear* at
the National and then, two days later, a seat in the stalls for the re-
vival of *Turandot* at the Coliseum. Much to look forward to, once
this wretched interview was over.

At last the lift hummed into life and one of the Society's younger
members, Giles Bloxham, appeared. At forty, Bloxham looked
twice that age. It took a kind of genius, Godolphin had once remarked when talking about Bloxham (he liked to report on the ab-
surdities of the Society, particularly when he was in his cups), to
look so dissipated and have nothing to regret for it.

"We're ready for you now," Bloxham said, indicating that Dowd should join him in the lift. "You realize," he said as they ascended, "that if you're ever tempted to breathe a word of what you see here, the Society will eradicate you so quickly and so thoroughly your mother won't even know you existed?"

This overheated threat sounded ludicrous delivered in Bloxham's nasal whine, but Dowd played the chastened functionary. "I perfectly understand," he said.

"It's an extraordinary step," Bloxham continued, "calling anyone who isn't a member to a meeting. But these are extraordinary times. Not that it's any of your business."

"Quite so," Dowd said, all innocence.

Tonight he'd take their condescension without argument, he thought, more confident by the day that something was coming that would rock this tower to its foundations. When it did, he'd have his revenge.

The lift door opened, and Bloxham ordered Dowd to follow him. The passages that led to the main suite were stark and uncarpeted; the room he was led into, the same. The drapes were drawn over all the windows; the enormous marble-topped table that dominated the room was lit by overhead lamps, the wash of their light thrown up on the five members, two of them women, sitting around it. To judge by the clutter of bottles, glasses, and overfilled ashtrays, and the brooding, weary faces, they had been debating for many hours. Bloxham poured himself a glass of water and took his place. There was one empty seat: Godolphin's. Dowd was not invited to occupy it but stood at the end of the table, mildly discomfited by the stares of his interrogators. Not one face among them would have been known by the populace at large. Though all of them had descended from families of wealth and influence, these were not public powers. The Society forbade any member to hold office or take as a spouse an individual who might invite or arouse the curiosity of the press. It worked in mystery, for the demise of mystery. Perhaps it was that paradox—more than any other aspect of its nature—which would finally undo it.

At the other end of the table from Dowd, sitting in front of a heap of newspapers doubtless carrying the Burke reports, sat a professorial man in his sixties, white hair oiled to his scalp. Dowd knew his name from Godolphin's description: Hubert Shales, dubbed The Sloth by Oscar. He moved and spoke with the caution of a glass-boned theologian.

"You know why you're here?" he said.

"He knows," Bloxham put in.

"Some problem with Mr. Godolphin?" Dowd ventured.

"He's not here," said one of the women to Dowd's right, her face emaciated beneath a confection of dyed black hair. Alice Tyrwhitt, Dowd guessed. "That's the problem."

"So I see," Dowd said.

"Where the hell is he?" Bloxham demanded.

"He's traveling," Dowd replied. "I don't think he anticipated a meeting."

"Neither did we," said Lionel Wakeman, flushed with the Scotch he'd imbibed, the bottle lying in the crook of his arm.

"Where's he traveling?" Tyrwhitt asked. "It's imperative we find him."

"I'm afraid I don't know," Dowd said. "His business takes him all over the world."

"Anything respectable?" Wakeman slurred.

"He's got a number of investments in Singapore," Dowd replied. "And in India. Would you like me to prepare a dossier? I'm sure he'd be—"

"Bugger the dossier!" Bloxham said. "We want him here! Now!"

"I'm afraid I don't know his precise whereabouts. Somewhere in the Far East."

The severe but not unalluring woman to Wakeman's left now entered the exchange, stabbing her cigarette in the ashtray as she spoke. This could only be Charlotte Feaver: Charlotte the Scarlet, as Oscar called her. She was the last of the Roxborough line, he'd said, unless she found a way to fertilize one of her girlfriends.

"This isn't some damn club he can visit when it fucking well suits him," she said.

"That's right," Wakeman put in. "It's a damn poor show."

Shales picked up one of the newspapers in front of him and pitched it down the table in Dowd's direction.

"I presume you've read about this body they found in Clerkenwell?" he said.

"Yes. I believe so."

Shales paused for several seconds, his sparrow eyes going from one member to another. Whatever he was about to say, its broaching had been debated before Dowd entered.

"We have reason to believe that this man Chant did not originate in this Dominion."

"I'm sorry?" Dowd said, feigning confusion. "I don't follow. Dominion?"

"Spare us your discretion," Charlotte Feaver said. "You know what we're talking about. Oscar hasn't employed you for twenty-five years and kept his counsel."

"I know very little," Dowd protested.

"But enough to know there's an anniversary imminent," Shales said.

My, my, Dowd thought, they're not as stupid as they look.

"You mean the Reconciliation?" he said.

"That's exactly what I mean. This coming midsummer—"

"Do we have to spell it out?" Bloxham said. "He already knows more than he should."

Shales ignored the interruption and was beginning again when a voice so far unheard, emanating from a bulky figure sitting beyond the reach of the light, broke in. Dowd had been waiting for this man, Matthias McGann, to say his piece. If the Tabula Rasa had a leader, this was he.

"Hubert?" he said. "May I?"

Shales murmured, "Of course."

"Mr. Dowd," said McGann, "I don't doubt that Oscar has been indiscreet. We all have our weaknesses. You must be his. Nobody here blames you for listening. But this Society was created for a very specific purpose and on occasion has been obliged to act with extreme severity in the pursuit of that purpose. I won't go into details. As Giles says, you're already wiser than any of us would like. But believe me, we will silence any and all who put this Dominion at risk."

He leaned forward. His face announced a man of good humor, presently unhappy with his lot.

"Hubert mentioned that an anniversary is imminent. So it is. And forces with an interest in subverting the sanity of this Dominion may be readying themselves to celebrate that anniversary. So far, this"—he pointed to the newspaper—"is the only evidence we'd found of such preparations, but if there are others they will be swiftly terminated by this Society and its agents. Do you understand?"

He didn't wait for an answer.

"This sort of thing is very dangerous," he went on. "People start to investigate. Academics. Esoterics. They start to question, and they start to dream."

"I could see how that would be dangerous," Dowd said.

"Don't smarm, you smug little bastard," Bloxham burst out. "We all know what you and Godolphin have been doing. Tell him, Hubert!"

"I've traced some artifacts of . . . nonterrestrial origin . . . that came my way. The trail, as it were, leads back to Oscar Godolphin."

"We don't know that," Lionel put in. "These buggers lie."

"I'm satisfied Godolphin's guilty," Alice Tyrwhitt said. "And this one with him."

"I protest," Dowd said.

"You've been dealing in magic," Bloxham hollered. "Admit it!" He rose and slammed the table. *Admit it!*

"Sit down, Giles," McGann said.

"Look at him," Bloxham went on, jabbing his thumb in Dowd's direction. "He's guilty as hell."

"I said *sit down*," McGann replied, raising his voice ever so slightly. Cowed, Bloxham sat. "You're not on trial here," McGann said to Dowd. "It's Godolphin we want."

"So find him," Feaver said.

"And when you do," Shales said, "tell him I've got a few items he may recognize."

The table fell silent. Several heads turned in Matthias McGann's direction. "I think that's it," he said. "Unless you have any remarks to make?"

"I don't believe so," Dowd replied.

"Then you may go."

Dowd took his leave without further exchange, escorted as far as the lift by Charlotte Feaver and left to make the descent alone. They were better informed than he'd imagined, but they were some way from guessing the truth. He turned over passages of the interview as he drove back to Regent's Park Road, committing them to memory for later recitation. Wakeman's drunken irrelevancies; Shales's indiscretion; McGann, smooth as a velvet scabbard. He'd repeat it all for Godolphin's edification, especially the cross-questioning about the absentee's whereabouts.

Somewhere in the East, Dowd had said. East Yzorddcrrcx, maybe, in the Kesparates built close to the harbor where Oscar liked to bargain for contraband brought back from Hakaridek or the islands. Whether he was there or some other place, Dowd had no way of fetching him back. He would come when he would come, and the Tabula Rasa would have to bide its time, though the longer he was away the more the likelihood grew of one of their number voicing the suspicion some of them surely nurtured: that Godolphin's dealings in talismans and wantons were only the tip of the iceberg. Perhaps they even suspected he took trips.

He wasn't the only Fifther who'd jaunted between Dominions, of course. There were many routes from Earth to the Reconciled Dominions, some safer than others but all used at one time or another, and not always by magicians. Poets had found their way over (and sometimes back, to tell the tale); so had a good number of priests over the centuries, and hermits, meditating on their essence so hard the In Ovo enveloped them and spat them into another world. Any soul despairing or inspired enough could get access. But few in Dowd's experience had made such a commonplace of it as Godolphin.

These were dangerous times for such jaunts, both here and there. The Reconciled Dominions had been under the control of

Yzordderrex's Autarch for over a century, and every time Godolphin returned from a trip he had new signs of unrest to report. From the margins of the First Dominion to Patashoqua and its satellite cities in the Fourth, voices were raised to stir rebellion. There was as yet no consensus on how best to overcome the Autarch's tyranny, only a simmering unrest which regularly erupted in riots or strikes, the leaders of such mutinies invariably found and executed. In fact, on occasion the Autarch's suppressions had been more Draconian still. Entire communities had been destroyed in the name of the Yzordderrexian Empire: tribes and small nations deprived of their gods, their lands, and their right to procreate, others, simply eradicated by pogroms the Autarch personally supervised. But none of these horrors had dissuaded Godolphin from traveling in the Reconciled Dominions. Perhaps tonight's events would, however, at least until the Society's suspicions had been allayed.

Tiresome as it was, Dowd knew he had no choice as to where he went tonight: to the Godolphin estate and the folly in its deserted grounds which was Oscar's departure place. There he would wait, like a dog grown lonely at its master's absence, until Godolphin's return. Oscar was not the only one who would have to muster some excuses in the near future; so would he. Killing Chant had seemed like a wise maneuver at the time—and, of course, an agreeable diversion on a night without a show to go to—but Dowd hadn't predicted the furor it would cause. With hindsight, that had been naïve. England loved murder, preferably with diagrams. And he'd been unlucky, what with the ubiquitous Mr. Burke of the Somme and a low quota of political scandals conspiring to make Chant posthumously famous. He would have to be prepared for Godolphin's wrath. But hopefully it would be subsumed in the larger anxiety of the Society's suspicions. Godolphin would need Dowd to help him calm these suspicions, and a man who needed his dog knew not to kick it too hard.

7

I

Gentle called Klein from the airport, minutes before he caught his flight. He presented Chester with a severely edited version of the truth, making no mention of Estabrook's murder plot but explaining that Jude was ill and had requested his presence. Klein didn't deliver the tirade that Gentle had anticipated. He simply observed, rather wearily, that if Gentle's word was worth so little after all the effort he, Klein, had put into finding work for him, it was perhaps best that they end their business relationship now. Gentle begged him to be a little more lenient, to which Klein said he'd call Gentle's studio in two days' time and, if he received no answer, would assume their deal was no longer valid.

"Your dick'll be the death of you," he commented as he signed off.

The flight gave Gentle time to think about both that remark and the conversation on Kite Hill, the memory of which still vexed him. During the exchange itself he'd moved from suspicion to disbelief to disgust and finally to acceptance of Estabrook's proposal. But despite the fact that the man had been as good as his word, providing ample funds for the trip, the more Gentle returned to the conversation in memory, the more that first response—suspicion— was reawakened. His doubts circled around two elements of Estabrook's story: the assassin himself (this Mr. Pie, hired out of nowhere) and, more particularly, around the man who'd introduced Estabrook to his hired hand: Chant, whose death had been media fodder for the past several days.

The dead man's letter was virtually incomprehensible, as Estabrook had warned, veering from pulpit rhetoric to opiate invention. The fact that Chant, knowing he was going to be murdered (that much *was* cogent), should have chosen to set these nonsenses down as vital information was proof of significant derangement. How much more deranged, then, a man like Estabrook, who did business with this crazy? And by the same token was Gentle not crazier still, employed by the lunatic's employer?

Amid all these fantasies and equivocations, however, there were two irreducible facts: death and Judith. The former had come to Chant in a derelict house in Clerkenwell; about that there was no ambiguity. The latter, innocent of her husband's malice, was probably its next target. His task was simple: to come between the two.

He checked into his hotel at 52nd and Madison a little after five in the afternoon, New York time. From his window on the fourteenth floor he had a view downtown, but the scene was far from welcoming. A gruel of rain, threatening to thicken into snow, had begun to fall as he journeyed in from Kennedy, and the weather reports promised cold and more cold. It suited him, however. The gray darkness, together with the horn and brake squeals rising from the intersection below, fitted his mood of dislocation. As with London, New York was a city in which he'd had friends once, but lost them. The only face he would seek out here was Judith's.

There was no purpose in delaying that search. He ordered coffee from Room Service, showered, drank, dressed in his thickest sweater, leather jacket, corduroys, and heavy boots, and headed out. Cabs were hard to come by, and after ten minutes of waiting in line beneath the hotel canopy, he decided to walk uptown a few blocks and catch a passing cab if he got lucky. If not, the cold would clear his head. By the time he'd reached 70th Street the sleet had become a drizzle, and there was a spring in his step. Ten blocks from here Judith was about some early evening occupation: bathing, perhaps, or dressing for an evening on the town. Ten blocks, at a minute a block. Ten minutes until he was standing outside the place where she was.

2

Marlin had been as solicitous as an erring husband since the attack, calling her from his office every hour or so, and several times suggesting that she might want to talk with an analyst, or at very least with one of his many friends who'd been assaulted or mugged on the streets of Manhattan. She declined the offer. Physically, she was quite well. Psychologically too. Though she'd heard that victims of attack often suffered from delayed repercussions—depression and sleeplessness among them—neither had struck her yet. It was the mystery of what had happened that kept her awake at night. Who was he, this man who knew her name, who got up from a collision that should have killed him outright and still managed to outrun a healthy man? And why had she projected upon his face the likeness of John Zacharias? Twice she'd begun to tell Marlin about the meeting in and outside Bloomingdale's; twice she'd rechanneled the conversation at the last moment, unable to face his benign condescension. This enigma was hers to unravel, and sharing it too soon, perhaps at all, might make the solving impossible.

In the meantime, Marlin's apartment felt very secure. There were two doormen: Sergio by day and Freddy by night. Marlin had given them both a detailed description of the assailant, and instructions to let nobody up to the second floor without Ms. Odell's permission, and even then they were to accompany visitors to the apartment door and escort them out if his guest chose not to see them. Nothing could harm her as long as she stayed behind closed doors. Tonight, with Marlin working until nine and a late dinner planned, she'd decided to spend the early evening assigning and wrapping the presents she'd accumulated on her various Fifth Avenue sorties, sweetening her labors with wine and music. Marlin's record collection was chiefly seduction songs of his sixties adolescence, which suited her fine. She played smoochy soul and sipped well-chilled Sauvignon as she pottered, more than content with her own company. Once in a while she'd get up from the chaos of ribbons and tissue and go to the window to watch the cold. The glass was misting. She didn't clear it. Let the world lose focus. She had no taste for it tonight.

There was a woman standing at one of the third-story windows when Gentle reached the intersection, just gazing out at the street. He watched her for several seconds before the casual motion of a hand raised to the back of her neck and run up through her long hair identified the silhouette as Judith. She made no backward glance to signify the presence of anyone else in the room. She simply sipped from her glass, and stroked her scalp, and watched the murky night. He had thought it would be easy to approach her, but now, watching her remotely like this, he knew otherwise.

The first time he'd seen her—all those years ago—he'd felt something close to panic. His whole system had been stirred to nausea as he relinquished power to the sight of her. The seduction that had followed had been both an homage and a revenge: an attempt to control someone who exercised an authority over him that defied analysis. To this day he didn't understand that authority. She was certainly a bewitching woman, but then he'd known others every bit as bewitching and not been panicked by them. What was it about Judith that threw him into such confusion now, as then? He watched her until she left the window; then he watched the window where she'd been; but he wearied of that, finally, and of the chill in his feet. He needed fortification: against the cold, against the woman. He left the corner and trekked a few blocks east until he found a bar, where he put two bourbons down his throat and wished to his core that alcohol had been his addiction instead of the opposite sex.

At the sound of the stranger's voice, Freddy, the night doorman, rose muttering from his seat in the nook beside the elevator. There was a shadowy figure visible through the ironwork filigree and bulletproof glass of the front door. He couldn't quite make out the face, but he was certain he didn't know the caller, which was unusual. He'd worked in the building for five years and knew the names of most of the occupants' visitors. Grumbling, he crossed the mirrored lobby, sucking in his paunch as he caught sight of himself. Then, with chilled fingers, he unlocked the door. As he opened it he realized his mistake. Though a gust of icy wind made his eyes water, blurring the caller's features, he knew them well enough. How could he not recognize his own brother? He'd been about to call him and find out what was going on in

Brooklyn when he'd heard the voice and the rapping on the door.

"What are you doing here, Fly?"

Fly smiled his missing-toothed smile. "Thought I'd just drop in," he said.

"You got some problem?"

"No, everything's fine," Fly said. Despite all the evidence of his senses, Freddy was uneasy. The shadow on the step, the wind in his eye, the very fact that Fly was here when he never came into the city on weekdays: it all added up to something he couldn't quite catch hold of.

"What you want?" he said. "You shouldn't be here."

"Here I am, anyway," Fly said, stepping past Freddy into the foyer. "I thought you'd be pleased to see me."

Freddy let the door swing closed, still wrestling with his thoughts. But they went from him the way they did in dreams. He couldn't string Fly's presence and his doubts together long enough to know what one had to do with the other.

"I think I'll take a look around," Fly was saying, heading towards the elevator.

"Wait up! You can't do that."

"What am I going to do? Set fire to the place?"

"I said *no*!" Freddy replied and, blurred vision notwithstanding, went after Fly, overtaking him to stand between his brother and the elevator. His motion dashed the tears from his eyes, and as he came to a halt he saw the visitor plainly. "You're not Fly!" he said.

He backed away towards the nook beside the elevator, where he kept his gun, but the stranger was too quick. He reached for Freddy and, with what seemed no more than a flick of his wrist, pitched him across the foyer. Freddy let out a yell, but who was going to come and help? There was nobody to guard the guard. He was a dead man.

Across the street, sheltering as best he could from the blasts of wind down Park Avenue, Gentle—who'd returned to his station barely a minute before—caught sight of the doorman scrabbling on the foyer floor. He crossed the street, dodging the traffic, reaching the door in time to see a second figure stepping into the elevator. He slammed his fist on the door, yelling to stir the doorman from his stupor.

"Let me in! For God's sake, let me in!"

Two floors above, Jude heard what she took to be a domestic argument and, not wanting somebody else's marital strife to sour her fine mood, was crossing to turn up the soul song on the turntable when somebody knocked on the door.

"Who's there?" she said.

The summons came again, not accompanied by any reply. She

turned the volume down instead of up and went to the door, which she'd dutifully bolted and chained. But the wine in her system made her incautious; she fumbled with the chain and was in the act of opening the door when doubt entered her head. Too late. The man on the other side took instant advantage. The door was slammed wide, and he came at her with the speed of the vehicle that should have killed him two nights before. There were only phantom traces of the lacerations that had made his face scarlet and no hint in his motion of any bodily harm. He had healed miraculously. Only the expression bore an echo of that night. It was as pained and as lost—even now, as he came to kill her—as it had been when they'd faced each other in the street. His hands reached for her, silencing her scream behind his palm.

"Please," he said.

If he was asking her to die quietly, he was out of luck. She raised her glass to break it against his face but he intercepted her, snatching it from her hand.

"Judith!" he said.

She stopped struggling at the sound of her name, and his hand dropped from her face.

"How the fuck do you know who I am?"

"I don't want to hurt you," he said. His voice was downy, his breath orange-scented. The perversest desire came into her head, and she cast it out instantly. This man had tried to kill her, and this talk now was just an attempt to quiet her till he tried again.

"Get away from me."

"I have to tell you—"

He didn't step away, nor did he finish. She glimpsed a movement behind him, and he saw her look, turning his head in time to meet a blow. He stumbled but didn't fall, turning his motion to an attack with balletic ease and coming back at the other man with tremendous force.

It wasn't Freddy, she saw. It was Gentle, of all people. The assassin's blow threw him back against the wall, hitting it so hard he brought books tumbling from the shelves, but before the assassin's fingers found his throat he delivered a punch to the man's belly that must have touched some tender place, because the assault ceased, and the attacker let him go, his eyes fixing for the first time on Gentle's face.

The expression of pain in his face became something else entirely: in some part horror, in some part awe, but in the greatest part some sentiment for which she knew no word. Gasping for breath, Gentle registered little or none of this but pushed himself up from the wall to relaunch his attack. The assassin was quick, however. He was at the door and out through it before Gentle could lay hands on him. Gentle took a moment to ask if Judith was all right—which she was—then raced in pursuit.

The snow had come again, its veil dropping between Gentle and Pie. The assassin was fast, despite the hurt done him, but Gentle was determined not to let the bastard slip. He chased Pie across Park Avenue and west on 80th, his heels sliding on the sleet-slickened ground. Twice his quarry threw him backward glances, and on the second occasion seemed to slow his pace, as if he might stop and attempt a truce, but then thought better of it and put on an extra turn of speed. It carried him over Madison towards Central Park. If he reached its sanctuary, Gentle knew, he'd be gone. Throwing every last ounce of energy into the pursuit, Gentle came within snatching distance. But even as he reached for the man he lost his footing. He fell headlong, his arms flailing, and struck the street hard enough to lose consciousness for a few seconds. When he opened his eyes, the taste of blood sharp in his mouth, he expected to see the assassin disappearing into the shadows of the park, but the bizarre Mr. Pie was standing at the curb, looking back at him. He continued to watch as Gentle got up, his face betraying a mournful empathy with Gentle's bruising. Before the chase could begin again he spoke, his voice as soft and melting as the sleet.

"Don't follow me," he said.

"You leave her . . . the fuck . . . alone," Gentle gasped, knowing even as he spoke he had no way of enforcing this edict in his present state.

But the man's reply was affirmation. "I will," he said. "But please, I beg you . . . forget you ever set eyes on me."

As he spoke he began to take a backward step, and for an instant Gentle's dizzied brain almost thought it possible the man would retreat into nothingness: be proved spirit rather than substance.

"Who are you?" he found himself asking.

"Pie 'oh' pah," the man returned, his voice perfectly matched to the soft expellations of those syllables.

"But who?"

"Nobody and nothing," came the second reply, accompanied by a backward step.

He took another and another, each pace putting further layers of sleet between them. Gentle began to follow, but the fall had left him aching in every joint, and he knew the chase was lost before he'd hobbled three yards. He pushed himself on, however, reaching one side of Fifth Avenue as Pie 'oh' pah made the other. The street between them was empty, but the assassin spoke across it as if across a raging river.

"Go back," he said. "Or if you come, be prepared. . . ."

Absurd as it was, Gentle answered as if there were white waters between them. "Prepared for what?" he shouted.

The man shook his head, and even across the street, with the sleet between them, Gentle could see how much despair and confusion there was on his face. He wasn't certain why the expression made his stomach churn, but churn it did. He started to cross the street, plunging a foot into the imaginary flood. The expression on the assassin's face changed: despair gave way to disbelief, and disbelief to a kind of terror, as though this fording was unthinkable, unbearable. With Gentle halfway across the street the man's courage broke. The shaking of the head became a violent fit of denial, and he let out a strange sob, throwing back his head as he did so. Then he retreated, as he had before, stepping away from the object of his terror—Gentle—as though expecting to forfeit his visibility. If there was such magic in the world—and tonight Gentle could believe it—the assassin was not an adept. But his feet could do what magic could not. As Gentle reached the river's other bank Pie 'oh' pah turned and fled, throwing himself over the wall into the park without seeming to care what lay on the other side: anything to be out of Gentle's sight.

There was no purpose in following any further. The cold was already making Gentle's bruised bones ache fiercely, and in such a condition the two blocks back to Jude's apartment would be a long and painful trek. By the time he made it the sleet had soaked through every layer of his clothing. With his teeth chattering, his mouth bleeding, and his hair flattened to his skull he could not have looked less appealing as he presented himself at the front door. Jude was waiting in the lobby, with the shame-faced doorman. She came to Gentle's aid as soon as he appeared, the exchange between them short and functional: Was he badly hurt? No. Did the man get away? Yes.

"Come upstairs," she said. "You need some medical attention."

3

There had been too much drama in Jude and Gentle's reunion already tonight for them to add more to it, so there was no gushing forth of sentiment on either side. Jude attended to Gentle with her usual pragmatism. He declined a shower but bathed his face and wounded extremities, delicately sluicing the grit from the palms of his hands. Then he changed into a selection of dry clothes she'd found in Marlin's wardrobe, though Gentle was both taller and

leaner than the absent lender. As he did so, Jude asked if he wanted
to have a doctor examine him. He thanked her but said no, he'd
be fine. And so he was, once dry and clean: aching, but fine.

"Did you call the police?" he asked, as he stood at the kitchen
door watching her brew Darjeeling.

"It's not worth it," she said. "They already know about this guy
from the last time. Maybe I'll get Marlin to call them later."

"This is his second try?" She nodded. "Well, if it's any comfort,
I don't think he'll try again."

"What makes you say that?"

"Because he looked about ready to throw himself under a car."

"I don't think that'd do him much harm," she said, and went on
to tell him about the incident in the Village, finishing up with the
assassin's miraculous recovery.

"He should be dead," she said. "His face was smashed up ... it
was a wonder he could even stand. Do you want sugar or milk?"

"Maybe a dash of Scotch. Does Marlin drink?"

"He's not a connoisseur like you."

Gentle laughed. "Is that how you describe me? The alcoholic
Gentle?"

"No. To tell the truth, I don't really describe you at all," she said,
slightly abashed. "I mean I'm sure I've mentioned you to Marlin
in passing, but you're ... I don't know ... you're a guilty secret."

This echo of Kite Hill brought his hirer to mind. "Have you spoken to Estabrook?" he said.

"Why should I do that?"

"He's been trying to contact you."

"I don't want to talk to him."

She put his tea down on the table in the living room, sought out
the Scotch, and set it beside the cup.

"Help yourself," she said.

"You're not having a dram?"

"Tea, but no whisky. My brain's crazed enough as it is." She
crossed back to the window, taking her tea. "There's so much I
don't understand about all of this," she said. "To start with, why are
you here?"

"I hate to sound melodramatic, but I really think you should sit
down before we have this discussion."

"Just tell me what's going on," she said, her voice tainted with
accusation. "How long have you been watching me?"

"Just a few hours."

"I thought I saw you following me a couple of days ago."

"Not me. I was in London until this morning."

She looked puzzled at this. "So what do you know about this
man who's trying to kill me?"

"He said his name was Pie 'oh' pah."

"I don't give a fuck what his name is," she said, her show of detachment finally dropping away. "Who is he? Why does he want to hurt me?"

"Because he was hired."

"He was *what?*"

"He was hired. By Estabrook."

Tea slopped from her cup as a shudder passed through her. "To kill me?" she said. "He hired someone to kill me? I don't believe you. That's crazy."

"He's obsessed with you, Jude. It's his way of making sure you don't belong to anybody else."

She drew the cup up to her face, both hands clutched around it, the knuckles so white it was a wonder the china didn't crack like an egg. She sipped, her face obscured. Then, the same denial, but more flatly: "I don't believe you."

"He's been trying to speak to you to warn you. He hired this man, then changed his mind."

"How do you know all of this?" Again, the accusation.

"He sent me to stop it."

"Hired you too?"

It wasn't pleasant to hear it from her lips, but yes, he said, he was just another hireling. It was as though Estabrook had set two dogs on Judith's heels—one bringing death, the other life—and let fate decide which caught up with her first.

"Maybe I will have some booze," she said, and crossed to the table to pick up the bottle.

He stood to pour for her but his motion was enough to stop her in her tracks, and he realized she was afraid of him. He handed her the bottle at arm's length. She didn't take it.

"I think maybe you should go," she said. "Marlin'll be home soon. I don't want you here. . . ."

He understood her nervousness but felt ill treated by this change of tone. As he'd hobbled back through the sleet a tiny part of him had hoped her gratitude would include an embrace, or at least a few words that would let him know she felt something for him. But he was tarred with Estabrook's guilt. He wasn't her champion, he was her enemy's agent.

"If that's what you want," he said.

"It's what I want."

"Just one request? If you tell the police about Estabrook, will you keep me out of it?"

"Why? Are you back at the old business with Klein?"

"Let's not get into why. Just pretend you never saw me."

She shrugged. "I suppose I can do that."

"Thank you," he said. "Where did you put my clothes?"

"They won't be dry. Why don't you just keep the stuff you're wearing?"

"Better not," he said, unable to resist a tiny jab. "You never know what Marlin might think."

She didn't rise to the remark, but let him go and change. The clothes had been left on the heated towel rack in the bathroom, which had taken some of the chill off them, but insinuating himself into their dampness was almost enough to make him retract his jibe and wear the absent lover's clothes. Almost, but not quite. Changed, he returned to the living room to find her standing at the window again, as if watching for the assassin's return.

"What did you say his name was?" she said.

"Something like Pie 'oh' pah."

"What language is that? Arabic?"

"I don't know."

"Well, did you tell him Estabrook had changed his mind? Did you tell him to leave me alone?"

"I didn't get a chance," he said, lamely.

"So he could still come back and try again?"

"Like I said, I don't think he will."

"He's tried twice. Maybe he's out there thinking, Third time lucky. There's something ... *unnatural* about him, Gentle. How the hell could he heal so fast?"

"Maybe he wasn't as badly hurt as he looked."

She didn't seem convinced. "A name like that ... he shouldn't be difficult to trace."

"I don't know, I think men like him ... they're almost invisible."

"Marlin'll know what to do."

"Good for Marlin."

She drew a deep breath. "I should thank you, though," she said, her tone as far from gratitude as it was possible to get.

"Don't bother," he replied. "I'm just a hired hand. I was only doing it for the money."

4

From the shadows of a doorway on 79th Street, Pie 'oh' pah watched John Furie Zacharias emerge from the apartment building, pull the collar of his jacket up around his bare nape, and scan the street north and south, looking for a cab. It was many years since the assassin's eyes had taken the pleasure they did now, seeing him. In the time between, the world had changed in so many ways. But this man looked unchanged. He was a constant, freed from alteration by his own forgetfulness; always new to himself, and therefore ageless. Pie envied him. For Gentle time was a vapor, dissolving hurt and self-knowledge. For Pie it was a sack into which each day, each hour, dropped another stone, bending the spine until it creaked. Nor, until tonight, had he dared entertain any hope of release. But here, walking away down Park Avenue, was a man in whose power it lay to make whole all broken things, even Pie's wounded spirit. Indeed, especially that. Whether it was chance or the covert workings of the Unbeheld that had brought them together this way, there was surely significance in their reunion.

Minutes before, terrified by the scale of what was unfolding, Pie had attempted to drive Gentle away and, having failed, had fled. Now such fear seemed stupid. What was there to be afraid of? Change? That would be welcome. Revelation? The same. Death? What did an assassin care for death? If it came, it came; it was no reason to turn from opportunity. He shuddered. It was cold here in the doorway; cold in the century too. Especially for a soul like his, that loved the melting season, when the rise of sap and sun made all things seem possible. Until now, he'd given up hope that such a burgeoning time would ever come again. He'd been obliged to commit too many crimes in this joyless world. He'd broken too many hearts. So had they both, most likely. But what if they were obliged to seek that elusive spring for the good of those they'd orphaned and anguished? What if it was their *duty* to hope? Then his denying of this near reunion, his fleeing from it, was just another crime to be laid at his feet. Had these lonely years made him a coward? Never.

Clearing his tears, he left the doorstep and pursued the disappearing figure, daring to believe as he went that there might yet be another spring, and a summer of reconciliations to follow.

8

WHEN HE GOT BACK TO THE HOTEL, Gentle's first instinct was to call Jude. She'd made her feelings towards him abundantly clear, of course, and common sense decreed that he leave this little drama to fizzle out, but he'd glimpsed too many enigmas tonight to be able to shrug off his unease and walk away. Though the streets of this city were solid, their buildings numbered and named, though the avenues were bright enough even at night to banish ambiguity, he still felt as though he was on the margin of some unknown land, in danger of crossing into it without realizing he was even doing so. And if *he* went, might Jude not also follow? Determined though she was to divide her life from his, the obscure suspicion remained in him that their fates were interwoven.

He had no logical explanation for this. The feeling was a mystery, and mysteries weren't his specialty. They were the stuff of after-dinner conversation, when—mellowed by brandy and candlelight—people confessed to fascinations they wouldn't have broached an hour earlier. Under such influence he'd heard rationalists confess their devotion to tabloid astrologies; heard atheists lay claim to heavenly visitations; heard tales of psychic siblings and prophetic deathbed pronouncements. They'd all been amusing enough, in their way. But this was something different. This was happening to him, and it made him afraid.

He finally gave in to his unease. He located Marlin's number and called the apartment. The lover boy picked up. He sounded agitated and became more so when Gentle identified himself.

"I don't know what your goddamn game is," he said.

"It's no game," Gentle told him.

"You just keep away from this apartment—"

"I've no intention—"

"—because if I see your face, I swear—"

"Can I speak to Jude?"

"Judith's not—"

"I'm on the other line," Jude said.

"Judith, put down the phone! You don't want to be talking with this scum."

"Calm down, Marlin."

"You heard her, Mervin. Calm down."

Marlin slammed down the receiver.

"Suspicious, is he?" Gentle said.

"He thinks this is all your doing."

"So you told him about Estabrook?"

"No, not yet."

"You're just going to blame the hired hand, is that it?"

"Look, I'm sorry about some of the things I said. I wasn't thinking straight. If it hadn't been for you maybe I'd be dead by now."

"No maybe about it," Gentle said. "Our friend Pie meant business."

"He meant *something,*" she replied. "But I'm not sure it was murder."

"He was trying to smother you, Jude."

"Was he? Or was he just trying to hush me? He had such a strange look—"

"I think we should talk about this face to face," Gentle said. "Why don't you slip away from lover boy for a late-night drink? I can pick you up right outside your building. You'll be quite safe."

"I don't think that's such a good idea. I've got packing to do. I've decided to go back to London tomorrow."

"Was that planned?"

"No. I'd just feel more secure if I was at home."

"Is Mervin going with you?"

"It's Marlin. And no, he isn't."

"More fool him."

"Look, I'd better go. Thanks for thinking of me."

"It's no hardship," he said. "And if you get lonely between now and tomorrow morning—"

"I won't."

"You never know. I'm at the Omni. Room one-oh-three. There's a double bed."

"You'll have plenty of room, then."

"I'll be thinking of you," he said. He paused, then added, "I'm glad I saw you."

"I'm glad you're glad."

"Does that mean you're not?"

"It means I've got packing to do. Good night, Gentle."

"Good night."

"Have fun."

He did what little packing of his own he had to do, then ordered up a small supper: a club sandwich, ice cream, bourbon, and coffee. The warmth of the room after the icy street and its exertions made him feel sluggish. He undressed and ate his supper naked in front of the television, picking the crumbs from his pubic hair like lice. By the time he got to the ice cream he was too weary to eat, so he downed the bourbon—which instantly took its toll—and retired to bed, leaving the television on in the next room, its sound turned down to a soporific burble.

His body and his mind went about their different businesses. The former, freed from conscious instruction, breathed, rolled, sweated, and digested. The latter went dreaming. First, of Manhattan served on a plate, sculpted in perfect detail. Then of a waiter, speaking in a whisper, asking if sir wanted *night;* and of night coming in the form of a blueberry syrup, poured from high above the plate and falling in viscous folds upon the streets and towers. Then, Gentle walking in those streets, between those towers, hand in hand with a shadow, the company of which he was happy to keep, and which turned when they reached an intersection and laid its feather finger upon the middle of his brow, as though Ash Wednesday were dawning.

He liked the touch and opened his mouth to lightly lick the ball of the shadow's hand. It stroked the place again. He shuddered with pleasure, wishing he could see into the darkness of this other and know its face. In straining to see, he opened his eyes, body and mind converging once again. He was back in his hotel room, the only light the flicker of the television, reflected in the gloss of a half-open door. Though he was awake the sensation continued, and to it was added sound: a milky sigh that excited him. There was a woman in the room.

"Jude?" he said.

She pressed her cool palm against his open mouth, hushing his inquiry even as she answered it. He couldn't distinguish her from the darkness, but any lingering doubt that she might belong to the dream from which he'd risen was dispatched as her hand went from his mouth to his bare chest. He reached up in the darkness to take hold of her face and bring it down to his mouth, glad that the murk concealed the satisfaction he wore. She'd come to him. After all the signals of rejection she'd sent out at the apartment—despite Marlin, despite the dangerous streets, despite the hour, despite their bitter history—she'd come, bearing the gift of her body to his bed.

Though he couldn't see her, the darkness was a black canvas, and he painted her there to perfection, her beauty gazing down on him. His hands found her flawless cheeks. They were cooler than her hands, which were on his belly now, pressing harder as she hoisted herself over him. There was everywhere in their exchange an exquisite synchronicity. He thought of her tongue and tasted it; he imagined her breasts, and she took his hands to them; he wished she would speak, and she spoke (oh, how she spoke), words he hadn't dared admit he'd wanted to hear.

"I had to do this . . ." she said.

"I know. I know."

"Forgive me."

"What's to forgive?"

"I can't be without you, Gentle. We belong to each other, like man and wife."

With her here, so close after such an absence, the idea of marriage didn't seem so preposterous. Why not claim her now and forever?

"You want to marry me?" he murmured.

"Ask me again another night," she replied.

"I'm asking you now."

She put her hand back upon that anointing place in the middle of his brow. "Hush," she said. "What you want now you might not want tomorrow. . . ."

He opened his mouth to disagree, but the thought lost its way between his brain and his tongue, distracted by the small circular motions she was making on his forehead. A calm emanated from the place, moving down through his torso and out to his fingertips. With it, the pain of his bruising faded. He raised his hands above his head, stretching to let bliss run through him freely. Released from aches he'd become accustomed to, his body felt new minted: gleaming invisibly.

"I want to be inside you," he said.

"How far?"

"All the way."

He tried to divide the darkness and catch some glimpse of her response, but his sight was a poor explorer and returned from the unknown without news. Only a flicker from the television, reflected in the gloss of his eye and thrown up against the blank darkness, lent him the illusion of a luster passing through her body, opaline. He started to sit up, seeking her face, but she was already moving down the bed, and moments later he felt her lips on his stomach, and then upon the head of his cock, which she took into her mouth by degrees, her tongue playing on it as she went, until he thought he would lose control. He warned her with a murmur, was released and, a breath later, swallowed again.

The absence of sight lent potency to her touch. He felt every motion of tongue and tooth in play upon him, his prick, particularized by her appetite, becoming vast in his mind's eye until it was his body's size: a veiny torso and a blind head lying on the bed of his belly wet from end to end, straining and shuddering, while she, the darkness, swallowed him utterly. He was only sensation now, and she its supplier, his body enslaved by bliss, unable to remember its making or conceive of its undoing. God, but she knew how he liked to be pleasured, taking care not to stale his nerves with repetition, but cajoling his juice into cells already brimming, until he was ready to come in blood and be murdered by her work, willingly.

Another skitter of light behind his eye broke the hold of sensation, and he was once again entire—his prick its modest length— and she not darkness but a body through which waves of iridescence seemed to pass. Only *seemed,* he knew. This was his sight-starved eyes' invention. Yet it came again, a sinuous light, sleeking her, then going out. Invention or not it made him want her more completely, and he put his arms beneath her shoulders, lifting her up and off him. She rolled over to his side, and he reached across to undress her. Now that she was lying against white sheets her form was visible, albeit vaguely. She moved beneath his hand, raising her body to his touch.

"Inside you . . ." he said, rummaging through the damp folds of her clothes.

Her presence beside him had stilled; her breathing lost its irregularity. He bared her breasts, put his tongue to them as his hands went down to the belt of her skirt, to find that she'd changed for the trip and was wearing jeans. Her hands were on the belt, almost as if to deny him. But he wouldn't be delayed or denied. He pulled the jeans down around her hips, feeling skin so smooth beneath his hands it was almost fluid; her whole body a slow curve, like a wave about to break over him.

For the first time since she'd appeared she said his name, tentatively, as though in this darkness she'd suddenly doubted he was real.

"I'm here," he replied. "Always."

"This is what you want?" she said.

"Of course it is. Of course," he replied, and put his hand on her sex.

This time the iridescence, when it came, was almost bright, and fixed in his head the image of her crotch, his fingers sliding over and between her labia. As the light went, leaving its afterglow on his blind eyes, he was vaguely distracted by a ringing sound, far off at first but closer with every repetition. The telephone, damn it! He did his best to ignore it, failed, and reached out to the bedside table where it sat, throwing the receiver off its cradle and returning to her in one graceless motion. The body beneath him was once again perfectly still. He climbed on top of her and slid inside. It was like being sheathed in silk. She put her hands up around his neck, her fingers strong, and raised her head a little way off the bed to meet his kisses. Though their mouths were clamped together he could hear her saying his name—*"Gentle? Gentle?"*—with that same questioning tone she'd had before. He didn't let memory divert him from his present pleasure, but found his rhythm: long, slow strokes. He remembered her as a woman who liked him to take his time. At the height of their affair they'd made love from dusk to dawn on several occasions, toying and teasing, stopping to bathe so they'd have the bliss of working up a second sweat. But this was an encounter that had none of the froth of those liaisons. Her fingers were digging hard at his back, pulling him onto her with each thrust. And still he heard her voice, dimmed by the veils of his self-consumption: "Gentle? Are you there?"

"I'm here," he murmured.

A fresh tide of light was rising through them both, the erotic becoming a visionary toil as he watched it sweep over their skin, its brightness intensifying with every thrust.

Again she asked him, "Are you there?"

How could she doubt it? He was never more present than in this act, never more comprehending of himself than when buried in the other sex.

"I'm here," he said.

Yet she asked again, and this time, though his mind was stewed in bliss, the tiny voice of reason murmured that it wasn't his lady who was asking the question at all, but the woman on the telephone. He'd thrown the receiver off the hook, but she was haranguing the empty line, demanding he reply. Now he listened. There was no mistaking the voice. It was Jude. And if Jude was on the line, who the fuck was he fucking?

Whoever it was, she knew the deception was over. She dug deeper into the flesh of his lower back and buttocks, raising her hips to press him deeper into her still, her sex tightening around his cock as though to prevent him from leaving her unspent. But he was sufficiently master of himself to resist and pulled out of her, his heart thumping like some crazy locked up in the cell of his chest.

"Who the hell are you?" he yelled.

Her hands were still upon him. Their heat and their demand, which had so aroused him moments before, unnerved him now. He threw her off and started to reach towards the lamp on the bedside table. She took hold of his erection as he did so and slid her palm along the shaft. Her touch was so persuasive he almost succumbed to the idea of entering her again, taking her anonymity as carte blanche and indulging in the darkness every last desire he could dredge up. She was putting her mouth where her hand had been, sucking him into her. He regained in two heartbeats the hardness he'd lost.

Then the whine of the empty line reached his ears. Jude had given up trying to make contact. Perhaps she'd heard his panting and the promises he'd been making in the dark. The thought brought new rage. He took hold of the woman's head and pulled her from his lap. What could have possessed him to want somebody he couldn't even see? And what kind of whore offered herself that way? Diseased? Deformed? Psychotic? He had to see. However repulsive, he had to see!

He reached for the lamp a second time, feeling the bed shake as the harridan prepared to make her escape. Fumbling for the switch, he brought the lamp off its perch. It didn't smash, but its beams were cast up at the ceiling, throwing a gauzy light down on the room below. Suddenly fearful she'd attack him, he turned without picking the lamp up, only to find that the woman had already claimed her clothes from the snarl of sheets and was retreating to the bedroom door. His eyes had been feeding on darkness and projections for too long, and now, presented with solid reality, they were befuddled. Half concealed by shadow the woman was a mire of shifting forms—face blurred, body smeared, pulses of iridescence, slow now, passing from toes to head. The only fixable element in this flux was her eyes, which stared back at him mercilessly.

He wiped his hand from brow to chin in the hope of sloughing the illusion off, and in these seconds she opened the door to make her escape. He leapt from the bed, still determined to get past his confusions to the grim truth he'd coupled with, but she was already halfway through the door, and the only way he could stop her was to seize hold of her arm.

Whatever power had deranged his senses, its bluff was called when he made contact with her. The roiling forms of her face resolved themselves like pieces of a multifaceted jigsaw, turning and turning as they found their place, concealing countless other configurations—rare, wretched, bestial, dazzling—behind the shell of a congruous reality. He knew the features, now that they'd come to rest. Here were the ringlets, framing a face of exquisite symmetry. Here were the scars that healed with such unnatural speed. Here were the lips that hours before had described their owner as nothing and nobody. It was a lie! This nothing had two functions at least: assassin and whore. This nobody had a name.

"Pie 'oh' pah!"

Gentle let go of the man's arm as though it were venomous. The form before him didn't redissolve, however, for which fact Gentle was only half glad. That hallucinatory chaos had been distressing, but the solid thing it had concealed appalled him more. Whatever sexual imaginings he'd shaped in the darkness—Judith's face, Judith's breasts, belly, sex—all of them had been an illusion. The creature he'd coupled with, almost shot his load into, didn't even share her sex.

He was neither a hypocrite nor a puritan. He loved sex too much to condemn any expression of lust, and though he'd discouraged the homosexual courtships he'd attracted, it was out of indifference, not revulsion. So the shock he felt now was fueled more by the power of the deceit worked upon him than by the sex of the deceiver.

"What have you done to me?" was all he could say. "What have you done?"

Pie 'oh' pah stood his ground, knowing perhaps that his nakedness was his best defense.

"I wanted to heal you," he said. Though it trembled, there was music in his voice.

"You put some drug in me."

"No!" Pie said.

"Don't give me *no*! I thought you were Judith! You let me think you were Judith!" He looked down at his hands, then up at the hard, lean body in front of him. "I felt *her,* not you." Again, the same complaint. "What have you done to me?"

"I gave you what you wanted," Pie said.

Gentle had no retort to this. In its way, it was the truth. Scowling, he sniffed his palms, thinking there might be traces of some drug in his sweat. But there was only the stench of sex on him, of the heat of the bed behind him.

"You'll sleep it off," Pie said.

"Get the fuck out of here," Gentle replied. "And if you go anywhere near Jude again, I swear . . . I *swear* . . . I'll take you apart."

"You're obsessed with her, aren't you?"

"None of your fucking business."

"It'll do you harm."

"Shut up."

"It will, I'm telling you."

"I told you," Gentle yelled, *"shut the fuck up!"*

"She doesn't belong to you," came the reply.

The words ignited new fury in Gentle. He reached for Pie and took him by the throat. The bundle of clothes dropped from the assassin's arm, leaving him naked. But he put up no defense; he simply raised his hands and laid them lightly on Gentle's shoulders. The gesture only infuriated Gentle further. He let out a stream of invective, but the placid face before him took both spittle and spleen without flinching. Gentle shook him, digging his thumbs into the man's throat to stop his windpipe. Still he neither resisted nor succumbed, but stood in front of his attacker like a saint awaiting martyrdom.

Finally, breathless with rage and exertion, Gentle let go his hold and threw Pie back, stepping away from the creature with a glimmer of superstition in his eyes. Why hadn't the fellow fought back or fallen? Anything but this sickening passivity.

"Get out," Gentle told him.

Pie still stood his ground, watching him with forgiving eyes.

"Will you get out?" Gentle said again, more softly, and this time the martyr replied.

"If you wish."

"I wish."

He watched Pie 'oh' pah stoop to pick up the scattered clothes. Tomorrow, this would all come clear in his head, he thought. He'd have shat this delirium out of his system, and these events—Jude, the chase, his near rape at the hands of the assassin—would be a tale to tell Klein and Clem and Taylor when he got back to London. They'd be entertained. Aware now that he was more naked than the other man, he turned to the bed and dragged a sheet off it to cover himself with.

There was a strange moment then, when he knew the bastard was still in the room, still watching him, and all he could do was wait for him to leave. Strange because it reminded him of other bedroom partings: sheets tangled, sweat cooling, confusion and self-reproach keeping glances at bay. He waited, and waited, and finally heard the door close. Even then he didn't turn, but listened to the room to be certain there was only one breath in it: his own. When he finally looked back and saw that Pie 'oh' pah had gone, he pulled the sheet up around him like a toga, concealing himself from the absence in the room, which stared back at him too much like a reflection for his peace of mind. Then he locked the suite door and stumbled back to bed, listening to his drugged head whine like the empty telephone line.

9

I

Oscar Esmond Godolphin always recited a little prayer in praise of democracy when, after one of his trips to the Dominions, he stepped back onto English soil. Extraordinary as those visits were—and as warmly welcomed as he found himself in the diverse Kesparates of Yzordderrex—the city-state was an autocracy of the most extreme kind, its excesses dwarfing the repressions of the country he'd been born in. Especially of late. Even his great friend and business partner in the Second Dominion, Hebbert Nuits-St.-Georges, called Peccable by those who knew him well, a merchant who had made substantial profit from the superstitious and the woebegone in the Second Dominion, regularly remarked that the order of Yzordderrex was growing less stable by the day and he would soon take his family out of the city, indeed out of the Dominion entirely, and find a new home where he would not have to smell burning bodies when he opened his windows in the morning. So far, it was only talk. Godolphin knew Peccable well enough to be certain that until he'd exhausted his supply of idols, relics, and jujus from the Fifth and could make no more profit, he'd stay put. And given that it was Godolphin himself who supplied these items—most were simply terrestrial trivia, revered in the Dominions because of their place of origin—and given that he would not cease to do so as long as the fever of collection was upon him and he could exchange such items for artifacts from the Imajica, Peccable's business would flourish. It was a trade in talismans, and neither man was likely to tire of it soon.

Nor did Godolphin tire of being an Englishman in that most un-English of cities. He was instantly recognizable in the small but influential circle he kept. A large man in every way, he was tall and big-bellied: bellicose when fondest, hearty when not. At fifty-two he had long ago found his style and was more than comfortable with it. True, he concealed his second and third chins beneath a gray-brown beard that only got an efficient trimming at the hands of Peccable's eldest daughter, Hoi-Polloi. True, he attempted to look a little more learned by wearing silver-rimmed spectacles that were dwarfed by his large face but were, he thought, all the more pedagoguish because they didn't flatter. But these were little deceits. They helped to make him unmistakable, which he liked. He wore his thinning hair short and his collars long, preferring for dress a clash of tweeds and a striped shirt; always a tie; invariably a waistcoat. All in all, a difficult sight to ignore, which suited him fine. Nothing was more likely to bring a smile to his face than being told he was talked about. It was usually with affection.

There was no smile on his face now, however, as he stepped out of the site of the Reconciliation—known euphemistically as the Retreat—to find Dowd sitting perched on a shooting stick a few yards from the door. It was early afternoon but the sun was already low in the sky, the air as chilly as Dowd's welcome. It was almost enough to make him turn around and go back to Yzordderrex, revolution or no.

"Why do I think you haven't come here with sparkling news?" he said.

Dowd rose with his usual theatricality. "I'm afraid you're absolutely correct," he said.

"Let me guess: the government fell! The house burned down." His face dropped. "Not my brother?" he said. "Not Charlie?" He tried to read Dowd's face. "What: dead? A massive coronary. When was the funeral?"

"No, he's alive. But the problem lies with him."

"Always has. Always has. Will you fetch my goods and chattels out of the folly? We'll talk as we walk. Go on in, will you? There's nothing there that's going to bite."

Dowd had stayed out of the Retreat all the time he'd waited for Godolphin (a wearisome three days), even though it would have given him some measure of protection against the bitter cold. Not that his system was susceptible to such discomforts, but he fancied himself an empathic soul, and his time on Earth had taught him to feel cold as an intellectual concept, if not a physical one, and he might have wished to take shelter. Anywhere other than the Retreat. Not only had many esoterics died there (and he didn't enjoy the proximity of death unless he'd been its bringer), but the Retreat was a passing place between the Fifth Dominion and the other four, including, of course, the home from which he was in permanent exile. To be so close to the door through which his home lay, and be prevented by the conjurations of his first keeper, Joshua Godolphin, from opening that door, was painful. The cold was preferable.

He stepped inside now, however, having no choice in the matter. The Retreat had been built in neoclassical style: twelve marble pillars rising to support a dome that called for decoration but had none. The plainness of the whole lent it gravity and a certain functionalism which was not inappropriate. It was, after all, no more than a station, built to serve countless passengers and now used by only one. On the floor, set in the middle of the elaborate mosaic that appeared to be the building's sole concession to prettification but was in fact the evidence of its true purpose, were the bundles of artifacts Godolphin brought back from his travels, neatly tied up by Hoi-Polloi Nuits-St.-Georges, the knots encrusted with scarlet sealing wax. It was her present delight, this business with the wax, and Dowd cursed it, given that it fell to him to unpack these treasures. He crossed to the center of the mosaic, light on his heels. This was tremulous terrain, and he didn't trust it. But moments later he emerged with his freight, to find that Godolphin was already marching out of the copse that screened the Retreat from both the house (empty, of course; in ruins) and any casual spy who peered over the wall. He took a deep breath and went after his master, knowing the explanation ahead would not be easy.

2

"So they've *summoned* me, have they?" Oscar said, as they drove back into London, the traffic thickening with the dusk. "Well, let them wait."

"You're not going to tell them you're here?"

"In my time, not in theirs. This is a mess, Dowdy. A wretched mess."

"You told me to help Estabrook if he needed it."

"Helping him hire an assassin isn't what I had in mind."

"Chant was very discreet."

"Death makes you that way, I find. You really have made a pig's ear of the whole thing."

"I protest," said Dowd. "What else was I supposed to do? You knew he wanted the woman dead, and you washed your hands of it."

"All true," said Godolphin. "She *is* dead, I assume?"

"I don't think so. I've been scouring the papers, and there's no mention."

"So why did you have Chant killed?"

Here Dowd was more cautious in his account. If he said too

little, Godolphin would suspect him of concealment. Too much, and the larger picture might become apparent. The longer his employer stayed in ignorance of the scale of the stakes, the better. He proffered two explanations, both ready and waiting.

"For one thing, the man was more unreliable than I'd thought. Drunk and maudlin half the time. And I think he knew more than was good for either you or your brother. He might have ended up finding out about your travels."

"Instead it's the Society that's suspicious."

"It's unfortunate the way these things turn out."

"Unfortunate, my arse. A total balls-up is what it is."

"I'm very sorry."

"I know you are, Dowdy," Oscar said. "The point is, where do we find a scapegoat?"

"Your brother?"

"Perhaps," Godolphin replied, cannily concealing the degree to which this suggestion found favor.

"When should I tell them you've come back?" Dowd asked.

"When I've made up a lie I can believe in," came the reply.

Back in the house in Regent's Park Road, Oscar took some time to study the newspaper reports of Chant's death before retiring to his treasure house on the third floor with both his new artifacts and a good deal to think about. A sizable part of him wanted to exit this Dominion once and for all. Take himself off to Yzordderrex and set up business with Peccable; marry Hoi-Polloi despite her crossed eyes; have a litter of kids and retire to the Hills of the Conscious Cloud, in the Third, and raise parrots. But he knew he'd yearn for England sooner or later, and a yearning man could be cruel. He'd end up beating his wife, bullying his kids, and eating the parrots. So, given that he'd always have to keep a foot in England, if only during the cricket season, and given that as long as he kept a presence here he would be answerable to the Society, he had to face them.

He locked the door of his treasure room, sat down amid his collection, and waited for inspiration. The shelves around him, which were built to the ceiling, were bowed beneath the weight of his trove. Here were items gathered from the edge of the Second Dominion to the limits of the Fourth. He had only to pick one of them up to be transported back to the time and place of its acquisition. The statue of the Etook Ha'chiit, he'd bartered for in a little town called Slew, which was now, regrettably, a blasted spot, its citizens the victims of a purge visited upon them for the crime of a song, written in the dialect of their community, suggesting that the Autarch of Yzordderrex lacked testicles.

Another of his treasures, the seventh volume of Gaud Maybel-lome's *Encyclopedia of Heavenly Signs,* originally written in the language of Third Dominion academics but widely translated for the delectation of the proletariat, he'd bought from a woman in the city of Jassick, who'd approached him in a gaming room, where he was attempting to explain cricket to a group of the locals, and said she recognized him from stories her husband (who was in the Autarch's army in Yzordderrex) had told.

"You're the English male," she'd said, which didn't seem worth denying.

Then she'd shown him the book: a very rare volume indeed. He'd never ceased to find fascination within its pages, for it was Maybellome's intention to make an encyclopedia listing all the flora, fauna, languages, sciences, ideas, moral perspectives—in short, anything that occurred to her—that had found their way from the Fifth Dominion, the Place of the Succulent Rock, through to the other worlds. It was a herculean task, and she'd died just as she was beginning the nineteenth volume, with no end in sight, but even the one book in Godolphin's possession was enough to guarantee that he would search for the others until his dying day. It was a bizarre, almost surreal volume. Even if only half the entries were true, or nearly true, Earth had influenced just about every aspect of the worlds from which it was divided. Fauna, for instance. There were countless animals listed in the volume which Maybellome claimed to be invaders from the other world. Some clearly were: the zebra, the crocodile, the dog. Others were a mixture of genetic strands, part terrestrial, part not. But many of these species (pictured in the book like fugitives from a medieval bestiary) were so outlandish he doubted their very existence. Here, for instance, were hand-sized wolves with the wings of canaries. Here was an elephant that lived in an enormous conch. Here was a literate worm that wrote omens with its thread-fine half-mile body. Wonderment upon wonderment. Godolphin only had to pick up the encyclopedia and he was ready to put on his boots and set off for the Dominions again.

What was self-evident from even a casual perusal of the book was how extensively the unreconciled Dominion had influenced the others. The languages of earth—English, Italian, Hindustani, and Chinese particularly—were known in some variation everywhere, though it seemed the Autarch—who had come to power in the confusion following the failed Reconciliation—favored English, which was now the preferred linguistic currency almost everywhere. To name a child with an English word was thought particularly propitious, though there was little or no consideration given to what the word actually meant. Hence Hoi-Polloi, for instance; this one of the less strange namings among the thousands Godolphin had encountered.

He flattered himself that he was in some small part responsible for such blissful bizarrities, given that over the years he'd brought all manner of influences through from the Succulent Rock. There was always a hunger for newspapers and magazines (usually preferred to books), and he'd heard of baptizers in Patashoqua who named children by stabbing a copy of the London *Times* with a pin and bequeathing the first three words they pricked upon the infant, however unmusical the combination. But he was not the only influence. He hadn't brought the crocodile or the zebra or the dog (though he would lay claim to the parrot). No, there had always been routes through from Earth into the Dominions, other than that at the Retreat. Some, no doubt, had been opened by Maestros and esoterics, in all manner of cultures, for the express purpose of their passing to and fro between worlds. Others were conceivably opened by accident, and perhaps remained open, marking the sites as haunted or sacred, shunned or obsessively protected. Yet others, these in the smallest number, had been created by the sciences of the other Dominions, as a means of gaining access to the heaven of the Succulent Rock.

In such a place, this near the walls of the Iahmandhas in the Third Dominion, Godolphin had acquired his most sacred possession: a Boston Bowl, complete with its forty-one colored stones. Though he'd never used it, the bowl was reputedly the most accurate prophetic tool known in the worlds, and now—sitting amid his treasures, with a sense growing in him that events on earth in the last few days were leading to some matter of moment—he brought the bowl down from its place on the highest shelf, unwrapped it, and set it on the table. Then he took the stones from their pouch and laid them at the bottom of the bowl. Truth to tell, the arrangement didn't look particularly promising: the bowl resembled something for kitchen use, plain fired ceramic, large enough to whip eggs for a couple of soufflés. The stones were more colorful, varying in size and shape from tiny flat pebbles to perfect spheres the size of an eyeball.

Having set them out, Godolphin had second thoughts. Did he even believe in prophecy? And if he did, was it wise to know the future? Probably not. Death was bound to be in there somewhere, sooner or later. Only Maestros and deities lived forever, and a man might sour the balance of his span knowing when it was going to end. But then, suppose he found in this bowl some indication as to how the Society might be handled? That would be no small weight off his shoulders.

"Be brave," he told himself, and laid the middle finger of each hand upon the rim, as Peccable, who'd once owned such a bowl and had it smashed by his wife in a domestic row, had instructed.

Nothing happened at first, but Peccable had warned him the bowls usually took some time to start from cold. He waited and waited. The first sight of activation was a rattling from the bottom of the bowl as the stones began to move against each other; the second a distinctly acidic odor rising to jab at his sinuses; the third, and most startling, the sudden ricocheting of one pebble, then two, then a dozen, across the bowl and back, several skipping higher than the rim. Their ambition increased by the movement, until all forty-one were in violent motion, so violent that the bowl began to move across the table, and Oscar had to take a firm hold of it to keep it from turning over. The stones struck his fingers and knuckles with stinging force, but the pain was made sweeter by the success that now followed, as the speed and motion of the multifarious shapes and colors began to describe images in the air above the bowl.

Like all prophecy, the signs were in the eye of the beholder, and perhaps another witness would have seen different forms in the blur. But what Godolphin saw seemed quite plain to him. The Retreat, for one, half hidden in the copse. Then himself, standing in the middle of the mosaic, either coming back from Yzordderrex or preparing to depart. The images lingered for only a brief time before changing, the Retreat demolished in the storm of stones and a new structure raised in the whirl: the tower of the Tabula Rasa. He fixed his eyes on the prophecy with fresh deliberation, denying himself the comfort of blinking to be certain he missed nothing. The tower as seen from the street gave way to its interior. Here they were, the wise ones, sitting around the table contemplating their divine duty. They were navel defluffers and snot rollers to a man. Not one of them would be capable of surviving an hour in the alleyways of East Yzordderrex, he thought, down by the harbor where even the cats had pimps. Now he saw himself step into the picture, and something he was doing or saying made the men and women before him jump from their seats, even Lionel.

"What's this?" Oscar murmured.

They had wild expressions on their faces, every one. Were they laughing? What had he done? Cracked a joke? Passed wind? He studied the prophecy more closely. No, it wasn't humor on their faces. It was horror.

"Sir?"

Dowd's voice from outside the door broke his concentration. He looked away from the bowl for a few seconds to snap, "Go away."

But Dowd had urgent news. "McGann's on the telephone," he said.

"Tell him you don't know where I am." Oscar snorted, returning his gaze to the bowl. Something terrible had happened in the time between his looking away and looking back. The horror remained on their faces, but for some reason he'd disappeared from the scene. Had they dispatched him summarily? God, was he dead on the floor? Maybe. There was something glistening on the table, like spilled blood.

"Sir!"

"Fuck off, Dowdy."

"They know you're here, sir."

They knew; *they knew*. The house was being watched, and they knew.

"All right," he said. "Tell him I'll be down in a moment."

"What did you say, sir?"

Oscar raised his voice over the din of the stones, looking away again, this time more willingly. "Get his whereabouts. I'll call him back."

Again, he returned his gaze to the bowl, but his concentration had faltered, and he could no longer interpret the images concealed in the motion of the stones. Except for one. As the speed of the display slowed he seemed to catch—oh, so fleetingly—a woman's face in the mêlée. His replacement at the Society's table, perhaps; or his dispatcher.

3

He needed a drink before he spoke to McGann. Dowd, ever the anticipator, had already mixed him a whisky and soda, but he forsook it for fear it would loosen his tongue. Paradoxically, what had been half revealed by the Boston Bowl helped him in his exchange. In extreme circumstances he responded with almost pathological detachment; it was one of his most English traits. He had thus seldom been cooler or more controlled than now, as he told McGann that yes, indeed, he had been traveling, and no, it was none of the Society's business where or about what pursuit. He would of course be delighted to attend a gathering at the tower the following day, but was McGann aware (indeed did he care?) that tomorrow was Christmas Eve?

"I never miss Midnight Mass at St. Martin-in-the-Fields," Oscar told him, "so I'd appreciate it greatly if the meeting could be concluded quickly enough to allow me time to get there and find a pew with a good view."

He delivered all of this without a tremor in the voice. McGann attempted to press him as to his whereabouts in the last few days, to which Oscar asked why the hell it mattered.

"I don't ask about your private affairs, now, do I?" he said, in a mildly affronted tone. "Nor, by the way, do I spy on your comings and goings. Don't splutter, McGann. You don't trust me and I don't trust you. I will take tomorrow's meeting as a forum to debate the privacy of the Society's members and a chance to remind the gathering that the name of Godolphin is one of the cornerstones of the Society."

"All the more reason for you to be forthright," McGann said.

"I'll be perfectly forthright," was Oscar's reply. "You'll have ample evidence of my innocence." Only now, with the war of wits won, did he accept the whisky and soda Dowd had mixed for him. "Ample and definitive." He silently toasted Dowd as he talked, knowing as he sipped it that there'd be blood shed before Christmas Day dawned. Grim as that prospect was, there was no avoiding it now.

When he put the phone down he said to Dowd, "I think I'll wear the herringbone suit tomorrow. And a plain shirt. White. Starched collar."

"And the tie?" Dowd asked, replacing Oscar's drained glass with a fresh one.

"I'll be going straight on to Midnight Mass," Oscar said.

"Black, then."

"Black."

10

I

The afternoon of the day following the assassin's appearance at Marlin's apartment a blizzard descended upon New York with no little ferocity, conspiring with the inevitable seasonal rush to make finding a flight back to England difficult. But Jude was not easily denied anything, especially when she'd set her mind firmly on an objective; and she was certain—despite Marlin's protestations—that leaving Manhattan was the most sensible thing to do.

She had reason on her side. The assassin had made two attempts upon her life. He was still at large. As long as she stayed in New York she would be under threat. But even if this had not been the case (and there was a part of her that still believed that he'd come that second time to explain, or apologize), she would have found an excuse for returning to England, just to be out of Marlin's company. He had become too cloying in his affections, his talk as saccharine as the dialogue from the Christmas classics on the television, his every gaze mawkish. He'd had this sickness all along, of course, but he'd worsened since the assassin's visit, and her tolerance for its symptoms, braced as she'd been by her encounter with Gentle, had dropped to zero. Once she'd put the phone down on him the previous night she'd regretted her skittish way with him, and after a heart-to-heart with Marlin in which she'd told him she wanted to go back to England, and he'd replied that it would all seem different in the morning and why didn't she just take a pill and lie down, she'd decided to call him back. By this time, Marlin was sound asleep. She'd left her bed, gone through to the living room, put on a single lamp, and made the call. It felt covert, which in a way it was. Marlin had not been pleased to know that one of her ex-lovers had attempted to play hero in his own apartment, and he wouldn't have been happy to find her making contact with Gentle at two in the morning. She still didn't know what had happened when she'd been put through to the room. The receiver had been picked up and then dropped, leaving her to listen with increasing fury and frustration to the sound of Gentle making love. Instead of putting the phone down there and then she'd listened, half wishing she could have joined the escapade. Eventually, after failing to distract Gentle from his labors, she'd hung up and traipsed back to her cold bed in a foul humor.

He'd called the next day, and Marlin had answered. She let him tell Gentle that if he ever saw hide or hair of Gentle in the building again he'd have him arrested as an accomplice to attempted murder.

"What did he say?" she'd asked when the conversation was done.

"Not very much. He sounded drunk."

She had not discussed the matter any further. Marlin was already sullen enough, after her breakfast announcement that she still intended to return to England that day. He'd asked her over and over: why? Was there something he could do to make her stay more comfortable? Extra locks on the doors? A promise that he wouldn't leave her side? None of these, of course, filling her with renewed enthusiasm for staying. If she told him once she told him two dozen times that he was quite the perfect host, and that he wasn't to take this personally, but she wanted to be back in her own house, her own city, where she would feel most protected from the assassin. He'd then offered to come back with her, so she wasn't returning to an empty house alone, at which point—running out of soothing phrases and patience—she'd told him that alone was exactly what she wanted to be.

And so here she was, one snail crawl through the blizzard to
Kennedy, a five-hour delay, and a flight in which she was wedged
between a nun who prayed aloud every time they hit an air pocket
and a child in need of worming, later. Her own sole possessor, in
an empty flat on Christmas Eve.

2

The painting in four contrary modes was there to greet Gentle
when he got back to the studio. His return had been delayed by
the same blizzard that had almost prevented Judith from leaving
Manhattan, and put him beyond the deadline Klein had set. But
his thoughts had not turned to his business dealings with Klein
more than once during the journey. They'd revolved almost entirely
around the encounter with the assassin. Whatever mischief Pie
'oh' pah had worked upon his system it had cleared by the following morning—his eyes were operating normally, and he was
lucid enough to deal with the practicalities of departure—but the
echoes of what he'd experienced still reverberated. Dozing on the
plane he felt the smoothness of the assassin's face in his fingertips,
the tumble of hair he'd taken to be Jude's over the back of his
hands. He could still smell the scent of wet skin and feel the weight
of Pie 'oh' pah's body on his hips, this so persuasive he had an erection apparent enough to draw a stare from one of the flight attendants. He reasoned that perhaps he would have to put fresh
sensation between these echoes and their origins: fuck them out,
sweat himself clean. The thought comforted him. When he dozed
again, and the memories returned, he didn't fight them, knowing
he had a means of scouring them from his system once he got back
to England.

Now he sat in front of the painting in four modes and flipped
through his address book looking for a partner for the night. He
made a few calls but couldn't have chosen a worse time to be setting up a casual liaison. Husbands were home; family gatherings
were in the offing. He was out of season.

He did eventually speak to Klein, who after some persuasion accepted his apologies and then went on to tell him there was to be
a party at Taylor and Clem's house the following day, and he was
sure Gentle would be welcome if he had no other plans.

"Everyone says it'll be Taylor's last," Chester said. "I know he'd
like to see you."

"I suppose I should go, then," Gentle said.

"You should. He's very sick. He's had pneumonia, and now can-
cer. He was always very fond of you, you know."

The association of ideas made fondness for Gentle sound like another disease, but he didn't comment on it, merely made arrangements to pick up Klein the following evening; and put down the phone, plunged into a deeper trough than ever. He'd known Taylor had the plague but hadn't realized people were counting the days to his demise. Such grim times. Everywhere he looked things were coming apart. There seemed to be only darkness ahead, full of blurred shapes and pitiful glances. The Age of Pie 'oh' pah, perhaps. The time of the assassin.

He didn't sleep, despite being tired, but sat up into the small hours with an object of study that he'd previously dismissed as fanciful nonsense: Chant's final letter. When he'd first read it, on the plane to New York, it had seemed a ludicrous outpouring. But there had been strange times since then, and they'd put Gentle in an apter mood for this study. Pages that had seemed worthless a few days before were now pored over, in the hope they'd yield some clue, encoded in the fanciful excesses of Chant's idiosyncratic and ill-punctuated prose, that would lead him to some fresh comprehension of the times and their movers. Whose god, for instance, was this Hapexamendios that Chant exhorted Estabrook to pray to and praise? He came trailing synonyms: the Unbeheld, the Aboriginal, the Wanderer. And what was the greater plan that Chant hoped in his final hours he was a part of?

I AM ready for death in this DOMINION, he'd written, *if I know that the Unbeheld has used me as His INSTRUMENT. All praise to HAPEXAMENDIOS. For He was in the Place of the Succulent Rock and left His children to SUFFER here, and I have suffered here and AM DONE with suffering.*

That at least was true. The man had known his death was imminent, which suggested he'd known his murderer too. Was it Pie 'oh' pah he'd been expecting? It seemed not. The assassin was referred to, but not as Chant's executioner. Indeed, in his first reading of the letter Gentle hadn't even realized it was Pie 'oh' pah who was being spoken of in this passage. But on this rereading it was completely apparent.

You have made a covenant with a RARE thing in this DOMINION or any other, and I do not know if this death nearly upon me is my punishment or my reward for my agency in that. But be circumspect in all your dealings with it, for such power is capricious, being a stew of kinds and possibilities, no UTTER thing, in any part of its nature, but pavonine and prismatic, an apostate to its core.

I was never the friend of this power—it has only ADORERS AND UNDOERS—but it trusted me as its representative and I have done it as much harm in these dealings as I have you. More,

I think; for it is a lonely thing, and suffers in this DOMINION as I have. You have friends who know you for the man you are and do not have to conceal your TRUE NATURE. Cling to them, and their love for you, for the Place of the Succulent Rock is about to shake and tremble, and in such a time all a soul has is the company of its loving like. I say this having lived in such a time, and am GLAD that if such is coming upon the FIFTH DOMINION again, I will be dead, and my face turned to the glory of the UNBEHELD.

All praise to HAPEXAMENDIOS.

And to you sir, in this moment, I offer my contrition and my prayers.

There was a little more, but both handwriting and the sentence structure deteriorated rapidly thereafter, as though Chant had panicked and scrawled the rest while putting on his coat. The more coherent passages contained enough hints to keep Gentle from sleep, however. The descriptions of Pie 'oh' pah were particularly alarming:

"a RARE thing . . . a stew of kinds and possibilities."

How was that to be interpreted, except as a verification of what Gentle's senses had glimpsed in New York?

If so, what was this creature that had stood before him, naked and singular, but concealed multitudes; this power Chant had said possessed no friends (*it has only ADORERS and UNDOERS,* he'd written) and had been done as much harm in these dealings (again, Chant's words) as Estabrook, to whom Chant had offered his contrition and his prayers? Not human, for certain. Not born of any tribe or nation Gentle was familiar with. He read the letter over and over again, and with each rereading the possibility of belief crept closer. He felt its proximity. It was fresh from the margins of that land he'd first suspected in New York. The thought of being there had made him fearful then. But it no longer did, perhaps because it was Christmas morning, and time for something miraculous to appear and change the world.

The closer they crept—both morning and belief—the more he regretted shunning the assassin when it had so plainly wanted his company. He had no clues to its mystery but those contained in Chant's letter, and after a hundred readings they were exhausted. He wanted more. The only other source was his memory of the creature's jigsaw face, and, knowing his propensity for forgetting, they'd start to fade all too soon. He had to set them down! That was the priority now: to set the vision down before it slipped away!

He threw the letter aside and went to stare at his *Supper at Emmaus.* Was any of those styles capable of capturing what he'd seen? He doubted it. He'd have to invent a new mode. Fired up by that

ambition, he turned the *Supper* on end and began to squeeze burnt
umber directly onto the canvas, spreading it with a palette knife
until the scene beneath was completely obscured. In its place was
now a dark ground, into which he started to gouge the outline of
a figure. He had never studied anatomy very closely. The male
body was of little aesthetic interest to him, and the female was so
mutable, so much a function of its own motion, or that of light
across it, that all static representation seemed to him doomed from
the outset. But he wanted to represent a protean form now, however impossible; wanted to find a way to fix what he'd seen at the
door of his hotel room, when Pie 'oh' pah's many faces had been
shuffled in front of him like cards in an illusionist's deck. If he could
fix that sight, or even begin to do so, he might yet find a way of controlling the thing that had come to haunt him.

He worked in a fair frenzy for two hours, making demands of
the paint he'd never made before, plastering it on with palette
knife and fingers, attempting to capture at least the shape and proportion of the thing's head and neck. He could see the image
clearly enough in his mind's eye (since that night no two remem-
berings had been more than a minute apart), but even the most
basic sketch eluded his hand. He was badly equipped for the task.
He'd been a parasite for too long, a mere copier, echoing other
men's visions. Now he finally had one of his own—only one, but
all the more precious for that—and he simply couldn't set it down.
He wanted to weep at this final defeat, but he was too tired. With
his hands still covered in paint, he lay down on the chilly sheets
and waited for sleep to take his confusions away.

Two thoughts visited him as he slipped into dreams. The first,
that with so much burnt umber on his hands he looked as though
he'd been playing with his own shit. The second, that the only way
to solve the problem on the canvas was to see its subject again in
the flesh, which thought he welcomed, and went to dreams relieved of his frauds and pieties, smiling to think of having the rare
thing's face before him once again.

II

THOUGH THE JOURNEY FROM Godolphin's house in Primrose Hill
to the Tabula Rasa's tower was short, and Dowd got him up to
Highgate on the dot of six, Oscar suggested they drive down
through Crouch End, then up through Muswell Hill, and back to
the tower, so that they'd arrive ten minutes late.

"We mustn't seem to be too eager to prostrate ourselves," he observed as they approached the tower for a second time. "It'll only make them arrogant."

"Shall I wait down here?"

"Cold and lonely? My dear Dowdy, out of the question. We'll ascend together, bearing gifts."

"What gifts?"

"Our wit, our taste in suits—well, *my* taste—in essence, ourselves."

They got out of the car and went to the porch, their every step monitored by cameras mounted above the door. The lock clicked as they approached, and they stepped inside. As they crossed the foyer to the lift, Godolphin whispered, "Whatever happens tonight, Dowdy, please remember—"

He got no further. The lift doors opened, and Bloxham appeared, as preening as ever.

"Pretty tie," Oscar said to him. "Yellow's your color." The tie was blue. "Don't mind my man Dowd here, will you? I never go anywhere without him."

"He's got no place here tonight," Bloxham said.

Again, Dowd offered to wait below, but Oscar would have none of it. "Heaven forfend," he said. "You can wait upstairs. Enjoy the view."

All this irritated Bloxham mightily, but Oscar was not an easy man to deny. They ascended in silence. Once on the top floor Dowd was left to entertain himself, and Bloxham led Godolphin through to the chamber. They were all waiting, and there was accusation on every face. A few—Shales, certainly, and Charlotte Feaver—didn't attempt to disguise their pleasure that the Society's most ebullient and unrepentant member was here finally called to heel.

"Oh, I'm sorry," Oscar said, as they closed the doors behind him. "Have you been waiting long?"

Outside, in one of the deserted antechambers, Dowd listened to his tinny little radio and mused. At seven the news bulletin brought a report of a motorway collision which had claimed the lives of an entire family traveling north for Christmas, and of prison riots that had ignited in Bristol and Manchester, with inmates claiming that presents from loved ones had been tampered with and destroyed by prison officers. There was the usual collection of war updates, then the weather report, which promised a gray Christmas, accompanied by a springlike balm. This would on past experience coax the crocuses out in Hyde Park, only to be spiked by frost in a few days' time. At eight, still waiting by the window, he heard a second bulletin correcting one of the reports from the first. A survivor had been claimed from the entangled vehicles on the motorway: a tot of three months, found orphaned but unscathed in the wreckage. Sitting in the cold gloom, Dowd began to weep quietly, which was an experience as far beyond his true emotional capacity as cold was beyond his nerve endings. But he'd trained himself in the craft of grief with the same commitment to feigning humanity as he had learning to shiver: his tutor, the Bard; *Lear* his favorite lesson. He cried for the child, and for the crocuses, and was still moist-eyed when he heard the voices in the chamber suddenly rise up in rage. The door was flung open, and Oscar called him in, despite shouts of complaint from some of the other members.

"This is an outrage, Godolphin!" Bloxham yelped.

"You drive me to it!" was Oscar's reply, his performance at fever pitch. Clearly he'd been having a bad time of it. The sinews in his neck stood out like knotted string; sweat gleamed in the pouches beneath his eyes; every word brought flecks of spittle. "You don't know the half of it!" he was saying. "Not the half. We're being conspired against, by forces we can barely conceive of. This man Chant was undoubtedly one of their agents. They can take human form!"

"Godolphin, this is absurd," Alice Tyrwhitt said.

"You don't believe me?"

"No, I don't. And I certainly don't want your bum-boy here listening to us debate. Will you please remove him from the chamber?"

"But he has evidence to support my thesis," Oscar insisted.

"Oh, does he?" said Shales.

"He'll have to show you himself," Oscar said, turning to Dowd. "You're going to have to show them, I'm afraid," he said, and as he spoke reached into his jacket.

An instant before the blade emerged, Dowd realized Godolphin's intent and started to turn away, but Oscar had the edge, and it came forth glittering. Dowd felt his master's hand on his neck and heard shouts of horror on all sides. Then he was thrown back across the table, sprawling beneath the lights like an unwilling patient. The surgeon followed through with one swift stab, striking Dowd in the middle of his chest.

"You want proof?" Oscar yelled, through Dowd's screams and the din of shouts around the table. "You want proof? Then here it is!"

His bulk put weight behind the blade, driving it first to the right, then to the left, encountering no obstruction from rib or breastbone. Nor was there blood; only a fluid the color of brackish water, that dribbled from the wounds and ran across the table. Dowd's head thrashed to and fro as this indignity was visited upon him, only once raising his gaze to stare accusingly at Godolphin, who was too busy about this undoing to return the look. Despite protests from all sides he didn't halt his labors until the body before him had been opened from the navel to throat, and Dowd's thrashings had ceased. The stench from the carcass filled the chamber: a pungent mixture of sewage and vanilla. It drove two of the witnesses to the door, one of them Bloxham, whose nausea overtook him before he could reach the corridor. But his gaggings and moans didn't slow Godolphin by a beat. Without hesitation he plunged his arm into the open body and, rummaging there, pulled out a fistful of gut. It was a knotty mass of blue and black tissue—final proof of Dowd's inhumanity. Triumphant, he threw the evidence down on the table beside the body, then stepped away from his handiwork, chucking the knife into the wound it had opened. The whole performance had taken no more than a minute, but in that time he'd succeeded in turning the chamber's table into a fish-market gutter.

"Satisfied?" he said.

All protest had been silenced. The only sound was the rhythmical hiss of fluid escaping an opened artery.

Very quietly McGann said, "You're a fucking maniac."

Oscar reached gingerly into his trouser pocket and teased out a fresh handkerchief. One of poor Dowd's last tasks had been its pressing. It was immaculate. He shook out its scalpel creases and began to clean his hands.

"How else was I going to prove my point?" he said. "You drove me to this. Now there's the evidence, in all its glory. I don't know what happened to Dowd—my bum-boy, I think you called him, Alice—but wherever he is this *thing* took his place."

"How long have you known?" Charlotte asked.

"I've suspected for the last two weeks. I was here in the city all the time, watching its every move while it—and you—thought I was disporting myself in sunnier climes."

"What the bugger is it?" Lionel wanted to know, prodding a scrap of alien entrail with his finger.

"God alone knows," Godolphin said. "Something not of this world, clearly."

"What did it want?" Alice said. "That's more to the point."

"At a guess, access to this chamber, which"—he looked at those around the table one by one—"I gather you granted it three days ago. I trust none of you was indiscreet." Furtive glances were exchanged. "Oh, you were," he said. "That's a pity. Let's hope it didn't have time to communicate any of its findings to its overlords."

"What's done's done," McGann said, "and we must all bear some part of the responsibility. Including you, Oscar. You should have shared your suspicions with us."

"Would you have believed me?" Oscar replied. "I didn't believe it myself at first, until I started to notice little changes in Dowd."

"Why you?" Shales said. "That's what I want to know. Why would they target you for this surveillance unless they thought you were more susceptible than the rest of us? Maybe they thought you'd join them. Maybe you *have.*"

"As usual, Hubert, you're too self-righteous to see your own frailties," Godolphin replied. "How do you know I *am* the only one they targeted? Could you swear to me every one of your circle is above suspicion? How closely do you watch your friends? Your family? Any one of them might be a part of this conspiracy."

It gave Oscar a perverse joy to sow these doubts. He saw them taking root already, saw faces that half an hour before had been puffed up with their own infallibility deflated by doubt. It was worth the risk he'd taken with these theatrics, just to see them afraid. But Shales wouldn't leave this bone alone.

"The fact remains this thing was in your employ," he said.

"We've heard enough, Hubert," McGann said softly. "This is no time for divisive talk. We've got a fight on our hands, and whether we agree with Oscar's methods or not—and just for the record, I don't—surely none of us can doubt his integrity." He glanced around the table. There were murmurs of accord on all sides. "God knows what a creature like this might have been capable of had it realized its ruse had been discovered. Godolphin took a very considerable risk on our behalf."

"I agree," Lionel said. He'd come around to Oscar's side of the table and placed a glass of neat malt whisky in the executioner's freshly wiped fingers. "Good man, I say," he remarked. "I'd have done the same. Drink up."

Oscar accepted the glass. *"Salut,"* he said, downing the whisky in one.

"I see nothing to celebrate," said Charlotte Feaver, the first to sit down at the table despite what lay upon it. She lit a fresh cigarette, expelling the smoke through pursed lips. "Assuming Godolphin's right, and this thing *was* attempting to get access to the Society, we have to ask *why.*"

"Ask away," Shales said dryly, indicating the corpse. "He's not going to be telling us very much. Which is no doubt convenient for some."

"How much longer do I have to endure this innuendo?" Oscar demanded.

"I said we've heard enough, Hubert," McGann remarked.

"This is a democratic gathering," Shales said, rising to challenge McGann's unspoken authority. "If I've got something to say—"

"You've already said it," Lionel remarked with well-lubricated vim. "Now why don't you just shut up?"

"The point is, what do we do now?" Bloxham said. He'd returned to the table, his chin wiped, and was determined to reassert himself following his unmanly display. "This is a dangerous time."

"That's why they're here," said Alice. "They know the anniversary's coming up, and they want to start the whole damn Reconciliation over again."

"Why try and penetrate the Society?" Bloxham said.

"To put a spoke in our wheels," Lionel said. "If they know what we're planning, they can outmaneuver us. By the way, was the tie furiously expensive?"

Bloxham looked down to see that his silk tie was comprehensively spattered with puke. Casting a rancorous look in Lionel's direction, he tore it from his neck.

"I don't see what they could find out from us anyway," said Charlotte Feaver, in her distracted manner. "We don't even know what the Reconciliation is."

"Yes, we do," Shales said. "Our ancestors were trying to put Earth into the same orbit as Heaven."

"Very poetic," Charlotte remarked. "But what does that *mean*, in concrete terms? Does anybody know?" There was silence. "I thought not. Here we are, sworn to prevent something we don't even understand."

"It was an experiment of some kind," Bloxham said. "And it failed."

"Were they all insane?" Alice said.

"Let's hope not," Lionel put in. "Insanity usually runs in the family."

"Well, I'm not crazy," Alice said. "And I'm damn sure my friends are as sane and normal and human as I am. If they were anything else, I'd know it."

"Godolphin," McGann said, "you've been uncharacteristically quiet."

"I'm soaking up the wisdom," Oscar replied.

"Have you reached any conclusions?"

"Things go in cycles," he said, taking his time to reply. He was as certain of his audience as any man could ever hope to be. "We're coming to the end of the millennium. Reason'll be supplanted by unreason. Detachment by sentiment. I think if I were a fledgling esoteric with a nose for history, it wouldn't be difficult to turn up details of what was attempted—the experiment, as Bloxham called it—and maybe get it into my head that the time was right to try again."

"Very plausible," said McGann.

"Where would such an adept get the information?" Shales inquired.

"Self-taught."

"From what source? We've got every tome of any value buried in the ground beneath us."

"*Every* one?" said Godolphin. "How can we be so sure?"

"Because there hasn't been a significant act of magic performed on earth in two centuries," was Shales' reply. "The esoterics are powerless; lost. If there'd been the least sign of magical activity we'd know about it."

"We didn't know about Godolphin's little friend," Charlotte pointed out, denying Oscar the pleasure of that irony dropping from his own lips.

"Are we even sure the library's intact?" Charlotte went on. "How do we know books haven't been stolen?"

"Who by?" said Bloxham.

"By Dowd, for one. They've never been properly catalogued. I know that Leash woman attempted it, but we all know what happened to her."

The tale of the Leash woman, who had been a member of the Society, was one of its lesser shames: a catalogue of accidents that had ended in tragedy. In essence, the obsessive Clara Leash had taken it upon herself to make a full account of the volumes in the Society's possession and had suffered a stroke while doing so. She'd lain for three days on the cellar floor. By the time she was discovered, she was barely alive and quite without her wits. She survived, however, and eleven years later was still a resident in a hospice in Sussex, witless as ever.

"It still shouldn't be that difficult to find out if the place has been tampered with," Charlotte said.

Bloxham agreed. "That should be looked into," he said.

"I take it you're volunteering," said McGann.

"And if they didn't get their information from downstairs," Charlotte said, "there are other sources. We don't believe we have every last book dealing with the Imajica in our hands, do we?"

"No, of course not," said McGann. "But the Society's broken the back of the tradition over the years. The cults in this country aren't worth a damn, we all know that. They cobble workings together from whatever they can scrape up. It's all piecemeal. Senseless. None of them have the wherewithal to conceive of a Reconciliation. Most of them don't even know what the Imajica is. They're putting hexes on their bosses at the bank."

Godolphin had heard similar speeches for years. Talk of magic in the Western World as a spent force: self-congratulatory accounts of cults that had been infiltrated and discovered to be groups of pseudo-scientists exchanging arcane theories in a language no two of them agreed upon; or sexual obsessives using the excuse of workings to demand favors they couldn't seduce from their

partners; or, most often, crazies in search of some mythology, however ludicrous, to keep them from complete psychosis. But among
the fakes, obsessives, and lunatics was there perhaps a man who
instinctively knew the route to the Imajica? A natural Maestro,
born with something in his genes that made him capable of rein-
venting the workings of the Reconciliation? Until now the possibility hadn't occurred to Godolphin—he'd been too preoccupied
by the secret that he'd lived with most of his adult life—but it was
an intriguing, and disturbing, thought.

"I believe we should take the risk seriously," he pronounced.
"However unlikely we think it is."

"What risk?" McGann said.

"That there *is* a Maestro out there. Somebody who understands
our forefathers' ambition and is going to find his own way of repeating the experiment. Maybe he doesn't want the books. Maybe
he doesn't *need* the books. Maybe he's sitting at home somewhere,
even now, working out the problems for himself."

"So what do we do?" said Charlotte.

"We purge," said Shales. "It pains me to say it, but Godolphin's
right. We don't know what's going on out there. We've kept an eye
on things from a distance, and occasionally arranged to have somebody put under permanent sedation, but we haven't purged. I
think we've got to begin."

"How do we go about that?" Bloxham wanted to know. He had
a zealot's gleam in his dishwater eyes.

"We've got our allies. We use them. We turn over every stone,
and if we find anything we don't like, we kill it."

"We're not an assassination squad."

"We have the finance to hire one," Shales pointed out. "And the
friends to cover the evidence if need be. As I see it, we have one
responsibility: to prevent, at all costs, another attempt at Reconciliation. That's what we were *born* to do."

He spoke with a total lack of melodrama, as though he were
reciting a shopping list. His detachment impressed the room. So
did the last sentiment, however blandly it was presented. Who
could fail to be stirred by the thought of such purpose, reaching
back over generations to the men who had gathered on this spot
two centuries before? A few bloodied survivors, swearing that
they, and their children, and their children's children, and so on
until the end of the world would live and die with one ambition
burning in their hearts: the prevention of another such apocalypse.

At this juncture McGann suggested a vote, and one was taken.
There were no dissenting voices. The Society was agreed that the
way forward lay in a comprehensive purge of all elements—
innocent or not—who might presently be tampering, or tempted to

tamper, with rituals intended to gain access to so-called Reconciled Dominions. All conventional religious structures would be excluded from this sanction, as they were utterly ineffectual and presented a useful distraction for some souls who might have been tempted towards esoteric practices. The shams and the profiteers would also be passed over. The pier-end palmists and fake psychics, the spiritualists who wrote new concertos for dead composers and sonnets for poets long since dust—all these would be left untouched. Only those who stood a chance of tripping over something Imajical, and acting upon it, would be rooted out. It would be an extensive and sometimes brutal business, but the Society was the equal of the challenge. This was not the first purge it had masterminded (though it would be the first of this scale); the structure was in place for an invisible but comprehensive cleansing. The cults would be the prime targets: their acolytes would be dispersed, their leaders bought off or incarcerated. It had happened before that England had been sluiced clean of every significant esoteric and thaumaturgist. Now it would happen again.

"Is the business of the day concluded?" Oscar asked. "Only Mass calls me."

"What's to be done with the body?" Alice Tyrwhitt asked.

Godolphin had his answer ready and waiting. "It's my mess and I'll clear it up," he said, with due humility. "I can arrange to have it buried in a motorway tonight, unless anybody has a better idea?"

There were no objections.

"Just as long as it's out of here," Alice said.

"I'll need some help to wrap it up and get it down to the car. Bloxham, would you oblige?"

Reluctant to refuse, Bloxham went in search of something to contain the carcass.

"I see no reason for us to sit and watch," Charlotte said, rising from her seat. "If that's the night's business, I'm going home."

As she headed to the door, Oscar took his cue to sow one last triumphant mischief.

"I suppose we'll be all thinking the same thing tonight," he said.

"What's that?" Lionel asked.

"Oh, just that if these things are as good at imitation as they appear to be, then we can't entirely trust each other from now on. I'm assuming we're all still human at the moment, but who knows what Christmas will bring?"

Half an hour later, Oscar was ready to depart for Mass. For all his earlier squeamishness, Bloxham had done well, returning Dowd's guts into the bowl of the carcass and mummifying the whole sorry slab in plastic and tape. He and Oscar had then lugged the corpse to the lift and, at the bottom, out of the tower to the car. It was a fine night, the moon a virtuous sliver in a sky rife with stars. As ever, Oscar took beauty where he could find it and, before setting off, halted to admire the spectacle.

"Isn't it stupendous, Giles?"

"It is indeed!" Bloxham replied. "It makes my head spin."

"All those worlds."

"Don't worry," Bloxham replied. "We'll make sure it never happens."

Confounded by this reply, Oscar looked across at the other man, to see that he wasn't looking at the stars at all but was still busying himself with the body. It was the thought of the coming purge he found stupendous.

"That should do it," Bloxham said, slamming the trunk and offering his hand for shaking.

Glad that he had the shadows to conceal his distaste, Oscar shook it, and bid the boor good night. Very soon, he knew, he would have to choose sides, and despite the success of tonight's endeavor, and the security he'd won with it, he was by no means sure that he belonged among the ranks of the purgers, even though they were certain to carry the day. But then if his place was not there, where *was* his place? This was a puzzlement, and he was glad he had the soothing spectacle of Midnight Mass to distract him from it.

Twenty-five minutes later, as he climbed the steps of St. Martin-in-the-Fields, he found himself offering up a little prayer, its sentiments not so very different from those of the carols this congregation would presently be singing. He prayed that hope was somewhere out there in the city tonight, and that it might come into his heart and scour him of his doubts and confusions, a light that would not only burn in him but would spread throughout the Dominions and illuminate the Imajica from one end to the other. But if such a divinity was near, he prayed that the songs had it wrong, because sweet as tales of Nativity were, time was short, and if hope was only a babe tonight then by the time it had reached redeeming age the worlds it had come to save would be dead.

12

I

Taylor Briggs had once told Judith that he measured out his life in summers. When his span came to an end, he said, it would be the summers he remembered and, counting them, count himself blessed among them. From the romances of his youth to the days of the last great orgies in the back rooms and bathhouses of New York and San Francisco, he could recall his career in love by sniffing the sweat from his armpits. Judith had envied him at the time. Like Gentle, she had difficulty remembering more than ten years of her past. She had no recollection of her adolescence whatsoever, nor her childhood; could not picture her parents or even name them. This inability to hold on to history didn't much concern her (she knew no other), until she encountered somebody like Taylor, who took such satisfaction from memory. She hoped he still did; it was one of the few pleasures left to him.

She'd first heard news of his sickness the previous July, from his lover, Clem. Despite the fact that he and Taylor had lived the same high life together, the plague had passed Clem by, and Jude had spent several nights with him, talking through the guilt he felt at what he saw as an undeserved escape. Their paths had diverged through the autumn months, however, and she was surprised to find an invitation to their Christmas party awaiting her when she got back from New York. Still feeling delicate after all that had happened, she'd rung up to decline, only to have Clem quietly tell her that Taylor was not expected to see another spring, never mind another summer. Would she not come, for his sake? She of course accepted. If any of her circle could make good times of bad it was Taylor and Clem, and she owed them both her best efforts in that endeavor. Was it perhaps because she'd had so many difficulties with the heterosexual males in her life that she relaxed in the company of men for whom her sex were not contested terrain?

At a little after eight in the evening of Christmas Day, Clem opened the door and ushered her in, claiming a kiss beneath the sprig of mistletoe in the hallway before, as he put it, the barbarians were upon her. The house had been decorated as it might have been a century earlier, tinsel, fake snow, and fairy lights forsaken in favor of evergreen, hung in such abundance around the walls and mantelpieces that the rooms were half forested. Clem, whose youth had outrun the toll of years for so long, was not such a healthy sight. Five months before he'd looked a fleshy thirty in a flattering light. Now he looked ten years older at least, his bright welcome and flattery unable to conceal his fatigue.

"You wore green," he said as he escorted her in to the lounge. "I told Taylor you'd do that. Green eyes, green dress."

"Do you approve?"

"Of course! We're having a pagan Christmas this year. *Dies natalis solis invictus.*"

"What's that?"

"The Birth of the Unconquered Sun," he said. "The Light of the World. We need a little of that right now."

"Do I know many people here?" she said, before they stepped into the hub of the party.

"Everybody knows you, darling," he said fondly. "Even the people who've never met you."

There were many faces she knew awaiting them, and it took her five minutes to get across to where Taylor was sitting, lord of all he surveyed, in a well-cushioned chair close to the roaring fire. She tried not to register the shock she felt at the sight of him. He'd lost almost all of what had once been a leonine head of hair, and every spare ounce of substance from the face beneath. His eyes, which had always been his most penetrating feature (one of the many things they'd had in common), seemed enormous now, as though to devour in the time he had left the sights his demise would deny him. He opened his arms to her.

"Oh, my sweet," he said. "Give me a hug. Excuse me if I don't get up."

She bent and hugged him. He was skin and bone; and cold, despite the fire close by.

"Has Clem got you some punch?"

"I'm on my way," Clem said.

"Get me another vodka while you're at it," Taylor said, imperious as ever.

"I thought we'd agreed—" Clem said.

"I know it's bad for me. But staying sober's worse."

"It's your funeral," Clem said, with a bluntness Jude found shocking. But he and Taylor eyed each other with a kind of adoring ferocity, and she saw in the look how Clem's cruelty was part of their mechanism for dealing with this tragedy.

"You wish," Taylor said. "I'll have an orange juice. No, make that a Virgin Mary. Let's be seasonal about it."

"I thought you were having a pagan celebration," Jude said as Clem headed away to fetch the drinks.

"I don't see why the Christians should have the Holy Mother," Taylor said. "They don't know what to do with her when they've got her. Pull up a chair, sweetie. I heard a rumor you were in foreign climes."

"I was. But I came back at the last minute. I had some problems in New York."

"Whose heart did you break this time?"

"It wasn't that kind of problem."

"Well?" he said. "Be a telltale. Tell Taylor."

This was a bad joke from way back, and it brought a smile to

Judith's lips. It also brought the story, which she'd come here swearing she'd keep to herself.

"Somebody tried to murder me," she said.

"You're jesting," he replied.

"I wish I was."

"What happened?" he said. "Spill the beans. I like hearing other people's bad news just at the moment. The worse, the better."

She slid her palm over Taylor's bony hand. "Tell me how *you* are first."

"Grotesque," he said. "Clem's wonderful, of course, but all the tender loving care in the world won't make me healthy. I have bad days and good days. Mostly bad lately. I am, as my ma used to say, not long for this world." He glanced up. "Look out, here comes Saint Clemence of the Bedpan. Change the subject. Clem, did Judy tell you somebody tried to kill her?"

"No. Where was this?"

"In Manhattan."

"A mugger?"

"No."

"Not someone you knew?" Taylor said.

Now she was on the point of telling the whole thing, and she wasn't sure she wanted to. But Taylor had an anticipatory gleam in his eye, and she couldn't bear to disappoint him. She began, her account punctuated by exclamations of delighted incredulity from Taylor, and she found herself rising to her audience as though this story were not the grim truth but a preposterous fiction. Only once did she lose her momentum, when she mentioned Gentle's name, and Clem broke in to say that he'd been invited tonight. Her heart tripped and took a beat to get back into its rhythm.

"Tell the rest," Taylor was exhorting her. "What happened?"

She went on with her story, but now, with her back to the door, she found herself wondering every moment if he was stepping through it. Her distraction took its toll on the narrative. But then perhaps a tale about murder told by the prey was bound to predictability. She wrapped it up with undue haste.

"The point is, I'm alive," she said.

"I'll drink to that," Taylor replied, passing his unsipped Virgin Mary back to Clem. "Maybe just a splash of vodka?" he pleaded. "I'll take the consequences."

Clem made a reluctant shrug and, claiming Jude's empty glass, wended his way back through the crowd to the drinks table, giving Jude an excuse for turning around and scanning the room. Half a dozen new faces had appeared since she'd sat down. Gentle was not among them.

"Looking for Mr. Right?" Taylor said. "He's not here yet."

She looked back to meet his amusement.

"I don't know who you're talking about," she said.

"Mr. Zacharias."

"What's so funny?"

"You and him. The most talked-about affair of the last decade. You know, when you mention him, your voice changes. It gets—"

"Venomous."

"Breathy. Yearning."

"I don't yearn for Gentle."

"My mistake," he said archly. "Was he good in bed?"

"I've had better."

"You want to know something I never told anybody?"

He leaned forward, the smile becoming more pained. She thought it was his aching body that brought the frown to his brow, until she heard his words.

"I was in love with Gentle from the moment I met him. I tried everything to get him into bed. Got him drunk. Got him high. Nothing worked. But I kept at him, and about six years ago—"

Clem appeared at this juncture, supplying Taylor and Jude with replenished glasses before heading off to welcome a fresh influx of guests.

"You slept with Gentle?" Jude said.

"Not exactly. I mean, I sort of talked him into letting me give him a blow job. He was very high. Grinning that grin of his. I used to worship that grin. So there I am," Taylor went on, as lascivious as he'd ever been when recounting his conquests, "trying to get him hard, and he starts . . . I don't know how to explain this . . . I suppose he began speaking in tongues. He was lying back on my bed with his trousers around his ankles, and he just started to talk in some other language. Nothing vaguely recognizable. It wasn't Spanish. It wasn't French. I don't know what it was. And you know what? I lost my hard-on, and he got one." He laughed uproariously, but not for long. The laugh went from his face, as he began again. "You know, I was a little afraid of him suddenly. I was actually afraid. I couldn't finish what I'd started. I got up and left him to it, lying there with his dick sticking up, speaking in tongues." He claimed her drink from her hand and took a throatful. The memory had clearly shaken him. There was a mottled rash on his neck, and his eyes were glistening.

"Did you ever hear anything like that from him?" She shook her head. "I only ask because I know you broke up very quickly. I wondered if he'd freaked you out for some reason."

"No. He just fucked around too much."

Taylor made a noncommittal grunt, then said, "I get these night sweats now, you know, and I have to get up sometimes at three in the morning and let Clem change the sheets. I don't know whether I'm awake or asleep half the time. And all kinds of memories are coming back to me. Things I haven't thought about in years. One of them was that. I can hear him, when I'm standing there in a pool of sweat. Hear him talking like he's possessed."

"And you don't like it?"

"I don't know," he said. "Memories mean different things to me now. I dream about my mother, and it's like I want to crawl back into her and be born all over again. I dream about Gentle, and I wonder why I let all these mysteries in my life go. Things it's too late to solve now. Being in love. Speaking in tongues. It's all one in the end. I haven't understood any of it." He shook his head and shook down tears at the same time. "I'm sorry," he said. "I always get maudlin at Christmas. Will you fetch Clem for me? I need the bathroom."

"Can't I help?"

"There's some things I still need Clem for. Thanks anyway."

"No problem."

"And for listening."

She threaded her way to where Clem was chatting and discreetly informed him of Taylor's request.

"You know Simone, don't you?" Clem said by way of an exit, and left Jude to talk.

She did indeed know Simone, though not well, and after the conversation she'd just had with Taylor, she found it difficult to whip up a social soufflé. But Simone was almost flirtatiously excessive in her responses, unleashing a gurgling laugh at the merest hint of a cue and fingering her neck as though to mark the places she wanted kissed. Jude was silently rehearsing a polite refusal when she caught Simone's glance, ill concealed in a particularly extravagant laugh, flitting towards somebody elsewhere in the crowd. Irritated to be cast as a stooge for the woman's vamping, she said, "Who is he?"

"Who's who?" Simone said, flustered and blushing. "Oh, I'm sorry. It's just some man who keeps staring at me."

Her gaze went back to her admirer, and as it did so Jude was seized by the utter certainty that if she were to turn now it would be Gentle's stare she intercepted. He was here, and up to his stale old tricks, threading himself a little string of gazes, ready to pluck the prettiest when he tired of the game.

"Why don't you just go near and talk to him," she said.

"I don't know if I should."

"You can always change your mind if a better offer comes along."

"Maybe I will," Simone said, and without making any further attempt at conversation she took her laugh elsewhere.

Jude fought the temptation to follow her progress for fully two seconds, then glanced around. Simone's wooer was standing beside the Christmas tree, smiling a welcome at his object of desire as she breasted her way through the crowd towards him. It wasn't Gentle after all, but a man she thought she remembered as Taylor's brother. Oddly relieved, and irritated at herself for being so, she headed towards the drinks table for a refill, then wandered out into the hallway in search of some cooler air. There was a cellist on the half landing, playing *In the Bleak Midwinter*, the melody and the instrument it was being played upon combining to melancholy effect. The front door stood open, and the air through it raised goose bumps. She went to close it, only to have one of the other listeners discreetly whisper, "There's somebody being sick out there."

She glanced into the street. There was indeed somebody sitting on the edge of the pavement, in the posture of one resigned to the dictates of his belly: head down, elbows on his knees, waiting for the next surge. Perhaps she made a sound. Perhaps he simply felt her gaze on him. He raised his head and looked around.

"Gentle. What are you doing out here?"

"What does it look like?" He hadn't looked too pretty last time she'd seen him, but he looked a damn sight worse now: haggard, unshaven, and waxy with nausea.

"There's a bathroom in the house."

"There's a wheelchair up there," Gentle said, with an almost superstitious look. "I'd prefer to be sick out here."

He wiped his mouth with the back of his hand. It was virtually covered in paint. So was the other, she now saw; and his trousers, and his shirt.

"You've been busy."

He misunderstood. "I shouldn't have drunk anything," he said.

"Do you want me to get you some water?"

"No, thanks. I'm going home. Will you say goodbye to Taylor and Clem for me? I can't face going back in. I'll disgrace myself." He got to his feet, stumbling a little. "We don't seem to meet under very pleasant circumstances, do we?" he said.

"I think I should drive you home. You'll either kill yourself or somebody else."

"It's all right," he said, raising his painted hands. "The roads are empty. I'll be fine." He started to rummage in his pocket for his car keys.

"You saved my life; let me return the favor."

He looked up at her, his eyelids drooping. "Maybe it wouldn't be such a bad idea."

She went back inside to say farewell on behalf of herself and Gentle. Taylor was back in his chair. She caught sight of him before he saw her. He was staring into middle distance, his eyes glazed. It wasn't sorrow she read in his expression, but a fatigue so profound it had wiped all feeling from him except, maybe, regret for unsolved mysteries. She went to him and explained that she'd found Gentle and that he was sick and needed taking home.

"Isn't he going to come and say goodbye?" Taylor said.

"I think he's afraid of throwing up all over the carpet, or you, or both."

"Tell him to call me. Tell him I want to see him soon." He took hold of Jude's hand, holding it with surprising strength. "Soon, tell him."

"I will."

"I want to see that grin of his one more time."

"There'll be lots of times," she said.

He shook his head. "Once will have to do," he replied softly.

She kissed him and promised she'd call to say she got home safely. On her way to the door she met Clem and once again made her apologies and farewells.

"Call me if there's anything I can do," she offered.

"Thanks, but I think it's a waiting game."

"Then we can wait together."

"Better just him and me," Clem said. "But I will call."

He glanced towards Taylor, who was once more staring at nothing.

"He's determined to hold on till spring. One more spring, he keeps saying. He never gave a fuck about crocuses till now." Clem smiled. "You know what's wonderful?" he said. "I've fallen in love with him all over again."

"That *is* wonderful."

"And now I'm going to lose him, just when I realize what he means to me. You won't make that mistake, will you?" He looked at her hard. "You know who I mean."

She nodded.

"Good. Then you'd better take him home."

2

The roads were as empty as he'd predicted, and it took only fifteen minutes to get back to Gentle's studio. He wasn't exactly coherent. On the way, the exchanges between them were full of gaps and discontinuities, as though his mind were running ahead of his tongue, or behind it. Drink wasn't the culprit. Jude had seen Gentle drunk on all forms of alcohol; it made him roaring, randy, and sanctimonious by turns. Never like this, with his head back against the seat, his eyes closed, talking from the bottom of a pit. One moment he was thanking her for looking after him, the next he was telling her not to mistake the paint on his hands for shit. It wasn't shit, he kept saying, it was burnt umber, and prussian blue, and cadmium yellow, but somehow when you mixed colors together, any colors, they always came out looking like shit eventually. This monologue dwindled into silence, from which, a minute or two later, a new subject emerged.

"I can't look at him, you know, the way he is . . ."

"Who?" Jude said.

"Taylor. I can't look at him when he's so sick. You know how much I hate sickness."

She'd forgotten. It amounted to a paranoia with him, fueled perhaps by the fact that though he treated his body with scant regard for its health he not only never sickened but hardly aged. Doubtless the collapse, when it came, would be calamitous: excess, frenzy, and the passage of years taking their toll in one fell swoop. Until that time he wanted no reminders of his physical frailty.

"Taylor's going to die, isn't he?" he said.

"Clem thinks very soon."

Gentle gave a heavy sigh. "I should spend some time with him. We were good friends once."

"There were rumors about you two."

"He spread them, not me."

"Just rumors, were they?"

"What do you think?"

"I think you've probably tried every experience that swam by at least once."

"He's not my type," Gentle said, not opening his eyes.

"You should see him again," she said. "You've got to face up to falling apart sooner or later. It happens to us all."

"Not to me it won't. When I start to decay, I'm going to kill myself. I swear." He made fists of his painted hands and raised them to his face, drawing the knuckles down over his cheeks. "I won't let it happen," he said.

"Good luck," she replied.

They drove the rest of the way without any further exchange between them, his passive presence on the passenger seat beside her making her uneasy. She kept thinking of Taylor's story and expecting him to start talking, unleashing a stream of lunacies. It wasn't until she announced that they'd arrived at the studio that she realized he'd fallen asleep. She stared at him awhile: at the smooth dome of his forehead and the delicate configuration of his lips. It was still in her to dote on him, no question of that. But what lay that way? Disappointment and frustrated rage. Despite Clem's words of encouragement she was almost certain it was a lost cause.

She shook him awake and asked him if she could use his bathroom before going on her way. The punch was heavy in her bladder. He was hesitant, which surprised her. The suspicion dawned that he'd already moved a female companion into the studio, some seasonal bird to be stuffed for Christmas and dumped by New Year. Curiosity made her press to be allowed in. Reluctant as he was, he could scarcely say no, of course, and she traipsed up the stairs after him, wondering as she went what the conquest was going to look like, only to find that the studio was empty. His sole companion was the painting that had so filthied his hands. He seemed genuinely upset that she'd set eyes on it and ushered her to the bathroom, more discomfited than if her first suspicions had been correct and one of his conquests had indeed been disporting herself on the threadbare couch. Poor Gentle. He was getting stranger by the day.

She relieved herself and emerged from the toilet to find the painting covered with a stained sheet and him looking furtive and fidgety, clearly eager to have her out of the place. She saw no reason not to be plain with him, and said, "Working on something new?"

"Nothing much," he said.

"I'd like to see."

"It's not finished."

"It doesn't matter to me if it's a fake," she said. "I know what you and Klein get up to."

"It's not a fake," he said, a fierceness in his voice and face she'd not seen so far tonight. "It's *mine.*"

"An original Zacharias?" she remarked. "This I *have* to see."

She reached for the sheet, before he could stop her, and flipped it up over the top of the canvas. She'd only had a glimpse of the picture as she'd entered, and from some distance. Up close, it was clear he'd worked on the canvas with no little ferocity. There were places where it had been punctured, as though he'd stabbed it with his palette knife or brush; other places where the paint was laid on with glutinous abandon, then thumbed and fingered to drive it before his will. All this to achieve the likeness of what? Two people, it seemed, standing face to face against a brutal sky, their flesh white, but shot through with jabs of livid color.

"Who are they?" she said.

"*They?*" he said, sounding almost surprised that she'd read the image thusly, then covering his response with a shrug. "Nobody," he said, "just an experiment," and pulled the sheet back down over the painting.

"Is it a commission?"

"I'd prefer not to discuss it," he said.

His discomfort was oddly charming. He was like a child who'd been caught about some secret ritual. "You're full of surprises," she said, smiling.

"Nah, not me."

Though the painting was out of sight he continued to look ill at ease, and she realized there was going to be no further discussion of the picture or its import.

"I'll be off, then," she said.

"Thanks for the lift," he replied, escorting her to the door.

"Do you still want to have that drink?" she said.

"You're not going back to New York?"

"Not immediately. I'll call you in a couple of days. Don't forget Taylor."

"What are you, my conscience?" he said, with too small a trace of humor to soften the weight of the reply. "I won't forget."

"You leave marks on people, Gentle. That's a responsibility you can't just shrug off."

"I'll try to be invisible from now on," he replied.

He didn't take her to the front door but let her head down the stairs alone, closing the studio door before she'd taken more than half a dozen steps. As she went, she wondered what misbegotten instinct had made her suggest drinks. Well, it was easily slipped out of, even assuming he remembered the suggestion had been made, which she doubted.

Once out in the street she looked up at the building to see if she could spot him through the window. She had to cross the road to do so, but from the opposite pavement she could see him standing in front of the painting, which he had once again unveiled. He was staring at it with his head slightly cocked. She couldn't be certain, but it looked as though his lips were moving; as though he were talking to the image on the canvas. What was he saying? she wondered. Was he coaxing some image forth from the chaos of paint? And if so, in which of his many tongues was he speaking?

13

I

She had seen two people where he'd painted one. Not a he, a she, or an it, but *they*. She'd looked at the image and seen past his conscious intention to a buried purpose, one he'd hidden even from himself. Now he went back to the canvas and looked at it again, with borrowed eyes, and there they were, the two she'd seen. In his passion to capture some impression of Pie 'oh' pah, he had painted the assassin stepping from shadow (or back into it), a stream of darkness running down the middle of his face and torso. It divided the figure from top to bottom, and its outer edges, ragged and lush, described the reciprocative forms of profiles, etched in white from the halves of what he'd intended to be a single face. They stared at each other like lovers, eyes looking forward in the Egyptian manner, the backs of their heads folded into shadow. The question was: Who *were* these two? What had he been trying to express, setting these faces thus, nose to nose?

He interrogated the painting for several minutes after she'd gone, preparing as he did so to attack the canvas again. But when it came to doing so, he lacked the strength. His hands were trembling, his palms clammy; his eyes could only focus upon the image indifferently well. He retreated from the picture, afraid to touch it in this weakened state for fear he'd undo what little he'd already achieved. A painting could escape so quickly. A few inept strokes and a likeness (to a face, to another painter's work) could flee the canvas and never be recaptured. Better to leave it alone tonight. To rest, and hope he was strong tomorrow.

He dreamed of sickness. Of lying in his bed, naked beneath a thin white sheet, shivering so hard his teeth chattered. Snow fell from the ceiling intermittently and didn't melt when it touched his flesh, because he was colder than the snow. There were visitors in his sickroom, and he tried to tell them how cold he was, but he had no power in his voice, and the words came out as gasps, as though he were struggling for his last breath. He began to fear that this dream condition was fatal; that snow and breathlessness would bury him. He had to act. Rise up from the hard bed and prove these mourners premature.

With painful slowness, he moved his hands to the edge of the mattress in the hope of pulling himself upright, but the sheets were slick with his final sweat, and he couldn't get a firm hold. Fear turned to panic, despair bringing on a new round of gasps, more desperate than the last. He struggled to make his situation plain, but the door of his sickroom stood wide, now, and all the mourners had disappeared through it. He could hear them in another room, talking and laughing. There was a patch of sun on the threshold, he saw. Next door it was summer. Here, there was only the heart-stopping cold, taking a firmer grip on him by the moment. He gave up attempting Lazarus and instead let his palms lie flat on the sheets and his eyes flutter closed. The sound of voices from the next room softened to a murmur. The noise of his heart dwindled. New sounds rose to replace it, however. A wind was gusting outside, and branches thrashed at the windows. Somebody's voice rose in prayer; another simply sobbed. What grief was this? Not his passing, surely. He was too minor to earn such lamentation. He opened his eyes again. The bed had gone; so had the snow. Lightning threw into silhouette a man who stood watching the storm.

"Can you make me forget?" Gentle heard himself saying. "Do you have the trick of that?"

"Of course," came the soft reply. "But you don't want it."

"No, what I want's death, but I'm too afraid of that tonight. That's the real sickness: fear of death. But I can live with forgetfulness, give me that."

"For how long?"

"Until the end of the world."

Another lightning flash burned out the figure in front of him, and then the whole scene. Gone; forgotten. Gentle blinked the afterimage of window and silhouette out of his eyes and, in doing so, passed between sleep and waking.

The room was cold, but not as icy as his deathbed. He sat upright, staring first at his unclean hands, then at the window. It was still night, but he could hear the sound of vehicles on the Edgware Road, their murmur reassuring. Already—distracted by sound and sight—the nightmare was fading. He was happy to lose it.

He shrugged off the bedclothes and went to the kitchen to find himself something to drink. There was a carton of milk in the refrigerator. He downed its contents—though the milk was ready to turn—aware that his churned system would probably reject it in short order. Quenched, he wiped his mouth and chin and went through to look at the painting again, but the intensity of the dream from which he'd just woken made a mockery of his efforts. He would not conjure the assassin by this crude magic. He could paint a dozen canvases, a hundred, and still not capture the ambiguities of Pie 'oh' pah. He belched, bringing the taste of bad milk back up into his mouth. What was he to do? Lock himself away and let this sickness in him—put there by the sight of the assassin—consume him? Or bathe, sweeten himself, and go out to find some faces to put between him and the memory? Both vain endeavors. Which left a third, distressing route. To find Pie 'oh' pah in the flesh: to face him, question him, have his fill of him, until every ambiguity was scoured away.

He went on staring at the painting while he turned this option over. What would it take to find the assassin? An interrogation of

Estabrook, for one. That wouldn't be too onerous a duty. Then a search of the city, to find the place Estabrook had claimed he couldn't recall. Again, no great hardship. Better than sour milk and sourer dreams.

Knowing that in the light of morning he might lose his present clarity of mind, and he was best to close off at least one route of retreat, he went to the paints, squeezed onto his palm a fat worm of cadmium yellow, and worked it into the still-wet canvas. It obliterated the lovers immediately, but he wasn't satisfied until he'd covered the canvas from edge to edge. The color fought for its brilliance, but it soon deteriorated, tainted by the darkness it was trying to obscure. By the time he'd finished, it was as if his attempt to capture Pie 'oh' pah had never been made.

Satisfied, he stood back and belched again. The nausea had gone from him. He felt strangely buoyant. Maybe sour milk suited him.

2

Pie 'oh' pah sat on the step of his trailer and stared up at the night sky. In their beds behind him, his adopted wife and children slept. In the heavens above him, the stars were burning behind a blanket of sodium-tinted cloud. He had seldom felt more alone in his long life than now. Since returning from New York he had been in a state of constant anticipation. Something was going to happen to him and his world, but he didn't know what. His ignorance pained him, not simply because he was helpless in the face of this imminent event, but because his inability to grasp its nature was testament to how his skills had deteriorated. The days when he could read futurities off the air had gone. He was more and more a prisoner of the here and now. That here, the body he occupied, was also less than its former glory. It was so long since he'd corresponded the way he had with Gentle, taking the will of another as the gospel of his flesh, that he'd almost lost the trick of it. But Gentle's desire had been potent enough to remind him, and his body still reverberated with echoes of their time together. Though it had ended badly he didn't regret snatching those minutes. Another such encounter might never come.

He wandered from his trailer towards the perimeter of the encampment. The first light of dawn was beginning to eat at the murk. One of the camp mongrels, back from a night of adventuring, squeezed between two sheets of corrugated iron and came wagging to his side. He stroked the dog's snout and tickled behind its battle-ravaged ears, wishing he could find his way back to his home and master so easily.

3

It was the oft-stated belief of Esmond Bloom Godolphin, the late father of Oscar and Charles, that a man could never have too many bolt holes, and of E.B.G.'s countless saws this was the only one Oscar had been significantly influenced by. He had not less than four places of occupation in London. The house in Primrose Hill was his chief residence, but there was also a *pied-à-terre* in Maida Vale, a smallish flat in Notting Hill, and the location he was presently occupying: a windowless warehouse concealed in a maze of derelict and near-derelict properties near the river.

It was not a place he was particularly happy to frequent, especially not on the day after Christmas, but over the years it had proved a secure haven for Dowd's two associates, the voiders, and it now served as a Chapel of Rest for Dowd himself. His naked corpse lay beneath a shroud on the cold concrete, with aromatic herbs, picked and dried on the slopes of the Jokalaylau, smoldering in bowls at his head and feet, after the rituals proscribed in that region. The voiders had shown little interest in the arrival of their leader's body. They were functionaries, incapable of anything but the most rudimentary thought processes. They had no physical appetites: no desire, no hunger or thirst, no ambition. They simply sat out the days and nights in the darkness of the warehouse and waited for Dowd to instruct them. Oscar was less than comfortable in their company, but could not bring himself to leave until this business was finished. He'd brought a book to read: a cricket almanac that he found soothing to peruse. Every now and then he'd get up and refuel the bowls. Otherwise there was little to do but wait.

It had already been a day and a half since he'd made such a show of taking Dowd's life: a performance of which he was justly proud. But the casualty that lay before him was a real loss. Dowd had been passed down the line of Godolphins for two centuries, bound to them until the end of time or of Joshua's line, whichever came first. And he had been a fine manservant. Who else could mix a whisky and soda so well? Who else knew to dry and powder between Oscar's toes with special care, because he was prone to fungal infections there? Dowd was irreplaceable, and it had pained Oscar considerably to take the brutal measures circumstance had demanded. But he'd done so knowing that while there was a slim possibility that he would lose his servant forever, an entity such as Dowd could survive a disemboweling as long as the rituals of Resurrection were readily and precisely followed. Oscar was not in ignorance of those rituals. He'd spent many lazy Yzordderrexian evenings on the roof of Peccable's house, watching the tail of the comet disappear behind the towers of the Autarch's palace, talking about the theory and practice of Imajical feits, writs, pneumas, uredos, and the rest. He knew the oils to pour into Dowd's carcass, and what blossoms to burn around the body. He even had in his treasure room a phonetic version of the ritual, set down by Peccable himself, in case Dowd was ever harmed. He had no idea how long the process would take, but he knew better than to peer beneath the sheet to see if the bread of life was rising. He could only bide his time and hope he'd done all that was necessary.

At four minutes past four, he had proof of his precision. A choking breath was drawn beneath the sheet, and a second later Dowd sat up. The motion was so sudden, and—after such a time—so unexpected, Oscar panicked, his chair tipping over as he rose, the almanac flying from his hand. He'd seen much in his time that the people of the Fifth would call miraculous, but not in a dismal room like this, with the commonplace world grinding on its way outside the door. Composing himself, he searched for a word of welcome, but his mouth was so dry he could have blotted a letter with his tongue. He simply stared, gaping and amazed.

Dowd had pulled the sheet off his face and was studying the hand with which he'd done so, his face as empty as the eyes of the voiders sitting against the opposite wall.

I've made a terrible error, Oscar thought. I've brought back the body, but the soul's gone out of him: Oh, Christ, what now?

Dowd stared on, blankly. Then, like a puppet into which a hand has been inserted, bringing the illusion of life and independent purpose to senseless stuff, he raised his head, and his face filled with expression. It was all anger. He narrowed his eyes and bared his teeth as he spoke.

"You did me a great wrong," he said. "A terrible wrong."

Oscar worked up some spittle, thick as mud. "I did what I deemed necessary," he replied, determined not to be cowed by the creature. It had been bound by Joshua never to do a Godolphin harm, much as it might presently wish to.

"What have I ever done to you that you humiliate me that way?" Dowd said.

"I had to prove my allegiance to the Tabula Rasa. You understand why."

"And must I continue to be humiliated?" he said. "Can I not at least have something to wear?"

"Your suit's stained."

"It's better than nothing," Dowd replied.

The garments lay on the floor a few feet from where Dowd sat, but he made no move to pick them up. Aware that Dowd was testing the limits of his master's remorse, but willing to play the game for a while at least, Oscar picked up the clothes and laid them within Dowd's reach.

"I knew a knife wasn't going to kill you," he said.

"It's more than I did," Dowd replied. "But that's not the point. I would have entered the game with you if that's what you'd wanted. Happily; *slavishly.* Entered and died for you." His tone was that of a man deeply and inconsolably affronted. "Instead, you conspire against me. You make me suffer like a common criminal."

"I couldn't afford for it to look like a charade. If they'd suspected it was stage-managed—"

"Oh, I see," Dowd replied. Unwittingly Oscar had caused even greater offense with this justification. "You didn't trust my actorly instincts. I've played every lead Quexos wrote: comedy, tragedy, farce. And you didn't trust me to carry off a petty little death scene!"

"All right, I was mistaken."

"I thought the knife stung badly enough. But *this*—"

"Please, accept my apologies. It was crude and hurtful. What can I do to heal the harm, eh? Name it, Dowdy. I feel I've violated the trust between us and I have to make good. Whatever you want, just name it."

Dowd shook his head. "It's not as easy as that."

"I know. But it's a start. Name it."

Dowd considered the offer for a full minute, staring not at Oscar but the blank wall. Finally, he said, "I'll start with the assassin, Pie 'oh' pah."

"What do you want with a mystif?"

"I want to torment it. I want to humiliate it. And finally, I want to kill it."

"Why?"

"You offered me whatever I wanted. Name it, you said. I've named it."

"Then you have carte blanche to do whatever you wish," Oscar said. "Is that all?"

"For now," Dowd said. "I'm sure something more will occur. Death's put some strange ideas in my head. But I'll name them as time goes by."

14

I

While it was to prove difficult for Gentle to prize from Estabrook
the details of the night journey that had taken him to Pie 'oh' pah,
it was not as difficult as getting in to see the man in the first place.
He went to the house around noon, to find the curtains at all the
windows meticulously drawn. He knocked and rang the bell for
several minutes, but there was no reply. Assuming Estabrook had
gone out for a constitutional, he left off his attempt and went to
find something to put into his stomach, which after being so thoroughly scorned the night before was echoing with its own emptiness. It was Boxing Day, of course, and there was no café or
restaurant open, but he located a small supermarket managed by
a family of Pakistanis, who were doing a fine trade supplying Christians with stale bread to break. Though the stock had disappeared
from many of the shelves, the store still had a tempting parade of
tooth decayers, and Gentle left with chocolate, biscuits, and cake
to satisfy his sweet tooth. He found a bench and sat down to subdue his hunger. The cake was too moist and heavy for his taste, so
he broke it up into pieces and threw it to the pigeons his meal had
attracted. The news soon spread that there was sustenance to be
had, and what had been an intimate picnic quickly turned into a
squabbling match. In lieu of loaves and fishes to subdue the mob,
Gentle tossed the rest of his biscuits into the midst of the feasters
and returned to Estabrook's house content with his chocolate. As
he approached he saw a motion at one of the upper windows. He
didn't bother to ring and knock this time, but simply called up at
the window.

"I want a word, Charlie! I know you're in there. Open up!"

When there was no sign of Estabrook obliging, he let his voice
ring out a little louder. There was very little competition from traffic, this being a holiday. His call was a clarion.

"Come on, Charlie, open up, unless you want me to tell the
neighbors about our little deal."

The curtain was drawn aside this time, and Gentle had his first
sight of Estabrook. A glimpse only, for the curtain was dropped
back into place a moment later. Gentle waited, and just as he was
about to start his haranguing afresh heard the front door being un-
bolted. Estabrook appeared, barefoot and bald. The latter was a
shock. Gentle hadn't known the man wore a toupée. Without it his

face was as round and white as a plate, his features set upon it like a child's breakfast. Eggs for eyes, a tomato nose, sausage lips: all swimming in a grease of fear.

"It's time we talked," Gentle said and, without waiting for an invitation, stepped inside.

He pulled no punches in his interrogation, making it plain from the outset that this was no social call. He needed to know where to find Pie 'oh' pah, and he wasn't going to be fobbed off with excuses. To aid Estabrook's memory he'd brought a battered street map of London. He set it down on the table between them.

"Now," he said. "We sit here until you've told where you went that night. And if you lie to me I swear I'm going to come back and break your neck."

Estabrook didn't attempt any obfuscation. His manner was that of a man who had passed many days in terror of a sound upon his step and was relieved, now that it had come, that his caller was merely human. His egg eyes were perpetually on the verge of breaking, and his hands trembled as he flipped the pages of the gazetteer, murmuring as he did so that he was sure of nothing but he would try to remember. Gentle didn't press too hard, but let the man make the journey again in memory, running his finger back and forth over the map as he did so.

They'd driven through Lambeth, he said, then Kennington and Stockwell. He didn't remember grazing Clapham Common, so he assumed they'd driven to the east of it, towards Streatham Hill. He remembered a church and sought out a cross on the map that would mark the place. There were several, but only one close to the other landmark he remembered, the railway line. At this point, he said he could offer nothing more by way of directions, only a description of the place itself: the corrugated iron perimeter, the trailers, the fires.

"You'll find it," he said.

"I'd better," Gentle replied.

He'd so far told Estabrook nothing about the circumstances that had brought him back here, though the man had several times asked if Judith was alive and well. Now he asked again.

"Please tell me," he said. "I've been straight with you, I swear I have. Won't you please tell me how she is?"

"She's alive and kicking," Gentle said.

"Has she mentioned me at all? She must have done. What did she say? Did you tell her I still love her?"

"I'm not your pimp," Gentle said. "Tell her yourself. If you can get her to talk to you."

"What am I going to do?" Estabrook said. He took hold of

Gentle's arm. "You're an expert with women, aren't you? Every-body says so. What can I do to make amends?"

"She'd probably be satisfied if you sent her your balls," Gentle said. "Anything less wouldn't be appropriate."

"You think it's funny."

"Trying to have your wife killed? No, I don't think that's very amusing. Changing your mind and wanting everything lovey-dovey again: *that's* hysterical."

"You wait till you love somebody the way I love Judith. If you're capable of that, which I doubt. You wait until you want somebody so badly your sanity hangs on it. You'll learn."

Gentle didn't rise to the remark. It was too close to his present state to be fully confessed, even to himself. But once out of the house, map in hand, he couldn't suppress a smile of pleasure that he had a way forward. It was already getting gloomy, as the mid-winter afternoon closed its fist on the city. But darkness loved lovers, even if the world no longer did.

2

At midday, with his unease of the previous night allayed not one jot, Pie 'oh' pah had suggested to Theresa that they should leave the encampment. The suggestion wasn't met with enthusiasm. The baby was sick with sniffles and had not stopped wailing since she'd woken; the other child was feverish too. This was no time to be going away, Theresa said, even if they had somewhere to go, which they didn't. We'll take the trailer with us, Pie replied; we'll just drive out of the city. To the coast, maybe, where the children would ben-efit from the cleaner air. Theresa liked that idea. Tomorrow, she said, or the day after, but not now.

Pie pressed the case, however, until she asked him what he was so nervous about. He had no answer to give; at least none that she'd care to hear. She understood nothing of his nature, nor questioned him about his past. He was simply a provider, someone who put food in the mouths of her children and his arms around her at night. But her question still hung in the air, so he answered it as best he could.

"I'm afraid for us," he said.

"It's that old man, isn't it?" Theresa replied. "The one who came to see you? Who was he?"

"He wanted a job done."

"And you did it?"

"No."

"So you think he's going to come back?" she said. "We'll set the dogs on him."

It was healthy to hear such plain solutions, even if—as now—
they didn't answer the problem at hand. His mystif soul was sometimes too readily drawn to the ambiguities that mirrored his true
self. But she chastened him; reminded him that he'd taken a face
and a function and, in this human sphere, a sex; that as far as she
was concerned he belonged in the fixed world of children, dogs,
and orange peel. There was no room for poetry in such straitened
circumstances; no time between hard dawn and uneasy dusk for
the luxury of doubt or speculation.

Now another of those dusks had fallen, and Theresa was putting
her cherished ones to bed in the trailer. They slept well. He had a
spell that he'd kept polished from the days of his power, a way of
speaking prayers into a pillow so they'd sweeten the sleeper's
dreams. His Maestro had asked for its comfort often, and Pie used
it still, two hundred years later. Even now Theresa was laying her
children's heads upon down suffused with cradle songs, secreted
there to guide them from the dark world into the bright.

The mongrel he'd met at the perimeter in the predawn gloom
was barking furiously, and he went out to calm it. Seeing him approach it pulled on its chain, scrabbling at the dirt to be closer to
him. Its owner was a man Pie had little contact with, a short-
tempered Scot who brutalized the dog when he could catch it. Pie
went down on his haunches to hush the creature, for fear its din
brought the owner out from his supping. The dog obeyed but continued to paw at Pie fretfully, clearly wanting to be loosed from its
leash.

"What's wrong, buster?" he said to it, scratching behind its war-
torn ears. "Have you got a lady out there?"

He looked up towards the perimeter as he spoke and caught the
fleeting glimpse of a figure stepping into shadow behind one of the
trailers. The dog had seen the interloper too. It set up a new round
of barking. Pie stood up again.

"Who's there?" he demanded.

A sound at the other end of the encampment claimed his attention momentarily: water splashing on the ground. No, not water.
The stench that reached his nostrils was that of petrol. He looked
back towards his own trailer. Theresa's shadow was on the blind,
her head bowed as she turned off the nightlight beside the children's bed. The stench was coming from that direction too. He
reached down and released the dog.

"Go, boy! Go! Go!"

It ran barking at a figure slipping out through a gap in the fence.
As it went Pie started towards his trailer, yelling Theresa's name.

Behind him, somebody shouted for him to shut up out there, but the curses were unfinished, erased by the boom and bloom of fire, twin eruptions that lit the encampment from end to end. He heard Theresa scream, saw flame surge up and around his trailer. The spilled fuel was only a fuse. Before he'd covered ten yards the mother lode exploded directly under the vehicle, the force sufficient to lift it off the ground and pitch it on its side.

Pie was blown over by a solid wave of heat. By the time he'd scrabbled to his feet the trailer was a solid sheet of flame. As he pitched himself through the baking air towards the pyre he heard another sobbing cry and realized it was his own, a sound he'd forgotten his throat could make but which was always the same, grief on grief.

Gentle had just sighted the church which had been Estabrook's last landmark when a sudden day broke on the street ahead, as though the sun had come to burn the night away. The car in front of his veered sharply, and he was only able to prevent a collision by mounting the pavement, bringing his own car to a juddering halt inches short of the church wall.

He got out and headed towards the fire on foot, turning a corner to head directly into the smoke, which veered and veered again as he ran, allowing him only glimpses of his destination. He saw a corrugated iron fence, and beyond it a host of trailers, most of which were already ablaze. Even if he'd not had Estabrook's description to confirm that this was indeed Pie 'oh' pah's home, the fact of its destruction would have marked it out. Death had preceded him here, like his shadow, thrown forward by a blaze at his back that was even brighter than the one that lay ahead. His knowledge of this other cataclysm, the one behind, had been a part of the business between himself and the assassin from the beginning. It had flickered in their first exchanges on Fifth Avenue; it had lit the fury that had sent him to debate with the canvas; and it had burned brightest in his dreams, in that room he'd invented (or remembered) where he'd begged Pie for forgetfulness. What had they experienced together that had been so terrible he'd wanted to forget his whole life rather than live with the fact? Whatever it was, it was somehow echoed in this new calamity, and he wished to God he could have his forgetfulness undone and know what crime he'd committed that brought upon innocents such punishment as this.

The encampment was an inferno, wind fanning flames that in turn inspired new wind, with flesh the toy of both. He had only piss and spittle against this conflagration—useless!—but he ran on towards it anyway, his eyes streaming as the smoke bit at them, not knowing what hope of survival he had, only certain that Pie was somewhere in this firestorm and to lose him now would be tantamount to losing himself.

There were some escapees, a pitiful few. He ran past them towards the gap in the fence through which they'd escaped. His route was by turns clear and confounded, as the wind brought choking smoke in his direction, then carried it away again. He pulled off his leather jacket and threw it over his head as primitive protection against the heat, then ducked through the fence. There was solid flame in front of him, making the way forward impassable. He tried to his left and found a gap between two blazing vehicles. Dodging between them, the smell of singeing leather already sharp in his nostrils, he found himself in the middle of the compound, a space relatively free of combustible material, and thus of fire. But on every side, the flames had hold. Only three of the trailers weren't blazing, and the veering wind would soon carry the flame in their direction. How many of the inhabitants had fled before the flames took hold he couldn't know, but it was certain there'd be no further escapees. The heat was nearly unbearable. It beat upon him from every side, cooking his thoughts to incoherence. But he held on to the image of the creature he'd come to find, determined not to desert the pyre until he had that face in his hands or knew beyond doubt it was ash.

A dog appeared from the smoke, barking hysterically. As it ran past him a fresh eruption of fire drove it back the way it had come, its panic escalating. Having no better route, he chased its tail through the chaos, calling Pie's name as he ran, though each breath he took was hotter than the last, and after a few such shouts the name was a rasp. He'd lost the dog in the smoke, and all sense of direction at the same time. Even if the way was still clear he no longer knew where it lay. The world was fire on every side.

Somewhere up ahead he heard the dog again, and thinking now that maybe the only life he'd claim from this horror was the hound's, he ran in search of it. Tears were pouring from his smoke-stung eyes; he could barely focus on the ground he was stumbling across. The barking stopped again, leaving him without a beacon. There was no way to go but forward, hoping the silence didn't mean the dog had succumbed. It hadn't. He spotted it ahead of him now, cowering in terror.

As he drew a breath to call it to him he saw the figure beyond it, stepping from the smoke. The fire had taken its toll on Pie 'oh' pah, but he was at least alive. His eyes, like Gentle's, streamed. There was blood at his mouth and neck and, in his arms, a forlorn bundle. A child.

"*Are there more?*" Gentle yelled.

Pie's reply was to glance back over his shoulder, towards a heap of debris that had once been a trailer. Rather than draw another lung-cooking breath to reply, Gentle started towards this bonfire but was intercepted by Pie, who passed over the child in his arms.

"Take her," he said.

Gentle threw aside his jacket and took the child.

"Now get out!" Pie said. *"I'll follow."*

He didn't wait to see his instruction obeyed but turned back towards the debris.

Gentle looked down at the child he was carrying. She was bloody and blackened, surely dead. But perhaps life could be pumped back into her if he was quick. What was the fastest route to safety? The way he'd come was blocked now, and the ground ahead littered with burning wreckage. Between left and right, he chose left, because he heard the incongruous sound of somebody whistling somewhere in the smoke: at least proof that breath could be drawn in that direction.

The dog came with him, but only for a few steps. Then it retreated again, despite the fact that the air was cooler by the step, and a gap in the flames was visible ahead. Visible, but not empty. As Gentle headed for the place a figure stepped out from behind one of the bonfires. It was the whistler, still practicing his craft, though his hair was burning and his hands, raised in front of him, were smoking ruins. He turned his head as he walked and looked at Gentle.

The tune he whistled was charmless, but it was sweet beside the stare he had. His eyes were like mirrors, reflecting the fires: they flared and smoked. This was the fire setter, he realized, or one of them. That was why it whistled as it burned, because this was its paradise. It didn't attempt to lay its carbonized hands on either Gentle or the child but walked on into the smoke, turning its stare back towards the blaze as it did so, leaving Gentle's route to the perimeter clear. The cooler air was heady; it dizzied him, made him stumble. He held on tight to the child, his only thought now to get it out into the street, in which endeavor he was aided by two masked firemen who'd seen his approach and came to meet him now, arms outstretched. One took the child from him; the other bore him up as his legs gave way beneath him.

"There's people alive in there!" he said, looking back towards the fire. "You've got to get them out!"

His rescuer didn't leave his side till he'd got Gentle through the fence and into the street. Then there were other hands to take charge. Ambulance attendants with stretchers and blankets, telling him that he was safe now and everything would be all right. But it wasn't, not as long as Pie was in the fire. He shrugged off the blanket and refused the oxygen mask they were ready to clamp to his face, insisting that he wanted no help. With so many others in need, they didn't waste time attempting to persuade him but went to aid those who were sobbing and shrieking on all sides. They were the lucky ones, who had voices to raise. He saw others being carried past who were too far gone to complain, and still others lying beneath makeshift shrouds on the pavement, blackened limbs jutting out here and there.

He turned his back on this horror and began to make his way around the edge of the encampment. The fence was being torn down to allow the hoses, which thronged the street like mating snakes, access to the fire. The engines pumped and roared, their reeling blue lights no competition for the fierce brightness of the fire itself. By that blaze he saw a substantial crowd had gathered to watch. They raised a cheer as the fence was toppled, sending plagues of fireflies up as it fell. He moved on as the firefighters advanced into the conflagration, bringing their hoses to bear on the heart of the fire. By the time he'd made a half circuit of the site and was standing opposite the breach they'd made, the flames were already in retreat in several places, smoke and steam replacing their fury. He watched them gain ground from his new vantage point, hoping for some glimpse of life, until the appearance of another two machines and a further group of firefighters drove him on around the perimeter, back to the place from which he'd emerged.

There was no sign of Pie 'oh' pah, either being carried from the blaze or standing among those few survivors who, like Gentle, had refused to be taken away to be tended. The smoke issuing from the fire's steady defeat was thickening, and by the time he got back to the row of bodies on the pavement—the number of which had doubled—the whole scene was barely visible through the pall. He looked down at the shrouded forms. Was one of them Pie 'oh' pah? As he approached the nearest of them a hand was laid on his shoulder, and he turned to face a policeman whose features were those of a boy soprano, smooth and troubled.

"Aren't you the one who brought out the kid?" he said.

"Yes. Is she all right?"

"I'm sorry, mate. I'm afraid she's dead. Was she your kid?"

He shook his head. "There was somebody else. A black guy with long curly hair. He had blood on his face. Has he come out of there?"

Formal language now: "I haven't seen anybody of that description."

Gentle looked back towards the bodies on the pavement.

"It's no use looking there," the policeman said. "They're all black now, whatever color they started out."

"I have to look," Gentle said.

"I'm telling you it's no use. You wouldn't recognize them. Why don't you let me put you in an ambulance? You need seeing to."

"No. I have to keep looking," Gentle said, and was about to move off when the policeman took hold of his arm.

"I think you'd be better away from the fence, sir," he said. "There's some danger of explosions."

"But he could still be in there."

"If he is, sir, I think he's gone. There's not much chance of anybody else coming out alive. Let me take you to the police line. You can watch from there."

Gentle shook off the man's hold.

"I'll go," he said. "I don't need an escort."

It took an hour for the fire to be finally brought under control, by which time it had little left to consume. During that hour all Gentle could do was wait behind the cordon and watch as the ambulances came and went, ferrying the last of the injured away and then taking the bodies. As the boy soprano had predicted, no further victims were brought out, dead or alive, though Gentle waited until all but a few late arrivals among the crowd had left, and the fire was almost completely doused. Only when the last of the firefighters emerged from the crematorium, and the hoses were turned off, did he give up hope. It was almost two in the morning. His limbs were burdened with exhaustion, but they were light beside the weight in his chest. To go heavyhearted was no poet's conceit: it felt as though the pump had turned to lead and was bruising the plush meat of his innards.

As he wandered back to his car he heard the whistling again, the same tuneless sound floating on the dirty air. He stopped walking and turned to all compass points, looking for the source, but the whistler was already out of sight, and Gentle was too weary to give chase. Even if he had, he thought, even if he'd caught it by its lapels and threatened to break its burned bones, what purpose would that have served? Assuming it had been moved by his threat (and pain was probably meat and drink to a creature that whistled as it burned) he'd be no more able to comprehend its reply than interpret Chant's letter: and for similar reasons. They were both escapees from the same unknown land, whose borders he'd grazed when he'd gone to New York; the same world that held the God Hapexamendios and had given birth to Pie 'oh' pah. Sooner or later he'd find a way to gain access to that state, and when he did all the mysteries would come clear: the whistler, the letter, the lover. He might even solve the mystery that he met most mornings in the shaving mirror: the face he thought he'd known well enough until recently, but whose code he now realized he'd forgotten and would not now remember without the help of the undiscovered God.

3

Back in the house in Primrose Hill, Godolphin sat up through the night and listened to the news bulletins reporting the tragedy. The number of dead rose every hour; two more victims had already perished in the hospital. Theories were being advanced everywhere as to the cause of the fire; pundits used the event to comment on the lax safety standards applied to sites where itinerants camped and demanded a full Parliamentary inquiry to prevent a repeat of such a conflagration.

The reports appalled him. Though he'd given Dowd leash enough to dispatch the mystif—and who knew what hidden agenda lay there?—the creature had abused the freedom he'd been granted. There would have to be punishment meted out for such abuse, though Godolphin was in no mood to plot that now. He'd bide his time, choose his moment. It would come. Meanwhile, Dowd's violence seemed to him further evidence of a disturbing pattern. Things he'd thought immutable were changing. Power was slipping from the possession of those who'd traditionally held it into the hands of underlings—fixers, familiars, and functionaries—who were ill equipped to use it. Tonight's disaster was symptomatic of that. But the disease had barely begun to take hold. Once it spread through the Dominions there'd be no stopping it. There had already been uprisings in Vanaeph and L'Himby, there were mutterings of rebellion in Yzordderrex; now there was to be a purge here in the Fifth Dominion, organized by the Tabula Rasa, a perfect background to Dowd's vendetta and its bloody consequences. Everywhere, signs of disintegration.

Paradoxically the most chilling of those signs was superficially an image of reconstruction: that of Dowd re-creating his face so that if he was seen by any member of the Society he'd not be recognized. It was a process he'd undertaken with each generation, but this was the first time any Godolphin had witnessed said process. Now Oscar thought back on it, he suspected Dowd had deliberately displayed his transformative powers, as further evidence of his newfound authority. It had worked. Seeing the face he'd grown so used to soften and shift at the will of its possessor was one of the most distressing spectacles Oscar had set eyes upon. The face Dowd had finally fixed was *sans* mustache and eyebrows, the head sleeker than his other, and younger: the face that of an ideal National Socialist. Dowd must also have caught that echo, because he later bleached his hair and bought several new suits, all apricot but of a much severer cut than those he'd worn in his earlier incarnation. He sensed the instabilities ahead as well as Oscar; he felt the rot in the body politic and was readying himself for a New Austerity.

And what more perfect tool than fire, the book burner's joy, the soul cleanser's bliss? Oscar shuddered to contemplate the pleasure Dowd had taken from his night's work, callously murdering innocent human families in pursuit of the mystif. He would return to the house, no doubt, with tears on his face and say he regretted the hurt he'd done to the children. But it would be a performance, a sham. There was no true capacity for grief or regret in the creature, and Oscar knew it. Dowd was deceit incarnate, and from now on Oscar knew he had to be on his guard. The comfortable years were over. Hereafter he would sleep with his bedroom door locked.

15

I

In her rage at his conspiracies Jude had contemplated several possible ways to revenge herself upon Estabrook, ranging from the bloodily intimate to the classically detached. But her nature never ceased to surprise her. All thoughts of garden shears and prosecutions dimmed in a short time, and she came to realize that the worst harm she could do him—given that the harm he'd intended to do her had been stopped in its tracks—was to ignore him. Why give him the satisfaction of her least interest in him? From now on he would be so far beneath her contempt as to be invisible. Having unburdened herself of her story to Taylor and Clem, she sought no further audience. From now on she wouldn't sully her lips with his name or let her thoughts dally with him for two consecutive seconds. At least, that was the pact she made with herself. It proved difficult to keep.

On Boxing Day she received the first of what were to be many calls from him, which she resolutely cut short the instant she recognized his voice. It wasn't the authoritative Estabrook she'd been used to hearing, and it took her three exchanges before she realized who was on the other end of the line, at which point she put down the receiver and let it lie uncradled for the rest of the day. The following morning he called again, and this time, just in case he was in any doubt, she told him, "I don't ever want to hear your voice again," and once more cut him off.

When she'd done so she realized he'd been sobbing as he spoke, which gave her no little satisfaction, and the hope that he wouldn't try again. A frail hope; he called twice that evening, leaving messages on her answering machine while she was out at a party flung by Chester Klein. There she heard news of Gentle, to whom she hadn't spoken since their odd parting at the studio. Chester, who was much the worse for vodka, told her plainly he expected Gentle to have a full-blown nervous breakdown in a short time. He'd spoken to the Bastard Boy twice since Christmas, and he was increasingly incoherent.

"What is it about all you men?" she found herself saying. "You fall apart so easily."

"That's because we're the more tragic of the sexes," Chester returned. "God, woman, can't you see how we *suffer*?"

"Frankly, no."

"Well, we do. Take it from me. We do."

"Is there any particular reason, or is it just free-form suffering?"

"We're all sealed up," Klein said. "Nothing can get in."

"So are women. What's the—"

"Women get *fucked*," Klein interrupted, pronouncing the word with a drunken ripeness. "Oh, you bitch about it, but you love it. Go on, admit it. You love it."

"So all men really want is to get fucked, is that it?" Jude said. "Or are you just talking personally?"

This brought a ripple of laughter from those who'd given up their chitchat to watch the fireworks.

"Not literally," Klein spat back. "You're not listening to me."

"I'm listening. You're just not making any sense."

"Take the church—"

"Fuck the church!"

"No, *listen!*" Klein said, teeth clenched. "I'm telling God's honest fucking truth here. Why do you think men invented the church, huh? *Huh?*"

His bombast had infuriated Jude to the point where she refused to reply. He went on, unperturbed, talking pedantically, as if to a slow student.

"Men invented the church so they could bleed for Christ. So they could be entered by the Holy Spirit. So they could be saved from being sealed up." His lesson finished, he leaned back in his chair, raising his glass. "In vodka veritas," he said.

"In vodka shit," Jude replied.

"Well, that's just typical of you, isn't it?" Klein's words slurred. "As soon as you're fucking beaten you start the insults."

She turned from him, shaking her head dismissively. But he still had a barb in his armory.

"Is that how you drive the Bastard Boy crazy?" he said.

She turned back on him, stung. "Keep him out of this," she snapped.

"You want to see *sealed up*?" Klein said. "There's your example. He's out of his head, you know that?"

"Who cares?" she said. "If he wants to have a nervous breakdown, he can have one."

"How very humanitarian of you."

She stood up at this juncture, knowing she was perilously close to losing her temper completely.

"I know the Bastard Boy's excuse," Klein went on. "He's anemic. He's only got enough blood for his brain or his prick. If he gets a hard-on, he can't remember his own name."

"I wouldn't know," Jude said, swilling the ice around in her glass.

"Is that your excuse too?" Klein went on. "Have you got something down there you haven't been telling us about?"

"If I had," she said, "you'd be the last to know."

And so saying, she deposited her drink, ice and all, down the front of his open shirt.

She regretted it afterwards, of course, and she drove home trying to invent some way of making peace with him without apologizing. Unable to think of any, she decided to let it lie. She'd had arguments with Klein before, drunk and sober. They were forgotten after a month; two at most.

She got in to find more messages from Estabrook awaiting her. He wasn't sobbing any more. His voice was a colorless dirge, delivered from what was clearly genuine despair. The first call was filled with the same pleas she'd heard before. He told her he was losing his mind without her and needed her with him. Wouldn't she at least talk to him, let him explain himself? The second call was less coherent. He said she didn't understand how many secrets he had, how he was smothered in secrets and it was killing him. Wouldn't she come back to see him, he said, even if it was just to collect her clothes?

That was probably the only part of her exit scene she would rewrite if she could play it over again. In her rage she'd left a goodly collection of personal items, jewelry and clothes, in Estabrook's possession. Now she imagined him sobbing over them, sniffing them; God knows, even wearing them. But peeved as she was not to have taken them with her, she was not about to bargain for them now. There would come a time when she felt calm enough to go back and empty the cupboards and the drawers, but not quite yet.

There were no further calls after that night. With the New Year
almost upon her, it was time to turn her attention to the challenge
of earning a crust come January. She'd given up her job at Van-
denburgh's when Estabrook had proposed marriage, and she'd
enjoyed his money freely while they were together, trusting—
naïvely, no doubt—that if they ever broke up he'd deal with her in
an honorable fashion. She hadn't anticipated either the profound
unease that had finally driven her from his side (the sense that she
was almost owned, and that if she stayed with him a moment longer
she'd never unshackle herself) or the vehemence of his revenge.
Again, there'd come a time when she felt able to deal with the mutual mud-slinging of a divorce, but, like the business with the
clothes, she wasn't ready for that turmoil yet, even though she
could hope for some monies from such a settlement. In the meanwhile, she had to think about employment.

Then, on December thirtieth, she received a call from
Estabrook's lawyer, Lewis Leader, a man she'd met only once but
who was memorable for his loquaciousness. It was not in evidence
on this occasion, however. He signaled what she assumed was his
distaste for her desertion of his client with a manner that teetered
on the rude. Did she know, he asked her, that Estabrook had been
hospitalized? When she told him she didn't, he replied that though
he was sure she didn't give a damn, he'd been charged with the duty
of informing her. She asked him what had happened. He briskly
explained that Estabrook had been found in the street in the early
hours of the twenty-eighth, wearing only one item of clothing. He
didn't specify what.

"Is he hurt?" she asked.

"Not physically," Leader replied. "But mentally he's in a bad
state. I thought you ought to know, even though I'm sure he
wouldn't want to see you."

"I'm sure you're right," Jude said.

"For what it's worth," Leader said, "he deserved better than
this."

He signed off with that platitude, leaving Jude to ponder on why
it was that the men she mated with turned out to be crazy. Just two
days earlier she'd been predicting that Gentle would soon be in the
throes of a nervous breakdown. Now it was Estabrook who was
under sedation. Was it her presence in their lives that drove them
to it, or was the lunacy in their blood? She contemplated calling
Gentle at the studio, to see that he was all right, but decided against
it. He had his painting to make love to, and she was damned if she
was going to compete for his attention with a piece of canvas.

One useful possibility did spring from the news Leader had
brought. With Estabrook in the hospital, there was nothing to stop

her from visiting the house and picking up her belongings. It was an apt project for the last day of December. She'd gather the remnants of her life from the lair of her husband and prepare to begin the New Year alone.

2

He hadn't changed the lock, perhaps in the hope that she'd come back one night and slip into bed beside him. But as she entered the house she couldn't shake the feeling of being a burglar. It was gloomy outside, and she switched on all the lights, but the rooms seemed to resist illumination, as though the smell of spoiled food, which was pungent, was thickening the air. She braved the kitchen in search of something to drink, before she began her packing, and found plates of rotting food stacked on every surface, most of them barely picked at. She opened first a window and then the refrigerator, where there were further rancid goods. There was also ice and water. She put both into a clean glass and got about her work.

There was as much disarray upstairs as down. Estabrook had apparently lived in squalor since her departure: the bed they'd shared a swamp of filthy sheets, the floor littered with soiled linen. There was no sign of any of her clothes among these heaps, however, and when she went through to the adjacent dressing room she found them all hanging in place, untouched. Determined to be done with this distasteful business in as short a time as possible, she found herself a set of suitcases and proceeded to pack. It didn't take long. With that labor performed she emptied her belongings from the drawers and packed those. Her jewelry was in the safe downstairs, and it was there she went once she'd finished in the bedroom, leaving the cases by the front door to be picked up as she left. Though she knew where Estabrook kept the key to the safe, she'd never opened it herself. It was a ritual he'd demanded be rigorously observed that on a night when she was to wear one of the pieces he'd given her he'd first ask her which she favored, then go and get it from the safe and put it around her neck, or wrist, or slip it through the lobe of her ear himself. With hindsight, a blatant power play. She wondered what kind of fugue state she'd been in when sharing his company, that she'd endured such idiocies for so long. Certainly the luxuries he'd bestowed upon her had been pleasurable, but why had she played his game so passively? It was grotesque.

The key to the safe was where she'd expected it to be, secreted at the back of the desk drawer in his study. The safe itself was behind an architectural drawing on the study wall, several elevations of a pseudoclassical folly the artist had simply marked as *The*

Retreat. It was far more elaborately framed than its merit deserved, and she had some difficulty lifting it. But she eventually succeeded and got into the safe it had concealed.

There were two shelves, the lower crammed with papers, the upper with small parcels, among which she assumed she would find her belongings. She took everything out and laid it all on the desk, curiosity overtaking the desire to have what was hers and be gone. Two of the packages clearly contained her jewelry, but the other three were far more intriguing, not least because they were wrapped in a fabric as fine as silk and smelled not of the safe's must but of a sweet, almost sickly, spice. She opened the largest of them first. It contained a manuscript, made up of vellum pages sewn together with an elaborate stitch. It had no cover to speak of but seemed to be an arbitrarily arrayed collection of sheets, their subject an anatomical treatise, or at least so she first assumed. On second glance she realized it was not a surgeon's manual at all but a pillow book, depicting lovemaking positions and techniques. Leafing through it she sincerely hoped the artist was locked up where he could not attempt to put these fantasies into practice. Human flesh was neither malleable nor protean enough to re-create what his brush and ink had set on the pages. There were couples intertwined like quarreling squid; others who seemed to have been blessed (or cursed) with organs and orifices of such strangeness and in such profusion they were barely recognizable as human.

She flicked back and forth through the sheets, her interest returning her to the double-page illustration at the center, which was laid out sequentially. The first picture showed a naked man and woman of perfectly normal appearance, the woman lying with her head on a pillow while the man knelt between her legs, applying his tongue to the underside of her foot. From that innocent beginning, a cannibalistic union ensued, the male beginning to devour the woman, starting with her legs, while his partner obliged him with the same act of devotion. Their antics defied both physics and physique, of course, but the artist had succeeded in rendering the act without grotesquerie, but rather in the manner of instructions for some extraordinary magical illusion. It was only when she closed the book, and found the images lingering in her head, that they distressed her, and to sluice them out she turned her distress into a righteous rage that Estabrook would not only purchase such bizarrenesses but hide them from her. Another reason to be well out of his company.

The second package contained a much more innocent item: what appeared to be a fragment of statuary the size of her fist. One facet had been crudely marked with what could have been a weeping eye, a lactating nipple, or a bud seeping sap. The other facets revealed the structure of the block from which the image had been carved. It was predominantly a milky blue, but shot through with fine seams of black and red. She liked the feel of it in her hand and only reluctantly put it down to pick up the third parcel. The contents of this were the prettiest find: half a dozen pea-sized beads, which had been obsessively carved. She'd seen oriental ivories worked with this level of care, but they'd always been behind museum glass. She took one of them to the window to study more closely. The artist had carved the bead to give the impression that it was in fact a ball of gossamer thread, wound upon itself. Curious, and oddly inviting. As she turned it over in her fingers, and over, and over, she found her concentration narrowing, focusing on the exquisite interweaving of threads, almost as though there were an end to be found in the ball, and if she could only grasp it with her mind she might unravel it and discover some mystery inside. She had to force herself to look away, or she was certain the bead's will would have overwhelmed her own, and she'd have ended up staring at its detail until she collapsed.

She returned to the desk and put the bead back among its fellows. Staring at it so intently had upset her equilibrium somewhat. She felt slightly dizzy, the litter she'd left on the desk slipping out of focus as she rifled through it. Her hands knew what she wanted, however, even if her conscious thought didn't. One of them picked up the fragment of blue stone, while her other strayed back to the bead she'd relinquished. Two souvenirs: why not? A piece of stone and a bead. Who could blame her for dispossessing Estabrook of such minor items when he'd intended her so much harm? She pocketed them both without further hesitation and set about wrapping up the book and the remaining beads, returning them to the safe and closing it, and replacing drawing and key. Then she picked up the cloth in which the fragment had been wrapped, pocketed that, took the jewelry, and returned to the front door, turning off the lights as she went. At the door she remembered she'd opened the kitchen window and headed back to close it. She didn't want the place burglarized in her absence. There was only one thief who had right of trespass here, and that was her.

3

She felt well satisfied with the morning's work and treated herself to a glass of wine with her spartan lunch, then started unpacking her loot. As she laid her hostage clothes out on the bed, her thoughts returned to the pillow book. She regretted leaving it now; it would have been the perfect gift for Gentle, who doubtless imagined he'd indulged every physical excess known to man. No matter. She'd find an opportunity to describe its contents to him one of these days and astonish him with her memory for depravity.

A call from Clem interrupted her work. He spoke so softly she had to strain to hear. The news was grim. Taylor was at death's door, he said, having two days before succumbed to another sudden bout of pneumonia. He refused to be hospitalized, however. His last wish, he'd said, was to die where he had lived.

"He keeps asking for Gentle," Clem explained. "And I've tried to telephone him but he doesn't answer. Do you know if he's gone away?"

"I don't think so," she said. "But I haven't spoken to him since Christmas Night."

"Could you try and find him for me? Or rather for Taylor? If you could maybe go round to the studio and rouse him? I'd go myself but I daren't leave the house. I'm afraid as soon as I step outside . . ." He faltered, tears in his breath. "I want to be here if anything happens."

"Of course you do. And of course I'll go. Right now."

"Thanks. I don't think there's much time, Judy."

Before she left she tried calling Gentle, but as Clem had already warned her, nobody answered. She gave up after two attempts, put on her jacket, and headed out to the car. As she reached into her pocket for the keys she realized she'd brought the stone and the bead with her, and some superstition made her hesitate, wondering if she should deposit them back inside. But time was of the essence. As long as they remained in her pocket, who was going to see them? And even if they did, what did it matter? With death in the air who was going to care about a few purloined bits and pieces?

She had discovered the night she'd left Gentle at the studio that he could be seen through the window if she stood on the opposite side of the street, so when he failed to answer the door, that was where she went to spy him. The room seemed to be empty, but the bare bulb was burning. She waited a minute or so and he stepped into view, shirtless and bedraggled. She had powerful lungs and used them now, hollering his name. He didn't seem to hear at first. But she tried again, and this time he looked in her direction, crossing to the window.

"Let me in!" she yelled. "It's an emergency."

The same reluctance she read in his retreat from the window was on his face when he opened the door. If he had looked bad at the party, he looked considerably worse now.

"What's the problem?" he said.

"Taylor's very sick, and Clem says he keeps asking for you."

Gentle looked bemused, as though he was having difficulty remembering who Taylor and Clem were.

"You have to get cleaned up and dressed," she said. "Furie, are you listening to me?"

She'd always called him Furie when she was irritated with him, and that name seemed to work its magic now. Though she'd expected some objection from him, given his phobia where sickness was concerned, she got none. He looked too drained to argue, his stare somehow unfinished, as though it had a place it wanted to rest but couldn't find. She followed him up the stairs into the studio.

"I'd better clean up," he said, leaving her in the midst of the chaos and going into the bathroom.

She heard the shower run. As ever, he'd left the bathroom door wide open. There was no bodily function, to the most fundamental, he'd ever shown the least embarrassment about, an attitude which had shocked her at first but which she'd taken for granted after a time, so that she'd had to relearn the laws of propriety when she'd gone to live with Estabrook.

"Will you find a clean shirt for me?" he called through to her. "And some underwear?"

It seemed to be a day for going through other people's belongings. By the time she'd found a denim shirt and a pair of over-washed boxer shorts, he was out of the shower, standing in front of the bathroom mirror combing his wet hair back from his brow. His body hadn't changed since she'd last looked at it naked. He was as lean as ever, his buttocks and belly tight, his chest smooth. His hooded prick drew her eye: the part that truly gave the lie to Gentle's name. It was no great size in this passive state, but it was pretty even so. If he knew he was being scrutinized he made no sign of it. He peered at himself in the mirror without affection, then shook his head.

"Should I shave?" he said.

"I wouldn't worry about it," she said. "Here's your clothes."

He dressed quickly, repairing to his bedroom to find a pair of boots, leaving her to idle in the studio while he did so. The painting of the couple she'd seen on Christmas Night had gone, and his equipment—paints, easel, and primed canvases—had been unceremoniously dumped in a corner. In their place, newspapers, many of their pages bearing reports on a tragedy she had only noted in passing: the death by fire of twenty-one men, women, and children in an arson attack in South London. She didn't give the reports close scrutiny. There was enough to mourn this gloomy afternoon.

Clem was pale but tearless. He embraced them both at the front door, then ushered them into the house. The Christmas decorations were still up, awaiting Twelfth Night, the perfume of pine needles sharpening the air.

"Before you see him, Gentle," Clem said. "I should explain that he's got a lot of drugs in his system, so he drifts in and out. But he wanted to see you so badly."

"Did he say why?" Gentle asked.

"He doesn't need a reason, does he?" Clem said softly. "Will you stay, Judy? If you want to see him when Gentle's been in ..."

"I'd like that."

While Clem took Gentle up to the bedroom, Jude went through to the kitchen to make a cup of tea, wishing as she did so that she'd had the foresight to tell Gentle as they drove about how Taylor had talked of him the week before, particularly the tale about his speaking in tongues. It might have provided Gentle with some sense of what Taylor needed to know from him now. The solving of mysteries had been much on Taylor's mind on Christmas Night. Perhaps now, whether drugged or not, he hoped to win some last reprieve from his confusion. She doubted Gentle would have any answers. The look she'd seen him give the bathroom mirror had been that of a man to whom even his own reflection was a mystery.

Bedrooms were only ever this hot for sickness or love, Gentle thought as Clem ushered him in: for the sweating out of obsession or contagion. It didn't always work, of course, in either case, but at least in love failure had its satisfactions. He'd eaten very little since he'd departed the scene in Streatham, and the stale heat made him feel light-headed. He had to scan the room twice before his eyes settled on the bed in which Taylor lay, so nearly enveloped was it by the soulless attendants of modern death: an oxygen tank with its tubes and mask; a table loaded with dressings and towels; another, with a vomit bowl, bedpan, and towels; and beside them a third, carrying medication and ointments. In the midst of this panoply was the magnet that had drawn them here, who now seemed very like their prisoner. Taylor was propped up on plastic-covered pillows, with his eyes closed. He looked like an ancient. His hair was thin, his frame thinner still, the inner life of his body—bone, nerve, and vein—painfully visible through skin the color of his sheet. It was all Gentle could do not to turn and flee before the man's eyes flickered open. Death was here again, so soon. A different heat this time, and a different scene, but he was assailed by the same mixture of fear and ineptitude he'd felt in Streatham.

He hung back at the door, leaving Clem to approach the bed first and softly wake the sleeper.

Taylor stirred, an irritated look on his face until his gaze found

Gentle. Then the anger at being called back into pain went from his brow, and he said, "You found him."

"It was Judy, not me," Clem said.

"Oh, Judy. She's a wonder," Taylor murmured.

He tried to reposition himself on the pillow, but the effort was beyond him. His breathing became instantly arduous, and he flinched at some discomfort the motion brought.

"Do you want a painkiller?" Clem asked him.

"No, thanks," he said. "I want to be clearheaded, so Gentle and I can talk." He looked across at his visitor, who was still lingering at the door. "Will you talk to me for a while, John?" he said. "Just the two of us?"

"Of course," Gentle said.

Clem moved from beside the bed and beckoned Gentle across. There was a chair, but Taylor patted the bed, and it was there Gentle sat, hearing the crackle of the plastic undersheet as he did so.

"Call if you need anything," Clem said, the remark directed not at Taylor but at Gentle. Then he left them alone.

"Could you pour me a glass of water?" Taylor asked.

Gentle did so, realizing as he passed it to Taylor that his friend lacked the strength to hold it for himself. He put it to Taylor's lips. There was a salve on them, which moistened them lightly, but they were still split, and puffy with sores. After a few sips Taylor murmured something.

"Enough?" Gentle said.

"Yes, thanks," Taylor replied. Gentle set the glass down. "I've had just about enough of everything. It's time it was all over."

"You'll get strong again."

"I didn't want to see you so we could sit and lie to each other," Taylor said. "I wanted you here so I could tell you how much I've been thinking about you. Night and day, Gentle."

"I'm sure I don't deserve that."

"My subconscious thinks you do," Taylor replied. "And, while we're being honest, the rest of me too. You don't look as if you're getting enough sleep, Gentle."

"I've been working, that's all."

"Painting?"

"Some of the time. Looking for inspiration, you know."

"I've got a confession to make," Taylor said. "But first, you've got to promise you won't be angry with me."

"What have you done?"

"I told Judy about the night we got together," Taylor said. He stared at Gentle as if expecting there to be some eruption. When there was none, he went on, "I know it was no big deal to you," he said. "But it's been on my mind a lot. You don't mind, do you?"

Gentle shrugged. "I'm sure it didn't come as any big surprise to her."

Taylor turned his hand palm up on the sheet, and Gentle took it. There was no power in Taylor's fingers, but he closed them round Gentle's hand with what little strength he had. His grip was cold.

"You're shaking," Taylor said.

"I haven't eaten in a while," Gentle said.

"You should keep your strength up. You're a busy man."

"Sometimes I need to float a little bit," Gentle replied.

Taylor smiled, and there in his wasted features was a phantom glimpse of the beauty he'd had.

"Oh, yes," he said. "I float all the time. I've been all over the room. I've even been outside the window, looking in at myself. That's the way it'll be when I go, Gentle. I'll float off, only that one time I won't come back. I know Clem's going to miss me—we've had half a lifetime together—but you and Judy will be kind to him, won't you? Make him understand how things are, if you can. Tell him how I floated off. He doesn't want to hear me talk that way, but you understand."

"I'm not sure I do."

"You're an artist," he said.

"I'm a faker."

"Not in my dreams, you're not. In my dreams you want to heal me, and you know what I say? I tell you I don't want to get well. I say I want to be out in the light."

"That sounds like a good place to be," Gentle said. "Maybe I'll join you."

"Are things so bad? Tell me. I want to hear."

"My whole life's fucked, Tay."

"You shouldn't be so hard on yourself. You're a good man."

"You said we wouldn't tell lies."

"That's no lie. You are. You just need someone to remind you once in a while. Everybody does. Otherwise we slip back into the mud, you know?"

Gentle took tighter hold of Taylor's hand. There was so much in him he had neither the form nor the comprehension to express. Here was Taylor pouring out his heart about love and dreams and how it was going to be when he died, and what did he, Gentle, have by way of contribution? At best, confusion and forgetfulness. Which of them was the sicker, then? he found himself thinking. Taylor, who was frail but able to speak his heart? Or himself, whole but silent? Determined he wouldn't part from this man without attempting to share something of what had happened to him, he fumbled for some words of explanation.

"I think I found somebody," he said. "Somebody to help me ... remember myself."

"That's good."

"I'm not sure," he said, his voice gossamer. "I've seen some things in the last few weeks, Tay ... things I didn't want to believe until I had no choice. Sometimes I think I'm going crazy."

"Tell me."

"There was someone in New York who tried to kill Jude."

"I know. She told me about it. What about him?" His eyes widened. "Is this the somebody?" he said.

"It's not a he."

"I thought Judy said it was a man."

"It's not a man," Gentle said. "It's not a woman, either. It's not even human, Tay."

"What is it then?"

"Wonderful," he said quietly.

He hadn't dared use a word like that, even to himself. But anything less was a lie, and lies weren't welcome here.

"I told you I was going crazy. But I swear if you had seen the way it changed ... it was like nothing on earth."

"And where is it now?"

"I think it's dead," Gentle replied. "I wasted too long to find it. I tried to forget I'd ever set eyes on it. I was afraid of what it was stirring up in me. And then when that didn't work I tried to paint it out of my system. But it wouldn't go. *Of course,* it wouldn't go. It was *part* of me by that time. And then when I finally went to find it ... it was too late."

"Are you sure?" Taylor said. Knots of discomfort had appeared on his face, as Gentle talked, and were tightening.

"Are you all right?"

"Yes, yes," he said. "I want to hear the rest."

"There's nothing else to hear. Maybe Pie's out there somewhere, but I don't know where."

"Is that why you want to float? Are you hoping—" He stopped, his breathing suddenly turning into gasps. "You know, maybe you *should* fetch Clem," he said.

"Of course."

Gentle went to the door, but before he reached it Taylor said, "You've got to understand, Gentle. Whatever the mystery is, you'll have to see it for us both."

With his hand on the door, and ample reason to beat a hasty retreat, Gentle knew he could still choose silence over a reply, could take his leave of the ancient without accepting the quest. But if he answered, and took it, he was bound.

"I'm going to understand," he said, meeting Taylor's despairing gaze. "We both are. I swear."

Taylor managed to smile in response, but it was fleeting. Gentle opened the door and headed out onto the landing. Clem was waiting.

"He needs you," Gentle said.

Clem stepped inside and closed the bedroom door. Feeling suddenly exiled, Gentle headed downstairs. Jude was sitting at the kitchen table, playing with a piece of rock.

"How is he?" she wanted to know.

"Not good," Gentle said. "Clem's gone in to look after him."

"Do you want some tea?"

"No, thanks. What I really need's some fresh air. I think I'll take a walk around the block."

There was a fine drizzle falling when he stepped outside, which was welcome after the suffocating heat of the sickroom. He knew the neighborhood scarcely at all, so he decided to stay close to the house, but his distraction soon got the better of that plan and he wandered aimlessly, lost in thought and the maze of streets. There was a freshness in the wind that made him sigh for escape. This was no place to solve mysteries. After the turn of the year everybody would be stepping up to a new round of resolutions and ambitions, plotting their futures like well-oiled farces. He wanted none of it.

As he began the trek back to the house he remembered that Jude had asked him to pick up milk and cigarettes on his journey, and that he was returning empty-handed. He turned and went in search of both, which took him longer than he expected. When he finally rounded the corner, goods in hand, there was an ambulance outside the house. The front door was open. Jude stood on the step, watching the drizzle. She had tears on her face.

"He's dead," she said.

He stood rooted to the spot a yard from her. "When?" he said, as if it mattered.

"Just after you left."

He didn't want to weep, not with her watching. There was too much else he didn't want to stumble over in her presence. Stony, he said, "Where's Clem?"

"With him upstairs. Don't go up. There's already too many people." She spied the cigarettes in his hand and reached for them. As her hand grazed his, their grief ran between them. Despite his intent, tears sprang to his eyes, and he went into her embrace, both of them sobbing freely, like enemies joined by a common loss or lovers about to be parted. Or else souls who could not remember whether they were lovers or enemies and were weeping at their own confusion.

16

I

Since the meeting at which the subject of the Tabula Rasa's library
had first been raised, Bloxham had several times planned to perform the duty he'd volunteered himself for and go into the bowels of the tower to check on the security of the collection. But he'd
twice put off the task, telling himself that there were more urgent
claims on his time: specifically, the organization of the Society's
Great Purge. He might have postponed a third time had the matter not been raised again, this in a casual aside from Charlotte
Feaver, who'd been equally vociferous about the safety of the
books at that first gathering and now offered to accompany him
on the investigation. Women baffled Bloxham, and the attraction
they exercised over him had always to be set beside the discomfort he felt in their company, but in recent days he'd felt an intensity of sexual need he'd seldom, if ever, experienced before. Not
even in the privacy of his own prayers did he dare confess the
reason. The Purge excited him—it roused his blood and his
manhood—and he had no doubt that Charlotte had responded to
this heat, even though he'd made no outward show of it. He
promptly accepted her offer, and at her suggestion they agreed to
meet at the tower on the last evening of the old year. He brought
a bottle of champagne.

"We may as well enjoy ourselves," he said, as they headed down
through the remains of Roxborough's original house, a floor of
which had been preserved and concealed within the plainer walls
of the tower.

Neither of them had ventured into this underworld for many
years. It was more primitive than either of them remembered.
Electric light had been crudely installed—cables from which bare
bulbs hung looped along the passages—but otherwise the place
was just as it had been in the first years of the Tabula Rasa. The
cellars had been built for the express purpose of housing the Society's collection; thus for the millennium. A fan of identical corridors spread from the bottom stairs, lined on both sides with
shelves that rose up the brick walls to the curve of the ceilings. The
intersections were elaborately vaulted, but otherwise there was no
decoration.

"Shall we break open the bottle before we start?" Bloxham suggested.

"Why not? What are we drinking from?"

His reply was to bring two fluted glasses from his pocket. She claimed them from him while he opened the bottle, its cork coming with no more than a decorous sigh, the sound of which carried away through the labyrinth and failed to return. Glasses filled, they drank to the Purge.

"Now we're here," Charlotte said, pulling her furs up around her, "what are we looking for?"

"Any sign of tampering or theft," Bloxham said. "Shall we split up or go together?"

"Oh, together," she replied.

It had been Roxborough's claim that these shelves carried every single volume of any significance in the hemisphere, and as they wandered together, surveying the tens of thousands of manuscripts and books, it was easy to believe the boast.

"How in hell's name do you suppose they gathered all this stuff up?" Charlotte wondered as they walked.

"I daresay the world was smaller then," Bloxham remarked. "They all knew each other, didn't they? Casanova, Sartori, the Comte de Saint-Germain. All fakes and buggers together."

"Fakes? Do you really think so?"

"Most of them," Bloxham said, wallowing in the ill-deserved role of expert. "There may have been one or two, I suppose, who knew what they were doing."

"Have you ever been tempted?" Charlotte asked him, slipping her arm through the crook of his as they went.

"To do what?"

"To see if any of it's worth a damn. To try raising a familiar or crossing into the Dominions."

He looked at her with genuine astonishment. "That's against every precept of the Society," he said.

"That's not what I asked," she replied, almost curtly. "I said, 'Have you ever been tempted?'"

"My father taught me that any dealings with the Imajica would put my soul in jeopardy."

"Mine said the same. But I think he regretted not finding out for himself at the end. I mean, if there's no truth in it, then there's no harm."

"Oh, I believe there's truth in it," Bloxham said.

"You believe there are other Dominions?"

"You saw that damn creature Godolphin cut up in front of us."

"I saw a species I hadn't seen before, that's all." She stopped and arbitrarily plucked a book from the shelves. "But I wonder sometimes if the fortress we're guarding isn't empty." She opened the book, and a lock of hair fell from it. "Maybe it's all invention," she said. "Drug dreams and fancy." She put the book back on the shelf and turned to face Bloxham. "Did you really invite me down here to check the security?" she murmured. "I'm going to be damn disappointed if you did."

"Not entirely," he said.

"Good," she replied, and wandered on, deeper into the maze.

2

Though Jude had been invited to a number of New Year's Eve parties, she'd made no firm commitment to attend any of them, for which fact, after the sorrows the day had brought, she was thankful. She'd offered to stay with Clem once Taylor's body had been taken from the house, but he'd quietly declined, saying that he needed the time alone. He was comforted to know she'd be at the other end of the telephone if he needed her, however, and said he'd call if he got too maudlin.

One of the parties she'd been invited to was at the house opposite her flat, and on the evidence of past years it would raise quite a din. She'd several times been one of the celebrants there herself, but it was no great hardship to be alone tonight. She was in no mood to trust the future, if what the New Year brought was more of what the old had offered.

She closed the curtains in the hope that her presence would go undetected, lit some candles, put on a flute concerto, and started to prepare something light for supper. As she washed her hands, she found that her fingers and palms had taken on a light dusting of color from the stone. She'd caught herself toying with it several times during the afternoon, and pocketed it, only to find minutes later that it was once again in her hands. Why the color it had left behind had escaped her until now, she didn't know. She rubbed her hands briskly beneath the tap to wash the dust off, but when she came to dry them found the color was actually brighter. She went into the bathroom to study the phenomenon under a more intense light. It wasn't, as she'd first thought, dust. The pigment seemed to be in her skin, like a henna stain. Nor was it confined to her palms. It had spread to her wrists, where she was sure her flesh hadn't come in contact with the stone. She took off her blouse and to her shock discovered there were irregular patches of color at her elbows as well. She started talking to herself, which she always did when she was confounded by something.

"What the hell is this? I'm turning blue? This is ridiculous."

Ridiculous, maybe, but none too funny. There was a crawl of panic in her stomach. Had she caught some disease from the stone?

Was that why Estabrook had wrapped it up so carefully and hidden it away?

She turned on the shower and stripped. There were no further stains on her body that she could find, which was some small comfort. With the water seething hot she stepped into the bath, working up a lather and rubbing at the color. The combination of heat and the panic in her belly was dizzying her, and halfway through scrubbing at her skin she feared she was going to faint and had to step out of the bath again, reaching to open the bathroom door and let in some cooler air. Her slick hand slid on the doorknob, however, and cursing she reeled around for a towel to wipe the soap off. As she did so she caught sight of herself in the mirror. Her neck was blue. The skin around her eyes was blue. Her brow was blue, all the way up into her hairline. She backed away from this grotesquerie, flattening herself against the steam-wetted tiles.

"This isn't real," she said aloud.

She reached for the handle a second time and wrenched at it with sufficient force to open the door. The cold brought gooseflesh from head to foot, but she was glad of the chill. Perhaps it would slap this self-deceit out of her. Shuddering with cold she fled the reflection, heading back into the candle-lit haven of the living room. There in the middle of the coffee table lay the piece of blue stone, its eye looking back at her. She didn't even remember taking it out of her pocket, much less setting it on the table in this studied fashion, surrounded by candles. Its presence made her hang back at the door. She was suddenly superstitious of it, as though its gaze had a basilisk's power and could turn her to similar stuff. If that was its business she was too late to undo it. Every time she'd turned the stone over she'd met its glance. Made bold by fatalism, she went to the table and picked the stone up, not giving it time to obsess her again but flinging it against the wall with all the power she possessed.

As it flew from her hand it granted her the luxury of knowing her error. It had taken possession of the room in her absence, had become more real than the hand that had thrown it or the wall it was about to strike. Time was its plaything, and place its toy, and in seeking its destruction she would unknit both.

It was too late to undo the error now. The stone struck the wall with a loud hard sound, and in that moment she was thrown out of herself, as surely as if somebody had reached into her head, plucked out her consciousness, and pitched it through the window. Her body remained in the room she'd left, irrelevant to the journey she was about to undertake. All she had of its senses was sight. That was enough. She floated out over the bleak street, shining wet in the lamplight, towards the step of the house opposite hers. A

quartet of party-goers—three young men with a tipsy girl in their
midst—was waiting there, one of the youths rapping impatiently
on the door. While they waited the burliest of the trio pressed
kisses on the girl, kneading her breasts covertly as he did so. Jude
caught glimpses of the discomfort that surfaced between the girl's
giggles; saw her hands make vain little fists when her suitor pushed
his tongue against her lips, then saw her open her mouth to him,
more in resignation than lust. As the door opened and the four
stumbled into the din of celebration, she moved away, rising over
the rooftops as she flew and dropping down again to catch glimpses
of other dramas unfolding in the houses she passed.

They were all, like the stone that had sent her on this mission,
fragments: slivers of dramas she could only guess at. A woman in
an upper room, staring down at a dress laid on a stripped bed; another at a window, tears falling from beneath her closed lids as she
swayed to music Jude couldn't hear; yet another rising from a table
of glittering guests, sickened by something. None of them women
she knew, but all quite familiar. Even in her short remembered life
she'd felt like all of them at some time or other: forsaken, powerless, yearning. She began to see the scheme here. She was going
from glimpse to glimpse as if to moments of her life, meeting her
reflection in women of every class and kind.

In a dark street behind King's Cross she saw a woman servicing
a man in the front seat of his car, bending to take his hard pink
prick between lips the color of menstrual blood. She'd done that
too, or its like, because she'd wanted to be loved. And the woman
driving past, seeing the whores on parade and righteously sickened
by them: that was her. And the beauty taunting her lover out in the
rain, and the virago applauding drunkenly above: she'd been in
those lives just as surely, or they in hers.

Her journey was nearing its end. She'd reached a bridge from
which there would perhaps have been a panoramic view of the city,
but that the rain in this region was heavier than it had been in Notting Hill, and the distance was shrouded. Her mind didn't linger
but moved on through the downpour—unchilled, unwetted—
towards a lightless tower that lay all but concealed behind a row
of trees. Her speed had dropped, and she wove between the foliage
like a drunken bird, dropping down to the ground and sinking
through it into a sodden and utter darkness.

There was a momentary terror that she was going to be buried
alive in this place; then the darkness gave way to light, and she was
dropping through the roof of some kind of cellar, its walls lined not
with wine racks but with shelves. Lights hung along the passage-
ways, but the air here was still dense, not with dust but with something she only understood vaguely. There was sanctity here, and

there was power. She had felt nothing like it in her life: not in St. Peter's, or Chartres, or the Duomo. It made her want to be flesh again, instead of a roving mind. To walk here. To touch the books, the bricks; to smell the air. Dusty it would be, but *such* dust: every mote wise as a planet from floating in this holy space.

The motion of a shadow caught her eye, and she moved towards it along the passageway, wondering as she went what volumes these were, stacked on every side. The shadow up ahead, which she'd taken to be that of one person, was of two, erotically entangled. The woman had her back to the books, her arms grasping the shelf above her head. Her mate, his trousers around his ankles, was pressed against her, making short gasps to accompany the jabbing of his hips. Both had their eyes closed; the sight of each other was no great aphrodisiac. Was this coupling what she'd come here to see? God knows, there was nothing in their labors to either arouse or educate her. Surely the blue eye hadn't driven her across the city gathering tales of womanhood just to witness this joyless intercourse. There had to be something here she wasn't comprehending. Something hidden in their exchange, perhaps? But no. It was only gasps. In the books that rocked on the shelves behind them? Perhaps.

She drifted closer to scrutinize the titles, but her gaze ran beyond spines to the wall against which they stood. The bricks were the same plain stuff as all along the passages. The mortar between had a stain in it she recognized, however: an unmistakable blue. Excited now, she drove her mind on, past the lovers and the books and through the brick. It was dark on the other side, darker even than the ground she'd dropped through to enter this secret place. Nor was it simply a darkness made of light's absence, but of despair and sorrow. Her instinct was to retreat from it, but there was another presence here that made her linger: a form, barely distinguishable from the darkness, lying on the ground in this squalid cell. It was bound—almost cocooned—its face completely covered. The binding was as fine as thread, and had been wound around the body with obsessive care, but there was enough of its shape visible for her to be certain that this, like the ensnared spirits at every station along her route, was also a woman.

Her binders had been meticulous. They'd left not so much as a hair or toenail visible. Jude hovered over the body, studying it. They were almost complementary, like corpse and essence, eternally divided; except that she had flesh to return to. At least she hoped she did; hoped that now she'd completed this bizarre pilgrimage, and had seen the relic in the wall, she'd be allowed to return to her tainted skin. But something still held her here. Not the darkness, not the walls, but some sense of unfinished business. Was a sign of veneration required of her? If so, what? She lacked the knees for genuflection, and the lips for hosannas; she couldn't stoop; she couldn't touch the relic. What was there left to do? Unless—God help her—she had to *enter* the thing.

She knew the instant she'd formed the thought that this was precisely why she'd been brought here. She'd left her living flesh to enter this prisoner of brick, cord, and decay, a thrice-bounded carcass from which she might never emerge again. The thought revolted her, but had she come this far only to turn back because this last rite distressed her too much? Even assuming she could defy the forces that had brought her here, and return to the house of her body against their will, wouldn't she wonder forever what adventure she'd turned her back on? She was no coward; she would enter the relic and take the consequences.

No sooner thought than done. Her mind sank towards the binding and slipped between the threads into the body's maze. She had expected darkness, but there was light here, the forms of the body's innards delineated by the milk-blue she'd come to know as the color of this mystery. There was no foulness, no corruption. It was less a charnel house than a cathedral, the source, she now suspected, of the sacredness that permeated this underground. But, like a cathedral, its substance was quite dead. No blood ran in these veins, no heart pumped, no lungs drew breath. She spread her intention through the stilled anatomy, to feel its length and breadth. The dead woman had been large in life, her hips substantial, her breasts heavy. But the binding bit into her ripeness everywhere, perverting the swell and sweep of her. What terrible last moments she must have known, lying blind in this filth, hearing the wall of her mausoleum being built brick by brick. What kind of crime hung on her, Jude wondered, that she'd been condemned to such a death? And who were her executioners, the builders of that wall? Had they sung as they worked, their voices growing dimmer as the brick blotted them out? Or had they been silent, half ashamed of their cruelty?

There was so much she wished she knew, and none of it answerable. She'd finished her journey as she'd begun it, in fear and confusion. It was time to be gone from the relic, and home. She willed herself to rise out of the dead blue flesh. To her horror, nothing happened. She was bound here, a prisoner within a prisoner. God help her, what had she done? Instructing herself not to panic, she concentrated her mind on the problem, picturing the cell beyond the binding, and the wall she'd passed so effortlessly through, and the lovers, and the passageway that led out to the open sky. But imagining was not enough. She had let her curiosity overtake her, spreading her spirit through the corpse, and now it had claimed that spirit for itself.

A rage began in her, and she let it come. It was as recognizable a part of her as the nose on her face, and she needed all that she was, every particular, to empower her. If she'd had her own body around her it would have been flushing as her heartbeat caught the rhythm of her fury. She even seemed to hear it—the first sound she'd been aware of since leaving the house—the pump at its hectic work. It was not imagined. She felt it in the body around her, a tremor passing through the long-stilled system as her rage ignited it afresh. In the throne room of its head a sleeping mind woke and knew it was invaded.

For Jude there was an exquisite moment of shared consciousness, when a mind new to her—yet sweetly familiar—grazed her own. Then she was expelled by its wakefulness. She heard it scream in horror behind her, a sound of mind rather than throat, which went with her as she sped from the cell, out through the wall, past the lovers shaken from their intercourse by falls of dust, out and up, into the rain, and into a night not blue but bitterest black. The din of the woman's terror accompanied her all the way back to the house, where, to her infinite relief, she found her own body still standing in the candle-lit room. She slid into it with ease, and stood in the middle of the room for a minute or two, sobbing, until she began to shudder with cold. She found her dressing gown and, as she put it on, realized that her wrists and elbows were no longer stained. She went into the bathroom and consulted the mirror. Her face was similarly cleansed.

Still shivering, she returned to the living room to look for the blue stone. There was a substantial hole in the wall where its impact had gouged out the plaster. The stone itself was unharmed, lying on the rug in front of the hearth. She didn't pick it up. She'd had enough of its delirium for one night. Avoiding its baleful glance as best she could, she threw a cushion over it. Tomorrow she'd plan some way of ridding herself of the thing. Tonight she needed to tell somebody what she'd experienced, before she began to doubt it. Someone a little crazy, who'd not dismiss her account out of hand; someone already half believing. Gentle, of course.

17

TOWARDS MIDNIGHT, THE TRAFFIC outside Gentle's studio dwindled to almost nothing. Anybody who was going to a party tonight had arrived. They were deep in drink, debate, or seduction, determined as they celebrated to have in the coming year what the going had denied them.

Content with his solitude, Gentle sat cross-legged on the floor, a bottle of bourbon between his legs and canvases propped up against the furniture all around him. Most of them were blank, but that suited his meditation. So was the future.

He'd been sitting in this ring of emptiness for about two hours, drinking from the bottle, and now his bladder needed emptying. He got up and went to the bathroom, using the light from the lounge to go by rather than face his reflection. As he shook the last drops into the bowl, that light went off. He zipped himself up and went back into the studio. The rain lashed against the window, but there was sufficient illumination from the street for him to see that the door out onto the landing stood inches ajar.

"Who's there?" he said.

The room was still for a moment; then he glimpsed a form against the window, and the smell of something burned and cold pricked his nostrils. The whistler! My God, it had found him!

Fear made him fleet. He broke from his frozen posture and raced to the door. He would have been through it and away down the stairs had he not almost tripped on the dog waiting obediently on the other side. It wagged its tail in pleasure at the sight of him and halted his flight. The whistler was no dog lover. So who was here?

Turning back, he reached for the light switch and was about to flip it on when the unmistakable voice of Pie 'oh' pah said, "Please don't. I prefer the dark."

Gentle's finger dropped from the switch, his heart hammering for a different reason. "Pie? Is that you?"

"Yes, it's me," came the reply. "I heard you wanted to see me, from a friend of yours."

"I thought you were dead."

"I was *with* the dead. Theresa and the children."

"Oh, God. Oh, God."

"You lost somebody too," Pie 'oh' pah said.

It was wise, Gentle now understood, to have this exchange in darkness: to talk, in shadow, of the grave and the lambs it had claimed.

"I was with the spirits of my children for a time. Your friend found me in the mourning place, spoke to me, told me you wanted to see me again. This surprises me, Gentle."

"As much as you talking to Taylor surprises me," Gentle replied, though after their conversation it shouldn't have done. "Is he happy?" he asked, knowing the question might be viewed as a banality, but wanting reassurance.

"No spirit is happy," Pie replied. "There's no release for them. Not in this Dominion or any other. They haunt the doors, waiting to leave, but there's nowhere for them to go."

"Why?"

"That's a question that's been asked for many generations, Gentle. And unanswered. As a child I was taught that before the Unbeheld went into the First Dominion there was a place there into which all spirits were received. My people lived in that Dominion then, and watched over that place, but the Unbeheld drove both the spirits and my people out."

"So the spirits have nowhere to go?"

"Exactly. Their numbers swell, and so does their grief."

He thought of Taylor, lying on his deathbed, dreaming of release, of the final flight into the Absolute. Instead, if Pie was to be believed, his spirit had entered a place of lost souls, denied both flesh and revelation. What price understanding now, when the end of everything was limbo?

"Who is this Unbeheld?" Gentle said.

"Hapexamendios, the God of the Imajica."

"Is He a God of this world too?"

"He was once. But He went out of the Fifth Dominion, through the other worlds, laying their divinities waste, until He reached the Place of Spirits. Then He drew a veil across that Dominion—"

"And became Unbeheld."

"That's what I was taught."

The formality and plainness of Pie 'oh' pah's account lent the story authority, but for all its elegance it was still a tale of gods and other worlds, very far from this dark room and the cold rain running on the glass.

"How do I know any of this is true?" Gentle said.

"You don't, unless you see it with your own eyes," Pie 'oh' pah replied. His voice when he said this was almost sultry. He spoke like a seducer.

"And how do I do that?"

"You must ask me direct questions, and I'll try to answer them. I can't reply to generalities."

"All right, answer this: Can you take me to the Dominions?"

"That I can do."

"I want to follow in the footsteps of Hapexamendios. Can we do that?"

"We can try."

"I want to see the Unbeheld, Pie 'oh' pah. I want to know why Taylor and your children are in Purgatory. I want to *understand* why they're suffering."

There was no question in this speech, therefore no reply except the other's quickening breath.

"Can you take us now?" Gentle said.

"If that's what you want."

"It's what I want, Pie. Prove what you've said is true, or leave me alone forever."

It was eighteen minutes to midnight when Jude got into her car to start her journey to Gentle's house. It was an easy drive, with the roads so clear, and she was several times tempted to jump red lights, but the police were especially vigilant on this night, and any infringement might bring them out of hiding. Though she had no alcohol in her system, she was by no means sure it was innocent of alien influences. She therefore drove as cautiously as at noon, and it took fully fifteen minutes to reach the studio. When she did she found the upper windows dark. Had Gentle decided to drown his sorrows in a night of high life, she wondered, or was he already fast asleep? If the latter, she had news worth waking him for.

"There are some things you should understand before we leave," Pie said, tying their wrists together, left to right, with a belt. "This is no easy journey, Gentle. This Dominion, the Fifth, is unreconciled, which means that getting to the Fourth involves risk. It's not like crossing a bridge. Passing over requires considerable power And if anything goes wrong, the consequences will be dire."

"Tell me the worst."

"In between the Reconciled Dominions and the Fifth is a state called the In Ovo. It's an ether, in which things that have ventured from their worlds are imprisoned. Some of them are innocent. They're there by accident. Some were dispatched there as a judgment. They're lethal. I'm hoping we'll pass through the In Ovo before any of them even notice we're there. But if we were to become separated—"

"I get the picture. You'd better tighten that knot. It could still work loose."

Pie bent to the task, with Gentle fumbling to help in the darkness.

"Let's assume we get through the In Ovo," Gentle said. "What's on the other side?"

"The Fourth Dominion," Pie replied. "If I'm accurate in my bearings, we'll arrive near the city of Patashoqua."

"And if not?"

"Who knows? The sea. A swamp."

"Shit."

"Don't worry. I've got a good sense of direction. And there's plenty of power between us. I couldn't do this on my own. But together . . ."

"Is this the only way to cross over?"

"Not at all. There are a number of passing places here in the Fifth: stone circles, hidden away. But most of them were created to carry travelers to some particular location. We want to go as free agents. Unseen, unsuspected."

"So why have you chosen Patashoqua?"

"It has . . . sentimental associations," Pie replied. "You'll see for yourself, very soon." The mystif paused. "You *do* still want to go?"

"Of course."

"This is as tight as I can get the knot without stopping our blood."

"Then why are we delaying?"

Pie's fingers touched Gentle's face. "Close your eyes."

Gentle did so. Pie's fingers sought out Gentle's free hand and raised it between them.

"You have to help me," the mystif said.

"Tell me what to do."

"Make a fist. Lightly. Leave enough room for a breath to pass through. Good. Good. All magic proceeds from breath. Remember that."

He did, from somewhere.

"Now," Pie went on. "Put your hand to your face, with your thumb against your chin. There are very few incantations in our workings. No pretty words. Just pneuma like this, and the will behind them."

"I've got the will, if that's what you're asking," Gentle said.

"Then one solid breath is all we need. Exhale until it hurts. I'll do the rest."

"Can I take another breath afterwards?"

"Not in this Dominion."

With that reply the enormity of what they were undertaking struck Gentle. They were leaving Earth. Stepping off the edge of the only reality he'd ever known into another state entirely. He grinned in the darkness, the hand bound to Pie's taking hold of his deliverer's fingers.

"Shall we?" he said.

In the murk ahead of him Pie's teeth gleamed in a matching smile.

"Why not?"

Gentle drew breath.

Somewhere in the house, he heard a door slamming and footsteps on the stairs leading up to the studio. But it was too late for interruptions. He exhaled through his hand, one solid breath which

Pie 'oh' pah seemed to snatch from the air between them. Something ignited in the fist the mystif made, bright enough to burn between its clenched fingers. . . .

At the door, Jude saw Gentle's painting almost made flesh: two figures, almost nose to nose, with their faces illuminated by some unnatural source, swelling like a slow explosion between them. She had time to recognize them both—to see the smiles on their faces as they met each other's gaze—then, to her horror, they seemed to turn inside out. She glimpsed wet red surfaces, which folded upon themselves not once but three times in quick succession, each fold diminishing their bodies, until they were slivers of stuff, still folding, and folding, and finally gone.

She sank back against the doorjamb, shock making her nerves cavort. The dog she'd found waiting at the top of the stairs went fearlessly to the place where they'd stood. There was no further magic there, to snatch him after them. The place was dead. They'd gone, the bastards, wherever such avenues led.

The realization drew a yell of rage from her, sufficient to send the dog scurrying for cover. She dearly hoped Gentle heard her, wherever he was. Hadn't she come here to share her revelations with him, so that they could investigate the great unknown together? And all the time he was preparing for his departure without her. Without her!

"How dare you?" she yelled at the empty space.

The dog whined in fear, and the sight of its terror mellowed her. She went down on her haunches.

"I'm sorry," she said to it. "Come here. I'm not cross with you. It's that little fucker Gentle."

The dog was reluctant at first but came to her after a time, its tail wagging intermittently as it grew more confident of her sanity. She rubbed its head, the contact soothing. All was not lost. What Gentle could do, she could do. He didn't have the copyright on adventuring. She'd find a way to go where he'd gone, if she had to eat the blue eye grain by grain to do so.

Church bells began to ring as she sat chewing this over, announcing in their ragged peals the arrival of midnight. Their clamor was accompanied by car horns in the street outside and cheers from a party in an adjacent house.

"Whoopee," she said quietly, on her face the distracted look that had obsessed so many of the opposite sex over the years. She'd forgotten most of them. The ones who'd fought over her, the ones who'd lost their wives in their pursuit of her, even those who'd sold their sanity to find her equal: all were forgotten.

History had never much engaged her. It was the future that glittered in her mind's eye, now more than ever.

The past had been written by men. But the future—pregnant with possibilities—the future was a woman.

I

Until the rise of Yzordderrex, a rise engineered by the Autarch for reasons more political than geographical, the city of Patashoqua, which lay on the edge of the Fourth Dominion, close to where the In Ovo marked the perimeter of the Reconciled worlds, had just claim to be the preeminent city of the Dominions. Its proud inhabitants called it *casje au casje,* simply meaning the hive of hives, a place of intense and fruitful labor. Its proximity to the Fifth made it particularly prone to influences from that source, and even after Yzordderrex had became the center of power across the Dominions it was to Patashoqua that those at the cutting edge of style and invention looked for the coming thing. Patashoqua had a variation on the motor vehicle in its streets long before Yzordderrex. It had rock and roll in its clubs long before Yzordderrex. It had hamburgers, cinemas, blue jeans, and countless other proofs of modernity long before the great city of the Second. Nor was it simply the trivialities of fashion that Patashoqua reinvented from Fifth Dominion models. It was philosophies and belief systems. Indeed, it was said in Patashoqua that you knew a native of Yzordderrex because he looked like you did yesterday and believed what you'd believed the day before.

As with most cities in love with the modern, however, Patashoqua had deeply conservative roots. Whereas Yzordderrex was a sinful city, notorious for the excesses of its darker Kesparates, the streets of Patashoqua were quiet after nightfall, its occupants in their own beds with their own spouses, plotting vogues. This mingling of chic and conservatism was nowhere more apparent than in architecture. Built as it was in a temperate region, unlike the semitropical Yzordderrex, the buildings did not have to be designed with any climatic extreme in mind. They were either elegantly classical, and built to remain standing until Doomsday, or else functions of some current craze, and likely to be demolished within a week.

But it was on the borders of the city where the most extraordinary sights were to be seen, because it was here that a second,

parasitical city had been created, peopled by inhabitants of the
Four Dominions who had fled persecution and had looked to
Patashoqua as a place where liberty of thought and action were
still possible. How much longer this would remain the case was a
debate that dominated every social gathering in the city. The
Autarch had moved against other towns, cities, and states which he
and his councils judged hotbeds of revolutionary thought. Some
of those cities had been razed; others had come under Yzordderrexian edict and all sign of independent thought crushed. The uni-
versity city of Hezoir, for instance, had been reduced to rubble, the
brains of its students literally scooped out of their skulls and
heaped up in the streets. In the Azzimulto the inhabitants of an entire province had been decimated, so rumor went, by a disease introduced into that region by the Autarch's representatives. There
were tales of atrocity from so many sources that people became
almost blasé about the newest horror, until, of course, somebody
asked how long it would be until the Autarch turned his unforgiv-
ing eyes on the hive of hives. Then their faces drained of color, and
people talked in whispers of how they planned to escape or defend
themselves if that day ever came; and they looked around at their
exquisite city, built to stand until Doomsday, and wondered just
how near that day was.

2

Though Pie 'oh' pah had briefly described the forces that haunted
the In Ovo, Gentle had only the vaguest impression of the dark
protean state between the Dominions, occupied as he was by a
spectacle much closer to his heart, that of the change that overtook
both travelers as their bodies were translated into the common currency of passage.

Dizzied by lack of oxygen, he wasn't certain whether these were
real phenomena or not. Could bodies open like flowers, and the
seeds of an essential self fly from them the way his mind told him
they did? And could those same bodies be remade at the other end
of the journey, arriving whole despite the trauma they'd under-
gone? So it seemed. The world Pie had called the Fifth folded up
before the travelers' eyes, and they went like transported dreams
into another place entirely. As soon as he saw the light, Gentle fell
to his knees on the hard rock, drinking the air of this Dominion
with gratitude.

"Not bad at all," he heard Pie say. "We did it, Gentle. I didn't
think we were going to make it for a moment, but we did it!"

Gentle raised his head, as Pie pulled him to his feet by the strap
that joined them.

"Up! Up!" the mystif said. "It's not good to start a journey on your knees."

It was a bright day here, Gentle saw, the sky above his head cloudless, and brilliant as the green-gold sheen of a peacock's tail. There was neither sun nor moon in it, but the very air seemed lucid, and by it Gentle had his first true sight of Pie since they'd met in the fire. Perhaps out of remembrance for those it had lost, the mystif was still wearing the clothes it had worn that night, scorched and bloodied though they were. But it had washed the dirt from its face, and its skin gleamed in the clear light.

"Good to see you," Gentle said.

"You, too."

Pie started to untie the belt that bound them, while Gentle turned his gaze on the Dominion. They were standing close to the summit of a hill, a quarter of a mile from the perimeters of a sprawling shantytown, from which a din of activity rose. It spread beyond the foot of the hill and halfway across a flat and treeless plain of ocher earth, crossed by a thronged highway that led his eye to the domes and spires of a glittering city.

"Patashoqua?" he said.

"Where else?"

"You were accurate, then."

"More than I dared hope. The hill we're standing on is supposed to be the place where Hapexamendios first rested when He came through from the Fifth. It's called the Mount of Lipper Bayak. Don't ask me why."

"Is the city under siege?" Gentle said.

"I don't think so. The gates look open to me."

Gentle scanned the distant walls, and indeed the gates were open wide. "So who are all these people? Refugees?"

"We'll ask in a while," Pie said.

The knot had come undone. Gentle rubbed his wrist, which was indented by the belt, staring down the hill as he did so. Moving between the makeshift dwellings below he glimpsed forms of being that didn't much resemble humanity. And, mingling freely with them, many who did. It wouldn't be difficult to pass as a local, at least.

"You're going to have to teach me, Pie," he said. "I need to know who's who and what's what. Do they speak English here?"

"It used to be quite a popular language," Pie replied. "I can't believe it's fallen out of fashion. But before we go any farther, I think you should know what you're traveling with. The way people respond to me may confound you otherwise."

"Tell me as we go," Gentle said, eager to see the strangers below up close.

"As you wish." They began to descend. "I'm a mystif; my name's Pie 'oh' pah. That much you know. My gender you don't."

"I've made a guess," Gentle said.

"Oh?" said Pie, smiling. "And what's your guess?"

"You're an androgyne. Am I right?"

"That's part of it, certainly."

"But you've got a talent for illusion. I saw that in New York."

"I don't like the word *illusion*. It makes me a guiser, and I'm not that."

"What then?"

"In New York you wanted Judith, and that's what you saw. It was *your* invention, not mine."

"But you played along."

"Because I wanted to be with you."

"And are you playing along now?"

"I'm not deceiving you, if that's what you mean. What you see is what I am, to you."

"But to other people?"

"I may be something different. A man sometimes. A woman others."

"Could you be white?"

"I might manage it for a moment or two. But if I'd tried to come to your bed in daylight, you'd have known I wasn't Judith. Or if you'd been in love with an eight-year-old, or a dog. I couldn't have accommodated that, except . . ."—the creature glanced around at him—". . . under very particular circumstances."

Gentle wrestled with this notion, questions biological, philosophical, and libidinous filling his head. He stopped walking for a moment and turned to Pie.

"Let me tell you what I see," he said. "Just so you know."

"Good."

"If I passed you on the street I believe I'd think you were a woman"—he cocked his head—"though maybe not. I suppose it'd depend on the light, and how fast you were walking." He laughed. "Oh, shit," he said. "The more I look at you the more I see, and the more I see—"

"The less you know."

"That's right. You're not a man. That's plain enough. But then . . ." He shook his head. "Am I seeing you the way you really are? I mean, is this the final version?"

"Of course not. There's stranger sights inside us both. You know that."

"Not until now."

"We can't go too naked in the world. We'd burn out each other's eyes."

"But this *is* you."

"For the time being."

"For what it's worth, I like it," Gentle said. "I don't know what I'd call you if I saw you in the street, but I'd turn my head. How's that?"

"What more could I ask for?"

"Will I meet others like you?"

"A few, maybe," Pie said. "But mystifs aren't common. When one is born, it's an occasion for great celebration among my people."

"Who are your people?"

"The Eurhetemec."

"Will they be here?" Gentle said, nodding towards the throng below.

"I doubt it. But in Yzordderrex, certainly. They have a Kesparate there."

"What's a Kesparate?"

"A district. My people have a city within the city. Or at least they had one. It's two hundred and twenty-one years since I was there."

"My God. How old are you?"

"Half that again. I know that sounds like an extraordinary span, but time works slowly on flesh touched by feits."

"Feits?"

"Magical workings. Feits, wantons, sways. They work their miracles even on a whore like me."

"Whoa!" said Gentle.

"Oh, yes. That's something else you should know about me. I was told—a long time ago—that I should spend my life as a whore or an assassin, and that's what I've done."

"Until now, maybe. But that's over."

"What will I be from now on?"

"My friend," Gentle said, without hesitation.

The mystif smiled. "Thank you for that."

The round of questions ended there, and side by side they wandered on down the slope.

"Don't make your interest too apparent," Pie advised as they approached the edge of this makeshift conurbation. "Pretend you see this sort of sight daily."

"That's going to be difficult," Gentle predicted.

So it was. Walking through the narrow spaces between the shanties was like passing through a country in which the very air had evolutionary ambition, and to breathe was to change. A hundred kinds of eye gazed out at them from doorways and windows, while a hundred forms of limb got about the business of the day—cooking, nursing, crafting, conniving, making fires and deals and love—and all glimpsed so briefly that after a few paces Gentle was obliged to look away, to study the muddy gutter they were walking in, lest his mind be overwhelmed by the sheer profusion of sights. Smells, too: aromatic, sickly, sour and sweet; and sounds that made his skull shake and his gut quiver.

There had been nothing in his life to date, either waking or sleeping, to prepare him for this. He'd studied the masterworks of great imaginers—he'd painted a passable Goya, once, and sold an Ensor for a little fortune—but the difference between paint and reality was vast, a gap whose scale he could not by definition have known until now, when he had around him the other half of the equation. This wasn't an invented place, its inhabitants variations on experienced phenomena. It was independent of his terms of reference: a place unto and of itself.

When he looked up again, daring the assault of the strange, he was grateful that he and Pie were now in a quarter occupied by more human entities, though even here there were surprises. What seemed to be a three-legged child skipped across their path only to look back with a face wizened as a desert corpse, its third leg a tail. A woman sitting in a doorway, her hair being combed by her consort, drew her robes around her as Gentle looked her way, but not fast enough to conceal the fact that a second consort, with the skin of a herring and an eye that ran all the way around its skull, was kneeling in front of her, inscribing hieroglyphics on her belly with the sharpened heel of its hand. He heard a range of tongues being spoken, but English seemed to be the commonest parlance, albeit heavily accented or corrupted by the labial anatomy of the speaker. Some seemed to sing their speech; some almost to vomit it up.

But the voice that called to them from one of the crowded alleyways off to their right might have been heard on any street in London: a lisping, pompous holler demanding they halt in their tracks. They looked in its direction. The throng had divided to allow the speaker and his party of three easy passage.

"Play dumb," Pie muttered to Gentle as the lisper, an overfed gargoyle, bald but for an absurd wreath of oiled kiss curls, approached.

He was finely dressed, his high black boots polished and his canary yellow jacket densely embroidered after what Gentle would come to know as the present Patashoquan fashion. A man much less showily garbed followed, an eye covered by a patch that trailed the tail feathers of a scarlet bird as if echoing the moment of his mutilation. On his shoulders he carried a woman in black, with silvery scales for skin and a cane in her tiny hands with which she tapped her mount's head to speed him on his way. Still farther behind came the oddest of the four.

"A Nullianac," Gentle heard Pie murmur.

He didn't need to ask if this was good news or bad. The creature was its own best advertisement, and it was selling harm. Its head resembled nothing so much as praying hands, the thumbs leading and tipped with lobster's eyes, the gap between the palms wide enough for the sky to be seen through it, but flickering, as arcs of energy passed from side to side. It was without question the ugliest living thing Gentle had ever seen. If Pie had not suggested they obey the edict and halt, Gentle would have taken to his heels there and then, rather than let the Nullianac get one stride closer to them.

The lisper had halted and now addressed them afresh. "What business have you in Vanaeph?" he wanted to know.

"We're just passing through," Pie said, a reply somewhat lacking in invention, Gentle thought.

"Who are you?" the man demanded.

"Who are *you?*" Gentle returned.

The patch-eyed mount guffawed and got his head slapped for his troubles.

"Loitus Hammeryock," the lisper replied.

"My name's Zacharias," Gentle said, "and this is—"

"Casanova," Pie said, which earned him a quizzical glance from Gentle.

"Zooical!" the woman said. "D'yee speakat te gloss?"

"Sure," said Gentle. "I speakat te gloss."

"Be careful," Pie whispered at his side.

"Bone! Bone!" the woman went on, and proceeded to tell them, in a language which was two parts English, or a variant thereof, one part Latin, and one part some Fourth Dominion dialect that consisted of tongue clicks and teeth tappings, that all strangers to this town, Neo Vanaeph, had to register their origins and intentions before they were allowed access: or, indeed, the right to depart. For all its ramshackle appearance, Vanaeph was no lawless stew, it appeared, but a tightly policed township, and this woman—who introduced herself in this flurry of lexicons as Pontiff Farrow—was a significant authority here.

When she'd finished, Gentle cast a confounded look in Pie's direction. This was proving more difficult terrain by the moment. Unconcealed in the Pontiff's speech was threat of summary execution if they failed to answer their inquiries satisfactorily. The executioner among this party was not hard to spot: he of the prayerful head—the Nullianac—waiting in the rear for his instructions.

"So," said Hammeryock. "We need some identification."

"I don't have any," Gentle said.

"And you?" he asked the mystif, which also shook its head.

"A Nullianac," Gentle heard Pie murmur.

He didn't need to ask if this was good news or bad. The creature was its own best advertisement, and it was selling harm. Its head resembled nothing so much as praying hands, the thumbs leading and tipped with lobster's eyes, the gap between the palms wide enough for the sky to be seen through it, but flickering, as arcs of energy passed from side to side. It was without question the ugliest living thing Gentle had ever seen. If Pie had not suggested they obey the edict and halt, Gentle would have taken to his heels there and then, rather than let the Nullianac get one stride closer to them.

The lisper had halted and now addressed them afresh. "What business have you in Vanaeph?" he wanted to know.

"We're just passing through," Pie said, a reply somewhat lacking in invention, Gentle thought.

"Who are you?" the man demanded.

"Who are *you?*" Gentle returned.

The patch-eyed mount guffawed and got his head slapped for his troubles.

"Loitus Hammeryock," the lisper replied.

"My name's Zacharias," Gentle said, "and this is—"

"Casanova," Pie said, which earned him a quizzical glance from Gentle.

"Zooical!" the woman said. "D'yee speakat te gloss?"

"Sure," said Gentle. "I speakat te gloss."

"Be careful," Pie whispered at his side.

"Bone! Bone!" the woman went on, and proceeded to tell them, in a language which was two parts English, or a variant thereof, one part Latin, and one part some Fourth Dominion dialect that consisted of tongue clicks and teeth tappings, that all strangers to this town, Neo Vanaeph, had to register their origins and intentions before they were allowed access: or, indeed, the right to depart. For all its ramshackle appearance, Vanaeph was no lawless stew, it appeared, but a tightly policed township, and this woman—who introduced herself in this flurry of lexicons as Pontiff Farrow—was a significant authority here.

When she'd finished, Gentle cast a confounded look in Pie's direction. This was proving more difficult terrain by the moment. Unconcealed in the Pontiff's speech was threat of summary execution if they failed to answer their inquiries satisfactorily. The executioner among this party was not hard to spot: he of the prayerful head—the Nullianac—waiting in the rear for his instructions.

"So," said Hammeryock. "We need some identification."

"I don't have any," Gentle said.

"And you?" he asked the mystif, which also shook its head.

"As you wish." They began to descend. "I'm a mystif; my name's Pie 'oh' pah. That much you know. My gender you don't."

"I've made a guess," Gentle said.

"Oh?" said Pie, smiling. "And what's your guess?"

"You're an androgyne. Am I right?"

"That's part of it, certainly."

"But you've got a talent for illusion. I saw that in New York."

"I don't like the word *illusion*. It makes me a guiser, and I'm not that."

"What then?"

"In New York you wanted Judith, and that's what you saw. It was *your* invention, not mine."

"But you played along."

"Because I wanted to be with you."

"And are you playing along now?"

"I'm not deceiving you, if that's what you mean. What you see is what I am, to you."

"But to other people?"

"I may be something different. A man sometimes. A woman others."

"Could you be white?"

"I might manage it for a moment or two. But if I'd tried to come to your bed in daylight, you'd have known I wasn't Judith. Or if you'd been in love with an eight-year-old, or a dog. I couldn't have accommodated that, except . . ."—the creature glanced around at him—". . . under very particular circumstances."

Gentle wrestled with this notion, questions biological, philosophical, and libidinous filling his head. He stopped walking for a moment and turned to Pie.

"Let me tell you what I see," he said. "Just so you know."

"Good."

"If I passed you on the street I believe I'd think you were a woman"—he cocked his head—"though maybe not. I suppose it'd depend on the light, and how fast you were walking." He laughed. "Oh, shit," he said. "The more I look at you the more I see, and the more I see—"

"The less you know."

"That's right. You're not a man. That's plain enough. But then . . ." He shook his head. "Am I seeing you the way you really are? I mean, is this the final version?"

"Of course not. There's stranger sights inside us both. You know that."

"Not until now."

"We can't go too naked in the world. We'd burn out each other's eyes."

"But this *is* you."

"For the time being."

"For what it's worth, I like it," Gentle said. "I don't know what I'd call you if I saw you in the street, but I'd turn my head. How's that?"

"What more could I ask for?"

"Will I meet others like you?"

"A few, maybe," Pie said. "But mystifs aren't common. When one is born, it's an occasion for great celebration among my people."

"Who are your people?"

"The Eurhetemec."

"Will they be here?" Gentle said, nodding towards the throng below.

"I doubt it. But in Yzordderrex, certainly. They have a Kesparate there."

"What's a Kesparate?"

"A district. My people have a city within the city. Or at least they had one. It's two hundred and twenty-one years since I was there."

"My God. How old are you?"

"Half that again. I know that sounds like an extraordinary span, but time works slowly on flesh touched by feits."

"Feits?"

"Magical workings. Feits, wantons, sways. They work their miracles even on a whore like me."

"Whoa!" said Gentle.

"Oh, yes. That's something else you should know about me. I was told—a long time ago—that I should spend my life as a whore or an assassin, and that's what I've done."

"Until now, maybe. But that's over."

"What will I be from now on?"

"My friend," Gentle said, without hesitation.

The mystif smiled. "Thank you for that."

The round of questions ended there, and side by side they wandered on down the slope.

"Don't make your interest too apparent," Pie advised as they approached the edge of this makeshift conurbation. "Pretend you see this sort of sight daily."

"That's going to be difficult," Gentle predicted.

So it was. Walking through the narrow spaces between the shanties was like passing through a country in which the very air had evolutionary ambition, and to breathe was to change. A hundred kinds of eye gazed out at them from doorways and windows, while a hundred forms of limb got about the business of the day—cooking, nursing, crafting, conniving, making fires and deals and love—and all glimpsed so briefly that after a few paces Gentle was

obliged to look away, to study the muddy gutter they were walking in, lest his mind be overwhelmed by the sheer profusion of sights. Smells, too: aromatic, sickly, sour and sweet; and sounds that made his skull shake and his gut quiver.

There had been nothing in his life to date, either waking or sleeping, to prepare him for this. He'd studied the masterworks of great imaginers—he'd painted a passable Goya, once, and sold an Ensor for a little fortune—but the difference between paint and reality was vast, a gap whose scale he could not by definition have known until now, when he had around him the other half of the equation. This wasn't an invented place, its inhabitants variations on experienced phenomena. It was independent of his terms of reference: a place unto and of itself.

When he looked up again, daring the assault of the strange, he was grateful that he and Pie were now in a quarter occupied by more human entities, though even here there were surprises. What seemed to be a three-legged child skipped across their path only to look back with a face wizened as a desert corpse, its third leg a tail. A woman sitting in a doorway, her hair being combed by her consort, drew her robes around her as Gentle looked her way, but not fast enough to conceal the fact that a second consort, with the skin of a herring and an eye that ran all the way around its skull, was kneeling in front of her, inscribing hieroglyphics on her belly with the sharpened heel of its hand. He heard a range of tongues being spoken, but English seemed to be the commonest parlance, albeit heavily accented or corrupted by the labial anatomy of the speaker. Some seemed to sing their speech; some almost to vomit it up.

But the voice that called to them from one of the crowded alleyways off to their right might have been heard on any street in London: a lisping, pompous holler demanding they halt in their tracks. They looked in its direction. The throng had divided to allow the speaker and his party of three easy passage.

"Play dumb," Pie muttered to Gentle as the lisper, an overfed gargoyle, bald but for an absurd wreath of oiled kiss curls, approached.

He was finely dressed, his high black boots polished and his canary yellow jacket densely embroidered after what Gentle would come to know as the present Patashoquan fashion. A man much less showily garbed followed, an eye covered by a patch that trailed the tail feathers of a scarlet bird as if echoing the moment of his mutilation. On his shoulders he carried a woman in black, with silvery scales for skin and a cane in her tiny hands with which she tapped her mount's head to speed him on his way. Still farther behind came the oddest of the four.

"Spies," the Pontiff hissed.

"No, we're just . . . tourists," Gentle said.

"Tourists?" said Hammeryock.

"We've come to see the sights of Patashoqua." He turned to Pie for support. "Whatever they are."

"The tombs of the Vehement Loki Lobb," Pie said, clearly scratching around for the glories Patashoqua had to offer, "and the Merrow Ti' Ti'."

That sounded pretty to Gentle's ears. He faked a broad smile of enthusiasm. "The Merrow Ti' Ti'!" he said. "Absolutely! I wouldn't miss the Merrow Ti' Ti' for all the tea in China."

"*China?*" said Hammeryock.

"Did I say China?"

"You did."

"Fifth Dominion," the Pontiff muttered. "Spiatits from the Fifth Dominion."

"I object strongly to that accusation," said Pie 'oh' pah.

"And so," said a voice behind the accused, "do I."

Both Pie and Gentle turned to take in the sight of a scabrous, bearded individual, dressed in what might generously have been described as motley and less generously as rags, standing on one leg and scraping shit off the heel of his other foot with a stick.

"It's the hypocrisy that turns my stomach, Hammeryock," he said, his expression a maze of wiles. "You two pontificate," he went on, eyeing his pun's target as he spoke, "about keeping the streets free from undesirables, but you do nothing about the dog shite!"

"This isn't your business, Tick Raw," Hammeryock said.

"Oh, but it is. These are my friends, and you've insulted them with your slurs and your suspicions."

"Friends, sayat?" the Pontiff murmured.

"Yes, ma'am. Friends. Some of us still know the difference between conversation and diatribe. I have friends, with whom I talk and exchange ideas. Remember *ideas?* They're what make life worth living."

Hammeryock could not disguise his unease, hearing his mistress thus addressed, but whoever Tick Raw was he wielded sufficient authority to silence any further objection.

"My dearlings," he said to Gentle and Pie, "shall we repair to my home?"

As a parting gesture he lobbed the stick in Hammeryock's direction. It landed in the mud between the man's legs.

"Clean up, Loitus," Tick Raw said. "We don't want the Autarch's heel sliding in shite, now, do we?"

The two parties then went their separate ways, Tick Raw leading Pie and Gentle off through the labyrinth.

"We want to thank you," Gentle said.

"What for?" Tick Raw asked him, aiming a kick at a goat that wandered across his path.

"Talking us out of trouble," Gentle replied. "We'll be on our way now."

"But you've got to come back with me," Tick Raw said.

"There's no need."

"Need? There's *every* need! Have I got this right?" he said to Pie. "Is there need or isn't there?"

"We'd certainly like the benefit of your insights," Pie said. "We're strangers here. Both of us." The mystif spoke in an oddly stilted fashion, as if it wanted to say more, but couldn't. "We need reeducating," it said.

"Oh?" said Tick Raw. "Really?"

"Who is this Autarch?" Gentle asked.

"He rules the Reconciled Dominions, from Yzordderrex. He's the greatest power in the Imajica."

"And he's coming here?"

"That's the rumor. He's losing his grip in the Fourth, and he knows it. So he's decided to put in a personal appearance. Officially, he's visiting Patashoqua, but this is where the trouble's brewing."

"Do you think he'll definitely come?" Pie asked.

"If he doesn't, the whole of the Imajica's going to know he's afraid to show his face. Of course that's always been a part of his fascination, hasn't it? All these years he's ruled the Dominions without anybody really knowing what he looks like. But the glamour's worn off. If he wants to avoid revolution he's going to have to prove he's a charismatic."

"Are you going to get blamed for telling Hammeryock we were your friends?" Gentle asked.

"Probably, but I've been accused of worse. Besides, it's almost true. Any stranger here's a friend of mine." He cast a glance at Pie. "Even a mystif," he said. "The people in this dung heap have no poetry in them. I know I should be more sympathetic. They're refugees, most of them. They've lost their lands, their houses, their tribes. But they're so concerned with their itsy-bitsy little sorrows they don't see the broader picture."

"And what *is* the broader picture?" Gentle asked.

"I think that's better discussed behind closed doors," Tick Raw said, and would not be drawn any further on the subject until they were secure in his hut.

It was spartan in the extreme. Blankets on a board for a bed; another board for a table; some moth-eaten pillows to squat on.

"This is what I'm reduced to," Tick Raw said to Pie, as though the mystif understood, perhaps even shared, his sense of humiliation. "If I'd moved on it might have been different. But I couldn't, of course."

"Why not?" Gentle asked.

Tick Raw gave him a quizzical look, glancing over at Pie, then looking back at Gentle again.

"I'd have thought that was obvious," he said. "I've kept my post. I'm here until a better day dawns."

"And when will that be?" Gentle inquired.

"You tell me," Tick Raw replied, a certain bitterness entering his voice. "Tomorrow wouldn't be too soon. This is no frigging life for a great sway-worker. I mean, look at it!" He cast his eyes around the room. "And let me tell you, this is the lap of luxury compared with some of the hovels I could show you. People living in their own excrement, grubbing around for food. And all in sight of one of the richest cities in the Dominions. It's obscene. At least I've got food in my belly. And I get some respect, you know. Nobody crosses me. They know I'm an evocator, and they keep their distance. Even Hammeryock. He hates me with a passion, but he'd never dare send the Nullianac to kill me, in case it failed and I came after him. Which I would. Oh, yes. Gladly. Pompous little fuck."

"You should just leave," Gentle said. "Go and live in Patashoqua."

"*Please,*" Tick Raw said, his tone vaguely pained. "Must we play games? Haven't I proved my integrity? I saved your lives."

"And we're grateful," Gentle said.

"I don't want gratitude," Tick Raw said.

"What do you want then? Money?"

At this, Tick Raw rose from his cushion, his face reddening, not with blushes but with rage.

"I don't deserve this," he said.

"Deserve *what?*" said Gentle.

"I've lived in shite," Tick Raw said, "but I'm damned if I'm going to eat it! All right, so I'm not a great Maestro. I wish I were! I wish Uter Musky was still alive, and he could have waited here all these years instead of me. But he's gone, and I'm all that's left! Take me or leave me!"

The outburst completely befuddled Gentle. He glanced across at Pie, looking for some guidance, but the mystif had hung its head.

"Maybe we'd better leave," Gentle said.

"Yes! Why don't you do that?" Tick Raw yelled. "Get the fuck out of here. Maybe you can find Musky's grave and resurrect him. He's out there on the mount. I buried him with these two hands!" His voice was close to cracking now. There was grief in it as well as rage. "You can dig him up the same way!"

Gentle started to get to his feet, sensing that any further words from him would only push Tick Raw closer to an eruption or a breakdown, neither of which he wanted to witness. But the mystif reached up and took hold of Gentle's arm.

"Wait," Pie said.

"The man wants us out," Gentle replied.

"Let me talk to Tick for a few moments," Pie said.

The evocator glared fiercely at the mystif.

"I'm in no mood for seductions," he warned.

The mystif shook its head, glancing at Gentle. "Neither am I."

"You want me out of here?" he said.

"Not for long."

Gentle shrugged, though he felt rather less easy with the idea of leaving Pie in Tick Raw's company than his manner suggested. There was something about the way the two of them stared and studied each other that made him think there was some hidden agenda here. If so, it was surely sexual, despite their denials.

"I'll be outside," Gentle said, and left them to their debate.

He'd no sooner closed the door than he heard the two begin to talk inside. There was a good deal of din from the shack opposite— a baby bawling, a mother attempting to hush it with an off-key lullaby—but he caught fragments of the exchange. Tick Raw was still in a fury.

"Is this some kind of punishment?" he demanded at one point; then, a few moments later: "Patient? How much more frigging patient do I have to be?"

The lullaby blotted out much of what followed, and when it quieted again, the conversation inside Raw's shack had taken another turn entirely.

"We've got a long way to go," Gentle heard Pie saying, "and a lot to learn." Tick Raw made some inaudible reply, to which Pie said, "He's a stranger here."

Again Tick murmured something.

"I can't do that," Pie replied. "He's my responsibility."

Now Tick Raw's persuasions grew loud enough for Gentle to hear.

"You're wasting your time," the evocator said. "Stay here with me. I miss a warm body at night."

At this Pie's voice dropped to a whisper. Gentle took a half step back towards the door and managed to catch a few of the mystif's words. It said *heartbroken,* he was sure; then something about faith. But the rest was a murmur too soft to be interpreted. Deciding he'd given the two of them long enough alone, he announced that he was coming back in and entered. Both looked up at him: somewhat guiltily, he thought.

"I want to get out of here," he announced.

Tick Raw's hand was at Pie's neck and remained there, like a staked claim.

"If you go," Tick told the mystif, "I can't guarantee your safety. Hammeryock will be wanting your blood."

"We can defend ourselves," Gentle said, somewhat surprised by his own certainty.

"Maybe we shouldn't be quite so hasty," Pie put in.

"We've got a journey to make," Gentle replied.

"Let her make up her own mind," Tick Raw suggested. "She's not your property."

At this remark, a curious look crossed Pie 'oh' pah's face. Not guilt now, but a troubled expression, softening into resignation. The mystif's hand went up to its neck and brushed off Tick Raw's hold.

"He's right," it said to Tick. "We do have a journey ahead of us."

The evocator pursed his lips, as if making up his mind whether to pursue this business any further or not. Then he said, "Well then. You'd better go."

He turned a sour eye on Gentle.

"May everything be as it seems, stranger."

"Thank you," said Gentle, and escorted Pie out of the hut into the mud and flurry of Vanaeph.

"Strange thing to say," Gentle observed as they trudged away from Tick Raw's hut. *"May everything be as it seems."*

"It's the profoundest curse a sway-worker knows," Pie replied.

"I see."

"On the contrary," Pie said, "I don't think you see very much."

There was a note of accusation in Pie's words which Gentle rose to.

"I certainly saw what you were up to," hc said. "You had half a mind to stay with him. Batting your eyes like a—" He stopped himself.

"Go on," Pie replied. "Say it. Like a *whore.*"

"That wasn't what I meant."

"No, please." Pie went on, bitterly. "You can lay on the insults. Why not? It can be very arousing."

Gentle shot Pie a look of disgust.

"You said you wanted education, Gentle. Well, let's start with *May everything be as it seems.* It's a curse, because if that were the case we'd all be living just to die, and mud would be king of the Dominions."

"I get it," Gentle said. "And you'd be just a whore."

"And you'd be just a faker, working for—"

Before the rest of the sentence was out of his mouth, a pack of animals ran out between two of the dwellings, squealing like pigs, though they looked more like tiny llamas. Gentle looked in the direction from which they'd come, and saw—advancing between the shanties—a sight to bring shudders.

"The Nullianac!"

"I see it!" Pie said.

As the executioner approached, the praying hands of its head opened and closed, as though kindling the energies between the palms to a lethal heat. There were cries of alarm from the houses around. Doors slammed. Shutters closed. A child was snatched from a step, bawling as it went. Gentle had time to see the executioner draw two weapons, with blades that caught the livid light of the arcs; then he was obeying Pie's instruction to run, the mystif leading the way.

The street they'd been on was no more than a narrow gutter, but it was a well-lit highway by comparison with the narrow alley they ducked into. Pie was light-footed; Gentle was not. Twice the mystif made a turn and Gentle overshot it. The second time he lost Pie entirely in the murk and dirt and was about to retrace his steps when he heard the executioner's blade slice through something behind him and glanced back to see one of the frailer houses folding up in a cloud of dust and screams, its demolisher's shape, lightning-headed, appearing from the chaos and fixing its gaze upon him. Its target sighted, it advanced with a sudden speed, and Gentle darted for cover at the first turn, a route that took him into a swamp of sewage which he barely crossed without falling, and thence into even narrower passages.

It would only be a matter of time before he chanced upon a cul-de-sac, he knew. When he did, the game would be up. He felt an itch at the nape of his neck, as though the blades were already there. This wasn't right! He'd barely been out of the Fifth an hour and he was seconds from death. He glanced back. The Nullianac had closed the distance between them. He picked up his pace, pitching himself around a corner and into a tunnel of corrugated iron, with no way out at the other end.

"Shite!" he said, taking Tick Raw's favorite word for his complaint. "Furie, you've killed yourself!"

The walls of the cul-de-sac were slick with filth, and high. Knowing he'd never scale them, he ran to the far end and threw himself against the wall there, hoping it might crack. But its builders (damn them!) had been better craftsmen than most in the vicinity. The wall rocked, and pieces of its fetid mortar fell about him, but all his efforts did was bring the Nullianac straight to him, drawn by the sound of his effort.

Seeing his executioner approaching, he pitched his body against the wall afresh, hoping for some last-minute reprieve. But all he got was bruises. The itch at his nape was an ache now, but through its pain he formed the despairing thought that this was surely the most ignominious of deaths, to be sliced up amid sewage. What had he done to deserve it? He asked it aloud.

"What have I done? What the fuck have I done?"

The question went unanswered; or did it? As his yells ceased he found himself raising his hand to his face, not knowing—even as he did so—why. There was simply an inner compulsion to open his palm and spit upon it. The spittle felt cold, or else his palm was hot. Now a yard away, the Nullianac raised its twin blades above its head. Gentle made a fist, lightly, and put it to his mouth. As the blades reached the top of their arc, he exhaled.

He felt his breath blaze against his palm, and in the instant before the blades reached his head the pneuma went from his fist like a bullet. It struck the Nullianac in the neck with such force it was thrown backwards, a livid spurt of energy breaking from the gap in its head and rising like earth-born lightning into the sky. The creature fell in the filth, its hands dropping the blades to reach for the wound. They never touched the place. Its life went out of it in a spasm, and its prayerful head was permanently silenced.

At least as shaken by the other's death as by the proximity of his own, Gentle got to his feet, his gaze going from the body in the dirt to his fist. He opened it. The spittle had gone, transformed into some lethal dart. A seam of discoloration ran from the ball of his thumb to the other side of his hand. That was the only sign of the pneuma's passing.

"Holy shite," he said.

A small crowd had already gathered at the end of the cul-de-sac, and heads appeared over the wall behind him. From every side came an agitated buzz that wouldn't, he guessed, take long to reach Hammeryock and Pontiff Farrow. It would be naïve to suppose they ruled Vanaeph with only one executioner in their squad. There'd be others; and here, soon. He stepped over the body, not caring to look too closely at the damage he'd done, but aware with only a passing glance that it was substantial.

The crowd, seeing the conquerer approach, parted. Some bowed, others fled. One said, "Bravo!" and tried to kiss his hand. He pressed his admirer away and scanned the alleys in every direction, hoping for some sign of Pie 'oh' pah. Finding none, he debated his options. Where would Pie go? Not to the top of the mount. Though that was a visible rendezvous, their enemies would spot them there. Where else? The gates of Patashoqua, perhaps, that the mystif had pointed out when they'd first arrived? It was as good a place as any, he thought, and started off, down through teeming Vanaeph towards the glorious city.

His worst expectations—that news of his crime had reached the Pontiff and her league—were soon confirmed. He was almost at the edge of the township, and within sight of the open ground that lay between its borders and the walls of Patashoqua, when a hue and cry from the streets behind announced a pursuing party. In his Fifth Dominion garb, jeans and shirt, he would be easily recognized if he started towards the gates, but if he attempted to stay within the confines of Vanaeph it would be only a matter of time before he was hunted down. Better to take the chance of running now, he decided, while he still had a lead. Even if he didn't make it to the gates before they came after him, they surely wouldn't dispatch him within sight of Patashoqua's gleaming walls.

He put on a fair turn of speed and was out of the township in less than a minute, the commotion behind him gathering volume. Though it was difficult to judge the distance to the gates in a light that lent such iridescence to the ground between, it was certainly no less than a mile; perhaps twice that. He'd not got far when the first of his pursuers appeared from the outskirts of Vanaeph, runners fresher and lighter than he, who rapidly closed the distance between them. There were plenty of travelers coming and going along the straight road to the gates. Some pedestrians, most in groups and dressed like pilgrims; other, finer figures, mounted on horses whose flanks and heads were painted with gaudy designs; still others riding on shaggy derivatives of the mule. Most envied however, and most rare, were those in motor vehicles, which, though they basically resembled their equivalents in the Fifth—a chassis riding on wheels—were in every other regard fresh inventions. Some were as elaborate as baroque altarpieces, every inch of their bodywork chased and filigreed. Others, with spindly wheels twice the height of their roofs, had the preposterous delicacy of tropical insects. Still others, mounted on a dozen or more tiny wheels, their exhausts giving off a dense, bitter fume, looked like speeding wreckage, asymmetrical and inelegant farragoes of glass and metalwork. Risking death by hoof and wheel, Gentle joined the traffic and put on a new spurt as he dodged between the vehicles. The leaders of the pack behind him had also reached the road. They were armed, he saw, and had no compunction about displaying their weapons. His belief that they wouldn't attempt to kill him among witnesses suddenly seemed frail. Perhaps the law of Vanaeph was good to the very gates of Patashoqua. If so, he was dead. They would overtake him long before he reached sanctuary.

But now, above the din of the highway, another sound reached him, and he dared a glance off to his left, to see a small, plain vehicle, its engine badly tuned, careering in his direction. It was open-topped, its driver visible: Pie 'oh' pah, God love him, driving like a man—or mystif—possessed. Gentle changed direction instantly, veering off the road and dividing a herd of pilgrims as he did so, and raced towards Pie's noisy chariot.

A chorus of whoops at his back told him the pursuers had also changed direction, but the sight of Pie had given heat to Gentle's heels. His turn of speed was wasted, however. Rather than slowing to let Gentle aboard, Pie drove on past, heading towards the hunters. The leaders scattered as the vehicle bore down upon them, but it was a figure Gentle had missed, being carried in a sedan chair, who was Pie's true target. Hammeryock, sitting on high, ready to watch the execution, was suddenly a target in his turn. He yelled to his bearers to retreat, but in their panic they failed to agree on a direction. Two pulled left, two right. One of the chair's arms splintered, and Hammeryock was pitched out, hitting the ground hard. He didn't get up. The sedan chair was discarded, and its bearers fled, leaving Pie to veer around and head back towards Gentle. With their leader felled, the scattered pursuers, most likely coerced into serving the Pontiffs in the first place, had lost heart. They were not sufficiently inspired to risk Hammeryock's fate and so kept their distance, while Pie drove back and picked up his gasping passenger.

"I thought maybe you'd gone back to Tick Raw," Gentle said, once he was aboard.

"He wouldn't have wanted me," Pie said. "I've had congress with a murderer."

"Who's that?"

"You, my friend, *you!* We're both assassins now."

"I suppose we are."

"And not much welcome in this region, I think."

"Where did you find the vehicle?"

"There's a few of them parked on the outskirts. They'll be in them soon enough, and after us."

"The sooner we're in the city the better, then."

"I don't think we'd be safe there for long," the mystif replied.

It had maneuvered the vehicle so that its snub nose faced the highway. The choice lay before them. Left, to the gates of Patashoqua. Right, down a highway which ran on past the Mount of Lipper Bayak to a horizon that rose, at the farthest limit of the eye, to a mountain range.

"It's up to you," Pie said.

Gentle looked longingly towards the city, tempted by its spires. But he knew there was wisdom in Pie's advice.

"We'll come back someday, won't we?" he said.

"Certainly, if that's what you want."

"Then let's head the other way."

The mystif turned the vehicle onto the highway, against the predominant flow of traffic, and with the city behind them they soon picked up speed.

"So much for Patashoqua," Gentle said as the walls became a mirage.

"No great loss," Pie remarked.

"But I wanted to see the Merrow Ti' Ti'," Gentle said.

"No chance," Pie returned.

"Why?"

"It was pure invention," Pie said. "Like all my favorite things, including myself. Pure invention!"

19

I

Though Jude had made an oath, in all sobriety, to follow Gentle wherever she'd seen him go, her plans for pursuit were stymied by a number of claims upon her energies, the most pressing of which was Clem's. He needed her advice, comfort, and organizational skills in the dreary, rainy days that followed New Year, and despite the urgency of her agenda she could scarcely turn her back on him. Taylor's funeral took place on January ninth, with a memorial service which Clem took great pains to perfect. It was a melancholy triumph: a time for Taylor's friends and relations to mingle and express their affections for the departed man. Jude met people she'd not seen in many years, and few, if any, failed to comment on the one conspicuous absentee: Gentle. She told everybody what she'd told Clem. That Gentle had been going through a bad time, and the last she'd heard he was planning to leave on holiday. Clem, of course, would not be fobbed off with such vague excuses. Gentle had left knowing that Taylor was dead, and Clem viewed his departure as a kind of cowardice. Jude didn't attempt to defend the wanderer. She simply tried to make as little mention of Gentle in Clem's presence as she could.

But the subject would keep coming up, one way or another. Sorting through Taylor's belongings after the funeral, Clem came upon three watercolors, painted by Gentle in the style of Samuel Palmer, but signed with his own name and dedicated to Taylor. Pictures of idealized landscapes, they couldn't help but turn Clem's thoughts back to Taylor's unrequited love for the vanished man, and Jude's to the place he had vanished for. They were among the few items that Clem, perhaps vengefully, wanted to destroy, but Jude persuaded him otherwise. He kept one in memory of Taylor, gave one to Klein, and gave the third to Jude.

Her duty to Clem not only took its toll upon her time but upon her focus. When, in the middle of the month, he suddenly announced that he was going to leave the next day for Tenerife, there to tan his troubles away for a fortnight, she was glad to be released from the daily duties of friend and comforter but found herself unable to rekindle the heat of ambition that had flared in her at the month's first hour. She had one unlikely touchstone, however: the dog. She only had to look at the mutt and she remembered—as though it were an hour ago—standing at the door of Gentle's flat and seeing the pair dissolving in front of her astonished eyes. And on the heels of that memory came thoughts of the news she had been carrying to Gentle that night: the dream journey induced by the stone that was now wrapped up and hidden from sight and seeing in her wardrobe. She was not a great lover of dogs, but she'd taken the mongrel home that night, knowing it would perish if she didn't. It quickly ingratiated itself, wagging a furious welcome when she returned home each night after being with Clem; sneaking into her bedroom in the early hours and making a nest for itself in her soiled clothes. She called it Skin, because it had so little fur, and while she didn't dote on it the way it doted on her, she was still glad of its company. More than once she found herself talking to it at great length, while it licked its paws or its balls, these monologues a means to refocus her thoughts without worrying that she was losing her mind. Three days after Clem's departure for sunnier climes, discussing with Skin how she should best proceed, Estabrook's name came up.

"You haven't met Estabrook," she told Skin. "But I'll guarantee you won't like him. He tried to have me killed, you know?"

The dog looked up from its toilet.

"Yes, I was amazed too," she said. "I mean, that's worse than an animal, right? No disrespect, but it is. I was his wife. I *am* his wife. And he tried to have me killed. What would you do, if you were me? Yes, I know, I should see him. He had the blue eye in his safe. And that book! Remind me to tell you about the book sometime. No, maybe I shouldn't. It'll give you ideas."

Skin settled his head on his crossed paws, gave a small sigh of contentment, and started to doze.

"You're a big help," she said. "I need some advice here. What do you say to a man who tried to have you murdered?"

Skin's eyes were closed, so she was obliged to furnish her own reply.

"I say: Hello, Charlie, why don't you tell me the story of your life?"

2

She called Lewis Leader the next day to find out whether Estabrook was still hospitalized. She was told he was, but that he'd been moved to a private clinic in Hampstead. Leader supplied details of his whereabouts, and Jude called to inquire both about Estabrook's condition and visiting hours. She was told he was still under close scrutiny but seemed to be in better spirits than he'd been, and she was welcome to come and see him at any time. There seemed little purpose in delaying the meeting. She drove up to Hampstead that very evening, through another tumultuous rainstorm, arriving to a welcome from the psychiatric nurse in charge of Estabrook's case, a chatty young man called Maurice who lost his top lip when he smiled, which was often, and talked with an almost indiscreet enthusiasm about the state of his patient's mind.

"He has good days," Maurice said brightly. Then, just as brightly: "But not many. He's severely depressed. He made one attempt to kill himself before he came to us, but he's settled down a lot."

"Is he sedated?"

"We help keep the anxiety controllable, but he's not drugged senseless. We can't help him get to the root of the problem if he is."

"Has he told you what that is?" she said, expecting accusations to be tossed in her direction.

"It's pretty obscure," Maurice said. "He talks about you very fondly, and I'm sure your coming will do him a great deal of good. But the problem's obviously with his blood relatives. I've got him to talk a little about his father and his brother, but he's very cagey. The father's dead, of course, but maybe you can shed some light on the brother."

"I never met him."

"That's a pity. Charles clearly feels a great deal of anger towards his brother, but I haven't got to the root of why. I will. It'll just take time. He's very good at keeping his secrets to himself, isn't he? But then you probably know that. Shall I take you along to see him? I *did* tell him you'd telephoned, so I think he's expecting you."

Jude was irritated that the element of surprise had been removed, that Estabrook would have had time to prepare his feints and fabrications. But what was done was done, and rather than snap at the gleeful Maurice for his indiscretion she kept her displeasure to herself. She might need the man's smiling assistance in the fullness of time.

Estabrook's room was pleasant enough. Spacious and comfortable, its walls adorned with reproductions of Monet and Renoir, it was a soothing space. Even the piano concerto that played softly in the background seemed composed to placate a troubled mind. Estabrook was not in bed but sitting by the window, one of the curtains drawn aside so he could watch the rain. He was dressed in pajamas and his best dressing gown, smoking. As Maurice had said, he was clearly awaiting his visitor. There was no flicker of surprise when she appeared at the door. And, as she'd anticipated, he had his welcome ready.

"At last, a familiar face."

He didn't open his arms to embrace her, but she went to him and kissed him lightly on both cheeks.

"One of the nurses will get you something to drink, if you'd like," he said.

"Yes, I'd like some coffee. It's bitter out there."

"Maybe Maurice'll get it, if I promise to unburden my soul."

"Do you?" said Maurice.

"I do. I promise. You'll know the secrets of my potty training by this time tomorrow."

"Milk and sugar?" Maurice asked.

"Just milk," Charlie said. "Unless her tastes have changed."

"No," she told him.

"Of course not. Judith doesn't change. Judith's eternal."

Maurice withdrew, leaving them to talk. There was no embarrassed silence. He had his spiel ready, and while he delivered it—a speech about how glad he was that she'd come, and how much he hoped it meant she would begin to forgive him—she studied his changed face. He'd lost weight and was without his toupée, which revealed in his physiognomy qualities she'd never seen before. His large nose and tugged-down mouth, with jutting over-large lower lip, lent him the look of an aristocrat fallen on hard times. She doubted that she'd ever find it in her heart to love him again, but she could certainly manage a twinge of pity, seeing him so reduced.

"I suppose you want a divorce," he said.

"We can talk about that another time."

"Do you need money?"

"Not at the moment."

"If you do—"

"I'll ask."

A male nurse appeared with coffee for Jude, hot chocolate for Estabrook, and biscuits. When he'd gone, she plunged into a confession. One from her, she reasoned, might elicit one from him.

"I went to the house," she said. "To collect my jewelry."

"And you couldn't get into the safe."

"Oh, no, I got in."

He didn't look at her, but sipped his chocolate noisily.

"And I found some very strange things, Charlie. I'd like to talk about them."

"I don't know what you mean."

"Some souvenirs. A piece of a statute. A book."

"No," he said, still not looking her way. "Those aren't mine. I don't know what they are. Oscar gave them to me to look after."

Here was an intriguing connection. "Where did Oscar get them?" she asked him.

"I didn't inquire," Estabrook said with a detached air. "He travels a lot, you know."

"I'd like to meet him."

"No, you wouldn't," he said hurriedly. "You wouldn't like him at all."

"Globe-trotters are always interesting," she said, attempting to preserve a lightness in her tone.

"I told you," he said. "You wouldn't like him."

"Has he been to see you?"

"No. And I wouldn't see him if he did. Why are you asking me these questions? You've never cared about Oscar before."

"He *is* your brother," she said. "He has some filial responsibility."

"Oscar? He doesn't care for anybody but himself. He only gave me those presents as a sop."

"So they *were* gifts. I thought you were just looking after them."

"Does it matter?" he said, raising his voice a little. "Just don't touch them, they're dangerous. You put them back, yes?"

She lied and told him she had, realizing any more discussion on the matter would only infuriate him further.

"Is there a view out of the window?" she asked him.

"Of the heath," he said. "It's very pretty on sunny days, apparently. They found a body there on Monday. A woman, strangled. I watched them combing the bushes all day yesterday and all day today: looking for clues, I suppose. In this weather. Horrible, to be out in this weather, digging around looking for soiled underwear or some such. Can you imagine? I thought: I'm damn lucky I'm in here, warm and cosy."

If there was any indication of a change in his mental processes it was here, in this strange digression. An earlier Estabrook would have had no patience with any conversation that was not serving a clear purpose. Gossip and its purveyors had drawn his contempt like little else, especially when he knew he was the subject of the tittle-tattle. As to gazing out of a window and wondering how others were faring in the cold, that would have been literally unthinkable two months before. She liked the change, just as she liked the newfound nobility in his profile. Seeing the hidden man revealed gave her faith in her own judgment. Perhaps it was this Estabrook she'd loved all along.

They spoke for a while more, without returning to any of the personal matters between them, and parted on friendly terms, with an embrace that was genuinely warm.

"When will you come again?" he asked her.

"In the next couple of days," she told him.

"I'll be waiting."

So the gifts she'd found in the safe had come from Oscar Godolphin. Oscar the mysterious, who'd kept the family name while brother Charles disowned it; Oscar the enigmatic; Oscar the globetrotter. How far afield had he gone, she wondered, to have returned with such outré trophies? Somewhere out of this world, perhaps, into the same remoteness to which she'd seen Gentle and Pie 'oh' pah dispatch themselves? She began to suspect that there was some conspiracy abroad. If two men who had no knowledge of each other, Oscar Godolphin and John Zacharias, knew about this other world and how to remove themselves there, how many others in her circle also knew? Was it information only available to men? Did it come with the penis and a mother fixation, as part of the male apparatus? Had Taylor known? Did Clem? Or was this some kind of family secret, and the part of the puzzle she was missing was the link between a Godolphin and a Zacharias?

Whatever the explanation, it was certain she would not get answers from Gentle, which meant she had to seek out brother Oscar. She tried by the most direct route first: the telephone directory. He wasn't listed. She then tried via Lewis Leader, but he claimed to have no knowledge of the man's whereabouts or fortunes, telling her that the affairs of the two brothers were quite separate, and he had never been called to deal with any matter involving Oscar Godolphin.

"For all I know," he said, "the man could be dead."

Having drawn a blank with the direct routes, she was thrown back upon the indirect. She returned to Estabrook's house and scoured it thoroughly, looking for Oscar's address or telephone number. She found neither, but she did turn up a photograph album Charlie had never shown to her, in which pictures of what she took to be the two brothers appeared. It wasn't difficult to distinguish one from the other. Even in those early pictures Charlie had the troubled look the camera always found in him, whereas

Oscar, younger by a few years, was nevertheless the more confident of the pair: a little overweight, but carrying it easily, smiling an easy smile as he hooked his arm around his brother's shoulders. She removed the most recent of the photographs from the album which pictured Charles at puberty or thereabouts, and kept it. Repetition, she found, made theft easier. But it was the only information about Oscar she took away with her. If she was to get to the traveler and find out in what world he'd bought his souvenirs, she'd have to work on Estabrook to do so. It would take time, and her impatience grew with every short and rainy day. Even though she had the freedom to buy a ticket anywhere on the planet, a kind of claustrophobia was upon her. There was another world to which she wanted access. Until she got it, Earth itself would be a prison.

3

Leader called Oscar on the morning of January seventeenth with the news that his brother's estranged wife was asking for information on his whereabouts.

"Did she say why?"

"No, not precisely. But she's very clearly sniffing after something. She's apparently seen Estabrook three times in the last week."

"Thank you, Lewis. I appreciate this."

"Appreciate it in hard cash, Oscar," Leader replied. "I've had a very expensive Christmas."

"When have you ever gone empty-handed?" Oscar said. "Keep me posted."

The lawyer promised to do so, but Oscar doubted he'd provide much more by way of useful information. Only truly despairing souls confided in lawyers, and he doubted Judith was the despairing type. He'd never met her—Charlie had seen to that—but if she'd survived his company for any time at all she had to have a will of iron. Which begged the question: Why would a woman who knew (presuming she did) that her husband had conspired to kill her, seek out his company, unless she had an ulterior motive? And was it conceivable that said motive was finding brother Oscar? If so, such curiosity had to be nipped in the bud. There were already enough variables at play, what with the Society's purge now under way, and the inevitable police investigation on its heels, not to mention his new majordomo Augustine (né Dowd), who was behaving in altogether too snotty a fashion. And of course, most volatile of these variables, sitting in his asylum beside the heath, Charlie himself, probably crazy, certainly unpredictable, with all manner of tidbits in his head which could do Oscar a lot of harm. It could be only a matter of time before he started to become talkative, and when he did, what better ear to drop his discretions into than that of his inquiring wife?

That evening he sent Dowd (he couldn't get used to that saintly Augustine) up to the clinic, with a basket of fruit for his brother.

"Find a friend there, if you can," he told Dowd. "I need to know what Charlie babbles about when he's being bathed."

"Why don't you ask him directly?"

"He hates me, that's why. He thinks I stole his mess of pottage when Papa introduced me into the Tabula Rasa instead of Charlie."

"Why did your father do that?"

"Because he knew Charlie was unstable, and he'd do the Society more harm than good. I've had him under control until now. He's had his little gifts from the Dominions. He's had you fawn upon him when he needed something out of the ordinary, like his assassin. This all started with that fucking assassin! Why couldn't you have just killed the woman yourself?"

"What do you take me for?" Dowd said with distaste. "I couldn't lay hands on a woman. Especially not a beauty."

"How do you know she's a beauty?"

"I've heard her talked about."

"Well, I don't care what she looks like. I don't want her meddling in my business. Find out what she's up to. Then we'll work out our response."

Dowd came back a few hours later, with alarming news. "Apparently she's persuaded him to take her to the estate."

"What? What?" Oscar bounded from his chair. The parrots rose up squawking in sympathy. "She knows more than she should. Shit! All that heartache to keep the Society out of our hair, and now this bitch comes along and we're in worse trouble than ever."

"Nothing's happened yet."

"But it will, it will! She'll wind him around her little finger, and he'll tell her everything."

"What do you want to do about it?"

Oscar went to hush the parrots. "Ideally?" he said, as he smoothed their ruffled wings. "Ideally I'd have Charlie vanish off the face of the earth."

"He had much the same ambition for her," Dowd observed.

"Meaning what?"

"Just that you're both quite capable of murder."

Oscar made a contemptuous grunt. "Charlie was only playing at it," he said. "He's got no balls! He's got no vision!" He returned to his high-backed chair, his expression sullen. "It's not going to hold, damn it," he said. "I can feel it in my gut. We've kept things neat and tidy so far, but it's not going to hold. Charlie has to be taken out of the equation."

"He's your brother."

"He's a burden."

"What I mean is: he's *your* brother. You should be the one to dispatch him."

Oscar's eyes widened. "Oh, my Lord," he said.

"Think what they'd say in Yzordderrex, if you were to tell them."

"What? That I killed my own brother? I don't see much charm in that."

"But that you did what you had to do, however unpalatable, to keep the secret safe." Dowd paused to let the idea blossom. "That sounds heroic to me. Think what they'll say."

"I'm thinking."

"It's your reputation in Yzordderrex you care about, isn't it, not what happens in the Fifth? You've said before that this world's getting duller all the time."

Oscar pondered this for a while. "Maybe I *should* slip away. Kill them both to make sure nobody ever knows where I've gone—"

"Where *we've* gone."

"—then slip away and pass into legend. Oscar Godolphin, who left his crazy brother dead beside his wife and disappeared. Oh, yes. That'd make quite a headline in Patashoqua." He mused a few moments more. "What's the classic sibling murder weapon?" he finally asked.

"The jawbone of an ass."

"Ridiculous."

"You'll think of something better."

"So I will. Make me a drink, Dowdie. And have one yourself. We'll drink to escape."

"Doesn't everybody?" Dowd replied, but the remark was lost on Godolphin, who was already plunged deep into murderous thought.

20

I

Gentle and Pie were six days on the Patashoquan Highway, days measured not by the watch on Pie's wrist but by the brightening and darkening of the peacock sky. On the fifth day the watch gave up the ghost anyway, maddened, Pie supposed, by the magnetic field surrounding a city of pyramids they passed. Thereafter, even though Gentle wanted to preserve some sense of how time was proceeding in the Dominion they'd left, it was virtually impossible. Within a few days their bodies were accommodating the rhythm of their new world, and he let his curiosity feast on more pertinent matters: chiefly, the landscape through which they were traveling.

It was diverse. In that first week they passed out of the plain into a region of lagoons—the Cosacosa—which took two days to cross, and thence into tracts of ancient conifers so tall that clouds hung in their topmost branches like the nests of ethereal birds. On the other side of this stupendous forest, the mountains Gentle had glimpsed days before came plainly into view. The range was called the Jokalaylau, Pie informed him, and legend had it that after the Mount of Lipper Bayak these heights had been Hapexamendios' next resting place as He'd crossed through the Dominions. It was no accident, it seemed, that the landscapes they passed through recalled those of the Fifth; they had been chosen for that similarity. The Unbeheld had strode the Imajica dropping seeds of humanity as He went—even to the very edge of His sanctum—in order to give the species He favored new challenges, and like any good gardener He'd dispersed them where they had the best hope of prospering. Where the native crop could be conquered or accommodated; where the living was hard enough to make sure only the most resilient survived, but the land fertile enough to feed their children; where rain came; where light came; where all the vicissitudes that strengthened a species by occasional calamity—tempest, earthquake, flood—were to hand.

But while there was much that any terrestrial traveler would have recognized, nothing, not the smallest pebble underfoot, was quite like its counterpart in the Fifth. Some of these disparities were too vast to be missed: the green-gold of the heavens, for instance, or the elephantine snails that grazed beneath the cloud-nested trees. Others were smaller but equally bizarre, like the wild dogs that ran along the highway now and then, hairless and shiny as patent leather; or grotesque, like the horned kites that swooped on any animal dead or near-dead on the road and only rose from their meals, purple wings opening like cloaks, when the vehicle was almost upon them; or absurd, like the bone-white lizards that congregated in their thousands along the edge of the lagoons, the urge to turn somersaults passing through their colonies in waves.

Perhaps finding some new response to these experiences was out of the question when the sheer proliferation of travelers' tales had all but exhausted the lexicon of discovery. But it nevertheless irritated Gentle to hear himself responding in clichés. The traveler moved by unspoilt beauty or appalled by native barbarism. The traveler touched by primitive wisdom or caught breathless by undreamt-of modernities. The traveler condescending; the traveler humbled; the traveler hungry for the next horizon or pining miserably for home. Of all these, perhaps only the last response never passed Gentle's lips. He thought of the Fifth only when it came up in conversation between himself and Pie, and that happened less and less as the practicalities of the moment pressed more heavily upon them. Food and sleeping quarters were easily come by at first, as was fuel for the car. There were small villages and hostelries along the highway, where Pie, despite an absence of hard cash, always managed to secure them sustenance and beds to sleep in. The mystif had a host of minor feits at its disposal, Gentle realized: ways to use its powers of seduction to make even the most rapacious hostelier pliant. But once they got beyond the forest, matters became more problematical. The bulk of the vehicles had turned off at the intersections, and the highway had degenerated from a well-serviced thoroughfare to a two-lane road, with more potholes than traffic. The vehicle Pie had stolen had not been designed for the rigors of long-distance travel. It started to show signs of fatigue, and with the mountains looming ahead it was decided they should stop at the next village and attempt to trade it in for a more reliable model.

"Perhaps something with breath in its body," Pie suggested.

"Speaking of which," Gentle said, "you never asked me about the Nullianac."

"What was there to ask?"

"How I killed it."

"I presumed you used a pneuma."

"You don't sound very surprised."

"How else would you have done it?" Pie said, quite reasonably. "You had the will, and you had the power."

"But where did I get it from?" Gentle said.

"You've always had it," Pie replied, which left Gentle nursing as many questions, or more, as he'd begun with. He started to formulate one, but something in the motion of the car began to nauseate him as he did so. "I think we'd better stop for a few minutes," he said. "I think I'm going to puke."

Pie brought the vehicle to a halt, and Gentle stepped out. The sky was darkening, and some night-blooming flower spiced the cooling air. On the slopes above them herds of pale-flanked beasts, relations of the yak but here called doeki, moved down through the twilight to their dormitory pastures, lowing as they came. The dangers of Vanaeph and the thronged highway outside Patashoqua seemed very remote. Gentle breathed deeply, and the nausea, like his questions, no longer vexed him. He looked up at the first stars. Some were red here, like Mars; others gold: fragments of the noon-day sky that refused to be extinguished.

"Is this Dominion another planet?" he asked Pie. "Are we in some other galaxy?"

"No. It's not space that separates the Fifth from the rest of the Dominions, it's the In Ovo."

"So, is the whole of planet Earth the Fifth Dominion, or just part of it?"

"I don't know," Pie said. "*All,* I assume. But everyone has a different theory."

"What's yours?"

"Well, when we move between the Reconciled Dominions, you'll see it's very easy. There are countless passing places between the Fourth and the Third, the Third and the Second. We'll walk into a mist, and we'll come out into another world. Simple. But I don't think the borders are fixed. I think they move over the centuries, and the shapes of the Dominions change. So maybe it'll be the same with the Fifth. If it's reconciled, the borders will spread, until the whole planet has access to the rest of the Dominions. The truth is, nobody really knows what the Imajica looks like, because nobody's ever made a map."

"Somebody should try."

"Maybe you're the man to do it," Pie said. "You were an artist before you were a traveler."

"I was a faker, not an artist."

"But your hands are clever," Pie replied.

"Clever," Gentle said softly, "but never inspired."

This melancholy thought took him back, momentarily, to Klein, and to the rest of the circle he'd left in the Fifth: to Jude, Clem, Estabrook, Vanessa, and the rest. What were they doing this fine night? Had they even noticed his departure? He doubted it.

"Are you feeling any better?" Pie inquired. "I see some lights down the road a little way. It may be the last outpost before the mountains."

"I'm in good shape," Gentle said, climbing back into the car.

They'd proceeded perhaps a quarter of a mile, and were in sight of the village, when their progress was brought to a halt by a young girl who appeared from the dusk to herd her doeki across the road. She was in every way a normal thirteen-year-old child but for one: her face, and those parts of her body revealed by her simple dress, were sleek with fawny down. It was plaited where it grew long at her elbows, and her temples, and tied in a row of ribbons at her nape.

"What village is this?" Pie asked, as the last of the doeki lingered in the road.

"Beatrix," she said, and without prompting added, "There is no better place in any heaven." Then, shooing the last beast on its way, she vanished into the twilight.

2

The streets of Beatrix weren't as narrow as those of Vanaeph, nor were they designed for motor vehicles. Pie parked the car close to the outskirts, and the two of them ambled into the village from there. The houses were unpretentious affairs, raised of an ocher stone and surrounded by stands of vegetation that were a cross between silver birch and bamboo. The lights Pie had spotted from a distance weren't those that burned in the windows, but lanterns that hung in these trees, throwing their mellow light across the streets. Just about every copse boasted its lantern trimmers— shaggy-faced children like the herder—some squatting beneath the trees, others perched precariously in their branches. The doors of almost all the houses stood open, and music drifted from several, tunes caught by the lantern trimmers and danced to in the dapple. Asked to guess, Gentle would have said life was good here. Slow, perhaps, but good.

"We can't cheat these people," Gentle said. "It wouldn't be honorable."

"Agreed," Pie replied.

"So what do we do for money?"

"Maybe they'll agree to cannibalize the vehicle for a good meal and a horse or two."

"I don't see any horses."

"A doeki would be fine."

"They look slow."

Pie directed Gentle's gaze up the heights of the Jokalaylau. The last traces of day still lingered on the snowfields, but for all their beauty the mountains were vast and uninviting.

"Slow and certain is safer up there," Pie said. Gentle took Pie's point. "I'm going to see if I can find somebody in charge," the mystif went on, and left Gentle's side to go and question one of the lantern trimmers.

Drawn by the sound of raucous laughter, Gentle wandered on a little farther, and turning a corner he found two dozen of the villagers, mostly men and boys, standing in front of a marionette theater that had been set up in the lee of one of the houses. The show they were watching contrasted violently with the benign atmosphere of the village. To judge by the spires painted on the backdrop the story was set in Patashoqua, and as Gentle joined the audience two characters, one a grossly fat woman, the other a man with the proportions of a fetus and the endowment of a donkey, were in the middle of a domestic tiff so frenzied the spires were shaking. The puppeteers, three slim young men with identical mustaches, were plainly visible above the booth and provided both the dialogue and the sound effects, the former larded with baroque obscenities. Now another character entered—this a hunchbacked sibling of Pulcinella—and summarily beheaded Donkey Dick. The head flew to the ground, where the fat woman knelt to sob over it. As she did so, cherubic wings unfolded from behind its ears and it floated up into the sky, accompanied by a falsetto din from the puppeteers. This earned applause from the audience, during which Gentle caught sight of Pie in the street. At the mystif's side was a jug-eared adolescent with hair down to the middle of his back. Gentle went to join them.

"This is Efreet Splendid," Pie said. "He tells me—wait for this—he tells me his mother has dreams about white furless men and would like to meet you."

The grin that broke through Efreet's facial thatch was crooked but beguiling.

"She'll like you," he announced.

"Are you sure?" Gentle said.

"Certainly!"

"Will she feed us?"

"For a furless whitey, anything," Efreet replied.

Gentle threw the mystif a doubtful glance. "I hope you know what we're doing," he said.

Efreet led the way, chattering as he went, asking mostly about Patashoqua. It was, he said, his ambition to see the great city. Rather than disappoint the boy by admitting that he hadn't stepped inside the gates, Gentle informed him that it was a place of untold magnificence.

"Especially the Merrow Ti' Ti'," he said.

The boy grinned and said he'd tell everybody he knew that he'd met a hairless white man who'd seen the Merrow Ti' Ti'. From such innocent lies, Gentle mused, legends came.

At the door of the house, Efreet stood aside, to let Gentle be first over the threshold. He startled the woman inside with his appearance. She dropped the cat she was combing and instantly fell to her knees. Embarrassed, Gentle asked her to stand, but it was only after much persuasion that she did so, and even then she kept her head bowed, watching him furtively from the corners of her small dark eyes. She was short—barely taller than her son, in fact—her face fine-boned beneath its down. Her name was Larumday, she said, and she would very happily extend to Gentle and his lady (as she assumed Pie to be) the hospitality of her house. Her younger son, Emblem, was coerced into helping her prepare food while Efreet talked about where they could find a buyer for the car. Nobody in the village had any use for such a vehicle, he said, but in the hills was a man who might. His name was Coaxial Tasko, and it came as a considerable shock to Efreet that neither Gentle nor Pie had heard of the man.

"Everybody knows Wretched Tasko," he said. "He used to be a king in the Third Dominion, but his tribe's extinct."

"Will you introduce me to him in the morning?" Pie asked.

"That's a long time off," Efreet said.

"Tonight then," Pie replied, and it was thus agreed between them.

The food, when it came, was simpler than the fare they'd been served along the highway but no less tasty for that: doeki meat marinated in a root wine, accompanied by bread, a selection of pickled goods—including eggs the size of small loaves—and a broth which stung the throat like chili, bringing tears to Gentle's eyes, much to Efreet's undisguised amusement. While they ate and drank—the wine strong, but downed by the boys like water—Gentle asked about the marionette show he'd seen. Ever eager to parade his knowledge, Efreet explained that the puppeteers were on their way to Patashoqua ahead of the Autarch's host, who were coming over the mountains in the next few days. The puppeteers were very famous in Yzordderrex, he said, at which point Larumday hushed him.

"But, Mams—" he began.

"I said *hush*. I won't have talk of that place in this house. Your father went there and never came back. Remember that."

"I want to go there when I've seen the Merrow Ti' Ti', like Mr. Gentle," Efreet replied defiantly, and earned a sharp slap on the head for his troubles.

"Enough," Larumday said. "We've had too much talk tonight. A little silence would be welcome."

The conversation dwindled thereafter, and it wasn't until the meal was finished and Efreet was preparing to take Pie up the hill to meet Wretched Tasko, that the boy's mood brightened and his spring of enthusiasms burst forth afresh. Gentle was ready to join them, but Efreet explained that his mother—who was presently out of the room—wanted him to stay.

"You should accommodate her," Pie remarked when the boy had headed out. "If Tasko doesn't want the car we may have to sell your body."

"I thought you were the expert on that, not me," Gentle replied.

"Now, now," Pie said, with a grin. "I thought we'd agreed not to mention my dubious past."

"So go," Gentle said. "Leave me to her tender mercies. But you'll have to pick the fluff from between my teeth."

He found Mother Splendid in the kitchen, kneading dough for the morrow's bread.

"You've honored our home, coming here and sharing our table," she said as she worked. "And please, don't think badly of me for asking, but . . ."—her voice became a frightened whisper—"what do you want?"

"Nothing," Gentle replied. "You've already been more than generous."

She looked at him balefully, as though he was being cruel, teasing her in this fashion.

"I've dreamt about somebody coming here," she said. "White and furless, like you. I wasn't sure whether it was a man or a woman, but now you're here, sitting at the table, I know it was you."

First Tick Raw, he thought, now Mother Splendid. What was it about his face that made people think they knew him? Did he have a doppelgänger wandering around the Fourth?

"Who do you think I am?" he said.

"I don't know," she replied. "But I knew that when you came everything would change."

Her eyes suddenly filled with tears as she spoke, and they ran down the silky fur on her cheeks. The sight of her distress in turn distressed him, not least because he knew he was the cause of it, but he didn't know why. Undoubtedly she had dreamt of him—the look of shocked recognition on her face when he'd first stepped over the threshold was ample evidence of that—but what did that fact signify? He and Pie were here by chance. They'd be gone again by morning, passing through the millpond of Beatrix leaving nary a ripple. He had no significance in the life of the Splendid household, except as a subject of conversation when he'd gone.

"I hope your life doesn't change," he said to her. "It seems very pleasant here."

"It is," she said, wiping the tears away. "This is a safe place. It's good to raise children here. I know Efreet will leave soon. He wants to see Patashoqua, and I won't be able to stop him. But Emblem will stay. He likes the hills, and tending the doeki."

"And you'll stay too?"

"Oh, yes. I've done my wandering," she said. "I lived in Yzordderrex, near the Oke T'Noon, when I was young. That's where I met Eloign. We moved away as soon as we were married. It's a terrible city, Mr. Gentle."

"If it's so bad, why did he go back there?"

"His brother joined the Autarch's army, and when Eloign heard he went back to try and make him desert. He said it brought shame on the family to have a brother taking a wage from an orphan-maker."

"A man of principle."

"Oh, yes," said Larumday, with fondness in her voice. "He's a fine man. Quiet, like Emblem, but with Efreet's curiosity. All the books in this house are his. There's nothing he won't read."

"How long has he been away?"

"Too long," she said. "I'm afraid perhaps his brother's killed him."

"A brother kill a brother?" Gentle said. "No. I can't believe that."

"Yzorderrex does strange things to people, Mr. Gentle. Even good men lose their way."

"Only men?" Gentle said.

"It's men who make this world," she said. "The Goddesses have gone, and men have their way everywhere."

There was no accusation in this. She simply stated it as fact, and he had no evidence to contradict it with. She asked him if he'd like her to brew tea, but he declined, saying he wanted to go out and take the air, perhaps find Pie 'oh' pah.

"She's very beautiful," Larumday said. "Is she wise as well?"

"Oh, yes," he said. "She's wise."

"That's not usually the way with beauties, is it?" she said. "It's strange that I didn't dream her at the table, too."

"Maybe you did, and you've forgotten."

She shook her head. "Oh, no, I've had the dream too many times, and it's always the same: a white furless someone sitting at my table, eating with me and my sons."

"I wish I could have been a more sparkling guest," he said.

"But you're just the beginning, aren't you?" she said. "What comes after?"

"I don't know," he said. "Maybe your husband, home from Yzorderrex."

She looked doubtful. "Something," she said. "Something that'll change us all."

3

Efreet had said the climb would be easy, and measuring it in terms of incline, so it was. But the darkness made an easy route difficult, even for one as light-footed as Pie 'oh' pah. Efreet was an accommodating guide, however, slowing his pace when he realized Pie was lagging behind and warning of places where the ground was uncertain. After a time they were high above the village, with the snow-clad peaks of the Jokalaylau visible above the backs of the hills in which Beatrix slept. High and majestic as those mountains were, the lower slopes of peaks yet more monumental were visible beyond them, their heads lost in cumulus. Not far now, the boy said, and this time his promises were good. Within a few yards Pie spotted a building silhouetted against the sky, with a light burning on its porch.

"Hey, Wretched!" Efreet started to call. "Someone to see you! Someone to see you!"

There was no reply forthcoming, however, and when they reached the house itself the only living occupant was the flame in the lamp. The door stood open; there was food on the table. But of Wretched Tasko there was no sign. Efreet went out to search around, leaving Pie on the porch. Animals corralled behind the house stamped and muttered in the darkness; there was a palpable unease.

Efreet came back moments later. "I see him up the hill! He's almost at the top."

"What's he doing there?" Pie asked.

"Watching the sky, maybe. We'll go up. He won't mind."

They continued to climb, their presence now noticed by the figure standing on the hill's higher reaches. "Who is this?" he called down.

"It's only Efreet, Mr. Tasko. I'm with a friend."

"Your voice is too loud, boy," the man returned. "Keep it low, will you?"

"He wants us to keep quiet," Efreet whispered.

"I understand."

There was a wind blowing on these heights, and its chill put the mystif in mind of the fact that neither Gentle nor itself had clothes appropriate to the journey that lay ahead of them. Coaxial clearly climbed here regularly; he was wearing a shaggy coat and a hat with fur ear warmers. He was very clearly not a local man. It would have taken three of the villagers to equal his mass or strength, and his skin was almost as dark as Pie's.

"This is my friend Pie 'oh' pah," Efreet whispered to him when they were at his side.

"Mystif," Tasko said instantly.

"Yes."

"Ah. So you're a stranger?"

"Yes."

"From Yzordderrex?"

"No."

"That's to the good, at least. But so many strangers, and all on the same night. What are we to make of it?"

"Are there others?" said Efreet.

"Listen," Tasko said, casting his gaze over the valley to the darkened slopes beyond. "Don't you hear the machines?"

"No. Just the wind."

Tasko's response was to pick the boy up and physically point him in the direction of the sound.

"Now *listen!*" he said fiercely.

The wind carried a low rumble that might have been distant thunder, but that it was unbroken. Its source was certainly not the village below, nor did it seem likely there were earthworks in the hills. This was the sound of engines, moving through the night.

"They're coming towards the valley."

Efreet made a whoop of pleasure, which was cut short by Tasko slapping his hand over the boy's mouth.

"Why so happy, child?" he said. "Have you never learned fear? No, I don't suppose you have. Well, learn it now." He held Efreet so tightly the boy struggled to be free. "Those machines are from Yzordderrex. From the Autarch. Do you understand?"

Growling his displeasure he let go, and Efreet backed away from him, at least as nervous of Tasko now as of the distant machines. The man hawked up a wad of phlegm and spat it in the direction of the sound.

"Maybe they'll pass us by," he said. "There are other valleys they could choose. They may not come through ours." He spat again. "Ach, well, there's no purpose in staying up here. If they come, they come." He turned to Efreet. "I'm sorry if I was rough, boy," he said. "But I've heard these machines before. They're the same that killed my people. Take it from me, they're nothing to whoop about. Do you understand?"

"Yes," Efreet said, though Pie doubted he did. The prospect of a visitation from these thundering things held no horror for him, only exhilaration.

"So tell me what you want, mystif," Tasko said as he started back down the hill. "You didn't climb all the way up here to watch the stars. Or maybe you did. Are you in love?"

Efreet tittered in the darkness behind them.

"If I were I wouldn't talk about it," Pie replied.

"So what, then?"

"I came here with a friend, from . . . some considerable distance, and our vehicle's nearly defunct. We need to trade it in for animals."

"Where are you heading?"

"Up into the mountains."

"Are you prepared for that journey?"

"No. But it has to be taken."

"The faster you're out of the valley the safer we'll be, I think. Strangers attract strangers."

"Will you help us?"

"Here's my offer, mystif," Tasko said. "If you leave Beatrix now, I'll see they give you supplies and two doeki. But you must be quick."

"I understand."

"If you go now, maybe the machines will pass us by."

4

Without anyone to lead him, Gentle had soon lost his way on the dark hill. But rather than turning around and heading back to await Pie in Beatrix, he continued to climb, drawn by the promise of a view from the heights and a wind to clear his head. Both took his breath away: the wind with its chill, the panorama with its sweep. Ahead, range upon range receded into mist and distance, the farthest heights so vast he doubted the Fifth Dominion could boast their equal. Behind him, just visible between the softer silhouettes of the foothills, were the forests which they'd driven through.

Once again, he wished he had a map of the territory, so that he could begin to grasp the scale of the journey they were undertaking. He tried to lay the landscape out on a page in his mind, like a sketch for a painting, with this vista of mountains, hills, and plain as the subject. But the fact of the scene before him overwhelmed his attempt to make symbols of it; to reduce it and set it down. He let the problem go and turned his eyes back towards the Jokalaylau. Before his gaze reached its destination, it came to rest on the hill slopes directly across from him. He was suddenly aware of the valley's symmetry, hills rising to the same height, left and right. He studied the slopes opposite. It was a nonsensical quest, seeking a sign of life at such a distance, but the more he squinted at the hill's face the more certain he became that it was a dark mirror, and that somebody as yet unseen was studying the shadows in which he stood, looking for some sign of him as he in his turn searched for them. The notion intrigued him at first, but then it began to make him afraid. The chill in his skin worked its way into his innards. He began to shiver inside, afraid to move for fear that this other, whoever or whatever it was, would see him and, in the seeing, bring calamity. He remained motionless for a long time, the wind coming in frigid gusts and bringing with it sounds he hadn't heard until now: the rumble of machinery; the complaint of unfed animals; sobbing. The sounds and the seeker on the mirror hill belonged together, he knew. This other had not come alone. It had engines and beasts. It brought tears.

As the cold reached his marrow, he heard Pie 'oh' pah calling his name, way down the hill. He prayed the wind wouldn't veer and carry the call, and thus his whereabouts, in the direction of the watcher. Pie continued to call for him, the voice getting nearer as the mystif climbed through the darkness. He endured five terrible minutes of this, his system racked by contrary desires: part of him desperately wanting Pie here with him, embracing him, telling him that the fear upon him was ridiculous; the other part in terror that Pie would find him and thus reveal his whereabouts to the creature on the other hill.

At last, the mystif gave up its search and retraced its steps down into the secure streets of Beatrix. Gentle didn't break cover, however. He waited another quarter of an hour until his aching eyes discovered a motion on the opposite slope. The watcher was giving up his post, it seemed, moving around the back of the hill. Gentle caught a glimpse of his silhouette as he disappeared over the brow, just enough to confirm that the other had indeed been human, at least in shape if not in spirit. He waited another minute, then started down the slope. His extremities were numb, his teeth chattering, his torso rigid with cold, but he went quickly, falling and descending several yards on his buttocks, much to the startlement of dozing doeki. Pie was below, waiting at the door of Mother Splendid's house. Two saddled and bridled beasts stood in the street, one being fed a palmful of fodder by Efreet.

"Where did you go?" Pie wanted to know. "I came looking for you."

"Later," Gentle said. "I have to get warm."

"No time," Pie replied. "The deal is we get the doeki, food, and coats if we go immediately."

"They're very eager to get rid of us suddenly."

"Yes, we are," said a voice from beneath the trees opposite the house. A black man with pale, mesmeric eyes stepped into view. "You're Zacharias?"

"I am."

"I'm Coaxial Tasko, called the Wretched. The doeki are yours. I've given the mystif some supplies to set you on your way, but please . . . tell nobody you've been here."

"He thinks we're bad luck," Pie said.

"He could be right," said Gentle. "Am I allowed to shake your hand, Mr. Tasko, or is that bad luck, too?"

"You may shake my hand," the man said.

"Thank you for the transport. I swear we'll tell nobody we were here. But I may want to mention you in my memoirs."

A smile broke over Tasko's stern features.

"You may do that too," he said, shaking Gentle's hand. "But not till I'm dead, huh? I don't like scrutiny."

"That's fair."

"Now, please . . . the sooner you're gone the sooner we can pretend we never saw you."

Efreet came forward, bearing a coat, which Gentle put on. It reached to his shins and smelled strongly of the animal who'd been born in it, but it was welcome.

"Mother says goodbye," the boy told Gentle. "She won't come out and see you." He lowered his voice to an embarrassed whisper. "She's crying a lot."

Gentle made a move towards the door, but Tasko checked him. "Please, Mr. Zacharias, no delays," he said. "Go now, with our blessing, or not at all."

"He means it," Pie said, climbing up onto his doeki, the animal casting a backward glance at its rider as it was mounted. "We have to go."

"Don't we even discuss the route?"

"Tasko has given me a compass and directions." The mystif pointed to a narrow trail that led up out of the village. "That's the way we take."

Reluctantly, Gentle put his foot in the doeki's leather stirrup and hoisted himself into the saddle. Only Efreet managed a goodbye, daring Tasko's wrath to press his hand into Gentle's.

"I'll see you in Patashoqua one day," he said.

"I hope so," Gentle replied.

That being the full sum of their farewells, Gentle was left with the sense of an exchange broken in midsentence, and now permanently unfinished. But they were at least going on from the village better equipped for the terrain ahead than they'd been when they entered.

"What was all that about?" Gentle asked Pie, when they were on the ridge above Beatrix, and the trail was about to turn and take its tranquil lamp-lit streets from sight.

"A battalion of the Autarch's army is passing through the hills, on its way to Patashoqua. Tasko was afraid the presence of strangers in the village would give the soldiers an excuse for marauding."

"So that's what I heard on the hill."

"That's what you heard."

"And I saw somebody on the other hill. I swear he was looking for me. No, that's not right. Not me, but somebody. That's why I didn't answer when you came looking for me."

"Any idea who it was?"

Gentle shook his head. "I just felt his stare. Then I got a glimpse of somebody on the ridge. Who knows? It sounds absurd now I say it."

"There was nothing absurd about the noises I heard. The best thing we can do is get out of this region as fast as possible."

"Agreed."

"Tasko said there was a place to the northeast of here, where the border of the Third reaches into this Dominion a good distance—maybe a thousand miles. We could shorten our journey if we made for it."

"That sounds good."

"But it means taking the High Pass."

"That sounds bad."

"It'll be faster."

"It'll be fatal," Gentle said. "I want to see Yzordderrex. I don't want to die frozen stiff in the Jokalaylau."

"Then we go the long way?"

"That's my vote."

"It'll add two or three weeks to the journey."

"And years to our lives," Gentle replied.

"As if we haven't lived long enough," Pie remarked.

"I've always held to the belief," Gentle said, "that you can never live too long or love too many women."

5

The doeki were obedient and surefooted mounts, negotiating the track whether it was churned mud or dust and pebbles, seemingly indifferent to the ravines that gaped inches from their hooves at one moment and the white waters that wound beside them the next. All this in the dark, for although the hours passed, and it seemed dawn should have crept up over the hills, the peacock sky hid its glory in a starless gloom.

"Is it possible the nights are longer up here than they were down on the highway?" Gentle wondered.

"It seems so," Pie said. "My bowels tell me the sun should have been up hours ago."

"Do you always calculate the passage of time by your bowels?"

"They're more reliable than your beard," Pie replied.

"Which direction is the light going to come from when it comes?" Gentle asked, turning in his saddle to scan the horizon.

As he craned around to look back the way they'd come, a murmur of distress escaped his lips.

"What is it?" the mystif said, bringing its beast to a halt and following Gentle's gaze.

It didn't need telling. A column of black smoke was rising from the cradle of the hills, its lower plumes tinged with fire. Gentle was already slipping from his saddle, and now he scrambled up the rock face at their side to get a better sense of the fire's location. He lingered only seconds at the top before scrambling down, sweating and panting.

"We have to turn back," he said.

"Why?"

"Beatrix is burning."

"How can you tell from this distance?" Pie said.

"I know, damn it! Beatrix is burning! We have to go back." He climbed onto his doeki and started to haul it around on the narrow path.

"Wait," said Pie. "Wait, for God's sake!"

"We have to help them," Gentle said, against the rock face. "They were good to us."

"Only because they wanted us out!" Pie replied.

"Well, now the worst's happened, and we have to do what we can."

"You used to be more rational than this."

"What do you mean, *used to be*? You don't know anything about me, so don't start making judgments. If you won't come with me, fuck you!"

The doeki was fully turned now, and Gentle dug his heels into its flanks to make it pick up speed. There had only been three or four places along the route where the road had divided. He was certain he could retrace their steps back to Beatrix without much problem. And if he was right, and it was the town that was burning up ahead, he would have the column of smoke as a grim marker.

The mystif followed, after a time, as Gentle knew it must. It was happy to be called a friend, but somewhere in its soul it was a slave.

They didn't speak as they traveled, which was not surprising given their last exchange. Only once, as they mounted a ridge that laid the vista of foothills before them, with the valley in which Beatrix nestled still out of sight but unequivocally the source of the smoke, did Pie 'oh' pah murmur, "Why is it always fire?" and Gentle realized how insensitive he'd been to his companion's reluctance to return. The devastation that undoubtedly lay before them was an echo of the fire in which its adopted family had perished— a matter that had gone undiscussed between them since.

"Shall I go from here without you?" he asked.

The mystif shook its head. "Together, or not at all," it said.

The route became easier to negotiate from there on. The inclines were mellower and the track itself better kept, but there was also light in the sky, as the long-delayed dawn finally came. By the time they finally laid their eyes on the remains of Beatrix, the peacock-tail glory Gentle had first admired in the heavens over Patashoqua was overhead, its glamour making grimmer still the scene laid below. Beatrix was still burning fitfully, but the fire had consumed most of the houses and their birch-bamboo arbors. He brought his doeki to a halt and scoured the place from this vantage point. There was no sign of Beatrix's destroyers.

"On foot from here?" Gentle said.

"I think so."

They tethered the beasts and descended into the village. The sound of lamentation reached them before they were within its perimeters, the sobbing, emerging as it did from the murk of the smoke, reminding Gentle of the sounds he'd heard while keeping his vigil on the hill. The destruction around them now was some-how a consequence of that sightless encounter, he knew. Though he'd avoided the eye of the watcher in the darkness, his presence had been suspected, and that had been enough to bring this calamity upon Beatrix.

"I'm responsible," he said. "God help me . . . I'm responsible."

He turned to the mystif, who was standing in the middle of the street, its features drained of blood and expression.

"Stay here," Gentle said. "I'm going to find the family."

Pie didn't register any response, but Gentle assumed what he'd said had been understood and headed off in the direction of the Splendids' house. It wasn't simply fire that had undone Beatrix. Some of the houses had been toppled unburned, the copses around them uprooted. There was no sign of fatalities, however, and Gentle began to hope that Coaxial Tasko had persuaded the villagers to take to the hills before Beatrix's violators had ap-peared out of the night. That hope was dashed when he came to the place where the Splendids' home had stood. It was rubble, like the others, and the smoke from its burning timbers had concealed from him until now the horror heaped in front of it. Here were the good people of Beatrix, shoveled together in a bleeding pile higher than his head. There were a few sobbing survivors at the heap, looking for their loved ones in the confusion of broken bod-ies, some clutching at limbs they thought they recognized, others simply kneeling in the bloody dirt, keening.

Gentle walked around the pile, searching among the mourners for a face he knew. One fellow he'd seen laughing at the show was cradling in his arms a wife or sister whose body was as lifeless as the puppets he'd taken such pleasure in. Another, a woman, was burrowing in among the bodies, yelling somebody's name. He went to help her, but she screamed at him to stay away. As he retreated he caught sight of Efreet. The boy was in the heap, his eyes open, his mouth—which had been the vehicle for such unalloyed enthusiasms—beaten in by a rifle butt or a boot. At that moment Gentle wanted nothing—not life itself—as much as he wanted the bastard who'd done this, standing in his sights. He felt the killing breath hot in his throat, itching to be merciless.

He turned from the heap, looking for some target, even if it wasn't the murderer himself. Someone with a gun or a uniform, a man he could call the enemy. He couldn't remember ever feeling this way before, but then he'd never possessed the power he had now—or rather, if Pie was to be believed, he'd had it without recognizing the fact—and agonizing as these horrors were, it was salve to his distress, knowing there was such a capacity for cleansing in him: that his lungs, throat, and palm could take the guilty out of life with such ease. He headed away from the cairn of flesh, ready to be an executioner at the first invitation.

The street twisted, and he followed its convolutions, turning a corner to find the way ahead blocked by one of the invaders' war machines. He stopped in his tracks, expecting it to turn its steel eyes upon him. It was a perfect death-bringer, armored as a crab, its wheels bristling with bloodied scythes, its turret with armaments. But death had found the bringer. Smoke rose from the turret, and the driver lay where the fire had found him, in the act of scrabbling from the machine's stomach. A small victory, but one that at least proved the machines had frailties. Come another day, that knowledge might be the difference between hope and despair. He was turning his back on the machine when he heard his name called, and Tasko appeared from behind the smoking carcass. Wretched he was, his face bloodied, his clothes filthy with dust.

"Bad timing, Zacharias," he said. "You left too late and now you come back, too late again."

"Why did they do this?"

"The Autarch doesn't need reasons."

"He was here?" Gentle said. The thought that the Butcher of Yzorddderrex had stood in Beatrix made his heart beat faster.

But Tasko said, "Who knows? Nobody's ever seen his face. Maybe he was here yesterday, counting the children, and nobody even noticed him."

"Do you know where Mother Splendid is?"

"In the heap somewhere."

"Jesus . . ."

"She wouldn't have made a very good witness. She was too crazy with grief. They left alive the ones who'd tell the story best. Atrocities need witnesses, Zacharias. People to spread the word."

"They did this as a warning?" Gentle said.

Tasko shook his huge head. "I don't know how their minds work," he said.

"Maybe we have to learn, so we can stop them."

"I'd prefer to die," the man replied, "than understand filth like that. If you've got the appetite, then go to Yzorddderrex. You'll get your education there."

"I want to help here," Gentle said. "There must be something I can do."

"You can leave us to mourn."

If there was any profounder dismissal, Gentle didn't know it. He searched for some word of comfort or apology, but in the face of such devastation only silence seemed appropriate. He bowed his head, and left Tasko to the burden of being a witness, returning up the street past the heap of corpses to where Pie 'oh' pah was standing. The mystif hadn't moved an inch, and even when Gentle came abreast of it, and quietly told it they should go, it was a long time before it looked round at him.

"We shouldn't have come back," it said.

"Every day we waste, this is going to happen again. . . ."

"You think you can stop it?" Pie said, with a trace of sarcasm.

"We won't go the long way around, we'll go through the mountains. Save ourselves three weeks."

"You *do,* don't you?" Pie said. "You think you can stop this."

"We won't die," Gentle said, putting his arms around Pie 'oh' pah. "I won't let us. I came here to understand, and I will."

"How much more of this can you take?"

"As much as I have to."

"I may remind you of that."

"I'll remember," Gentle said. "After this, I'll remember everything."

21

I

The Retreat at the Godolphin estate had been built in an age of follies, when the oldest sons of the rich and mighty, having no wars to distract them, amused themselves spending the gains of generations on buildings whose only function was to flatter their egos.

Most of these lunacies, designed without care for basic architectural principles, were dust before their designers. A few, however, became noteworthy even in neglect, either because somebody associated with them had lived or died in notoriety or because they were the scene of some drama.

The Retreat fell into both categories. Its architect, Geoffrey Light, had died within six months of its completion, choked by a bull's pizzle in the wilds of West Riding, a grotesquerie which attracted some attention—as did the retirement from the public eye of Light's patron, Lord Joshua Godolphin, whose decline into insanity was the talk of court and coffeehouse for many years. Even at his zenith he'd attracted gossip, mainly because he kept the company of magicians. Cagliostro, the Comte de St. Germain, and even Casanova (reputedly no mean thaumaturgist) had spent time on the estate, as well as a host of lesser-known practitioners.

His Lordship had made no secret of his occult investigations, though the work he was truly undertaking was never known to the gossips. They assumed he kept company with these mountebanks for their entertainment value. Whatever his reasons, the fact that he retired from sight so suddenly drew further attention to his last indulgence, the folly Light had built for him. A diary purporting to have belonged to the choked architect appeared a year after his demise, containing an account of the Retreat's construction. Whether it was the genuine article or not, it made bizarre reading. The foundations had been laid, it said, under stars calculated to be particularly propitious; the masons—sought and hired in a dozen cities—had been sworn to silence with an oath of Arabic ferocity. The stones themselves had been individually baptized in a mixture of milk and frankincense, and a lamb had been allowed to wander through the half-completed building three times, the altar and font placed where it had laid its innocent head.

Of course these details were soon corrupted by repetition, and Satanic purpose ascribed to the building. It became babies' blood that was used to anoint the stone, and a mad dog's grave that marked the spot where the altar was built. Sealed up behind the high walls of his sanctum, it was doubtful that Lord Godolphin even knew that such rumors were circulating until, two Septembers after his withdrawal, the inhabitants of Yoke, the village closest to the estate, needing a scapegoat to blame the poor harvest upon and inflamed by a passage from Ezekiel delivered from the pulpit of the parish church, used the Sunday afternoon to mount a crusade against the Devil's work and climbed the gates of the estate to raze the Retreat. They found none of the promised blasphemies: no inverted cross, no altar stained with virginal blood. But having trespassed they did what damage they could inflict out of sheer frustration, finally setting a bonfire of baled hay in the middle of the great mosaic. All the flames did was lick the place black, and the Retreat earned its nickname from that afternoon: the Black Chapel; or, Godolphin's Sin.

2

If Jude had known anything about the history of Yoke, she might well have looked for signs of its echoes in the village as she drove through. She would have had to look hard, but the signs were there to be found. There was scarcely a house within its bounds that didn't have a cross carved into the keystone above the door or a horseshoe cemented into the doorstep. If she'd had time to linger in the churchyard she would have found, inscribed on the stones there, entreaties to the good Lord that He keep the Devil from the living even as he gathered the dead to His Bosom, and on the board beside the gate a notice announcing that next Sunday's sermon would be "The Lamb in Our Lives," as though to banish any lingering thought of the infernal goat.

She saw none of these signs, however. It was the road and the man at her side—with occasional words of comfort directed towards the dog on the back seat—that consumed her attention. Getting Estabrook to bring her here had been a spur-of-the-moment inspiration, but there was sound logic behind it. She would be his freedom for a day, taking him out of the clinic's stale heat into the bracing January air. It was her hope that out in the open he might talk more freely about his family, and more particularly about brother Oscar. What better place to innocently inquire about the Godolphins and their history than in the grounds of the house Charlie's forefathers had built?

The estate lay half a mile beyond the village, along a private road that led to a gateway besieged, even in this sterile season, by a green army of bushes and creepers. The gates themselves had long ago been removed and a less elegant defense against trespasses raised: boards and corrugated iron covered with barbed wire. The storms of early December had brought down much of this barricade, however, and once the car was parked, and they both approached the gateway—Skin bounding ahead, yapping joyously—it became apparent that as long as they were willing to brave brambles and nettles, access could be readily gained.

"It's a sad sight," she remarked. "It must have been magnificent."

"Not in my time," Estabrook said.

"Shall I beat the way through?" she suggested, picking up a fallen branch and stripping off the twigs to do so.

"No, let me," he replied, relieving her of the switch and clearing a path for them by flaying the nettles mercilessly.

Jude followed in his green wake, a kind of exhilaration seizing her as she drew closer to stepping between the gateposts, a feeling she ascribed to the sight of Estabrook so heartily engaged in this adventure. He was a very different man to the husk she'd seen slumped in a chair two weeks before. As she clambered through the debris of fallen timbers he offered her his hand, and like lovers in search of some trysting place they slipped through the broken barrier into the estate beyond.

She was expecting an open vista: a driveway leading the eye to the house itself. Indeed, once she might have enjoyed just such a view. But two hundred years of ancestral insanities, mismanagement, and neglect had given symmetry over to chaos, parkland to pampas. What had once been artfully placed copses, built for shady dalliance, had spread and become choked woods. Lawns once leveled to perfection were wildernesses now. Several other members of England's landed gentry, finding themselves unable to sustain the family manse, had turned their estates into safari parks, importing the fauna of lost empire to wander where deer had grazed in better-heeled times. To Jude's eye the effect of such efforts was always bathetic. The parks were always too tended, the oaks and sycamores an inappropriate backdrop for lion or baboon. But here, she thought, it was possible to imagine wild beasts roaming. It was like a foreign landscape, dropped in the middle of England.

It was a long walk to the house, but Estabrook was already leading the way, with Skin as scout. What visions were in Charlie's mind's eye, Jude wondered, that drove him on with such gusto? The past, perhaps: childhood visits here? Or further back still, to the days of High Yoke's glory, when the route they were taking had been raked gravel, and the house ahead a gathering place for the wealthy and the influential?

"Did you come here a lot when you were little?" she asked him as they plowed through the grass.

He looked around at her with a moment's bewilderment, as though he'd forgotten she was with him.

"Not often," he said. "I liked it, though. It was like a playground. Later on, I thought about selling it, but Oscar would never let me. He had his reasons, of course...."

"What were they?" she asked him lightly.

"Frankly, I'm glad we left it to run to seed. It's prettier this way."

He marched on, wielding his branch like a machete. As they drew closer to the house, Jude could see what a pitiful state it was in. The windows were gone, the roof was reduced to a timber lattice, the doors teetered on their hinges like drunks. All sad enough in any house, but near tragic in a structure that had once been so magnificent. The sunlight was getting stronger as the clouds cleared, and by the time they stepped through the porch it was pouring through the lattice overhead, its geometry a perfect foil for the scene below. The staircase, albeit rubble-strewn, still rose in a sweep to a half landing, which had once been dominated by a window fit for a cathedral. It was smashed now, by a tree toppled many winters before, the withered extremities of which lay on the spot where the lord and lady would have paused before descending to greet their guests. The paneling of the hallway and the corridors that led off it was still intact, and the boards solid beneath their feet. Despite the decay of the roof, the structure didn't look unsound. It had been built to serve Godolphins in perpetuity, the fertility of land and loin preserving the name until the sun went out. It was flesh that had failed it, not the other way about.

Estabrook and Skin wandered off in the direction of the dining room, which was the size of a restaurant. Jude followed a little way, but found herself drawn back to the staircase. All she knew about the period in which the house had flourished she'd culled from films and television, but her imagination rose to the challenge with astonishing ardor, painting mind pictures so intense they all but displaced the dispiriting truth. When she climbed the stairs, indulging, somewhat guiltily, her dreams of aristocracy, she could see the hallway below lit with the glow of candles, could hear laughter on the landing above and—as she descended—the sigh of silk as her skirts brushed the carpet. Somebody called to her from a doorway, and she turned expecting to see Estabrook, but the caller was imagined, and the name too. Nobody had ever called her Peachplum.

The moment unsettled her slightly, and she went after Estabrook, as much to reacquaint herself with solid reality as for his company. He was in what had surely been a ballroom, one wall of which was a line of ceiling-high windows, offering a view across terraces and formal gardens to a ruined gazebo. She went to his side and put her arm through his. Their breaths became a common cloud, gilded by the sun through the shattered glass.

"It must have been so beautiful," she said.

"I'm sure it was." He sniffed hard. "But it's gone forever."

"It could be restored."

"For a fortune."

"You've got a fortune."

"Not that big."

"What about Oscar?"

"No. This is mine. He can come and go, but it's mine. That was part of the deal."

"What deal?" she said. He didn't reply. She pressed him, with words and proximity. "Tell me," she said. "Share it with me."

He took a deep breath. "I'm older than Oscar, and there's a family tradition—it goes back to the time when this house was intact—which says the oldest son, or daughter if there are no sons, becomes a member of a society called the Tabula Rasa."

"I've never heard of it."

"That's the way they'd like it to stay, I'm sure. I shouldn't be telling you any of this, but what the hell? I don't care any more. It's all ancient history. So . . . I was supposed to join the Tabula Rasa, but I was passed over by Papa in favor of Oscar."

"Why?"

Charlie made a little smile. "Believe it or not, they thought I was unstable. Me? Can you imagine? They were afraid I'd be indiscreet." The smile became a laugh. "Well, fuck them all. I'll *be* indiscreet."

"What does the Society do?"

"It was founded to prevent . . . let me remember the words exactly . . . to prevent *the tainting of England's soil.* Joshua loved England."

"Joshua?"

"The Godolphin who built this house."

"What did he think this taint was?"

"Who knows? Catholics? The French? He was crazy, and so were most of his friends. Secret societies were in vogue back then—"

"And it's still in operation?"

"I suppose so. I don't talk to Oscar very often, and when I do it's not about the Tabula Rasa. He's a strange man. In fact, he's a lot crazier than me. He just hides it better."

"You used to hide it very well, Charlie," she reminded him.

"More fool me. I should have let it out. I might have kept you." He put his hand up to her face. "I was stupid, Judith. I can't believe my luck that you've forgiven me."

She felt a pang of guilt, hearing him so moved by her manipulations. But they'd at least borne fruit. She had two new pieces for the puzzle: the Tabula Rasa and its raison d'être.

"Do you believe in magic?" she asked him.

"Do you want the old Charlie or the new one?"

"The new. The crazy."

"Then yes, I think I do. When Oscar used to bring his little presents round, he'd say to me, 'Have a piece of the miracle.' I used to throw most of them out, except for the bits and pieces you found. I didn't want to know where he got them."

"You never asked him?" she said.

"I did, finally. One night when you were away and I was drunk, he came round with that book you found in the safe, and I asked him outright where he got this smut from. I wasn't ready to believe what he told me. You know what made me ready?"

"No. What?"

"The body on the heath. I told you about it, didn't I? I watched them digging around in the muck and the rain for two days and I kept thinking, What a fucking life this is! No way out except feet first. I was ready to slit my wrists, and I probably would have done it except that you appeared, and I remembered the way I felt about you when I first saw you. I remembered feeling as though something miraculous was happening, as though I was reclaiming something I'd lost. And I thought, If I believe in one miracle I may as well believe in them all. Even Oscar's. Even his talk about the Imajica, and the Dominions in the Imajica, and the people there, and the cities. I just thought, Why not . . . embrace it all before I lose the chance? Before I'm a body lying out in the rain."

"You won't die in the rain."

"I don't care where I die, Jude, I care where I live, and I want to live in some kind of hope. I want to live with you."

"Charlie," she chided softly, "we shouldn't talk about that now."

"Why not? What better time? I know you brought me here because you've got questions of your own you want answering, and I don't blame you. If I'd seen that damn assassin come after me, I'd be asking questions too. But think about it, Judy, that's all I'm asking. Think about whether the new Charlie's worth a little bit of your time. Will you do that?"

"I'll do that."

"Thank you," he said, and taking the hand she'd tucked through his arm, he kissed her fingers.

"You've heard most of Oscar's secrets now," he said. "You may as well know them all. See the little wood way over towards the wall? That's his little railway station, where he takes the train to wherever he goes."

"I'd like to see it."

"Shall we stroll over there, ma'am?" he said. "Where did the dog go?" He whistled, and Skin came pounding in, raising golden dust. "Perfect. Let's take the air."

3

The afternoon was so bright it was easy to imagine what bliss this place would be, even in its present decay, come spring or high summer, with dandelion seeds and birdsong in the air and the evenings long and balmy. Though she was eager to see the place Estabrook had described as Oscar's railway station, she didn't force the pace.

They strolled, just as Charlie had suggested, taking time to cast an appreciative glance back towards the house. It looked even grander from this aspect, with the terraces rising to the row of ball-room windows. Though the wood ahead was not large, the under-growth and the sheer density of trees kept their destination from sight until they were under the canopy and treading the damp rot of last September's fall. Only then did she realize what building this was. She'd seen it countless times before, drawn in elevation and hanging in front of the safe.

"The Retreat," she said.

"You recognize it?"

"Of course."

Birds sang in the branches overhead, misled by the warmth and tuning up for courtship. When she looked up it seemed to her the branches formed a fretted vault above the Retreat, as if echoing its dome. Between the two, vault and song, the place felt almost sacred.

"Oscar calls it the Black Chapel," Charlie said. "Don't ask me why."

It had no windows and, from this side, no door. They had to walk around it a few yards before the entrance came in sight. Skin was panting at the step, but when Charlie opened the door the dog de-clined to enter.

"Coward," Charlie said, preceding Jude over the threshold. "It's quite safe."

The sense of the numinous she'd felt outside was stronger still inside, but despite all that she'd experienced since Pie 'oh' pah had come for her life, she was still ill prepared for mystery. Her moder-nity burdened her. She wished there was some forgotten self she could dredge from her crippled history, better equipped for this. Charlie had his bloodline even if he'd denied his name. The thrushes in the trees outside resembled absolutely the thrushes who'd sung here since these boughs had been strong enough to bear them. But she was adrift, resembling nobody; not even the woman she'd been six weeks ago.

"Don't be nervous," Charlie said, beckoning her in.

He spoke too loudly for the place; his voice carried around the vast bare circle and came back to meet him magnified. He seemed not to notice. Perhaps it was simply familiarity that bred this in-difference, but she thought not. For all his talk of embracing the miraculous, Charlie was still a pragmatist, fixed in the particular. Whatever forces moved here, and she felt them strongly, he was dead to their presence.

Approaching the Retreat she'd thought the place windowless, but she'd been wrong. At the intersection of wall and dome ran a ring of windows, like a halo fitted to the chapel's skull. Small though they were, they let in sufficient light to strike the floor and rise up into the middle of the space, where the luminescence converged above the mosaic. If this was indeed a place of departure, that rarefied spot was the platform.

"It's nothing special, is it?" Charlie observed.

She was about to disagree, searching for a way to express what she was feeling, when Skin began barking outside. This wasn't the excited yapping with which he'd announced each new pissing place along the way, but a sound of alarm. She started towards the door, but the hold the chapel had on her slowed her response, and Charlie was out before she'd reached the step, calling to the dog to be quiet. He stopped barking suddenly.

"Charlie?" she said.

There was no reply. With the dog quieted she heard a greater quiet. The birds had stopped singing.

Again she said, "Charlie?" and as she did so somebody stepped into the doorway. It was not Charlie; this man, bearded and heavy, was a stranger. But her system responded to the sight of him with a shock of recognition, as though he was some long lost comrade. She might have thought herself crazy, except that what she felt was echoed on his face. He looked at her with narrowed eyes, turning his head a little to the side.

"You're Judith?"

"Yes. Who are you?"

"Oscar Godolphin."

She let her shallow breaths go, in favor of a deeper draft.

"Oh . . . thank God," she said. "You startled me. I thought . . . I don't know what I thought. Did the dog try and attack you?"

"Forget the dog," he said, stepping into the chapel. "Have we met before?"

"I don't believe so," she said. "Where's Charlie? Is he all right?"

Godolphin continued to approach her, his step steady. "This confuses things," he said.

"What does?"

"Me . . . knowing you. You being whoever you are. It confuses things."

"I don't see why," she said. "I'd wanted to meet you, and I asked Charlie several times if he'd introduce us, but he always seemed reluctant. . . ." She kept chattering, as much to defend herself from his appraisal as for communication's sake. She felt if she fell silent she'd forget herself utterly, become his object. "I'm very pleased we finally get to talk."

He was close enough to touch her now. She put out her hand to shake his.

"It really is a pleasure," she said.

Outside, the dog began barking again, and this time its din was followed by a shout.

"Oh, God, he's bitten somebody," Jude said, and started towards the door.

Oscar took hold of her arm, and the contact, light but proprietorial, checked her. She looked back towards him, and all the laughable clichés of romantic fiction were suddenly real and deadly serious. Her heart was beating in her throat; her cheeks were beacons; the ground seemed uncertain beneath her feet. There was no pleasure in this, only a sickening powerlessness she could do nothing to defend herself against. Her only comfort—and it was small— was the fact that her partner in this dance of desire seemed almost as distressed by their mutual fixation as she.

The dog's din was abruptly cut short, and she heard Charlie yell her name. Oscar's glance went to the door, and hers went with it, to see Estabrook, armed with a cudgel of wood, gasping at the threshold. Behind him, an abomination: a half-burned creature, its face caved in (Charlie's doing, she saw; there were scraps of its blackened flesh on the cudgel) reaching blindly for him.

She cried out at the sight, and he stepped aside as it lurched forward. It lost its balance on the step and fell. One hand, fingers burned to the bone, reached for the doorjamb, but Charlie brought his weapon down on its wounded head. Skull shards flew; silvery blood preceded its head to the step, as its hand missed its purchase and it collapsed on the threshold.

She heard Oscar quietly moan.

"You fuckhead!" Charlie said.

He was panting and sweaty, but there was a gleam of purpose in his eye she'd never seen the like of.

"Let her go," he said.

She felt Oscar's grip go from her arm and mourned its departure. What she'd felt for Charlie had been only a prophecy of what she felt now; as if she'd loved him in remembrance of a man she'd never met. And now that she had, now that she'd heard the true voice and not its echo, Estabrook seemed like a poor substitute, for all his tardy heroism.

Where these feelings came from she didn't know, but they had the force of instinct, and she would not be gainsaid. She stared at Oscar. He was overweight, overdressed, and doubtless overbearing: not the kind of individual she'd have sought out, given the choice. But for some reason she didn't yet comprehend, she'd had that choice denied. Some urge profounder than conscious desire had claimed her will. The fears she had for Charlie's safety, and indeed for her own, were suddenly remote: almost abstractions.

"Take no notice of him," Charlie said. "He's not going to hurt you."

She glanced his way. He looked like a husk beside his brother, beset by tics and tremors. How had she ever loved him?

"Come here," he said, beckoning to her.

She didn't move, until Oscar said, "Go on."

More out of obedience to his instruction than any wish to go, she started to walk towards Charlie.

As she did so another shadow fell across the threshold. A severely dressed young man with dyed blond hair appeared at the door, the lines of his face perfect to the point of banality.

"Stay away, Dowd," Oscar said. "This is just Charlie and me."

Dowd looked down at the body on the step, then back at Oscar, offering two words of warning: "He's dangerous."

"I know what he is," Oscar said. "Judith, why don't you step outside with Dowd?"

"Don't go near that little fucker," Charlie told her. "He killed Skin. And there's another of those things out there."

"They're called voiders, Charles," Oscar said. "And they're not going to harm a hair on her beautiful head. Judith. Look at me." She looked around at him. "You're not in danger. You understand? Nobody's going to hurt you."

She understood and believed him. Without looking back at Charlie, she went to the door. The dog killer moved aside, offering her a hand to help her over the voider's corpse, but she ignored it and went out into the sun with a shameful lightness in her heart and step. Dowd followed her as she walked from the chapel. She felt his stare.

"Judith . . ." he said, as if astonished.

"That's me," she replied, knowing that to lay claim to that identity was somehow momentous.

Squatting in the humus a little way from them she saw the other voider. It was idly perusing the body of Skin, running its fingers over the dog's flank. She looked away, unwilling to have the strange joy she felt soured by morbidity.

She and Dowd had reached the edge of the wood, where she had an unhindered view of the sky. The sun was sinking, gaining color as it fell and lending a new glamour to the vista of park, terraces, and house.

"I feel as though I've been here before," she said.

The thought was strangely soothing. Like the feelings she had towards Oscar, it rose from some place in her she didn't remember owning, and identifying its source was not for now as important as accepting its presence. That she did, gladly. She'd spent so much of her recent life in the grip of events that lay outside her power to control, it was a pleasure to touch a source of feeling that was so deep, so instinctive, she didn't need to analyze its intentions. It was part of her, and therefore good. Tomorrow, maybe, or the day after, she'd question its significance more closely.

"Do you remember anything specific about this place?" Dowd asked her.

She mused on this for a time, then said, "No. It's just a feeling of . . . belonging."

"Then maybe it's better not to remember," came the reply. "You know memory. It can be very treacherous."

She didn't like this man, but there was merit in his observation. She could barely remember ten years of her own span; thinking back beyond that would be near impossible. If the recollections came, in the fullness of time, she'd welcome them. But for now she had a brimming cup of feelings, and perhaps they were all the more attractive for their mystery.

There were raised voices from the chapel, though the echo within and the distance without made comprehension impossible.

"A little sibling rivalry," Dowd remarked. "How does it feel being a woman contested over?"

"There's no contest," she replied.

"They don't seem to think so," he said.

The voices were shouts now, rising to a pitch, then suddenly subdued. One of them went on talking—Oscar, she thought—interrupted by exhortations from the other. Were they bargaining over her, throwing their bids back and forth? She started to think she should intervene. Go back to the chapel and make her allegiance, irrational as it was, quite plain. Better to tell the truth now than let Charlie bargain away his goods and chattels only to discover the prize wasn't his to have. She turned and began to walk towards the chapel.

"What are you doing?" said Dowd.

"I have to talk to them."

"Mr. Godolphin told you—"

"I heard him. I have to talk to them."

Off to her right she saw the voider rise from its haunches, its eyes not on her but on the open door. It sniffed the air, then let out a whistle as plaintive as a whine and started toward the building with a loping, almost bestial, gait. It reached the door before Jude, stepping on its dead brother in its haste to be inside. As she came within a couple of yards of the door she caught the scent that had set it whining. A breeze—too warm for the season and carrying perfumes too strange for this world—came to meet her out of the chapel, and to her horror she realized that history was repeating itself. The train between the Dominions was being boarded inside, and the wind she smelled was blowing along the track from its destination.

"Oscar!" she yelled, stumbling over the body as she threw herself inside.

The travelers were already dispatched. She saw them passing from view like Gentle and Pie 'oh' pah, except that the voider, desperate to go with them, was pitching itself into the flux of passage. She might have done the same, but that its error was evident. Caught in the flux, but too late to be taken where the travelers had gone, its whistle became a screech as it was unknitted. Its arms and head, thrust into the knot of power which marked the place of departure, began to turn inside out. Its lower half, untouched by the power, convulsed, its legs scrambling for purchase on the mosaic as it tried to retrieve itself. Too late. She saw its head and torso unveiled, saw the skin of its arms stripped and sucked away.

The power that trapped it quickly died. But it was not so lucky. With its arms still clutching at the world it had perhaps glimpsed as its eyes went from its head, it dropped to the ground, the blue-black stew of its innards spilling across the mosaic. Even then, gutted and blind, its body refused to cease. It thrashed in its coils like the victims of a *grand mal.*

Dowd stepped past her, approached the passing place cautiously for fear the flux had left an echo, but, finding none, drew a gun from inside his jacket and, eyeing some vulnerable place in the mess at his feet, fired twice. The voider's throes slowed, then stopped. Sighing heavily, Dowd stepped away from the body and returned to where Jude stood.

"You shouldn't be here," he said. "None of this is for your eyes."

"Why not? I know where they've gone."

"Oh, do you?" he said, raising a quizzical eyebrow. "And where's that?"

"To the Imajica," she said, affecting complete familiarity with the notion, though it still astonished her.

He made a tiny smile, though she wasn't sure whether it was one of acceptance or subtle mockery. He watched her study him, almost basking in her scrutiny, taking it, perhaps, for simple admiration.

"And how do you know about the Imajica?" he inquired.

"Doesn't everybody?"

"I think you know better than that," he replied. "Though how *much* better, I'm not entirely sure."

She was something of an enigma to him, she suspected, and, as long as she remained so, might hope to keep him friendly.

"Do you think they made it?" she asked.

"Who knows? The voider may have spoilt their passage by trying to tag along. They may not have reached Yzordderrex."

"So where will they be?"

"In the In Ovo, of course. Somewhere between here and the Second Dominion."

"And how will they get back?"

"Simple," he said. "They won't."

4

So they waited. Or, rather, she waited, watching the sun disappear behind trees blotted with rookeries, and the evening stars appearing as light bringers in its place. Dowd busied himself dealing with the bodies of the voiders, dragging them out of the chapel, making a simple pyre of dead wood, and burning them upon it. He showed not the least concern that she was witnessing this, which was a lesson and perhaps a warning to her. He apparently assumed she was part of the secret world he and the voiders occupied, not subject to the laws and moralities the rest of the world was bounded by. In seeing all she'd seen, and passing herself off as expert in the ways of the Imajica, she had become a conspirator. There was no way back after this, to the company she'd kept and the life she'd known; she belonged to the secret, every bit as much as the secret belonged to her.

That of itself would be no great loss if Godolphin returned. He would help her find her way through the mysteries. If he didn't return, the consequences were less palatable. To be obliged to keep Dowd's company, simply because they were fellow marginals, would be unbearable. She would surely wither and die. But then if Godolphin was not in her life, what could that matter? From ecstasy to despair in the space of an hour. Was it too much to hope the pendulum would swing back the other way before the day was out?

The chill was adding to her misery, and—having no other source of warmth—she went over to the pyre, preparing to retreat if the scent or the sight was too offensive. But the smoke, which she'd expected to smell of burning meat, was almost aromatic, and the forms in the fire unrecognizable. Dowd offered her a cigarette, which she accepted, lighting it from a branch plucked from the edge of the fire.

"What were they?" she asked him, eyeing the remains.

"You've never heard of voiders?" he said. "They're the lowest of the low. I brought them through from the In Ovo myself, and I'm no Maestro, so that gives an idea of how gullible they are."

"When it smelled the wind—"

"Yes, that was rather touching, wasn't it?" Dowd said. "It smelled Yzordderrex."

"Maybe it was born there."

"Very possibly. I've heard it said they're made of collective desire, but that's not true. They're revenge children. Got on women who were working the Way for themselves."

"Working the Way isn't good?"

"Not for your sex, it isn't. It's strictly forbidden."

"So somebody who breaks the law's made pregnant as revenge?"

"Exactly. You can't abort voiders, you see. They're stupid, but they fight, even in the womb. And killing something you gave birth to is strictly against the women's codes. So they pay to have the voiders thrown into the In Ovo. They can survive there longer than just about anything. They feed on whatever they can find, including each other. And eventually, if they're lucky, they get summoned by someone in this Dominion."

So much to learn, she thought. Perhaps she should cultivate Dowd's friendship, however charmless he was. He seemed to enjoy parading his knowledge, and the more she knew the better prepared she'd be when she finally stepped through the door into Yzordderrex. She was about to ask him something more about the city when a gust of wind, blowing from out of the chapel, threw a flurry of sparks up between them.

"They're coming back," she said, and started towards the building.

"Be careful," Dowd said. "You don't know it's them."

His warning went unheeded. She went to the door at a run, and reached it as the spicy summer wind died away. The interior of the chapel was gloomy, but she could see a single figure standing in the middle of the mosaic. It staggered towards her, its breathing ragged. The light from the fire caught it as it came within two yards of her. It was Oscar Godolphin, his hand up to his bleeding nose.

"That bastard," he said.

"Where is he?"

"Dead," he said plainly. "I had to do it, Judith. He was crazy. God alone knows what he might have said or done. . . ." He put his arm towards her. "Will you help me? He damn near broke my nose."

"I'll take him," Dowd said possessively. He stepped past her, fetching a handkerchief from his pocket to put to Oscar's nose. It was waved away.

"I'll survive," Oscar said. "Let's just get home." They were out of the chapel now, and Oscar was eyeing the fire.

"The voiders," Dowd explained.

Oscar threw a glance at Judith. "He made you pyre-watch with him?" he said. "I'm so sorry." He looked back at Dowd, pained.

"That's no way to treat a lady," he said. "We're going to have to do better in future."

"What do you mean?"

"She's coming to live with us. Aren't you, Judith?"

She hesitated a shamelessly short time; then she said, "Yes, I am."

Satisfied, he went over to look at the pyre.

"Come back tomorrow," she heard him tell Dowd. "Scatter the ashes and bury the bones. I've got a little prayer book Peccable gave me. We'll find something appropriate in there."

While he spoke she stared into the murk of the chapel, trying to imagine the journey that had been taken from here, and the city at the other end from which that tantalizing wind had blown. She would be there one day. She'd lost a husband in pursuit of passage, but from her present perspective that seemed like a negligible loss. There was a new order of feeling in her, founded at the sight of Oscar Godolphin. She didn't yet know what he would come to mean to her, but perhaps she could persuade him to take her away with him, someday soon.

Eager as she was to create in her mind's eye the mysteries that lay beyond the veil of the Fifth, Jude's imagination, for all its fever, could never have conjured the reality of that journey. Inspired by a few clues from Dowd, she had imagined the In Ovo as a kind of wasteland, where voiders hung like drowned men in deep-sea trenches, and creatures the sun would never see crawled towards her, their paths lit by their own sickly luminescence. But the inhabitants of the In Ovo beggared the bizarreness of any ocean floor. They had forms and appetites that no book had ever set down. They had rages and frustrations that were centuries old.

And the scenes she'd imagined awaiting her on the other side of that prison were also very different from those she'd created. If she'd traveled on the Yzordderrexian Express she'd would not have been delivered into the middle of a summer city but into a dampish cellar, lined with the merchant Peccable's forbidden cache of charms and petrifications. In order to reach the open air, she would have had to climb the stairs and pass through the house itself. Once she'd reached the street, she'd have found some of her expectations satisfied at least. The air was warm and spicy there, and the sky was bright. But it was not a sun that blazed overhead, it was a comet, trailing its glory across the Second Dominion. And if she stared at it a moment, then looked down at the street, she'd have found its reflection glittering in a pool of blood. Here was the spot where the brawl between Oscar and Charlie had ended, and where the defeated brother had been left.

He had not remained there for very long. News of a man dressed in foreign garb and dumped in the gutter had soon spread, and before the last of his blood had drained from his body three individuals never before seen in this Kesparate had come to claim him. They were Dearthers, to judge by their tattoos, and had Jude been standing on Peccable's step watching the scene, she would have been touched to see how reverently they treated their burden as they spirited it away. How they smiled down at that bruised and lolling face. How one of them wept. She might also have noticed—though in the flurry of the street this detail might have escaped her eye—that though the defeated man lay quite still in the cradle his bearers made of their limbs, his eyes closed, his arms trailing until they were folded across his chest, said chest was not entirely motionless.

Charles Estabrook, abandoned for dead in the filth of Yzorddderrex, left its streets with enough health in his body to be dubbed a loser, not a corpse.

22

I

The days following Pie and Gentle's second departure from Beatrix seemed to shorten as they climbed, supporting the suspicion that the nights in the Jokalaylau were longer than those in the lowlands. It was impossible to confirm that this was so, because their two timekeepers—Gentle's beard and Pie's bowels—became increasingly unreliable as they climbed, the former because Gentle ceased to shave, the latter because the travelers' desire to eat, and thus their need to defecate, dwindled the higher they went. Far from inspiring appetite, the rarefied air became a feast in itself, and they traveled for hour upon hour without their thoughts once turning to physical need. They had each other's company, of course, to keep them from completely forgetting their bodies and their purpose, but more reliable still were the beasts on whose shaggy backs they rode. When the doeki grew hungry they simply stopped, and would not be bullied or coaxed into moving from whatever bush or piece of pasture they'd found until they were sated. At first, this was an irritation, and the riders cursed as they slipped from their saddles on such occasions, knowing they had an idling hour ahead while the animals grazed. But as the days passed and the air grew thinner, they came to depend upon the rhythm of the doekis' digestive tracts and made such stopping places mealtimes for themselves.

It soon became apparent that Pie's calculations as to the length of this journey had been hopelessly optimistic. The only part of the mystif's predictions that experience was confirming was the hardship. Even before they reached the snow line, both riders and mounts were showing signs of fatigue, and the track they were following became less visible by the mile as the soft earth chilled and froze, refusing the traces of those who had preceded them. With the prospect of snowfields and glaciers ahead, they rested the doeki for a day and encouraged the beasts to gorge themselves on what would be the last available pasture until they reached the other side of the range.

Gentle had called his mount Chester, after dear old Klein, with whom it shared a certain ruminative charm. Pie declined to name the other beast, however, claiming it was bad luck to eat anything you knew by name, and circumstances might very well oblige them to dine on doeki meat before they reached the borders of the Third Dominion. That small disagreement aside, they kept their exchanges frictionless when they set off again, both consciously skirting any discussion of the events in Beatrix or their significance. The cold soon became aggressive, the coats they'd been given barely adequate defense against the assault of winds that blew up walls of dusty snow so dense they often obliterated the way ahead. When that happened Pie pulled out the compass—the face of which looked more like a star map to Gentle's untutored eye—and assessed their direction from that. Only once did Gentle remark that he hoped the mystif knew what it was doing, earning such a withering glance for his troubles it silenced him utterly on the matter thereafter.

Despite weather that was worsening by the day—making Gentle think wistfully of an English January—good fortune did not entirely desert them. On the fifth day beyond the snow line, in a lull between gusts, Gentle heard bells ringing, and following the sound they discovered a group of half a dozen mountain men, tending to a flock of a hundred or more cousins to the terrestrial goat, these shaggier by far and purple as crocuses. The herders spoke no English, and only one of them, whose name was Kuthuss and who boasted a beard as shaggy and as purple as his beasts (leading Gentle to wonder what marriages of convenience had occurred in these lonely uplands), had any words in his vocabulary that Pie could comprehend. What he told was grim. The herders were bringing their herds down from the High Pass early because the snow had covered ground the beasts would have grazed for another twenty days in a normal season. This was not, he repeated several times, a normal season. He had never known the snow to come so early or fall so copiously; never known the winds to be so bitter. In essence, he advised them not to attempt the route ahead. It would be tantamount to suicide. Pie and Gentle talked this advice over. The journey was already taking far longer than they'd anticipated. If they went back down below the snow line, tempting as the prospect of relative warmth and fresh food was, they were wasting yet more time. Days when all manner of horrors could be unfolding: a hundred villages like Beatrix destroyed, and countless lives lost.

"Remember what I said when we left Beatrix?" Gentle said.

"No, to be honest, I don't."

"I said we wouldn't die, and I meant it. We'll find a way through."

"I'm not sure I like this messianic conviction," Pie said. "People with the best intentions die, Gentle. Come to think of it, they're often the first to go."

"What are you saying? That you won't come with me?"

"I said I'd go wherever you go, and I will. But good intentions won't impress the cold."

"How much money have we got?"

"Not much."

"Enough to buy some goatskins off these men? And maybe some meat?"

A complex exchange ensued in three languages—with Pie translating Gentle's words into the language Kuthuss understood and Kuthuss in turn translating for his fellow herders. A deal was rapidly struck; the herders seemed much persuaded by the prospect of hard cash. Rather than give over their own coats, however, two of them got about the business of slaughtering and skinning four of the animals. The meat, they cooked and shared among the group. It was fatty and underdone, but neither Gentle nor Pie declined, and it was washed down with a beverage they brewed from boiled snow, dried leaves, and a dash of liquor which Pie understood Kuthuss to have called the piss of the goat. They tasted it in spite of this. It was potent, and after a shot of it—downed like vodka—Gentle remarked that if this made him a piss-drinker, so be it.

The next day, having been supplied with skins, meat, and the makings of several pots of the herders' beverage, plus a pan and two glasses, they made their inarticulate farewells and parted company. The weather closed in soon after, and once again they were lost in a white wilderness. But their spirits had been buoyed up by the meeting, and they made steady progress for the next two and a half days, until, as twilight approached on the third, the animal Gentle was riding started to show signs of exhaustion, its head

drooping, its hooves barely able to clear the snow they were trudg-
ing through.

"I think we'd better rest him," Gentle said.

They found a niche between boulders so large they were almost
hills in themselves, and lit a fire to brew up some of the herders'
liquor. It, more than the meat, was what had sustained them
through the most demanding portions of the journey so far, but try
as they might to use it sparingly, they had almost consumed their
modest supply. As they drank they talked about what lay ahead.
Kuthuss' predictions were proving correct. The weather was worsening all the time, and the chances of encountering another living
soul up here if they were to get into difficulty were surely zero. Pie
took a moment to remind Gentle of his conviction that they
weren't going to die; come blizzard, come hurricane, come the
echo of Hapexamendios Himself, down from the mountain.

"And I meant what I said," Gentle replied. "But I can still fret
about it, can't I?" He put his hands closer to the fire. "Any more
in the piss pot?"

"I'm afraid not."

"I tell you, when we come back this way"—Pie made a wry
face—"we will, we will. When we come back this way we've got to
get the recipe. Then we can brew it back on earth."

They'd left the doeki a little distance away and heard now a lowing sound.

"Chester!" Gentle said, and went to the beasts.

Chester was lying on its side, its flank heaving. Blood streamed
from its mouth and nose, melting the snow it poured upon.

"Oh, shit, Chester," Gentle implored, "don't die."

But he'd no sooner put what he hoped was a comforting hand
on the doeki's flank than it turned its glossy brown eye towards
him, let out one final moan, and stopped breathing.

"We just lost fifty percent of our transport," he said to Pie.

"Look on the bright side. We gained ourselves a week of meat."

Gentle glanced back towards the dead animal, wishing he'd
taken Pie's advice and never named the beast. Now when he
sucked its bones he'd be thinking of Klein.

"Will you do it or should I?" he said. "I suppose it should be me.
I named him, I should skin him."

The mystif didn't argue, only suggested that it should move the
other animal out of sight of the scene, in case it too lost all will to
live, seeing its comrade disemboweled. Gentle agreed, and watched
while Pie led the fretting creature away. Wielding the blade they'd
been given as they left Beatrix, he then set about his butchering.
He rapidly discovered that neither he nor the knife were equal to
the task. The doeki's hide was thick, its fat rubbery, its meat tough.

After an hour of hacking and tearing he'd only managed to strip the hide from the upper half of its back leg and a small portion of its flank. He was sticky with its blood and sweating inside his coat of furs.

"Shall I take over?" Pie suggested.

"No," Gentle snapped, "I can do it," and continued to labor in the same inept fashion, the blade dulled by now and the muscles driving it weary.

He waited a decent interval, then got up and went back to the fire where Pie was sitting, gazing into the flames. Disgruntled by his defeat, he tossed the knife down in the melting snow beside the fire.

"I give up," he said. "It's all yours."

Somewhat reluctantly, Pie picked up the knife, proceeded to sharpen it on the rock face, then went to work. Gentle didn't watch. Repulsed by the blood that had spattered him, he elected to brave the cold and wash it off. He found a place a little way from the fire where the ground was untrammeled, removed his coat and shirt, and knelt down to bathe in the snow. His skin crawled at the chill, but some urge to self-mortification was satisfied by this testing of will and flesh, and when he'd cleaned his hands and face he rubbed the pricking snow into his chest and belly, though the doeki's fluids hadn't stained him there. The wind had dropped in the last little while, and the sky visible between the rocks was more gold than green. He was seized by the need to stand unencumbered in its light, and without putting his coat back on he clambered up over the rocks to do so. His hands were numb, and the climb was more arduous than he'd anticipated, but the scene above and below him when he reached the top of the rock was worth the effort. No wonder Hapexamendios had come here on His way to His resting place. Even gods might be inspired by such grandeur. The peaks of the Jokalaylau receded in apparently infinite procession, their white slopes faintly gilded by the heavens they reached for. The silence could not have been more utter.

This vantage point served a practical as well as an aesthetic purpose. The High Pass was plainly visible. And so, some distance off to the right, was a sight perplexing enough for him to call the mystif up from its work. A glacier, its surface shimmering, lay a mile or more from the rock. But it wasn't the spectacle of such frozen enormity that claimed Gentle's eye, it was the presence within the ice of a litter of darker forms.

"You want to go and find out what they are?" the mystif said, washing its bloodied hands in the snow.

"I think we should," Gentle replied. "If we're walking in the

Unbeheld's footsteps, we should make it our business to see what
He saw."

"Or what He caused," Pie said.

They descended, and Gentle put his shirt and coat back on. The
clothes were warm, having been left beside the fire, and he was glad
of that comfort, but they also stank of his sweat and of the animals
whose backs they'd been stripped from, and he half wished he
could go naked, rather than be burdened by another hide.

"Have you finished with the skinning?" Gentle asked Pie as they
set off, going by foot rather than waste the energies of their remaining vehicle.

"I've done what I can," Pie replied, "but it's crude. I'm no
butcher."

"Are you a cook?" Gentle asked.

"Not really. Why'd you ask?"

"I've been thinking about food a lot, that's all. You know, after
this trip I may never eat meat again. The fat! The gristle! It turns
my stomach thinking about it."

"You've got a sweet tooth."

"You noticed. I'd kill for a plate of profiteroles right now, swimming in chocolate sauce." He laughed. "Listen to me. The glories
of Jokalaylau laid before us and I'm obsessing on profiteroles."
Then again, deadly serious. "Do they have chocolate in Yzordderrex?"

"By now, I'm sure they do. But my people eat plainly, so I never
got an addiction for sugar. Fish, on the other hand—"

"Fish?" said Gentle. "I've no taste for it."

"You'll get one in Yzordderrex. There's restaurants down by the
harbor ..." The mystif's talk turned into a smile. "Now I'm sounding like you. We must both be sick of doeki meat."

"Go on," Gentle said. "I want to see you salivate."

"There are restaurants down by the harbor where the fish is so
fresh it's still flapping when they take it into the kitchen."

"That's a recommendation?"

"There's nothing in the world as good as fresh fish," Pie said. "If
the catch is good you've got a choice of forty, maybe fifty, dishes.
From tiny jepas to squeffah my size and bigger."

"Is there anything I'd recognize?"

"A few species. But why travel all this way for a cod steak when
you could have squeffah? Or better, there's a dish I have to order
for you. It's a fish called an ugichee, which is almost as small as a
jepas, and it lives in the belly of another fish."

"That sounds suicidal."

"Wait, there's more. The second fish is often eaten whole by
a bloater called a coliacic. They're ugly, but the meat melts like

butter. So if you're lucky, they'll grill all three of them together, just the way they were caught—"

"One inside the other?"

"Head, tail, the whole caboodle."

"That's disgusting."

"And if you're very lucky—"

"Pie—"

"—the ugichee's a female, and you find, when you cut through all three layers of fish—"

"—her belly's full of caviar."

"You guessed it. Doesn't that sound tempting?"

"I'll stay with my chocolate mousse and ice cream."

"How is it you're not fat?"

"Vanessa used to say I had the palate of a child, the libido of an adolescent, and the—well, you can guess the rest. I sweat it out making love. Or at least I used to."

They were close to the edge of the glacier now, and their talk of fish and chocolate ceased, replaced by a grim silence, as the identity of the forms encased in the ice became apparent. They were human bodies, a dozen or more. Ice-locked around them, a collection of debris: fragments of blue stone; immense bowls of beaten metal; the remnants of garments, the blood on them still bright. Gentle clambered and skidded across the top of the glacier until the bodies were directly beneath him. Some were buried too deeply to be studied, but those closer to the surface—faces upturned, limbs fixed in attitudes of desperation—were almost too visible. They were all women, the youngest barely out of childhood, the oldest a naked many-breasted hag who'd perished with her eyes still open, her stare preserved for the millennium. Some massacre had occurred here, or farther up the mountain, and the evidence been thrown into this river while it still flowed. Then, apparently, it had frozen around the victims and their belongings.

"Who are they?" Gentle asked. "Any idea?" Though they were dead, the past tense didn't seem appropriate for corpses so perfectly preserved.

"When the Unbeheld passed through the Dominions, He overthrew all the cults He deemed unworthy. Most of them were sacred to Goddesses. Their oracles and devotees were women."

"So you think Hapexamendios did this?"

"If not him, then His agents, His Righteous. Though on second thought He's supposed to have walked here alone, so maybe this is His handiwork."

"Then whoever He is," Gentle said, looking down at the child in the ice, "He's a murderer. No better than you or me."

"I wouldn't say that too loudly," Pie advised.

"Why not? He's not here."

"If this *is* His doing, He may have left entities to watch over it."

Gentle looked around. The air could not have been clearer. There was no sign of motion on the peaks or the snow-fields gleaming below. "If they're here I don't see 'em," he said.

"The worst are the ones you can't see," Pie replied. "Shall we go back to the fire?"

2

They were weighed down by what they'd seen, and the return journey took longer than the outward. By the time they made the safety of their niche in the rocks, to welcoming grunts from the surviving doeki, the sky was losing its golden sheen and dusk was on its way. They debated whether to proceed in darkness and decided against it. Though the air was calm at present, they knew from past experience that conditions on these heights were unpredictable. If they attempted to move by night, and a storm descended from the peaks, they'd be twice blinded and in danger of losing their way. With the High Pass so close, and the journey easier, they hoped, once they were through it, the risk was not worth taking.

Having used up the supply of wood they'd collected below the snow line, they were obliged to fuel the fire with the dead doeki's saddle and harness. It made for a smoky, pungent, and fitful blaze, but it was better than nothing. They cooked some of the fresh meat, Gentle observing as he chewed that he had less compunction about eating something he'd named than he thought, and brewed up a small serving of the herders' piss liquor. As they drank, Gentle returned the conversation to the women in the ice.

"Why would a God as powerful as Hapexamendios slaughter defenseless women?"

"Whoever said they were defenseless?" Pie replied. "I think they were probably very powerful. Their oracles must have sensed what was coming, so they had their armies ready—"

"Armies of women?"

"Certainly. Warriors in their tens of thousands. There are places to the north of the Lenten Way where the earth used to move every fifty years or so and uncover one of their war graves."

"They were all slaughtered? The armies, the oracles—"

"Or driven so deep into hiding they forgot who they were after a few generations. Don't look so surprised. It happens."

"One God defeats how many Goddesses? Ten, twenty—"

"Innumerable."

"How?"

"He was One, and simple. They were many, and diverse."

"Singularity is strength—"

"At least in the short term. Who told you that?"

"I'm trying to remember. Somebody I didn't like much: Klein, maybe."

"Whoever said it, it's true. Hapexamendios came into the Dominions with a seductive idea: that wherever you went, whatever misfortune attended you, you needed only one name on your lips, one prayer, one altar, and you'd be in His care. And He brought a species to maintain that order once He'd established it. Yours."

"Those women back there looked human enough to me."

"So do I," Pie reminded him. "But I'm not."

"No . . . you're pretty diverse, aren't you?"

"I was once. . . ."

"So that puts you on the side of the Goddesses, doesn't it?" Gentle whispered.

The mystif put its finger to his lips.

Gentle mouthed one word by way of response: "Heretic."

It was very dark now, and they both settled to studying the fire. It was steadily diminishing as the last of Chester's saddle was consumed.

"Maybe we should burn some fur," Gentle suggested.

"No," said Pie. "Let it dwindle. But keep looking."

"At what?"

"Anything."

"There's only you to look at."

"Then look at me."

He did so. The privations of the last many days had seemingly taken little toll on the mystif. It had no facial hair to disfigure the symmetry of its features, nor had their spartan diet pinched its cheeks or hollowed its eyes. Studying its face was like returning to a favorite painting in a museum. There it was: a thing of calm and beauty. But, unlike the painting, the face before him, which presently seemed so solid, had the capacity for infinite change. It was months since the night when he'd first seen that phenomenon. But now, as the fire burned itself out and the shadows deepened around them, he realized the same sweet miracle was imminent. The flicker of dying flame made the symmetry swim; the flesh before him seemed to lose its fixedness as he stared and stirred it.

"I want to watch," he murmured.

"Then watch."

"But the fire's going out. . . ."

"We don't need light to see each other," the mystif whispered. "Hold on to the sight."

Gentle concentrated, studying the face before him. His eyes

ached as he tried to hold onto it, but they were no competition for
the swelling darkness.

"Stop looking," Pie said, in a voice that seemed to rise from the
decay of the embers. "Stop looking, and *see.*"

Gentle fought for the sense of this, but it was no more susceptible to analysis than the darkness in front of him. Two senses were
failing him here—one physical, one linguistic—two ways to embrace the world slipping from him at the same moment. It was like
a little death, and a panic seized him, like the fear he'd felt some
midnights waking in his bed and body and knowing neither: his
bones a cage, his blood a gruel, his dissolution the only certainty.
At such times he'd turned on all the lights, for their comfort. But
there were no lights here. Only bodies, growing colder as the fire
died.

"Help me," he said. The mystif didn't speak. "Are you there, Pie?
I'm afraid. Touch me, will you? *Pie?*"

The mystif didn't move. Gentle started to reach out in the darkness, remembering as he did so the sight of Taylor lying on a pillow from which they'd both known he'd never rise again, asking
for Gentle to hold his hand. With that memory, the panic became
sorrow: for Taylor, for Clem, for every soul sealed from its loved
ones by senses born to failure, himself included. He wanted what
the child wanted: knowledge of another presence, proved in touch.
But he knew it was no real solution. He might find the mystif in
the darkness, but he could no more hold on to its flesh forever than
he could hold the senses he'd already lost. Nerves decayed, and fingers slipped from fingers at the last.

Knowing this little solace was as hopeless as any other, he withdrew his hand and instead said, "I love you."

Or did he simply think it? Perhaps it was thought, because it was
the idea rather than the syllables that formed in front of him, the
iridescence he remembered from Pie's transforming self shimmering in a darkness that was not, he vaguely understood, the
darkness of the starless night but his mind's darkness; and this
seeing not the business of eye and object but his exchange with a
creature he loved, and who loved him back.

He let his feelings go to Pie, if there was indeed a going, which
he doubted. Space, like time, belonged to the other tale—to the
tragedy of separation they'd left behind. Stripped of his senses
and their necessities, almost unborn again, he knew the mystif's
comfort as it knew his, and that dissolution he'd woken in terror
of so many times stood revealed as the beginning of bliss.

A gust of wind, blowing between the rocks, caught the embers
at their side, and their glow became a momentary flame. It brightened the face in front of him, and the sight summoned him back

from his unborn state. It was no great hardship to return. The place they'd found together was out of time and could not decay, and the face in front of him, for all its frailty (or perhaps because of it), was beautiful to look at. Pie smiled at him but said nothing.

"We should sleep," Gentle said. "We've got a long way to go tomorrow."

Another gust came along, and there were flecks of snow in it, stinging Gentle's face. He pulled the hood of his coat up over his head and got up to check on the welfare of the doeki. It had made a shallow bed for itself in the snow and was asleep. By the time he got back to the fire, which had found some combustible morsel and was devouring it brightly, the mystif was also asleep, its hood pulled up around its head. As he stared down at the visible crescent of Pie's face, a simple thought came: that though the wind was moaning at the rock, ready to bury them, and there was death in the valley behind and a city of atrocities ahead, he was happy. He lay down on the hard ground beside the mystif. His last thought as sleep came was of Taylor, lying on a pillow which was becoming a snow-field as he drew his final breaths, his face growing translucent and finally disappearing, so that when Gentle slipped from consciousness, it was not into darkness but into the whiteness of that deathbed, turned to untrodden snow.

23

I

Gentle dreamed that the wind grew harsher and brought snow down off the peaks, fresh minted. He nevertheless rose from the relative comfort of his place beside the ashes, and took off his coat and shirt, took off his boots and socks, took off his trousers and underwear, and naked walked down the narrow corridor of rock, past the sleeping doeki, to face the blast. Even in dreams, the wind threatened to freeze his marrow, but he had his sights set on the glacier, and he had to go to it in all humility, bare-loined, bare-backed, to show due respect for those souls who suffered there. They had endured centuries of pain, the crime against them unrevenged. Beside theirs, his suffering was a minor thing.

There was sufficient light in the wide sky to show him his way, but the wastes seemed endless, and the gusts worsened as he went, several times throwing him over into the snow. His muscles cramped and his breath shortened, coming from between his numbed lips in hard, small clouds. He wanted to weep for the pain of it, but the tears crystallized on the ledge of his eye and would not fall.

Twice he stopped, because he sensed that there was something more than snow on the storm's back. He remembered Pie's talk of agents left in this wilderness to guard the murder site and, though he was only dreaming and knew it, he was still afraid. If these entities were charged to keep witnesses from the glacier, they would not simply drive the wakeful off but the sleeping too; and those who came as he came, in reverence, would earn their special ire. He studied the spattered air, looking for some sign of them, and once thought he glimpsed a form overhead that would have been invisible but that it displaced the snow: an eel's body with a tiny ball of a head. But it was come and gone too quickly for him to be certain he'd even seen it.

The glacier was in sight, however, and his will drove his limbs to motion, until he was standing at its edge. He raised his hands to his face and wiped the snow from his cheeks and forehead, then stepped onto the ice. The women gazed up at him as they had when he'd stood here with Pie 'oh' pah, but now, through the dust of snow blowing across the ice, they saw him naked, his manhood shrunk, his body trembling; on his face and lips a question he had half an answer to. Why, if this was indeed the work of Hapexamendios, had the Unbeheld, with all His powers of destruction, not obliterated every last sign of His victims? Was it because they were women or, more particularly, women of power? Had He brought them to ruin as best He could—overturning their altars and unseating their temples—but at the last been unable to wipe them away? And if so, was this ice a grave or merely a prison?

He dropped to his knees and laid his palms on the glacier. This time he definitely heard a sound in the wind, a raw howl somewhere overhead. The invisibles had entertained his dreaming presence long enough. They saw his purpose and were circling in preparation for descent. He blew against his palm and made a fist before the breath could slip, then raised his arm and slammed his hand against the ice, opening it as he did so.

The pneuma went off like a thunderclap. Before the tremors had died he snatched a second breath and broke it against the ice; then a third and fourth in quick succession, striking the steely surface so hard that had the pneuma not cushioned the blow he'd have broken every bone from wrist to fingertip. But his efforts had effect. There were hairline cracks spreading from the point of impact.

Encouraged, he began a second round of blows, but he'd delivered only three when he felt something take hold of his hair, wrenching his head back. A second grip instantly seized his raised arm. He had time to feel the ice splintering beneath his legs; then he was hauled up off the glacier by wrist and hair. He struggled against the claim, knowing that if his assaulters carried him too high death was assured; they'd either tear him apart in the clouds or simply drop him. The hold on his head was the less secure of the two, and his gyrations were sufficient to slip it, though blood ran down his brow.

Freed, he looked up at the entities. There were two, six feet long, their bodies scantily fleshed spines sprouting innumerable ribs, their limbs twelvefold and bereft of bone, their heads vestigial. Only their motion had beauty: a sinuous knotting and unknotting. He reached up and snatched at the closer of the two heads. Though it had no discernible features, it looked tender, and his hand had sufficient echo of the pneumas it had discharged to do harm. He dug his fingers into the flesh of the thing, and it instantly began to writhe, coiling its length around its companion for support, its limbs flailing wildly. He twisted his body to the left and right, the motion violent enough to wrench him free. Then he fell, a mere six feet but hard, onto slivered ice. The breath went from him as the pain came. He had time to see the agents descending upon him, but none in which to escape. Waking or sleeping, this was the end of him, he knew; death by these limbs had jurisdiction in both states.

But before they could find his flesh, and blind him, and unman him, he felt the shattered glacier beneath him shudder, and with a roar it rose, throwing him off its back into the snow. Shards pelted down upon him, but he peered up through their hail to see that the women were emerging from their graves, clothed in ice. He hauled himself to his feet as the tremors increased, the din of this unshackling echoing off the mountains. Then he turned and ran.

The storm was discreet and quickly drew its veil over the resurrection, so that he fled not knowing how the events he'd begun had finished. Certainly the agents of Hapexamendios made no pursuit; or, if they did, they failed to find him. Their absence comforted him only a little. His adventures had done him harm, and the distance he had to cover to get back to the camp was substantial. His run soon deteriorated into stumbling and staggering, blood marking his route. It was time to be done with this dream of endurance, he thought, and open his eyes; to roll over and put his arms around Pie 'oh' pah; to kiss the mystif's cheek and share this vision with it. But his thoughts were too confounded to take hold of wakefulness long enough for him to rouse himself, and he dared not lie down in the snow in case a dreamed death came to him before morning woke him. All he could do was push himself on, weaker by the step, putting out of his head the possibility that he'd lost his way and that the camp didn't lie ahead but off in another direction entirely.

He was looking down at his feet when he heard the shout, and his first instinct was to peer up into the snow above him, expecting one of the Unbeheld's creatures. But before his eyes reached his zenith they found the shape approaching him from his left. He stopped and studied the figure. It was shaggy and hooded, but its arms were outspread in invitation. He didn't waste what little energy he had calling Pie's name. He simply changed his direction and headed towards the mystif as it came to meet him. It was the faster of the two, and as it came it shrugged off its coat and held it open, so that he fell into its luxury. He couldn't feel it; indeed he could feel little, except relief. Borne up by the mystif he let all conscious thought go, the rest of the journey becoming a blur of snow and snow, and Pie's voice sometimes, at his side, telling him that it would be over soon.

"Am I awake?" He opened his eyes and sat up, grasping hold of Pie's coat to do so. "Am I awake?"

"Yes."

"Thank God! Thank God! I thought I was going to freeze to death."

He let his head sink back. The fire was burning, fed with fur, and he could feel its warmth on his face and body. It took a few seconds to realize the significance of this. Then he sat up again and realized he was naked: naked and covered with cuts.

"I'm not awake," he said. "Shit! I'm not awake!"

Pie took the pot of herders' brew from the fire, and poured a cup.

"You didn't dream it," the mystif said. It handed the cup over to Gentle. "You went to the glacier, and you almost didn't make it back."

Gentle took the cup in raw fingers. "I must have been out of my mind," he said. "I remember thinking: I'm dreaming this, then taking off my coat and my clothes . . . why the hell did I do that?"

He could still recall struggling through the snow and reaching the glacier. He remembered pain, and splintering ice, but the rest had receded so far he couldn't grasp it. Pie read his perplexed look.

"Don't try and remember now," the mystif said. "It'll come back when the moment's right. Push too hard and you'll break your heart. You should sleep for a while."

"I don't fancy sleeping," he said. "It's a little too much like dying."

"I'll be here," Pie told him. "Your body needs rest. Let it do what it needs to do."

The mystif had been warming Gentle's shirt in front of the fire, and now helped him put it on, a delicate business. Gentle's joints were already stiffening. He pulled on his trousers without Pie's help, however, up over limbs that were a mass of bruises and abrasions.

"Whatever I did out there I certainly made a mess of myself," he remarked.

"You heal quickly," Pie said. This was true, though Gentle couldn't remember sharing that information with the mystif. "Lie down. I'll wake you when it's light."

Gentle put his head on the small heap of hides Pie had made as a pillow and let the mystif pull his coat up over him.

"Dream of sleeping," Pie said, laying a hand on Gentle's face. "And wake whole."

2

When Pie shook him awake, what seemed mere minutes later, the sky visible between the rock faces was still dark, but it was the gloom of snow-bearing cloud rather than the purple black of a Jokalaylaurian night. He sat up feeling wretched, aching in every bone.

"I'd kill for coffee," he said, resisting the urge to torture his joints by stretching. "And warm *pain au chocolat.*"

"If they don't have it in Yzordderrex, we'll invent it," Pie said.

"Did you brew up?"

"There's nothing left to burn."

"And what's the weather like?"

"Don't ask."

"That bad?"

"We should get a move on. The thicker the snow gets, the more difficult it'll be to find the pass."

They roused the doeki, which made plain its disgruntlement at having to breakfast on words of encouragement rather than hay, and, with the meat Pie had prepared the day before loaded, left the shelter of the rock and headed out into the snow. There had been a short debate before they left as to whether they should ride or not, Pie insisting that Gentle should do so, given his present delicacy, but he'd argued that they might need the doeki's strength to carry them both if they got into worse difficulties, and they should preserve such energies as it still possessed for such an emergency. But he soon began to stumble in snow that was waist high in places,